HIDDEN ORDER

HIDDEN ORDER

A THRILLER

Brad Thor

POCKET BOOKS

New York   London   Toronto   Sydney   New Delhi

Pocket Books
A Division of Simon & Schuster, Inc.
1230 Avenue of the Americas
New York, NY 10020

This Pocket Books export edition November 2013

POCKET and colophon are trademarks of Simon & Schuster, Inc.

For information about special discounts for bulk purchases, please contact Simon & Schuster Special Sales at 1-866-506-1949 or business@simonandschuster.com.

The Simon & Schuster Speakers Bureau can bring authors to your live event. For more information or to book an event, contact the Simon & Schuster Speakers Bureau at 1-866-248-3049 or visit our website at www.simonspeakers.com.

Manufactured in the United States of America

10   9   8   7   6   5   4   3   2   1

ISBN 978-1-4767-6436-8
ISBN 978-1-4767-1711-1 (ebook)

To Cindy Jackson Baker—
whom I met on a train overseas,
who helped give me my start in publishing,
and to whom I will always be grateful

"Things do not happen. Things are made to happen."

—John F. Kennedy

PROLOGUE

C laire Marcourt should have gone to bed hours ago. She should have ignored the second bottle of white burgundy in the fridge, placed her empty wineglass in the sink, and headed upstairs. But the forty-five-year-old was feeling nostalgic. And the more she drank, the more nostalgic she became. Picking up the bottle, she stepped outside.

The night was warm and the ocean air carried with it the scent of magnolias. Just beyond her pool, foamy waves tumbled onto the quiet beach.

Her pool. It was hard for Claire Marcourt to believe how far one family could come in a generation. Her mother had cleaned houses on Sea Island. Now Claire owned one and was being considered for one of the most powerful positions in the world. *Only in America,* she thought to herself.

It was heartbreaking that her mother hadn't lived to see everything Claire had accomplished—her career, her handsome husband and their three beautiful children, the Sea Island house with its stately oaks covered in Spanish moss, all of it. She would have been so proud.

As it was, she hadn't even seen Claire graduate from college. Cancer had taken her and, in its wake, had left Claire with a growing fear that she too might someday be prematurely taken from her family.

Pouring another glass, she set the bottle on the outdoor table and walked to the edge of the patio. She was becoming maudlin. Focusing on the ocean, she took a long sip and closed her eyes. As the waves rolled onto the beach, she reflected on what a blessing it was to be able to come back to Georgia and escape the sirens and traffic of Manhattan. The family didn't get down to Sea Island enough these days. Everyone was so busy. The funny thing, though, was that once Paul and the kids were here, no one wanted to leave.

She couldn't blame them. The island was for them not only a source of strength, but also of revival. It was the one place where they all felt truly at home, truly safe.

Listening to the waves, she was reminded of a poem about the area by Sidney Lanier called "The Marshes of Glynn."

Take courage from the land which God has given you, which has always nourished you, and which is still there, and be comforted.

Claire smiled and opened her eyes; her budding melancholy swept out to sea on a receding wave. She needed to think about that poem, and this place more often. Work had all but consumed her and it wasn't going to get any easier if things went in the direction she thought they were about to.

Draining the last of the wine from her glass, she stood there admiring the power of the ocean for a moment, lost in her own thoughts.

She never noticed the figure that stepped out of the darkness and onto her patio. He was powerful and moved quickly, clamping a gloved hand over her mouth. Before she knew what had happened, she felt a prick, almost like being stung, and her body went limp. She not only couldn't move a muscle, she couldn't make a sound.

The man removed his hand from her mouth, bent down, and slung her over his shoulder.

She could feel her heart pounding in her chest. *What is going on?* she screamed in the silence of her mind. *Why me? What does he want? Where is he taking me?*

It didn't take long for her last question to be answered. Staring down past the man's dark trousers and thick, black boots, she could see the flagstone path turn to sand. He was taking her to the beach. *Why the beach? Does he need some isolated spot where he can do whatever it is he is going to do to me?*

A couple of hundred yards away, Claire began to see the outline of something else and her heart began to pound even faster.

Pulled up onto the beach was an inflatable, gray Zodiac boat. Claire was deathly afraid of open water, particularly the open ocean. It was one thing to have a house on the coast with a view of the ocean; it was something entirely different to be out on the water. But Claire had no choice in what was about to happen.

Laying her down inside the Zodiac, the man pulled the bow around and dragged the boat into the ocean.

She could feel the moment it was floated and lifted up off the sand. A wave of nausea swept over her and she wanted to throw up, but her body didn't comply. It was as if it weren't even her body anymore. As if she were in a coma and no one knew she was actually awake.

As her attacker climbed into the boat and started its engine, Claire's fear of the open ocean was replaced by another fear, or, more properly stated, a resignation—whoever this man was and whatever his intent, she was never going to see her family again.

Seven miles south, the Zodiac entered St. Simons Sound and continued on. At the tip of a narrow point of wooded land was the entrance to a small, winding creek. The man killed the main engine and switched to a smaller, quieter motor. There could be no witnesses.

His assignment was almost complete. By the time anyone realized Claire Marcourt was missing, the plan would already be unrolling and there'd be nothing anyone could do.

He glanced down at the woman as he removed a weatherized Iridium satellite phone and dialed a string of digits.

When the call was answered, he identified himself.

"Hotel Sierra?" a man's voice asked on the other end.

They spoke in code, using the military alphabet. Hotel represented the letter *H,* which in this communication stood for *hostage.* Sierra stood for *S,* as in *secure.*

"Affirmative. Hotel Sierra."

"ID Lima." *Identify location.*

"Lima three," the man in the Zodiac replied, indicating he had arrived at the creek.

"Roger. Lima three," the voice replied. "Charlie Mike." *Continue mission.*

"Roger. Charlie Mike."

With those words, Claire Marcourt's fate was sealed and the rest of the operation was officially set in motion.

CHAPTER 1

L ydia Ryan looked up from her tablet as a waiter set a drink in front of her. "I didn't order this," she said.

"No, ma'am," replied the waiter. "It is from the gentleman."

Ryan shut down the tablet and cautiously glanced around the sleek, chrome-and-leather-accented room. She didn't see anyone looking back at her. "What gentleman?"

As the waiter smiled, a man seated in the area behind her said, "*This* gentleman." Ryan recognized the voice almost immediately.

"May I join you?" he asked as she turned around to face him.

Before she could respond, the man had already stood, his own drink in hand, and was walking around to her.

While paths did sometimes cross in the intelligence world, Ryan knew better than to believe in coincidences. The fact that she and Nafi Nasiri, deputy chief of the Jordanian General Intelligence Department, were in the same airport lounge was no accident.

He was in his late forties, tall, with medium-length black hair and re-fined, handsome features. He came from a wealthy family related to the King and had been educated in England and the United States. He had a penchant for dark Italian suits and his shoes were always highly polished. On his left wrist he wore the same elegant Patek Philippe watch that Ryan remembered.

"It's good to see you again, Lydia," he said as he set a briefcase down and took the seat facing her.

"It's been a long time, Nafi."

"Even so, you haven't changed at all. You're still as beautiful as ever."

Still the player, she thought to herself as she smiled and shook her head. "How's the shoulder?" she asked, beating him to the punch.

Reaching across his body, he massaged his right shoulder. "I find the changes in barometric pressure difficult, particularly before it rains."

Three years ago, Nasiri had knocked her to the ground as a suicide bomber was about to detonate. He had taken shrapnel in his upper arm and had used the injury ever since as an attempt to guilt her into sleeping with him. "That's too bad. I guess it's a good thing you live in the desert, huh?"

Nasiri smiled. He had worked with multiple female intelligence agents over the years and had been able to break all of them down—all of them except Ryan.

She was like no woman he had ever met. The stunning product of a Greek mother and Irish father, she was tall—at least five foot, ten inches—with a mane of thick, dark hair framing an aristocratic face, illuminated by two large, deep green eyes. The fact that she had never said yes to him made him want her all the more.

She was also a highly adept field operative. Despite only being in her early thirties, she had proven herself on multiple occasions to be just as courageous, just as skilled, and just as deadly as her male counterparts. He could only imagine how exceptional she would be in bed.

Ryan took notice of him drinking her in with his eyes and decided to cut to the chase. "What are the odds that you and I would both be passing through Frankfurt?"

Nasiri smiled. "I needed to see you."

"So this isn't fate, then?" she replied, pursing her lips in a disappointed pout.

"Unfortunately, no," he said, his buoyant, casual demeanor gone. His tone now was more professional, almost urgent. "May we speak someplace more discreet?" he continued. "I've reserved one of the private conference rooms for us."

"What's going on, Nafi?"

"Please," he said, standing.

"I was going to get something to eat before my flight."

"There's already food in the room."

Ryan had no idea what this was about, but he had definitely piqued her curiosity. "Well, seeing as how you've gone to so much trouble, how could a lady say no?"

Gathering up their belongings, the pair made their way toward the conference room. Once inside, Nasiri closed the drapes as Ryan perused the assortment of appetizers that had been laid out. She prepared a plate of food and, after looking at the available beverages, poured herself a glass of mineral water. Wine was out of the question. She liked Nasiri, but she wasn't going to let her guard down around him. On the airplane back home, she could have a couple of glasses of wine if she wanted. Right now she intended to be all business.

After sitting down, she placed her napkin in her lap and had just taken a bite of smoked duck when Nasiri took the chair across from her and, apropos of nothing, asked, "Is Jordan next on your list?"

She had no idea what he was talking about. Swallowing her food, she said, "Excuse me?"

"Is Jordan next?"

"I don't understand. Next for what?"

"C'mon, Lydia," Nasiri replied. "We know each other well enough; we've seen some very bad things together. We shouldn't play games."

"Nafi, no one is playing games here. You need to be specific with me. What are you talking about?"

Reaching down, he removed a folder from his briefcase and slid it across the conference table. "These pictures were taken three days ago."

Now he really *had* piqued her interest. Moving her plate aside, she drew the folder to her and flipped it open. The exhalation of breath that escaped her lips, as well the word *shit* upon seeing the first of the photos, was both unintentional and unprofessional.

"I guess we don't need to argue whether or not those are *former* teammates."

They were in fact old teammates of hers. They had been part of a covert program that specialized in orchestrating social, political, and organizational instability abroad. Their primary expertise was in the Muslim world. In addition to developing elaborate plots designed to create chaos inside organizations like Al-Qaeda, the Taliban, Hamas, Al-Shabaab, and the Iranian Revolutionary Guard, they had also been active in the rendering of terrorists to disavowed black sites under the continuation of America's supposedly discontinued extraordinary rendition program.

In the program, code-named "Eclipse," the CIA team had broken every rule in the book. And the more rules they broke, the more successes they racked up. It was a self-perpetuating cycle that had turned the team into success addicts—and like real addicts, they kept searching for bigger and bigger highs by going after bigger targets and launching more audacious operations. In the team members' minds, they could do no wrong.

The funny thing about believing you can do no wrong is that you quickly begin doing nothing *but* wrong. It had started with small infractions as standards slipped, such as getting sloppy with reporting or sneaking alcohol along on ops. From there it grew into misappropriating Agency assets like Black Hawk helicopters for bighorn sheep hunts in the Hindu Kush, all the way to some members of the coed team developing off-limits personal relationships and sleeping with each other.

These were men and women whose reputations on the covert side of the intelligence community were quickly outstripping their actual abilities. They were the CIA's golden children, a mixture of analysts and gunslingers, who had not only started believing their own press releases, but in the deadly fog of the global war on terror had begun to see themselves as almost immortal. They were careening toward a cliff with no one to pump the brakes. That was precisely when fate stepped in.

Without the knowledge of the Italian government, they had attempted to snatch a high-ranking Al-Qaeda member off the streets of Rome and a shootout had erupted. Associates of the terrorist had opened fire, killing five Italian citizens, two of them police officers. It was the end of the Eclipse program. All of the members had been cut loose from the Central Intelligence Agency. All of them, that is, but Lydia Ryan.

"Where were these pictures taken?" she asked.

"Cyprus."

"And you said *three* days ago?"

"Yes," replied Nasiri. "The only person missing is you."

"I have nothing to do with them anymore."

"But that's your old team, is it not?" he asked.

"Sure, but all of them were cut loose. You *know* that."

"Do I? I'm not so sure anymore. The CIA didn't cut *you* loose, did they?"

"That's different," Ryan argued.

He leaned back in his chair, unconvinced. "Really? *Different how?*"

"I was assigned to police that team. They were good, but they were also a bunch of cowboys. People don't last long at Langley if you don't follow the rules."

"Interesting. I seem to remember you breaking a lot of the rules yourself."

"No," Ryan admonished him. "What you *remember* is an imbecile of a CIA station chief and an American ambassador with a Pollyannaish worldview. Everything we did, *everything,* there was clearance for, especially the things we kept quiet from those two. It's hard enough doing the work you and I do without having to fight our own people in the process."

Nasiri shrugged. "I guess I'll have to take your word for it."

She looked at him. "What the hell is that supposed to mean?"

"It means, my dear Lydia, that even by your own admission your destabilization team was very skilled. Yet despite that skill, someone chose to shut it down and fire all of its members. All the members, that is, except for you. If I recall correctly, you got promoted. Case officer now, isn't it?"

Glancing at her watch, Ryan said, "If there's a point to all of this, Nafi, I suggest you get to it."

"The point is that your entire CIA destabilization team, minus your 'policing' presence, was seen in Cyprus three days ago meeting with two men that my country is very nervous about."

"These two?" she asked, pointing at one of the photographs. "Who are they?"

"Senior members of the Jordanian Muslim Brotherhood."

Suddenly, it hit her. "Wait a second. You think that the United States is planning to topple Jordan?"

Nasiri raised his hands palms up and tilted his head to the side. "If you were in our position, with governments falling all around you, what would *you* think?"

"I think a country like Jordan should be confident enough to trust its allies. That's what I think."

The Jordanian leaned forward and repeated his original question. "Is Jordan going to be the next Middle Eastern country to be overthrown?"

"There could be any number of reasons for that meeting in Cyprus."

"Really?" he stated, reaching down and removing two more folders from his briefcase. He held them out over the table and then let them drop. "Would any of those reasons be the same, or different, for why your team was seen in both Egypt and Libya before those governments collapsed?"

She would've stressed again that it wasn't "her team," but she was too stunned by his remarks to utter the words. The Americans in those photos had not only been let go from the CIA; they had been let go with prejudice along with *big* black marks in their records. *What was this all about?*

Lydia Ryan was good at reading people, so whatever intelligence Nafi Nasiri had, she could see he was one hundred percent confident in it. Which meant, by extension, so was his boss, and very likely, the King of Jordan himself. Otherwise, Nafi wouldn't have been sent here to meet with her like this.

"I don't know what to say," she finally offered.

The Jordanian pushed the folders across the table to her. "Tell me you'll read what's in these files."

"Of course, but—"

"And that you'll get me some answers."

"Nafi, I can't make you any promises."

Nasiri looked at her, his face implacable. Reaching down, he removed a final folder from his briefcase, but he didn't open it. He didn't push it across the table, either. He just sat there tapping his index finger on the cover.

"I'm sorry to have to do this," he finally said.

"Sorry for what?"

"Understand that we take any threat to the survival of the Kingdom of Jordan very seriously."

There was now another tone in his voice, and she didn't like it. "What's in the folder, Nafi?"

The Jordanian lifted the cover, but only high enough so that he could see inside. From where she was sitting, Ryan couldn't make out a thing.

"Over the winter, we infiltrated a terror cell that has been moving bomb makers, bomb materials, and martyrs into Syria via Lebanon. While inside the cell, our asset learned of an advanced plot targeting the United States."

Ryan's eyes went wide. "You've known of an attack being mounted against the United States and this is the first you're telling us? Give me that file. I want to see what's in it."

Nasiri shook his head. "We've been monitoring the situation."

"*Monitoring the situation,* my ass," said Ryan, her anger growing. "You know what, Nafi? Fuck you, and fuck your monitoring. You can't sit on information like that."

"We didn't want to come to you until we were *confident.*"

"This is blackmail. The Kingdom of Jordan is blackmailing the United States. That's what's going on here. You're not going to give me what I want, until you get what you want."

The Jordanian slid the file back into his briefcase and stood.

Ryan's blood was boiling. She knew her emotions were getting the better of her and that that was wrong, but she couldn't control her anger. "You haven't given me a shred of proof. What makes you think my superiors will even believe you?"

Nasiri frowned as he reached the conference room door. "I think a country like America should be confident enough to trust its allies. That's what I think. Have a good flight home, Lydia."

With that, the Jordanian was gone, and in his wake, the CIA had been dropped into a nightmare involving a terrorist plot that might or might not exist, and no way to even begin running it to ground.

CHAPTER 2

From the beginning, everyone had told Scot Harvath that his plan not only was flawed and would never work, but was absolutely insane. The three men who disagreed had been hired on the spot.

Parachuting onto the rear deck of the supertanker *Sienna Star* was considered a kamikaze mission, but they'd made it. One of the team members was injured on the landing, but they still managed to retake the ship and free its crew. What they hadn't bargained for, though, was that the tanker's captain had been smuggled to shore earlier as an insurance policy against any such rescue attempt. This had placed Harvath and his team in a very difficult position.

The assignment called for the successful recapture of the ship and the recovery of the *entire* crew. In order to beat out the other private contractors for the job, Harvath's boss had proposed an exorbitant fee, but with the caveat that the ship's owners owed them nothing unless the operation was one hundred percent successful.

As a former Navy SEAL with a storied career now working for a private intelligence agency, he lived for this kind of work. That said, it was an extremely risky operation and it wasn't the first they had been forced to take. Recently, his employer and the company's namesake, Reed Carlton, had been targeted for assassination. The killers had also targeted the Carlton Group's top operations personnel. Harvath and Carlton had been lucky enough to survive, but they had lost so many key players that their organization was unable to function at its previous level and ended up losing its biggest and sole government contract with the Defense Department. Because of that loss, they had been forced to take any and all assignments—sometimes under ridiculous terms—in order to rebuild their organization.

The Old Man, as Harvath referred to Carlton, had put everything on the line for this assignment, advancing a small fortune that included funding a secondary team out in the Gulf of Aden to conduct drone reconnaissance on the *Sienna Star* for the last week and a half.

Despite this surveillance, though, no one had realized that the pirates had smuggled the captain off the tanker. It wasn't until Harvath and his team had retaken the ship that they discovered his absence. At that point, they were left with only one option. They had to recover him.

Their hope was that the last thing the pirates would ever expect was that their pursuers would risk following them to their own village.

As was typical with Somalis, the pirates had imported engineers—mostly from Kenya—who could operate the hijacked vessels until their owners, or more often their insurance companies, paid whatever ransom was being asked for. In the case of the *Sienna Star,* though, the tanker's navigator had been murdered in the initial throes of the hijacking and the ship's owners wanted to send a message. They wanted all of the pirates killed.

Considering that the Somalis had murdered a crew member, Harvath didn't have a problem with that. If any of them posed a threat, they'd be dealt with accordingly. That was exactly how his team had handled retaking the ship. The Kenyan engineer recruited by the pirates was another matter entirely.

Not only had he been helpful on board the *Sienna Star,* but Mukami had assisted Harvath in drawing up a rescue plan for the captain. He knew where the pirates were holding him and had even offered to take Harvath there, if the price was right. Harvath had agreed to his terms.

Mukami had come up with the idea to turn the tables on the pirates by hijacking their own supply boat when it came out to resupply the tanker with food, water, and fresh khat.

In addition to getting paid, the man had requested only one additional item. He had asked that his cousin Pili, also an engineer from Kenya and who would be coming out on the resupply boat, not be harmed. Harvath had agreed to that as well.

Leaving their injured colleague plus an additional man behind to hold the *Sienna Star*, Harvath and his remaining teammate—a former SEAL named Matt Sanchez—used a smiling and waving Mukami as bait and successfully took the pirates' resupply boat when it pulled up alongside the tanker. Within seconds of the three dead Somalis being tossed out of the resupply boat, the great white sharks that infested the Gulf of Aden tore the corpses to shreds.

Mukami's cousin, Pili, simply thought he was coming out to take over the *Sienna Star* for a few days. The shooting of the three pirates had taken him completely by surprise. He was in a state of quasi-shock, and so Mukami piloted the resupply boat into port.

As Harvath and Sanchez checked and cleaned their weapons, they went over the plan with Mukami once more.

They would berth at the northern end of the small harbor where the supply boats normally picked up and dropped off. The car Pili and Mukami shared was already there waiting. While Pili stayed with the boat, Mukami would drive Harvath and Sanchez past the house the pirates owned, in order to give them a quick look. He would then drop them off around the corner and continue on to the house himself.

It wasn't unusual for the Kenyan engineer, upon arriving back in port, to show up at the walled compound to be paid, before proceeding on to his hotel. Usually, the pirates invited him to drink, smoke the hookah, and gamble with them. If they did so tonight, Harvath had told him to accept their offer.

Mukami was carrying a satellite phone Harvath had given him, along with a plausible excuse for it. If the phone was discovered, he would state that the *Sienna Star* was experiencing an electrical issue and that he needed to be available should his cousin require technical assistance.

Once inside, Mukami was to try to ascertain where the Greek captain was being held and transmit that information to Harvath and Sanchez. The two former SEALs would handle the rest.

When they were done going over the operation, Harvath had a personal question for Mukami. "Why?"

"What do you mean, *why*?" the Kenyan replied.

"Why do all this? Why work with the pirates?"

"For the same reason everyone else does. For money."

"But the pirates are bad people."

"Unfortunately, in Africa," said Mukami, "we don't have the luxury of deciding from whom we take our money."

"But you and your cousin seem like good guys. You're educated. You're polite. You speak multiple languages. For men like you, there have to be other ways to make money."

"No, not true. Not for the kind of money we need."

"I don't understand," said Harvath.

"My sister and Pili's sister went abroad. They paid bad men to smuggle them into Europe. They were told they would be given jobs and would be starting over with an opportunity for a better life. It was a lie. They were trafficked. That was two years ago. We have not seen or heard from them since. The men tell us that for more money they can get our sisters back. This is why we have been working for anyone who will pay us, and pay us well."

It was one of the millions of heartbreaking stories that existed throughout the third world. It was also none of his business and Harvath was sorry he'd asked. A hush fell over the boat and there was only the sound of the diesel engines as they made their way toward shore.

When the resupply boat pulled into the pirates' port it was well past midnight. The pier they tied up to was completely deserted, except for a few other supply boats, their crews long since returned home for the evening. On the other side of the tiny harbor they could see a stem-to-stern string of pirate mother ships and fast attack boats. While Somali piracy may have been down overall, this village still seemed to be making a very good living at it.

Peering out of the boat's wheelhouse, Harvath and Sanchez took one last look up and down the pier before allowing Mukami to disembark and ready his vehicle. Pili would stay aboard and wait for everyone to return.

They watched Mukami walk down the dock to a battered brown Mercedes sedan with one white door and a missing rear window. Once the car was fired up and running, he turned the lights off and then back on to signal the coast was clear.

After one more thorough look around the harbor, Harvath and Sanchez stepped out of the wheelhouse and onto the dock. Though they had taken steps to disguise themselves with Somali clothing they'd found aboard the *Sienna Star,* they would never fool anyone up close. That was fine by both men, though, as they didn't plan to get personal with anyone other than the people they intended to kill.

As soon as his passengers were inside the car, Mukami turned onto a side street and made for the pirates' stronghold. He knew better than to drive up the narrow main drag.

The village wasn't very big, but judging from the satellite dishes clustered on the rooftops, as well as the expensive foreign cars parked in front of some rather impressive compounds, Harvath's opinion about the profitability of the local piracy trade had been right on the money.

Mukami slowed as they approached one such stronghold and told Harvath and Sanchez it was coming up on the left. Music could be heard from inside and lights could be seen from the upper windows. There were no guards in front, which Sanchez immediately remarked upon.

"They're pirates," replied Mukami. "They have many, many guns. Who would be dumb enough to steal from them?"

Just because it hadn't ever happened didn't mean it wouldn't, and the fact that even Somalis suffered from normalcy bias made Harvath shake his head. The pirates were about to learn a very painful and hopefully very expensive lesson.

Pulling around the block, Mukami dropped his passengers at an abandoned fisherman's shack, its windows missing and its roof caved in.

"You know what to do?" Harvath asked.

Mukami nodded and, before Harvath could ask another question, drove off.

Sanchez watched the old Mercedes recede into the darkness. "Do you think he can keep his shit together?"

Harvath nodded. "He's nervous, but I've made it worth his while. He'll do it. Let's get inside."

The two men hid themselves in the dilapidated dwelling and waited.

Twenty minutes later, they received a text message from Mukami. The captain was at the compound and was being kept in a room on the first floor. There were at least thirty men inside.

Sanchez let out a quiet whistle. "Thirty. That's a lot of man-skirts."

"That's a lot of guns."

"And RPGs."

"*And RPGs,*" Harvath agreed. "Let's see if we can't peel some of them off. Ready?"

Sanchez nodded as Harvath switched frequencies on his radio to hail the heavily armed support boat that had been doing the reconnaissance on the tanker. It was now hovering just out of sight offshore. "Shotgun, this is Norseman. Do you copy? Over."

A moment later, the response came back. "Norseman, this is Shotgun. We copy. Over."

"You are cleared hot. I repeat. You are cleared hot. Bring the rain. Over."

"Roger that, Norseman. Shotgun is cleared hot. Bringing the rain. Ninety seconds. Shotgun out."

Looking at Sanchez, Harvath said, "Beers are on me when we're done."

Sanchez smiled. "Roger that. Let's roll."

CHAPTER 3

Harvath and Sanchez stepped from the shack and listened. They were close enough that they could hear the RPGs as they began to be fired from the Shotgun team on board the support boat. They could feel the ground tremble as one after another of the mother ships and their fast attack craft down at the port exploded. Instantly, the village erupted in pandemonium.

Harvath and Sanchez took advantage of the mayhem to advance unseen on the pirate stronghold. They held up behind a parked car and watched as at least twenty men poured out of the compound and rushed down to the harbor. They gave it another sixty seconds and when no one else came out, they decided to go in.

The gate had been left wide open and Harvath slipped inside first, followed by Sanchez. They split the pie, with Harvath engaging two pirates to the left and Sanchez one to the right. Utilizing speed, surprise, and overwhelming violence of action, they kept moving and firing as they pressed on into the main structure.

From inside the house, a frightened Somali hopped up on khat began firing before the two Americans had even neared the door. As Harvath returned fire with his suppressed MP7, Sanchez flanked the Somali and shot him through a window, killing him instantly.

Entering the structure, the firefight continued as three Somalis on a balcony overlooking the living room fired on them. This time it was Sanchez who returned fire while Harvath attempted to maneuver for a cleaner shot. The only problem was, he couldn't get one. From their high ground position, the Somalis had total control of the room, and they knew it.

Harvath searched for a way to take them out, and then it came to him. Signaling Sanchez, he counted to three and then charged across the living room.

While Sanchez kept them pinned down, unable to return fire, Harvath slipped beneath the wooden balcony, pointed his weapon straight up, and fired. The high-velocity rounds of the MP7 tore through the planks, chewing the pirates above to bits.

As soon as Sanchez gave him the "all clear," he stepped from under the balcony and moved back across the living room.

There were two hallways available to them and Harvath was about to suggest they take the one to the right when two more skinnies popped out of a room at the end of the hall to their left. He and Sanchez dropped both Somalis instantly.

Hoping that was the room where the captain of the *Sienna Star* was being held, Harvath and Sanchez moved quickly for it.

At the door, Sanchez reached for the knob and when Harvath nodded, threw it open.

Inside, they found the last remaining Somali pirate along with two other men—the Greek tanker captain and the Kenyan engineer who had led them into the village. The satellite phone Harvath had given him was sitting in his lap, and pressed against Mukami's head was the barrel of the pirate's AK-47.

Before Harvath could shout *wait,* urge calm, or even get off a shot of his own, the pirate pulled his trigger and the air was filled with a pink mist as the wall beyond the bed was splattered with blood, bone, and pieces of Mukami's brain.

As the Kenyan engineer's body fell to the ground, Harvath unloaded his weapon into the Somali pirate. He didn't stop until his magazine was empty.

"Damn it," he said. "Damn it. Damn it. Damn it!"

Sanchez didn't reply. There was nothing he could say. Instead, he turned and faced the hallway to make sure they didn't get ambushed from behind.

As he tried to get his anger under control, Harvath stepped forward and picked up the radio. Putting his game face back on, he looked at the Greek captain and said, "Captain Velopoulos, we're here to take you home. Please stay as close to us as possible and do exactly as we say. Do you understand?"

The captain nodded, and after retrieving Mukami's car keys Harvath and Sanchez moved the Greek quickly out of the building and into the courtyard.

While Sanchez stepped out to study the street beyond the wall, Harvath radioed the Shotgun team, giving them a description of the Mercedes they'd be driving, as well as their ETA to the harbor.

"Roger that, Norseman," came the response. "We'll see you in the port in two minutes. Shotgun out."

They laid the captain down on the floor in back, while Harvath drove and Sanchez rode in the passenger seat.

It took only half a block until they began to see the flames from the burning boats down in the harbor climbing high into the night sky.

"They're not going to be very happy to see us when we get there," Sanchez said.

Harvath, still upset about the Kenyan being killed, pressed down hard on the accelerator and replied, "Fuck them."

Sanchez nodded and activated his radio. "Shotgun, this is Streak. ETA to exfil point sixty seconds. Over."

"Roger that, Streak. Be advised the port is crawling with skinnies. Over."

"Understood. Just be there. Over."

"We'll be there, don't worry. Shotgun out."

Sanchez looked at Harvath. "You ready for this?"

Harvath gripped the steering wheel tighter. "Just watch."

The Mercedes came screaming down the narrow main street into the port. As people ran in every direction, Harvath leaned on the horn to move them out of his path. While it might have been the somewhat humane thing to do, it also succeeded in drawing a hell of a lot of attention, particularly from the pirates gathered on the beach, who were watching their ships burn.

After glancing into the backseat, Sanchez said, "I hope our passenger has comfortable shoes. It's going to be a long walk from the parking lot."

"Who says we're stopping in the parking lot?" replied Harvath as he pointed the Mercedes toward the dock and picked up even more speed.

"You've got to be kidding—" Sanchez began, but was interrupted by a hail of gunfire that tore up their right rear quarter-panel.

As the Mercedes barreled through a stack of crates at the front of the pier, Sanchez returned fire at the heavily armed Somalis on the beach.

Activating his radio, he said, "Shotgun. Shotgun. This is Streak. We have contact. Multiple armed skinnies on the beach. You are cleared hot. We need you now. Over."

"Roger that, Streak. Shotgun coming up on your three o'clock."

Before breaking transmission, Sanchez and Harvath looked over to see the Shotgun team and their boat come almost parallel with them out on the water and open up on the men on the beach via a devastating minigun mounted on the bow of their boat.

Racing down the dock, Harvath brought the Mercedes skidding to a stop next to the resupply boat and leapt out. Taking cover, he aimed his MP7 toward the end of the pier and instructed Sanchez to get the tanker captain out of the car and onto the boat.

Once the captain was safely on board, Sanchez returned with a rag that had been soaked in some sort of chemical. After opening the Mercedes's gas cap he shoved it halfway in, removed a lighter, and ignited what was hanging out, saying to Harvath, "Let's get the hell out of here."

The two men untied the resupply boat and jumped on. As soon as Pili saw that Harvath and Sanchez were aboard and they were clear of the pier, he spun the craft around and made for the mouth of the harbor. The Shotgun team was right behind and covered their six o'clock all the way out.

The last thing any of them saw were the few surviving pirates who foolishly rushed down the dock firing wildly from their AK-47s. One of them even took a knee, mounted an RPG on his shoulder and was just about to fire, when the Mercedes exploded, taking the pier and everything else with it.

CHAPTER 4

Having reinstated Captain Velopoulos and debriefed the crew, Harvath and his team scuttled their weapons and slipped off the *Sienna Star* about forty-five minutes before INTERPOL boarded near the Kenyan port of Mombasa.

They were met by a crooked customs official arranged for by the Old Man. He stamped their passports and directed them to a waiting vehicle, which drove them to the airport.

The only deviation from their departure plan was that instead of flying home commercially with his teammates, Harvath was now going back via a private jet that was already waiting for him. Carlton was reluctant to give him many details, even over an encrypted satellite phone. He simply said he needed Harvath back as quickly as possible.

Harvath knew better than to question him. The Old Man was a legend in the espionage business. With more than three decades at the CIA, he had helped establish the Agency's counterterrorism center before retiring and starting his own private enterprise. If he said he needed him back right away, he needed him back right away.

While Harvath didn't like the idea of not personally seeing his team safely out of the country, they were all exceptional operators and big boys who could handle clearing passport control and getting on the correct flight. It goes without saying that they hazed Harvath for having his "own private jet" and being "too good" to fly commercial with them. It was nothing more than male chop-busting. None of the men held it against him. They understood that in this line of work, time wasn't only money—it could mean the difference between saving or losing lives.

Consoling himself with the fact that all his guys had flown private at some point in their lives, that thought quickly faded as he cleared passport control, walked out onto the tarmac, and saw his plane. While his men may have flown private before, he was pretty confident none of them had ever flown like this.

Even Harvath, who had gotten used to being moved from country to country on high-end private jets from Gulfstreams, Cessnas, and Hawkers, to Bombardiers, Dassaults, and Embraers, had never seen anything like it.

With its long, pointed nose and swept-back wings, the Aerion Supersonic Business Jet resembled a smaller, futuristic Concorde that had been designed for private use. A pilot, copilot, and flight attendant were waiting at the base of the air-stairs.

They introduced themselves and the captain gave Harvath a quick tour of the aircraft's exterior. Designed by an American aerospace firm in Reno, Nevada, the Aerion SBJ had a maximum speed of Mach 1.8 or 1,186 miles per hour and a range of up to 5,300 miles.

The captain explained that while over the water, their maximum supersonic cruise speed would be Mach 1.6; over land, they would have to slow to just under Mach 1.2 in order to continue supersonic travel, but without the boom, or "boomless" as he put it.

The man was full of interesting information and told Harvath everything except to whom the $90 million aircraft belonged. It sure didn't belong to the Old Man, but it was obviously somehow connected to the reason Carlton needed him back in D.C. as quickly as possible.

As the captain rejoined the copilot to complete his preflight check, Harvath was handed off to the flight attendant. She was an attractive redhead named Natalie. Her English was excellent, but he picked up on her

Swedish accent immediately. His call sign of Norseman wasn't given to him because he looked like some sort of Viking. In fact, with his brown hair and blue eyes, he looked more German than anything else. The Norseman call sign came from his early days in the SEALs when he had dated a string of Scandinavian Airlines flight attendants. What had started as a good-natured joke had stuck with him throughout his career. He didn't have any complaints, though. There were much worse things an operator could be named for.

Natalie escorted him up the stairs and into the aircraft. It was luxuriously appointed with large leather seats and intricate burled wood accents. At just over six and a half feet wide and thirty feet long, the cabin more than accommodated the five-foot-ten Harvath.

After showing him the galley, the lavatory, and the area at the rear of the aircraft that could be closed off for a private sleeping compartment, Natalie offered him something to drink. He smiled to himself as he thought about how many buddies of his got on a plane like this and went right for the top shelf of the bar either because they were insecure and wanted to appear like they belonged on a private jet, or because they wanted to take advantage of whoever was footing the bill. That wasn't his style. He was more than comfortable in his own skin and didn't give a damn what anyone thought of him. He also knew well enough that the aircraft wouldn't be provisioned with anything its owners didn't want him to enjoy.

Having been in the mood for a beer for over a week, that was exactly what he asked for.

"A beer drinker," Natalie replied with a smile. "I like that."

Harvath watched as she turned and walked up the aisle toward the galley. There was nothing like a woman in uniform, particularly a flight attendant's uniform. The scarf tied around the neck was always the coup de grâce for him. It radiated a confidence and sexiness that got him every time.

When Natalie returned with his drink, she explained the meal services, the in-flight entertainment options, and also handed him an iPad that was wirelessly connected to the plane's satellite Internet system.

He didn't plan on watching any movies. He planned on sleeping. Before disembarking the *Sienna Star* he had grabbed a quick shower and shaved, but that was it. It had been more than twenty-four hours since he had last slept. Knowing the Old Man the way he did, he was going to be expected to hit the ground running when the plane landed, so now was the time to get some rest.

Once the plane had taken off and had reached its cruising altitude, Natalie served Harvath a quick meal and then prepared the sleeping area. Despite how incredibly well insulated and quiet the aircraft was, she had left a pair of earplugs along with an eye mask and pair of silk pajamas. Thanking her, Harvath stepped inside and slid the doors closed behind him.

He wasn't a pajamas kind of guy. Hanging up his clothes, he slid between the sheets and closed his eyes. He was still wound up and no sooner had his eyes shut than a picture of Mukami getting his brains blown out floated across his mind. He had to force himself to think of something else.

He tried several things, finally settling on an image of Natalie. From there his mind drifted to other things and ten minutes later he fell into a deep, dark sleep.

CHAPTER 5

When Harvath awoke, it was once again to a mental picture of Natalie. Perhaps it was because she was gently knocking on his door. With only one stop for refueling, they had made the entire trip in less than ten hours.

After dressing, Harvath availed himself of the courtesy vanity kit in the lav to brush his teeth and clean up. When he stepped out, Natalie had a meal ready for him. He was able to get through only half of it before the pilot announced that they needed to prepare for landing and would be on the ground shortly.

He grabbed a couple more bites and then thanked Natalie as she cleared everything away. Looking out the window, he was surprised to see the sun almost in the same place as when they had left Kenya. It was amazing how traveling backward across time zones, especially in such a fast aircraft, could make it seem like the day had stood absolutely still.

Equally amazing was the fact that they were landing at Reagan National Airport and not Dulles International. The only international corporate jet flights allowed to land at Reagan were those originating at foreign airports with U.S. Customs and Border Protection preclearance facilities. Mombasa definitely didn't qualify. Whoever had arranged this flight had a lot of pull somewhere.

Once they had landed and the plane had taxied to a stop, the crew assembled at the door to say goodbye to their passenger. As Harvath thanked them, the copilot handed him a small gift box. "A souvenir from your flight," he said.

Looking inside, Harvath found a detailed display model of the Aerion SBJ, right down to this aircraft's signature paint job. "Thank you," he replied.

"And you won't want to forget this," Natalie added, handing him the vanity kit from the lav.

Unlike his mother, as well as many of the women he had dated, Harvath wasn't a "travel size" guy. He didn't keep hotel soaps or shampoos, nor did he keep the complimentary vanity kits when traveling first class. That said, he didn't want to hurt Natalie's feelings and so accepted the kit with a smile and a thank-you. He could toss it once he was off the plane.

After he'd cleared customs and passport control, a courtesy vehicle picked him up for the short drive over to Signature Flight Support. It was a "Fixed Base Operator" facility where he'd have a chance to clean up before one of his Carlton Group colleagues drove him into D.C. for his meeting with the Old Man.

As he arrived at the FBO, he saw that it was one of Carlton's protégés, Sloane Ashby, who had been sent there to pick him up.

Leaning against her car, with her high cheekbones, smoky gray eyes, and hair pulled back in a ponytail, she looked like the country club wife of some handsome young banker. It would be a mistake, though, to judge this book by its cover.

Sloane was not only brilliant, having graduated at the top of her class from Northwestern University with a dual major in math and chemistry; she was also highly skilled as a winter athlete, having competed in both figure skating and snowboarding. She was also one hell of an operator.

As a former member of the U.S. Freestyle Ski Team, Harvath told his colleagues that what he liked most about her was her prowess in winter sports, but none of them believed him. They all assumed that what he "liked" about her was that she was hot. In other words, even people trained to know better still fell prey to the mistake of judging her solely by what they saw on the surface.

Carlton, on the other hand, had very different reasons for liking her. In addition to admiring her academic and athletic abilities, he respected her because, despite her family's ability to cover all of her college expenses, she had insisted on paying her own way and had rocketed through the ROTC program. She had signed up insisting that she be promised combat duty. She went on to complete two tours in Afghanistan, killing more enemy combatants than all the women in the theater combined (not to mention many of the men). But when some glossy magazine ran an unauthorized cover story on her, it placed a huge bull's-eye on her back and brought her combat career to a screeching halt.

The Taliban and Al-Qaeda were both offering big rewards for her head on a pike and the Department of Defense had no other choice but to deny her request for a third tour. Without missing a beat, and as bold as brass, she requested to be sent immediately to Iraq before all the action ended there. She was turned down, though, once again.

She ended up being detailed to North Carolina's Fort Bragg, where she worked with the all-female Delta detachment known as the Athena Project. Despite her young age, she was an excellent instructor. Everyone knew, though, that her heart and her talent lay in being an operator. She was quite vocal about the fact that if it weren't for the Islamic bounty on her head and the subsequent PR nightmare her capture or killing would cause, she'd still be out whacking and stacking Muslim terrorists like cordwood. Neither political correctness, nor empathy for the risk aversion of her commanders, was part of her DNA.

Because of that, the United States Army had a love/hate relationship with Sloane Ashby. They loved the fact that they could push a super-attractive, athletic, young American woman as an Army success story, but they hated that she repeatedly suggested, in public, that the Army had no balls and was caving to the terrorists by not letting her return to the fight.

She was definitely a headache for the Department of Defense, but there were many other people in D.C. who absolutely loved her. To the chagrin of her superiors, Ashby was invited to lots of powerful, insider cocktail parties where she freely spoke her mind. It was at one such party where she had met Reed Carlton.

They chatted for over an hour about world events, politics, and the military. The next day they then met for a three-hour lunch. By the end of the month, the Old Man had worked his magic. Ashby was honorably discharged from the military and forty-eight hours later she had been hired on at the Carlton Group.

Under normal circumstances, she wouldn't have been relegated to doing airport pickups, but these weren't normal circumstances for the organization and everyone was chipping in. While she did have a hard-charging style, she was still a team player.

"Hey, old man," she said as Harvath stepped out of the courtesy vehicle.

Old man? He might have been in his forties, but he was nowhere near "old," especially when all of them worked for a literal "old" man like Reed Carlton. That said, she never missed a chance to needle him. He didn't see himself as old at all and it grated on him when she called him that.

"I brought you something from Africa," he said without missing a beat.

Suddenly, Ashby softened. "Really?" she asked with an almost child-like naïveté. "What is it?"

"This," Harvath replied, holding up his middle finger.

Ashby laughed. There wasn't even a hint of anger. She could admire a good joke, even one at her own expense and she never let it dent her ego. She was good at rolling with the punches.

She was also good at sizing up people and situations. It was scary both in how bright she was and how rapidly she could analyze something and figure out what was going on. Harvath hated to admit it, but she was probably much smarter and quicker than he had ever been.

"At least you have something to hang this on," Sloane said, reaching through the window of her car and pulling out a garment bag.

Harvath walked over to her. "Where'd that come from?"

"This?" she asked, looking down through the opening at the top of the bag. "I think somebody mugged a pimp or maybe a TV weatherman."

"Very funny," he replied, extending his hand. "How'd you get into my house?"

Sloane lifted her right foot and executed a quick snap kick. "I used my size-six Manolo skeleton key."

Sassy. Harvath liked sassy. In fact, he liked it almost as much as he did Scandinavian flight attendants with scarves tied around their necks. But only *almost*. Sloane Ashby was not only too young for him; she was also a colleague. What's more, Reed Carlton—who had very likely given her the key and alarm code for his house—had made it quite clear that he expected Harvath to maintain a strictly professional relationship with her. Someday she was going to go on to do some incredible things for their agency, even more than she already had for the country. By that point, God willing, she would be reporting to Harvath. The Old Man didn't want any messy entanglements between them screwing up their performance.

"If I get home," Harvath said as he accepted the garment bag, "and find any of my Kool & the Gang records missing, there's going to be hell to pay."

Ashby shook her head. "No one got near your *phon-o-graph,* grandpa," she replied, drawing the words out slowly like she was speaking to someone hard of hearing. "No need to worry. E-v-e-r-y-thing is okay. Your Drool & the Gang will still be there when the bus brings you back to the home after bingo."

Now it was Harvath's turn to laugh. Sloane Ashby was a wiseass and could give as good as she got. She reminded him a lot of himself at that age—cocky, and way too sure of herself. Even so, he enjoyed mixing it up with her. Because the Old Man had been so adamant about not getting romantic with her, Harvath looked at her like a younger sister and treated her accordingly.

"Here," he said, handing her the box with the SBJ model in it. "I really did get you something."

Sloane opened the lid, looked inside, and rolled her eyes. "Wow. What a guy. You really know what women want. It's a wonder some girl hasn't snapped you up yet."

"It isn't for lacking of trying," Harvath replied as he tucked the vanity kit under his arm, smiled, and then turned and walked inside the FBO to grab a quick shower and change into his fresh clothes.

CHAPTER 6

The staff of the FBO welcomed Harvath and after checking him in, offered him use of the facility's shower, which he accepted.

The steam from the hot water quickly filled the bathroom. Next to a nice, thick cheeseburger, there was nothing he looked forward to more after an overseas trip than a long, hot American shower. It just felt different.

Stepping into the stall, he closed his eyes and let the water pound against his sore body. The work he did was both mentally and physically demanding. He took extremely good care of himself and it showed. He was in better shape than most men half his age. Nevertheless, he was getting older and he knew it. He could still carry out the ops just fine; it was the recovery time that was beginning to take longer. Someday, he was going to have to face the facts that this tended to be a younger man's game and consider moving in a different direction. The Old Man had told him as much, and was grooming him to take over the business someday. As far as Harvath was concerned, though, that day was still a long way away.

He could have stood there in the shower forever, allowing his half-hypnotized mind to drift in the heat and the steam, but there was work to do. Taking a deep breath, he flipped the temperature selector all the way to cold and exhaled. As the icy water hit his skin, he forced himself to count to thirty.

Harvath was convinced that the amount of cold that SEALs were forced to endure over the course of their careers eventually made them unable to deal with it at all. His observations were anecdotal at best, but he knew way too many guys who had opted for warm-weather climates after getting out and who never set foot anywhere else even remotely cold for the rest of their lives.

He was determined to never let anything, much less cold, beat him and so he stood in the shower every morning and punched cold right in the face. Of course it punched him right back, but it was like getting a double espresso for free and it always left him feeling invigorated. Today was no different.

Climbing out of the shower, he dried off and tied the towel around his waist. On his right side was a bruise he hadn't noticed or felt any pain from until now. It must have come during the taking of the tanker or rescuing the captain in Somalia. You bump into tons of things in close quarters battle and don't notice until after the fact. He was afraid to look down and see what his legs looked like. The joke in close quarters battle, or CQB, was that the shinbone's only purpose was to find furniture in a darkened room.

Harvath glanced in the mirror. His face was tanned from the training they had done down in the Gulf of Mexico before leaving for Somalia. His neck and forearms were, too. A few days of R&R to tan the rest of his body would be pleasant and for a moment, he allowed himself the delusion that maybe the Old Man's new client had an easy job for them someplace nice. That caused him to smile. The Carlton Group wasn't in the "easy job" business. And as far as "someplace nice" was concerned, as long as it was someplace "nicer" than the pit of human misery and suffering that was Somalia, he'd be thrilled.

Noticing that he'd missed a spot while shaving, he bypassed the cheap, plastic disposable razors sitting in a glass jar on the bathroom counter and unzipped the vanity kit from the private jet. He was glad he'd held on to it. Not only was their razor a lot nicer, but Natalie had slipped her phone number inside at some point as well.

When he was done touching up his shave, he unzipped the garment bag. He had guessed by the weight that there was a pair of shoes inside and sure enough there was. Ashby had thought of everything, right down to a shirt and tie combination he probably wouldn't have made on his own, but which actually looked pretty nice.

Exiting the building and walking over to her car, he received an approving whistle. "Don't you look handsome."

"There were plenty of white shirts in my closet, you know."

"And they were all boring. You look great," she said, straightening the knot in his tie. "Don't let anyone tell you different."

Harvath tossed his garment bag with his other clothes into her trunk and then got in the passenger seat. "Where are we going?"

"Mr. Carlton is waiting for you downtown," she said, starting the car and pulling out of the parking lot.

"Where exactly?"

"C Street between 22nd and 21st."

Harvath pulled up the location in his mind's eye. "The State Department?"

"No," said Ashby. "Across the street. The Einstein Memorial."

"Any idea why?"

"I don't know. Have you done anything so stupid recently that he'd want to beat you to death in front of a statue of Albert Einstein as a lesson to the rest of us?"

Harvath laughed. It was true. The Old Man didn't suffer fools lightly and he was taken to making examples of smart people who made dumb decisions or did stupid things.

Sloane took her eyes off the road to look at him. "You're actually running through your mind what you've done lately, aren't you?"

"No, I'm not."

"The hell you aren't. I was pulling your leg and you actually think it's a possibility."

Harvath dismissed her with a wave. "Pay attention to the road."

"What a fitting end that would be," she replied, ignoring him. "Beaten to death at the feet of Albert Einstein for being a frickin' moron."

"Why don't we find something else to talk about?" he offered.

"Like what?" she asked as they merged onto the road for D.C.

"I don't care. Regale me," Harvath replied, adding, "As long as it's not about shopping, your girlfriends, or your love life."

"If you wanted to ride in silence, why didn't you just say so?"

She was pulling his leg. "Fine," he said. "You pretend to be interesting and I'll pretend to care. Sound good?"

Ashby smiled. "Aren't we just like an old married couple? And by old married couple, I mean a couple where some young hot girl hooks up with some *really* old guy only because he's filthy rich and she knows he's going to die at any moment now."

Harvath shook his head and leaned the seat way back like he was going to sleep. When she reached out and slapped him across the chest, he relented and told her to pick a topic.

She raised a few of the current problems their organization was having and how they might fix them, and despite their capacity for verbal jabs, the rest of the drive resulted in an excellent conversation.

CHAPTER 7

After conducting a circuitous surveillance detection route, also known as an SDR, Ashby pulled up in front of the Albert Einstein memorial and wished Harvath good luck.

"And by the way," she said, as he got out of the car and was about to shut the door, "if the boss does decide to kill you, do you think it would be okay if I took your parking space back at the office?"

"Here's a tip," he said as he leaned back into the car. "The only nutcrackers men actually enjoy are the ones you see at Christmastime. Keep that in mind and you might find a husband someday."

Ashby mimicked a massive overbite and replied, "Do you think I'll get a purty man? I sure do hope so."

Harvath shook his head and closed the door to the sound of the young woman laughing at her own joke. *Wiseass,* he smirked to himself. That sense of humor was going to get her into trouble. He wished he could save her some future heartache, but if she was anything like him, she was going to have to learn the hard way.

He spotted the Old Man sitting on one of the far benches and made a loop around the memorial, taking everything and everyone in before deciding it was safe to approach his boss and sit down.

"You sure took your time," Carlton snapped. "I've been sitting here like a moron for over forty-five minutes feeding the damn pigeons."

"I'm fine," Harvath replied. "Thank you for asking, sir."

"Don't be a smart aleck. What's with that shirt? All of your white ones at the cleaners?"

Reed Carlton put the "old" in old school. He had always worn Brooks Brothers suits, white shirts, and very conservative ties, which was exactly how he was attired now. A tan overcoat sat folded on the bench next to him along with a copy of the *Wall Street Journal*, a cup of coffee and a bag from which he must have been feeding the pigeons pieces of a muffin.

"This is what Ashby brought from my house," said Harvath.

"Women," the Old Man responded with a dismissive shake of his head. "I should have sent a man to pick up your clothes."

Harvath knew Carlton liked Ashby and didn't really mean the remark, but he was in a bad mood for some reason.

"We need to get going," he said.

"Where to? Across the street to State?"

Carlton chuckled as he stood and gathered his things. "Those people could screw up a one-car funeral. After all the headaches they put us through back when I was at the CIA, there isn't enough money in the world for me to take them as a client. Not even now."

Harvath doubted that, but he knew better than to argue with him. "So if not State, who are we going to see?"

Carlton pointed up C Street with his chin and began walking. "What do you know about the Federal Reserve?"

"The Fed? Let me see. I know that they technically don't print our money."

"Technically, they also don't make ice cream, but that's not what I asked."

Wow, the Old Man has a burr under his saddle. Assuming that it was the Fed who had sent the plane to pick him up, he was tempted to say that they had a very nice aircraft, but he bit his tongue and replied, "The Federal Reserve establishes our monetary policy."

"That's a better answer. What does it mean?"

"They set the interest rates at which banks borrow money."

"Is that all?" asked Carlton. "That's the extent of your knowledge of the Federal Reserve?"

"I think it's actually beyond the extent of most people's knowledge. Not many care about the Fed."

"They *should*."

Harvath couldn't argue with that. Americans should care about a lot of things. He wasn't quite sure, however, how high the Federal Reserve ought to be on that list.

"What did you study in school again? It wasn't economics, was it?"

The Old Man knew perfectly well what he had studied. The economics remark was a jab.

"I studied political science and military history."

"Did they give you any John Adams to read out there in Southern California?"

"Of course. The Revolutionary War and the history of the Republic was a key focus. We read all the Founders."

"Good," Carlton replied. "Then you can tell me what Adams identified to Jefferson as one of America's greatest weaknesses?"

"*One of America's greatest weaknesses*?" he repeated as he thought about it for a second. "Based on our context here, I'm going to assume it has something to do with banking."

"It does. Adams saw people's complete ignorance when it came to money, credit, and circulation as a serious deficiency."

"That's a new one by me. What does it have to do with why we're having a meeting at the Federal Reserve, though?"

"Have you even picked up a paper since you've been gone?" the Old Man asked.

"Didn't exactly have a lot of newsstands where we were."

Carlton's visage softened. "I'm sorry. I owe you an 'attaboy' for that job."

He had never been comfortable with praise, fulsome or otherwise. "No, you don't, sir."

"Yes, I do. That was a hard operation and you did remarkably well. You got handed a bushel basket of lemons with that captain having been smuggled into port and you still made lemonade. You and your team did, though, leave a lot of dead Somalis."

"No, sir. We left a lot of dead *pirates*."

"I understand," the Old Man said with a nod. "And better them than a single one of you, but my problem right now is that some French human rights organization caught wind of it and they're trying to put the pieces together and make some international incident out of it. Had everything been contained to the ship, that would have been one thing, but going into Somalia and that village has created a whole different set of headaches."

"We had no choice. They'd killed the navigator and we had every reason to believe they'd do the same thing to the captain," Harvath insisted.

"Of course, but I want you to listen to me. You did the *right* thing. That captain would have been murdered had you left him there. We all know that. Nevertheless, the owners of the *Sienna Star* are nervous. They never okayed the shore raid and now they're worried that this whole thing is going to blow up in their faces. They've boxed us into a corner by refusing to release any payment until this whole thing goes away."

He now understood why the Old Man was in such a bad mood. "I don't know what to say."

"Don't say anything."

"I feel responsible, though, about the payment being held up."

Carlton lifted his hand, his face tensing up again. "I gave the green light for you to launch. I will handle this. In the meantime, let's focus on what's in front of us."

Harvath nodded. "You asked if I'd seen a paper since I've been gone. I haven't. What's up?"

The Old Man handed him his copy of the *Wall Street Journal*. It had been folded over to an article inside. "You can read it if you want, but there's not a lot of detail. A week ago, the chairman of the Federal Reserve had a heart attack and died."

Harvath looked at the man's picture. He had seen him on TV and in a few news articles over the last couple of years. "I'm sorry for his family."

"So am I, but that's not why we've been asked to this meeting."

"What's the reason, then?"

"The President of the United States in this situation is given a very closely guarded, some even say secret list, and from that list he picks who the next Federal Reserve chairman will be. Last night, all of the people on that list disappeared."

Harvath was astounded. "All of them? *Just gone?*"

Carlton nodded. "The body of one, a woman named Claire Marcourt, was found this morning."

"Where? What happened to her?"

The Old Man stopped walking. They were now parallel with the enormous white marble Federal Reserve Building, which took up an entire D.C. block. Pointing to a discreet side entrance, he said, "That's what we're here to discuss."

CHAPTER 8

Phil Durkin leaned back in his chair, closed his eyes, and pressed the heels of his hands against his temples as he tried to think. "For all we know, Nafi didn't have a single thing in that folder. Or maybe he had his wife's grocery list or the lease for his mistress's apartment in Amman."

"He wasn't bluffing, Phil," Lydia Ryan said to her former supervisor. "If you'd been sitting across from him like I was, you would've seen he was dead serious."

"Think he might give you the information if you slept with him?"

"Go fuck yourself, Phil," Ryan responded in disgust. "Better yet, why don't you go fuck Nafi Nasiri and see if he'll pillow-talk the plot over to *you*."

"I'm not seriously suggesting you sleep with Nasiri to get the intel, Lydia."

"Oh, really? Because that's *exactly* what it just sounded like to me. In fact I ought to take this up to the seventh floor right now and have them run your ass up a flagpole. You're beyond sick."

Durkin laughed as he leaned forward and focused on Ryan. "You have no idea what sick is."

"I'm looking at you, so I've got a pretty good picture in my head."

"Yeah, I'm the first guy in all of history to have too much to drink at an office Christmas party and make a pass at a coworker. I'm the devil."

"First of all, we weren't coworkers, you were my *supervisor*. And secondly, what you did wasn't some booze-fueled pass," she said, remembering how he had pulled her into an empty office, forced his hand under her dress, and tried to pull her panties off. "It bordered on charges being filed and you know it."

"It's not healthy to live in the past, Lydia. You've got to let it go."

"You'd like that, wouldn't you. In fact, I bet you'd like it if I left the Agency altogether."

"What I'd like, is if you didn't run your mouth so much. It's not like I skated. I got suspended without pay *and* my wife left me."

"Brenda left you because you're an asshole and drinking only made you worse. The Agency should have cut you loose, but you manipulated the crap out of them and blamed all of your bad behavior on being an alcoholic so they sent you to rehab instead. Speaking of which, do you even bother going to AA meetings anymore?"

"That's none of your damn business."

"Fair enough," Ryan replied with a shrug. "I can only imagine how much they get in the way of drinking."

"Can we get to the point? I've got a lot of other work to do."

"*Get to the point?* What do I have to do? Draw you a picture? The Jordanians aren't going to share until we give them something."

Durkin shrugged and looked at her. "None of the guys they're asking about work here anymore. The Eclipse program was disassembled. What do you want me to do?"

"Let me see," she replied. "This is the Central Intelligence Agency. We have assets and liaison relationships around the world. Hmmmmm. Maybe try to find them?"

"You seem to have forgotten that the Eclipse program technically didn't exist. I can't now just unilaterally launch an operation to hunt down a group of American citizens who were photographed having lunch on Cyprus."

"Who were also placed in Egypt and Libya before the turmoil there."

"I hate to break it to you, Lydia, but visiting any of those countries isn't a crime."

Ryan couldn't believe what she was hearing. "How about lunching with two high-ranking Jordanian Muslim Brotherhood officials?"

"Also not a crime."

"This is serious, Phil. This isn't the kind of thing the Agency should be playing chicken over."

"I'm not saying it isn't serious."

Ryan locked eyes with her former boss. "Maybe you don't know Nafi Nasiri very well, but I do. Trust me, he doesn't bluff."

"I know Nafi Nasiri better than you think."

"If you did, then you'd know that he doesn't walk out on limbs without knowing exactly how strong they are and what he can grab if necessary on the way down."

"Things are changing," Durkin pontificated. "And if there's one thing the Arabs don't like, besides the Jews and the rest of us, it's change."

"I'm telling you, Phil, this is a survival issue for the Jordanians. They think they could be the next country to collapse and that we might be behind it. They're an ally. We shouldn't mess with them. Let's help them."

Again, the man shrugged. "What else do you want me to do? I told you that I'll personally hand the terrorism plot allegation over to our Jordanian and Syrian desks. We'll see what they come up with."

Despite their relationship, Ryan had expected more buy-in from him. "Why not horse-trade with Nafi a little? Aren't you even the slightest bit interested in what our old team might be up to? Let's at least open a file on them."

"The only jobs they'd ever be able to find are in the private contracting world. That whole team was made up of cowboys and more than a couple of bullshit artists, which means they're probably selling some hybrid package of intel gathering and personal security services. They never liked discipline and they didn't like rules, which means no reputable American company would ever hire them. They've either bamboozled some loosey-goosey foreign outfit to take them on, or they've hung their own shingle. Either way, they are persona non grata at this agency and I don't give a rat's ass what they're up to. They're simply not even worth thinking about."

While she hated to admit it, there was a lot of logic to what Durkin was saying. "Let's assume that you're right; that they're out there selling their services as private contractors. What's the harm in quietly looking around, compiling a case file, and passing it off to the Jordanians?"

Durkin adopted a more sympathetic tone, but it was still patronizing. "Lydia, I want to help. Believe me. But you're talking about private U.S. citizens. You know how the director feels about this kind of thing. We can't investigate them without some sort of a justification."

"So you're saying *no*."

The man nodded. "That's what I'm saying. I'm sorry."

"I'm sorry, too," said Ryan as she stood up from the couch and walked to the door.

"Tell Nasiri you're trying. In the meantime, let's see if our people can run down this 'plot' he's uncovered."

"And if we can't run it down?"

"Then hopefully, he'll do the right thing and come clean with you."

"I'm not going to hold my breath."

"You never know," Durkin said. "He may surprise you."

Ryan was halfway out the door when she turned around and asked, "Why wasn't I let go with the rest of the team when they were fired?"

"Why do you think?"

She shrugged. "I certainly broke my fair share of rules, just like the rest of them."

"That's the way the team was set up. You were expected to color outside the lines in order to get results."

"But why keep me and not the others?"

"Because unlike the others, you didn't ask for that assignment. You got put there as a babysitter. We knew you'd have to break a few rules, but we also knew where your loyalties were."

"*We?*" she asked, "Or *you?*"

"What are you saying?"

"Did I get some sort of special treatment that the others didn't get? Is that why you thought you could come on to me the way you did?"

"No," he replied, shaking his head. "That was me being stupid. You're still here because both the CIA and I value your talent. Nothing more. Now stop letting Nafi Nasiri mess with your head. You're too smart to be manipulated like that."

Coming from anyone else, it would have been a nice compliment. Nevertheless, she remained professional. "Thank you."

"You're welcome. Now go."

Once Ryan had left his office and the door had fully closed behind her, Durkin picked up his secure telephone and dialed. When a man's voice answered on the other end the CIA man said, "We've got a problem. A big one."

CHAPTER 9

The security at the headquarters of the Federal Reserve was similar to security at government buildings throughout the nation's capital. Uniformed men with sidearms were posted at the entrances, as well as at the checkpoints inside.

Harvath and Carlton were required to pass through a full-body imaging machine before being allowed to proceed to a reception desk near a plush waiting area. "I should have warned you, but I'm glad you didn't bring any weapons," said the Old Man.

"Who said I didn't bring any?" replied Harvath.

For a moment, Carlton couldn't tell if he was pulling his leg or not. He decided to let it go and walked over to the reception desk.

Harvath admired the building's interior. Even by Washington standards, it was impressive. With its polished marble and modernist interpretation of Beaux Arts style, if this was supposed to be an awe-inspiring temple to money, its architects had succeeded.

After giving their names to the receptionist, Carlton rejoined Harvath. "Ever been here before?" the Old Man asked.

Harvath shook his head. "No. I've been to the Treasury and about every other federal building in town, but not this one."

"This one isn't federal."

"What do you mean?"

"The Federal Reserve is a private organization. They gave themselves the title *Federal Reserve* to sound more official, but they're not part of the government by any stretch of the imagination."

"But, I always thought—"

The Old Man cut him off as someone approached from the other side of the lobby. "Here's the gentleman we're meeting with."

The man was in his late forties, with short hair graying at the temples and a pronounced beak of a nose. He wore a well-tailored gray suit with an understated tie and a plain white pocket square. His shoes shone like mirrors.

"Good morning," the man said as he walked up and extended his hand. "I'm Monroe Lewis." His fingers were long and slim like a pianist's and he spoke with the muted patrician accent of an old New England family.

Harvath and Carlton both shook the man's hand. "Thank you for coming so quickly," he said. Looking at Harvath he added, "Especially you. I hope you found the plane comfortable."

"It was more than comfortable. Thank you," Harvath replied. Closer now, he noticed that the man had undergone some sort of modest cosmetic surgery; either Botox or a lift of some sort, which had tightened the skin across his face. Harvath wasn't a fan of cosmetic surgery for men. While some guys might be able to get away with a little, there were others who didn't know when to stop and whose faces ended up looking like they'd seen more knives than a grill at a Benihana.

Lewis was accompanied by a protective detail made up of three solidly built men in dark suits. Scanning the lobby, Harvath could make out at least two more, their heads on swivels, as they took in every person and every movement in the cavernous space.

"I have our conference room available," Lewis offered. "Shall we go upstairs?"

Carlton nodded and the Federal Reserve man led the way. As they walked, he pointed out different pieces of the Fed's history adorning the walls, and made polite small talk. He was quite knowledgeable about the organization, having worked there for more than two decades. His path to the Fed had begun with a quote from Karl Marx he discovered in high school—*Money plays the largest role in determining the course of history.*

Monroe Lewis had been a shy, frail boy of modest upbringing and lofty ambitions. He would never captain a football team or lead men into battle. He didn't possess those skills. His strength lay neither in his muscles nor his character, but in his mind.

He was a voracious reader whose escape had always been books. And while outsiders saw him as perfectly suited for a career in academia, he knew academia was far too small a stage. One did not impact the course of history from some university campus. To impact history, one needed to be at the epicenter of where history was made. For him, that epicenter was the Federal Reserve.

Arriving at the conference room, he showed his guests in and asked his security detail to remain outside.

It was an enormous rectangular room with an almost thirty-foot mahogany table running down the center. Along one wall was a large marble fireplace and suspended above the table was an ornate chandelier that looked to be at least a thousand pounds.

"I suppose, given the situation, the security is a necessary precaution," he said, closing the door and crossing to Harvath and Carlton, "but it does take some getting used to."

"Always better to have it and not need it," said Harvath.

"Indeed," Lewis replied. "Indeed. Can I offer you gentlemen some coffee?"

The old spy and his number two accepted china cups with saucers and joined Lewis at the long inlaid conference table. As they pulled out their chairs, there was a knock followed by the door opening.

"Ah, William," Lewis said as a man walked in with a folder tucked beneath his arm. "Thank you for joining us." Turning to Harvath and Carlton he introduced the new arrival, "This is Will Jacobson, our director of security."

Jacobson was a large man in his late fifties. He was fit, with thick arms outlined by the sleeves of his almost too tight navy blue suit. He had silver hair that was neatly combed, and dark, almost slitlike eyes. He carried himself with an air of self-importance.

After shaking hands, they all sat back down and Lewis handed control of the meeting to Jacobson.

"Thank you, Mr. Lewis," he said, staring across the table and sizing up his two outsiders. "As you've probably heard, one week ago Federal Reserve Chairman Wallace Sawyer passed away."

"How did he die?" asked Harvath.

Jacobson, who didn't enjoy being interrupted, shot him a look. "Heart attack."

"Has the cause of death been confirmed?"

"Yes, by the coroner. Though it wasn't released to the press, Chairman Sawyer, who was sixty-six years old at the time of his death, had an underlying heart condition."

"Where was he when it happened?"

"You realize you weren't brought here to talk about Chairman Sawyer," Jacobson said curtly, irritation evident in his tone.

Lewis raised his hand to calm the security director. "It's okay, Will. Please answer their questions."

Jacobson took a deep breath and let it out. "He was leaving a restaurant in Bethesda with his wife."

"Did he travel with a security detail?"

"Yes. They were with him that night," he replied and then waited for any follow-up questions. When none were asked, he continued. "After the chairman's passing, the vice chairman was made temporary chair."

"And that would be Mr. Lewis?"

Monroe Lewis shook his head. "No, I'm not the vice chair. I report to the Board of Governors and help oversee day-to-day operations. Essentially, I function as a chief operating officer."

Harvath looked at Carlton and then back at Lewis. "I apologize. The structure is a little confusing."

Lewis smiled. "That's quite all right. It's actually not that difficult. The Board of Governors has seven members, all appointed by the President of the United States and confirmed by the Senate. They serve a fourteen-year term. From these seven members, the President selects a chairman and a vice chairman."

"Has the President ever appointed a chairman from outside the Board of Governors?"

"Yes, there is a precedent for that."

"So he could select you for instance?"

Lewis laughed. "I suppose anything is possible, but that's not how it happens. The chairman usually is selected from the Board of Governors."

"And what exactly do they do?" Harvath asked.

"They oversee the twelve district Federal Reserve banks."

"Which do what?"

"They represent the twelve districts the Federal Reserve has divided the nation into. Their job is to help implement monetary policy as established by the Federal Reserve's Federal Open Market Committee." He could see Harvath's eyes glazing over. "The Open Market Committee focuses on establishing interest rates and dealing with the nation's money supply. They also oversee the Federal Reserve's purchase and sale of U.S. Treasury securities. And to keep it simple, the district Federal Reserve banks help regulate the banks in their area. Does that make sense?"

Not really, thought Harvath, but he didn't want to look any dumber than he already felt. "Got it," he lied, figuring they'd get to his own area of expertise soon enough. "Please continue."

"As a thirty-thousand-foot view, that's pretty much it."

"And shortly after Chairman Sawyer died, your top five candidates to replace him disappeared, and one of them turned up murdered this morning."

Lewis nodded.

"It looks like someone is trying to send you a message."

"You can say that again," replied Jacobson, as he removed a hideous photograph from his file and slid it across the table.

CHAPTER 10

T he terrible image was a police evidence photo of a woman who had been mutilated and apparently beaten to death. She was lying atop a bed of logs, her ears missing, with some sort of sign hung around her neck.

"This is Claire Marcourt?" the Old Man asked, his voice filled with pity for the woman.

The security chief nodded solemnly. "Her body was found early this morning on Jekyll Island, about forty-five minutes from her vacation home on Sea Island down in Georgia."

"How'd you get a copy of the photo?" Harvath asked, examining it.

"We have some influence down there."

"Any idea why they cut off her ears?" Carlton inquired. "Could she have heard something she wasn't supposed to?"

The security chief shrugged. "For all we know, the symbolism is the exact opposite. Maybe someone felt she wasn't listening as she should."

"Do you have a better picture of whatever this sign is around her neck?"

Jacobson pulled another photo from his folder and slid it across the table. Harvath picked it up while the Old Man pulled a pair of glasses from his breast pocket. Before he'd even slipped them on, he heard a quiet gust of air blown from Harvath's mouth.

"What is it?"

Harvath handed the tight shot of the sign around the dead woman's neck to his boss. Upon it had been painted a skull and crossbones with a crown floating above. The sign was streaked in blood, as if the victim's bloody fingers had slid down it. Carlton read aloud the words painted beneath: "The Tree of Liberty must be refreshed from time to time with the blood of patriots and tyrants." Looking up from the photo, he stated, "I've heard that before. Who said it?"

"Thomas Jefferson," Harvath replied.

"Exactly," the security chief confirmed. "We think we're dealing with some sort of anti–Federal Reserve extremist group."

"What do these other letters mean here at the bottom? *S.O.L.*"

"S.O.L. is an abbreviation for multiple sayings and phrases: statute of limitations, standard of living, sooner or later, speed of light. It could mean anything."

The Old Man changed tack and asked a different question, "As far as you know, Mrs. Marcourt was kidnapped from home, correct?"

"According to her husband, that's what we understand. Yes."

"Did he have any additional insight, any clues as to who might have taken her or why?"

"No," replied the security chief. "He was asleep, as were their children. Claire had been up drinking wine. There was no sign of forced entry. She liked to sit out near their pool. We're assuming that may be where she was when she was kidnapped."

"Why take her to Jekyll Island?"

"On that point, we're pretty confident we know why. Jekyll Island is where the Federal Reserve Act, back in 1910, was originally outlined in a series of complicated meetings. You'd never know that, though, by listening to the conspiracy nuts. As far as they're concerned, the meetings had everything but devil-worshipping masses and animal sacrifices."

"That bad, huh?" said Harvath, picking up on what a hot-button issue this was for the security chief.

"Was there a certain degree of secrecy around the meetings, of course there was. Considering the sensitivity of what they were trying to do, why would that be strange? If I had been their security director back then, I would have advised them to do exactly what they did and stay as far under the radar as possible. We keep a lot of the day-to-day stuff here quiet because we have to, for security reasons, but that just fuels the crazies. You have no idea what a colossal pain in the ass those people are. Not a day goes by that we're not dealing with something they're stirring up."

"I can imagine," said the Old Man, who followed up with another question. "Have there been any ransom demands?"

"We're not sure," he replied, sliding another picture across the table. "This was also found at the scene."

It was a picture of Claire Marcourt's severed ears, propped up and bracketing an odd note that read *Today is already the tomorrow which the bad economist yesterday urged us to ignore.*

Harvath lined up the photo of the ears and note alongside the tight shot of the sign. The writing was exactly the same. "Any idea what it's supposed to mean?"

"I assume it means someone doesn't like how the Fed is handling the economy. It's just a quote from some dead economist named Henry Hazlitt."

Harvath doubted it was "just a quote." It obviously held significance for whoever had written it. Placing the crime scene photo of Claire Marcourt's body with the other two pictures, he remarked, "How about the local police, do they have any clues to go on? Witnesses? CCTV footage?"

"Nothing," the security chief replied. "Whoever did this went to great lengths to make sure they didn't leave any evidence behind."

He found that hard to believe, too. There was always evidence. It was just a matter of how well trained you were to look for it. Harvath studied the photos for a few more moments before saying, "I'm not exactly sure why we're here. The FBI must already be all over this."

He could feel the Old Man bristle next to him, but he didn't care. The question needed to be asked.

"Yes," Lewis offered. "The FBI is already involved, but we want to make sure we're bringing in every resource we can to prevent anyone else from being killed."

Jacobson added, "I have contacts at the Bureau and I know how it works. If we have any hope of bringing this to a rapid resolution, we need to have someone familiar with the system who, how do I say this delicately? Someone who's not afraid to work outside it."

Harvath didn't reply. He let Jacobson's words float in the air above the conference room table.

"We also need someone who can keep quiet," Lewis stated.

Now we're getting to the heart of what this is really about, thought Harvath.

"You need to understand," Lewis continued, "that there are several forces arrayed against the Federal Reserve who want to see us gone, and it's not just citizens. There are members of Congress as well. Granted they're not very powerful or very well organized, but a scandal of this magnitude could help put some wind in their sails and we don't want that."

"With all due respect, how are you going to hide it? You've already got five kidnappings, one of which has turned into a murder."

"We're trying very hard to keep it out of the press. So far, we've been successful."

"There's no way that'll hold," Harvath replied.

"We've asked the families and law enforcement for their cooperation, and so far they've been on board, but now with a murder things are going to be different," Jacobson said. "We've got maybe forty-eight hours, seventy-two tops before this story is everywhere."

Lewis nodded and Jacobson pulled a sheet of paper from his file and pushed it across to their guests. "This is a list of the missing candidates."

Harvath and the Old Man studied it together.

Marcourt, Claire—New York City
Mitchell, Betsy—Seattle
Penning, Herman—Boston
Renner, Jonathan—San Francisco
Whalen, Peter—Chicago

"I've never heard of any of these people," Harvath finally said.

"Me neither," the Old Man replied. "Who are they?"

"Private sector people. Investment banking mostly," said Lewis. "Because of the trouble the economy has been having and the way fingers have been pointed at us, we were considering bringing our next chairman or chairwoman from outside of the Federal Reserve. Sort of a breath of fresh air as it were."

Harvath looked at him. "How many people knew these were your top picks?"

"It was quietly known inside the organization."

"And outside of it?"

"The candidates themselves knew, and there were some financial reporters who had speculated on who might be on our list, though as far as we know, no one had come close to winnowing it down to our five."

"And the Bureau is aware of all of this?"

"All of it," said Jacobson. "They've already begun interviewing everyone here who had any knowledge of things. Our number-one goal is getting the kidnap victims recovered and making sure the perpetrators are dealt with. That's why we're having this meeting with you."

"*Dealt with*?" Harvath repeated. "I'm sorry, but what exactly is it that you think we do?"

The Old Man put his hand on Harvath's forearm. "They came to us because of our kidnap and ransom expertise."

Harvath knew that wealthy companies and individuals often brought in kidnapping specialists to augment the efforts of the FBI. "There are plenty of people who do K-and-R," he stated. "Why us specifically?"

"Because," said Lewis. "We want the best and you came very highly recommended."

"By whom?"

"I think the response you're searching for," the Old Man corrected Harvath, "is thank you."

"That's all right," Lewis said. "Mr. Harvath, Stephanie Gallo has been a personal friend of mine for many years. She was also a friend of Chairman Sawyer's before he passed away. When her daughter was kidnapped while doing aid work in Afghanistan, you were the person the President personally recommended she hire to cut through all the red tape and bring her back alive, which is exactly what you did."

Harvath remembered the case. The Taliban had captured Gallo's daughter Julia and were holding her hostage in exchange for the release of a very dangerous Al-Qaeda operative. Not many people knew of Harvath's involvement, much less that the President had quietly recommended him to the Gallo family.

"We don't discuss our clients or any of our operations," he replied.

"And I respect that," Lewis stated. "Like I said, we need someone who can keep quiet."

The Old Man tapped Harvath on the forearm again. "It's okay. The Gallo family knows that we're meeting with Mr. Lewis."

"Even so," said Harvath, "that was Afghanistan. This is the United States. The rules are different, *a lot* different. I'm not saying we can't help, but without a ransom demand this is almost entirely a law enforcement function. There's only so much a K-and-R team will be allowed to do."

"You'll have all of our resources at your disposal," said Lewis, "including the aircraft, which is being held at Reagan with a fresh crew standing by."

Harvath wasn't exactly sure how to respond. He had several more questions, none of which were appropriate to ask in front of Lewis and Jacobson. He needed to speak with the Old Man privately. The prospective clients, though, were not content to afford him that opportunity.

"Unfortunately, we don't have the luxury of time for you to think this over," Lewis stated. "I need to know now, whether you're in or you're out."

Before Harvath could respond, Reed Carlton answered for both of them. "We're in."

CHAPTER 11

"They're a client with a license to print their own money," said Carlton as he drove toward Harvath's home on the outskirts of Alexandria, Virginia. He was in a much better mood now that their meeting was over and they had the assignment. "That's not something that falls into your lap every day."

"*Technically,*" Harvath replied, "they don't *print* their own money. And, as a wise man once told me, they don't make ice cream, either."

"What's the matter with you all of a sudden?"

"I don't know."

"Well, snap out of it. Between this job and once we get paid on the *Sienna Star,* we'll be back in the black."

"What are you charging Monroe Lewis?"

"I'm not charging him, I'm charging the Federal Reserve. I came in high because I expected him to negotiate us down on our fee, but he didn't. He's even wiring us half of everything up front. You, though, for some reason seemed bound and determined to kill this deal. If I'd had my weapon, I might have put a bullet in you right there myself."

Harvath shook his head. "None of this bothers you?"

"Of course it bothers me. Every assignment we take bothers me. Each one has its share of headaches and blind alleys. That's why people call us. But despite all the problems, we always find a way through. It's what we do."

It's what I do, thought Harvath. And while he didn't discount the Old Man's genius, Carlton didn't do much if any fieldwork anymore. It was always Harvath who was being sent into shitholes around the world having to face danger on a regular basis. There was a ton of it he loved, but there was some he was starting to dislike.

"Listen, for Monroe Lewis and his crew money is *literally* no object. At some point, someone in the press is going to connect the dots and this is going to be a huge story. In fact, I don't even know how long they'll be able to keep the murder down in Georgia quiet. When this thing does go supernova on them, they're going to want to appear to have done everything they could, which includes bringing in a K-and-R team to assist the FBI. They're hedging their bets."

The Old Man was right. Harvath didn't want to dwell on it. "Where do we begin?" he asked.

Carlton signaled and merged into a faster-moving lane. "Jacobson gave us his file with everything on the kidnappings plus what they have on the murder. I think we ought to start there."

"Speaking of which, did you notice how her body was laid out?"

"On the bed of logs? Weird, huh?"

"Not so much weird as purposeful," Harvath replied.

"Why do you say that?"

"Because whoever killed her was sending a very specific message."

"Of course they were," the Old Man stated. "They're some wacko group that thinks the Fed is comprised of a bunch of tyrants."

"It's not just the line from Jefferson about the tree of liberty. It's also the skull and crossbones with the crown above it. And there's something with those logs that bothers me, too."

"Like what?"

"I want to double-check it when we get back to the house. It may not be anything."

• • •

Harvath's property sat above the Potomac, just south of George Washington's Mount Vernon. The modest estate, called Bishop's Gate, was a former Anglican church dating back to the Revolutionary War and was one of hundreds of properties owned by the United States Navy. Out of gratitude for his service to the United States, a previous president had arranged a ninety-nine-year lease for Harvath. All that was required was that he restore and maintain the property in a manner befitting its historic value. His rent was established at one dollar per annum.

With all of the places he had lived as an adult, nothing had ever felt truly like home to him until Bishop's Gate. Not someone particularly given to a belief in fate, he made a discovery on the day he took possession of the property that caused him to wonder if his tenancy wasn't somehow preordained.

In the attic of the rectory, he had come across a sign. On a beautifully carved piece of wood was the Latin motto of the Anglican missionaries. It was almost as if it had been left there for him. When he read the words that so perfectly summed up what he did and who he was, Scot knew he had found his refuge—TRANSIENS ADIUVA NOS—*I go overseas to give help*.

He removed the sign from the attic and hung it in his entry hall so he could read it each time he came or went.

Stepping inside, he told Carlton to help himself to whatever he could find in the kitchen and that he would join him there in a few minutes.

He turned and walked down the opposite hall to his study. Once he got there, he stood looking at the shelves and shelves of books. Everything was in perfect alphabetical order by author. When he had first moved in, he thought that was the best way to organize his vast library. Only now did he wish he had grouped things by subject matter.

One of Harvath's passions was American History, particularly the years surrounding the Revolutionary War. He had loved that piece of America's past since he was a boy. In fact, had his two majors in college not kept him so busy, he might have considered adding an American history minor.

It took him a few minutes to find what he was looking for, but once he had all the books stacked on his desk, he picked them up and headed for the kitchen.

Carlton had found probably the only two food items in the entire house that seemed to weather Harvath's long trips away without spoiling—pickled herring and Wasa Crispbread—yet another throwback to his Scandinavian-themed dating days.

Setting the books on the kitchen table, Harvath grabbed a beer from the fridge and joined the Old Man.

"What's all this?" Carlton asked.

"Research," replied Harvath as he twisted the top off his beer and sent the cap sailing toward the sink.

"*Books?* Why don't you use the Internet like everyone else?"

He shook his head. It was ironic that he'd be the one championing books, while the Old Man touted the Internet. "The Web's pretty good, but it doesn't have everything. When it comes to historical items, books are still the best bet."

Harvath opened the uppermost book from his stack and began leafing through it. When he figured out that it wasn't the one he wanted, he set it aside, and opened another. Soon enough, he came to the page he was looking for.

"Let me see the tight shot of the sign hung around Claire Marcourt's neck," he said without taking his eyes from the book.

Opening the folder on the table, Reed Carlton fished out the picture and handed it to Harvath. "Here you go."

"Thanks," Harvath replied as he took it and set it inside, right next to the image he was looking at. He then turned the book so the Old Man could see.

"They're almost a perfect match."

Harvath nodded. "Except Claire Marcourt's doesn't have the words *Death to Tyranny* underneath."

"Which would have been redundant considering the line from Jefferson."

"I agree. That's probably why they left it out."

Carlton stared at the image. "That's been bothering me ever since we saw it at the Fed. I know I should remember that crown over the skull and bones, but I don't."

The man was a walking encyclopedia about almost everything. It wasn't often that Harvath knew something that Carlton didn't and when that happened, Harvath often ribbed the older man over it. Carlton may have been his boss, but he had grown to be like a second father to him. Harvath's own father had died not long after he had graduated from high school. The two hadn't been on good terms. Harvath's father, also a U.S. Navy SEAL, had been against Scot's pursuing a career in professional sports, despite his son's success on the competition circuit and acceptance to the U.S. Ski Team.

Like father, like son, Harvath had been bound and determined to do what he wanted to do. Ignoring his father's wishes, he pursued his athletic career, and their relationship suffered dramatically because of it. They fell into a cold silence, with Harvath's mother doing everything she could to keep the family together. The frosty détente collapsed when Harvath's father was killed in a training accident.

Harvath's athletic career collapsed soon after. No matter how hard he tried, he couldn't get his head back into competition. The crushing guilt was more than he could bear. He knew he had let his father down. No matter how many friends and coaches spoke to him, his mind couldn't be changed. He abandoned sports and decided to return to school.

After graduating cum laude from the University of Southern California, he joined the Navy and was eventually accepted into BUD/S. It was the most grueling experience Harvath had ever undergone, but the idea that if his father could do it, he could do it propelled him forward.

His athletic prowess and ironclad determination saw him excel. He graduated at the top of his class and was assigned to SEAL Team Two, also known as the Polar SEALs, where his proficiency in skiing was an exceptional asset.

As much as he enjoyed his Team Two colleagues, he wasn't seeing enough action with them to keep him happy and so he applied for the storied SEAL Team Six.

Harvath had built a bit of a rep for himself, but even so, SEAL Team Six was very, very particular about whom they allowed to join their ranks. As much as the rest of the SEAL community was loath to admit it, SEAL Team Six was in a class all its own.

It was one of the most elite organizations in the world and one of the most difficult to be accepted into. You had to prove you not only deserved to be there, but also wanted it more than anything else. The members of SEAL Six didn't make it easy. In fact, they did everything they could to discourage Harvath. None of it worked. In the middle of an endurance exercise designed so that there was no way anyone could complete it, they realized he was either going to join their ranks or die trying and they ended the audition. Scot Harvath had won his probationary place among their ranks.

Language proficiency was not something SEALs were particularly known for, but Harvath's aptitude was quickly recognized and encouraged. He was sent to school for any language he showed talent for, or interest in, including Arabic and Russian.

His skill at SEAL Team Six won the attention of the Secret Service, who recruited him to the White House to help bolster their anti- and counterterrorism expertise. From there, the president at the time realized Harvath had a special set of skills that could better serve the nation in an offensive capacity. That was how Harvath wound up with a top-secret program hidden away at the Department of Homeland Security. It was one of the most forward-thinking and aggressive projects the United States had ever come up with. As long as the terrorists refused to play by any rules, Harvath wasn't expected to, either. He was set loose upon them without mercy.

When the administration changed, Harvath's program was discontinued and he was let go. That's when the Old Man had picked him up and had taken his training to an entirely new level. The career intelligence officer had taught Harvath everything he knew. Then he sent Harvath out to train with the best shooters, hand-to-hand combat instructors, interrogators, and former spies, among other dark arts specialists. By the time Harvath was done, he was one of the most formidable counterterrorism and intelligence operatives to ever ply the trade. In short, he was an Apex predator—an animal at the top of the food chain who hunted, yet was so fearsome, he himself was not hunted.

Be that as it may, Harvath had spent the last couple of years in awe of the Old Man. No matter how much he had seen and done in his career, he felt he would never accomplish as much as what Carlton had done.

"So, are you going to keep me in suspense or are you going to tell me what we're looking at?" the Old Man asked.

Harvath smiled.

"What's so funny?" Carlton said.

"I just figured at a prestigious university like Brown with a catchall major like *Western Civilization*, you would have learned at least a little about the Stamp Act."

CHAPTER 12

"The Stamp Act was a tax on any piece of paper printed in the colonies—newspapers, licenses, legal documents, anything and everything, even playing cards. The Brits claimed it was necessary in order to pay for the thousands of troops it had protecting the colonies' back door near the Appalachian Mountains. The colonists, though, had a greater fear than invaders from the frontier. They were afraid that if this tax was allowed to pass unchallenged, there'd be a tidal wave of taxes to follow, and all without any colonial input," said Harvath.

"Taxation without representation," replied the Old Man.

"Precisely. In an act of defiance, the colonists refused it. Instead, they began drawing their own stamp on their printed materials. They used a skull and crossbones, and eventually some added a crown floating above it to represent tyrannical Britain."

"Death to tyranny."

Harvath nodded.

"What do you think the 'S.O.L.' stands for? Is it Latin or something?"

"I don't think so," he said, reaching for another book and flipping through its pages. "I think it has to do with the bloody streaks left on the sign by Claire Marcourt's fingers."

"Why do you think those two are connected? Maybe she grasped at the sign in her death throes."

"It doesn't make any sense to hang a sign around someone's neck until they're dead," Harvath replied. "Why go to all the trouble of the sign, just to have the victim mess it up? If you're going to kill somebody, you kill them and then hang it around their neck."

"So the bloody streaks were put there on purpose? Just like the logs the body was put on?"

"If I can find the right picture, I'll show you, and then you tell me what you think."

The Old Man waited while Harvath flipped through two more books until he found it. When he did, he placed the police photo of the sign that had been hung around Marcourt's neck beneath the image of a flag in his new book and spun them around to show him.

"What am I looking at here?" the Old Man asked.

"A flag with nine vertical stripes; five red and four white," responded Harvath as he splayed the fingers of his right hand, placed them on the table, and slowly drew them toward himself like Claire Marcourt's bloody fingers sliding down the sign.

"You think that woman's bloody finger streaks look like that flag?"

"I don't know. You tell me."

Carlton studied both pictures for a few moments. The irritation was back in his voice again. "I think it's a stretch."

"Fair enough," said Harvath as he removed the police photo in order to reveal the caption beneath the flag. "How about now?"

The Old Man leaned forward and peered at the writing. "Hold on," he said, pulling his glasses from his suit pocket and putting them on. "The caption says this is the flag of the Sons of Liberty?" A fraction of a second later he put it together. "Sons of Liberty—S.O.L."

Harvath sat back and took a long, satisfied sip of his beer.

"Who are they?"

Setting the bottle on the table, Harvath flipped forward a couple of pages in the book. "They were America's first organized resistance," he said. "A group of patriots, inspired by what they saw as the tyranny of the Stamp Act who banded together to fight British oppression. Their most famous operation was one of my favorites—the Boston Tea Party."

The old spymaster sat for a moment appreciating one of America's greatest historical moments and then replied, "You think whoever's behind all of this is styling themselves as some sort of modern Sons of Liberty movement?"

"I do," said Harvath as he reached for his last book and opened it. "Ever heard of the Pine Tree Riot?"

Carlton shook his head.

"One of the reasons the Brits were the most powerful empire in the world was because of their command of the high seas—via both their navy and their merchant vessels. They were building ships at an incredible clip and white pine trees were considered the best species from which to make soaring, single-stick masts. Because the British Isles had been stripped almost entirely clean of white pines, they passed a law in the colonies that made it illegal to cut down any white pine here more than twelve inches in diameter.

"This angered lots of colonial loggers, builders, and sawmill owners. Many of them just ignored the law. In fact, it became highly fashionable among the colonists to thumb their noses at Britain by installing floors made of white pine and showing off that their boards were at least a foot wide or wider."

"What does that have to do with the logs Claire Marcourt was found on?"

Harvath pointed to the photo and the thickest log in the stack. "See the arrow chalked on this one?"

The Old Man peered at it and nodded as Harvath paraphrased the accompanying text.

"When the crown sent its 'Surveyors of the King's Woods' on inspections, any trees found to have been cut down in violation of the edict were marked with a big, thick arrow just like in that photo. Anyone found to be in possession of white pines, considered property of the crown, was heavily fined.

"In 1772, a surveyor for the crown uncovered a mill owner in Weare,

New Hampshire, named Ebenezer Mudgett, who had been cutting down white pines that should have been reserved for the king. Mudgett was fined, but he refused to pay, so the county sheriff, along with his deputy, rode out and arrested him.

"Mudgett must have been a hell of a salesman, because he convinced the sheriff to release him that night with the promise that he'd show up in the morning to pay his bail."

"He didn't show up, did he?" said Carlton with a laugh.

"No, he showed up, all right," Harvath replied, "but with somewhere between twenty to forty men. They arrived, their faces blackened with soot, just before dawn at Quimby's Inn, where the sheriff and his deputy were staying."

"I assume it didn't end well. What happened?"

"They beat the sheriff and his deputy with tree switches, and then shaved the manes of their horses. And here's the kicker: they cut off the horses' ears to send a message and make them worthless."

The Old Man screwed his face up in disgust. "That's horrible."

"I agree one hundred percent."

"Were they ever caught?"

"You bet," said Harvath, "and they were all prosecuted, but they only received a small fine. And because the punishment was so lenient, some think it encouraged more resistance and actually set the stage for the Boston Tea Party less than two years later."

"So again, the message this group is sending now, is what? That the Federal Reserve is a tyrant like King George and they're going to handle it by kidnapping and murdering people until it is shut down?"

"Or until they're caught. But I think I may have an idea as to how we can catch them."

CHAPTER 13

L ydia Ryan remembered the first time she had ever seen Camp
Peary, the nine-thousand-acre military base near Williamsburg,
Virginia, referred to by CIA personnel as "the Farm." She, along
with twelve other recruits, had been transported there on a crisp fall
morning in a white passenger van with blacked-out windows to begin
their CIA training. Out of those twelve, only five would make it all the
way through.

Much of the curriculum harkened back to the heyday of the CIA's
predecessor, the Office of Strategic Services, or OSS, and was heavy with
paramilitary instruction. From weapons and explosives to parachuting and land navigation, there were times when the recruits questioned
whether they had signed up for a career in intelligence, or the military.
The tradecraft, which would form the bulk of what they'd be learning,
wouldn't come till later.

The first month at the Farm was all about what the recruits were made
of and how badly they wanted to be there. It was a particularly sadistic
version of boot camp and involved nothing but physical conditioning and
hand-to-hand combat. Every exercise, whether it was a run, a timed ruck-

sack march, accelerated PT, or even the obstacle course, was designed to get as many students to drop out as possible.

Instructors yelled, berated, and constantly got right up into their charges' faces telling them that they didn't belong at the Agency and should aim for something easier, like the FBI.

In preparation for the yearlong Basic Operations Course, Ryan had searched for any information she could find on what to expect and how to make it through. There was next to nothing available, so she read a stack of books on the rigorous selection processes for the Navy SEALs, the Army's Special Forces, and the British SAS.

What she learned was that they were all very similar. The idea was to stress trainees to such a degree that no matter what they encountered in the real world, they'd be able to adapt and overcome. While the SEAL, Green Beret, SAS soldier, or CIA operative unquestionably plied a physical trade, success or failure would always come down to their mental mettle. If you steadfastly refused to quit, you rapidly narrowed your options to only winning. That was the type of personality a sovereign nation could put millions of training dollars into and then drop into the field, confident that those operatives would see their assignment through.

Ryan's intelligence, determination, and physical abilities were quickly realized. Her beauty was simply icing on the cake. Even without makeup, she was a striking woman, not someone who naturally blended in and was easily forgotten. That fact, though, could be dealt with. Ryan could be taught how to mask her good looks. On the other hand, taking a less appealing woman and trying to make her as attractive as Ryan was next to impossible without plastic surgery.

There was also an intangible aura about her, a magnetism that couldn't be taught. In short, she was a one-in-a-million recruit whose gifts weren't fully apparent until she began the Basic Operations Course. Once her talents were on display, it was up to one man to make sure they were noted and leveraged to their maximum potential. It was that man that Ryan had now returned to the Farm to see.

In addition to being a lead instructor for the Basic Operations Course, Bob McGee was also a spotter. Before she arrived, he had read Ryan's file cover to cover, just as he did the files of every other recruit being considered for eventual placement in the CIA's National Clandestine Service.

The NCS was charged with a myriad of missions, including the collection of foreign intelligence and the development of clandestine human intelligence assets. But it was the planning and execution of covert operations that most interested McGee.

A former Delta Force operative who had joined the CIA after leaving the Army, McGee was tasked with flagging prospective candidates for a secretive branch of the Clandestine Service called the Special Activities Division (SAD). Based on her jacket, Ryan had looked pretty good on paper, but it wasn't until he saw her in action that he appreciated how good she really was.

There was no way, though, that he was going to put his stamp of approval on her without making sure she was completely up to the task. So he had made it his personal mission to push her harder than all the others.

As recruits were prohibited from sharing personal information with each other, they were left with little to talk about other than their training. McGee's treatment of Ryan quickly became the hottest topic of conversation in the short window they had for R&R each night.

Most of the students believed McGee was a woman-hater. The prevailing wisdom was that somewhere in his past some woman had crushed him so badly that he now reveled in torturing female recruits. Ryan was an obvious choice, as she was the best-looking in class and either reminded McGee of the woman who had jilted him, or she somehow made him feel inferior.

A couple of other recruits, one an undergrad psychology major, had a different take and likened McGee's behavior to that of kindergarten boys who pull the hair of the girls they secretly like. None of them, though, suspected that Ryan was being tested for something bigger than a junior NCS officer, not even after she was removed from their ranks and the Basic Operations Course altogether.

She was moved into the CIA's Special Activities Division, which handled tactical paramilitary operations and covert political action, as well as destabilization efforts, psychological and economic warfare.

While the paramilitary side of SAD drew primarily from Tier One operators such as the SEALs and Delta, there was a tremendous amount of danger on the political action side and its members needed to be highly skilled. Once McGee was convinced that Ryan had the right stuff for SAD, he had her approved and transferred into a tailored training program, which he personally oversaw. As such, he became her mentor at the Agency and the person she had always been able to count on for good advice, as well as less-than-stellar career counseling.

During her problems with Phil Durkin, it had been McGee who suggested saving a lot of time and trouble by just putting a bullet in his head and dumping him in a quarry somewhere. Ryan didn't doubt for a moment that McGee was serious. He had never liked Durkin and he liked him even less for preying on his star student. In fact, though she couldn't prove it, Ryan suspected that it was McGee who had made Durkin's wife, Brenda, aware of her husband's sordid advances.

Stopping now just outside her mentor's office, Ryan raised her hand to knock on the door, when McGee's voice boomed from the other side. "It's open."

CHAPTER 14

B ob McGee was a tall man in his late fifties who ran four days a week and spent the other three in the gym. He sported a thick mustache, which, like his wavy hair, had somehow managed to escape the ravages of time. There were some who said that the only thing stronger than the forces of aging was McGee's vanity, along with a bottle of hair color he kept hidden away somewhere.

When the door opened, he looked up from his desk and saw Lydia Ryan standing in his doorway. "So this is how it ends," he said with a smile. "Well, at least they didn't send a stranger. I don't suppose it would make any difference if I offered you half the money, would it?"

Ryan shook her head and smiled back. "You should have disappeared when you had the chance, Bob."

"And give up all of this?" he asked, sweeping his arms out and taking in his tiny office. "Not a chance."

She laughed and they met in the center of the room, where he gave her a big hug. Once they were done saying hello, he offered her one of the chairs in front of his desk while he took the other. "What's so top secret that we couldn't discuss it over a secure phone? This isn't about that jackass Durkin again, is it? I told you, you should have shot him and dumped him in a shallow grave."

"Technically, you said I should've dumped him in a quarry."

McGee grinned. "Even better. No, wait. Shoot him, plant pocket litter on him from a gay bar, and then dump him. The Agency hates that kind of stuff and would never dig too deep. You'd get off scot-free."

"Pocket litter, check. If and when I shoot him, I'll remember that."

"So what's Durkin done now?"

Ryan took a deep breath. "I don't know that he's done anything."

"Then what's the problem?"

"How much time do you have?"

McGee leaned back in his chair, put his hands behind his head, and made himself comfortable. "As much time as you need."

After recounting everything to McGee, and sharing with him the materials Nafi Nasiri had given her in Frankfurt, she waited for her mentor to respond with something insightful that would help her figure out a way forward.

"What a friggin' disaster," he finally said.

"That's it? That's all you've got to say?"

"What do you want me to say?"

"I want you to make some sort of suggestion about how we're going to handle this."

McGee sat forward in his chair. "*We?* Why is this suddenly my problem?"

"Damn it, Bob. I need your help. This is serious."

"I'll make it easy for you. I think your pal at Jordanian Intelligence is pulling your chain. There's no way they'd play chicken with a potential terrorist attack. Not a chance in hell."

"So you think he's making it up?" said Ryan.

"I think everybody's making things up."

"You mean Durkin?"

McGee nodded. "Your destab team was top notch, but they broke the cardinal rule—they got caught."

"But they all got canned."

"No way," he replied. "They may have been scrubbed from the rolls, but there's no way Durkin let those guys go. They were too good. From what I heard, they had multiple reprimands. You were considered a by-the-book player and attaching you to that team was a last-ditch effort to rein them in. When things went south, they were shut down." McGee made air quotes as he said the words *shut down*.

"But Durkin told me to my face that he has no idea what they're up to or where they are."

"C'mon, Ryan. Don't be so naïve. He's a spook, just like you. He's paid to lie to people."

McGee was right. "I don't get it. We're just supposed to ignore potentially actionable intel from the Jordanians?"

"How well do you know Nasiri?"

"Very well. He took a shoulder full of shrapnel for me. Probably saved my life," she replied.

"And you trust him?"

"I wouldn't be wasting my time, or yours, if I didn't. Listen, I agree. I think holding back information on a terrorism plot is particularly bad form for an ally, but if our positions were reversed I'd do the exact same thing. In fact, I'd probably do more."

McGee flipped slowly through the material again as he spoke. "If this is legitimate, it's pretty damning, regardless of whether or not your old team is still working for Durkin. If it can be proven that the United States not only cooked up and carried out the Arab Spring, but is continuing to topple governments throughout the Middle East, that's going to cause an international firestorm. It'll sink this administration."

"I don't care about the political ramifications. What I care about is stopping a terrorist attack from being carried out on U.S. soil. We're not going to get any help from the Jordanians without giving them something in return."

"Why not take this to someone above Durkin?"

"You don't think I already thought of that? What if I'm wrong? What if the Jordanians *are* playing me? I'll look like a fool. Worse, I could end up looking like I cooked this whole thing up just to embarrass Durkin."

McGee shook his head. "You can't go tearing after this without some sort of approval. You have to get someone to sprinkle holy water on it."

"And who's going to do that?"

He tapped the folder against his knee as he ran the possibilities through his mind. "What if I could get you into the director's office?"

Ryan laughed. "Who do you think I was contemplating going over Durkin's head to? The DCI's a tyrant. He hates when the chain of command isn't followed. He'll just kick it back to Durkin and pin a pink slip to my back with a knife."

"I'm not talking about the Director of Central Intelligence. I'm talking about the other director—the DCI's boss."

"The Director of National Intelligence?"

McGee nodded.

"How do you have that kind of pull?" she asked.

"I'm an important guy."

Ryan laughed again. "Yeah, right."

"Your lack of faith aside, if I can make a meeting with the DNI happen, are you interested?"

"What makes you think he won't kick it back to our director, who'll then fire me for violating the chain of command?"

"Because I'll protect you."

"Protect me how?" asked Ryan.

"The DNI and I go back a long way and he owes me some favors. I'll make sure you've got cover."

"If you can guarantee cover, I'm in."

As McGee leaned over his desk to reach for the phone, he shooed Ryan out of his office. "Give me twenty minutes."

Nodding, she stepped out into the hall. Coming to see McGee had been the right thing to do. She had felt it even before walking into his office. The only problem was that walking *out* of his office, she was now feeling something else and it troubled her more than the prospect of being chewed out for violating the CIA chain of command, or even being fired.

She was gripped by the fear that no matter what strings her mentor might pull, it wouldn't matter, because they were already too far behind to catch up.

CHAPTER 15

Harvath pulled up in front of the chipped brick warehouse and checked the rusted numbers above the door against the address the Old Man had given him. He appeared to be at the right place.

Though he normally didn't leave anything of value in his SUV, he did a quick visual sweep of the seats just to make sure. This neighborhood wasn't exactly in the town's garden district and the last thing he wanted to do was tempt some passing thug into a quick smash-and-grab.

Preparing to exit the vehicle, he adjusted his weapon. He was convinced that one of the biggest reasons D.C. was so dangerous was that its citizens weren't allowed to defend themselves and legally carry firearms. The criminals knew this and took full advantage. A proponent of the belief that it was better to be judged by twelve than carried by six, Harvath always carried his .45-caliber H&K USP Compact in a custom Blackhawk "Check Six" holster placed securely behind his right hip, wherever he was. One of the few exceptions was that afternoon when he had gone straight from the airport to the Federal Reserve Building. As a rule, any weapons used overseas stayed overseas.

By and large, most of the rules Harvath lived by served him well. Some, though, were more difficult to reconcile with circumstances than others. His maxim that there was no such thing as a perfect crime was a prime example. Whether it was a terrorist attack, a kidnapping, or a murder, there were always clues to be found. But in the case of the kidnapped Fed candidates, the clues were proving to be extremely hard to find.

With some help from the Old Man, Harvath had turned his study into a makeshift war room and they officially launched their investigation. They began with what Harvath had hoped would be the easiest and quickest route to uncovering potential suspects—the Internet.

Though he didn't know much about the Fed, he did know that their critics were fairly outspoken. Some of the better known ran the gamut from pundits to business leaders and members of Congress, while the lesser known were simply day-to-day citizens. He used every mix of search terms he could come up with. He began with a generic search for the "Sons of Liberty" and because of its historical relevance was gifted with over a million prospective returns.

He tried to narrow it down by adding the term "Federal Reserve" to the search and ended up with just over thirteen thousand possibilities. From there, he added the names of the kidnapped candidates and hit a digital wall. As best he could tell, none of the terms appeared together, at least not openly anywhere on the Web.

Stripping out the "Sons of Liberty" from his search, he entered the hostages' names along with the term "Federal Reserve." He even tried adding the Henry Hazlitt quote about today being the "tomorrow" that the bad economist told us to ignore. The results were a mixed bag and not very helpful. There wasn't anyone, at least not on the open Internet, calling for any of the victims to be harmed, much less killed.

Harvath turned his attention to the police reports. He had been through Claire Marcourt's file a hundred times. It felt like there was something missing, but he just couldn't put his finger on it.

He read through the reports of the other kidnap victims, searching for some common thread, but the only thing he seemed to be able to come up with was that the kidnappings had been very well executed. They had all happened on the same night, but in different cities, which meant that multiple teams had to have been used. That was a plus, as far as Harvath was concerned. The more people involved in any plot, the greater the chances were that one of them would screw up. The challenge, however, was allocating enough assets to a case in order to see the screw-up the moment it happened, jump on it, and leverage it to your advantage.

The Carlton Group, though, didn't have many assets, much less extra ones they could move from project to project, as they'd been forced to let most of their people go. At the moment, Harvath was it, conducting the entire investigation himself out of his house, with his study acting as ground zero and the overflow spilling into the hall.

Even the Old Man was limited by how much time he could spare. He had spent a few hours with Harvath on the assignment before having to leave to deal with the fallout from the *Sienna Star* operation.

Though he didn't come right out and say it, Carlton had also been troubled by Claire Marcourt's murder. Harvath could see it in his face and by how much time he had spent with the file. He'd scanned all the contents onto his laptop and uploaded them onto a secure FTP site before walking outside to place a lengthy phone call. When he came back in and announced that he was leaving, he handed Harvath a slip of paper with the address for a warehouse and *WWII* written on it.

The initials stood for William Wise II. "He's expecting you," the Old Man had said on his way out the door.

"Expecting me for what? Who is he?"

"He used to work for the Agency, brilliant guy. Knows something about everything. I gave him the file. He might have some insight."

Harvath tried to ask what kind of work Wise had done and what made him so special, but Carlton was in a hurry and gone before the conversation could go any further. He figured he'd learn soon enough.

Walking up to the front of the building, Harvath noticed several low-visibility security precautions. While they may have been in response to the neighborhood's crime rate, Harvath suspected there might be another, much more realistic reason. Whoever this Bill Wise person was, he had some very dangerous enemies.

CHAPTER 16

Bill Wise looked like Santa Claus crossed with one of the toughest bikers the Hell's Angels had ever produced. He had white hair, a thick white beard, and towered over Harvath by a good five inches and an additional seventy-five pounds.

He wore dark jeans, a pair of black Frye boots, and a faded Dallas Cowboys jersey. On his right wrist was a copper bracelet—the kind used for warding off arthritis, and on his left was an expensive Panerai diver's watch.

As Harvath stepped inside, Wise stole a quick glance toward the street, closed the door, and then offered his hand.

"Thanks for seeing me on such short notice, Mr. Wise."

"First of all, it's *Doctor* Wise and second of all, give me a break with all the formalities," he replied with a smile. "If Peaches says you're okay, then that's good enough for me."

Peaches was the nickname the Old Man had been known by back in the day. According to legend, he was one of the roughest interrogators the Central Intelligence Agency had ever produced. He had a reputation for taking the hardest cases, the worst of the worst, and could be absolutely brutal with the enemy. It was said that if lives hung in the balance and time was of the essence, Reed Carlton was the man you wanted on the job. The fact that he was willing to go to some pretty extraordinary lengths in his interrogations had earned him the amusing and also chilling sobriquet of Peaches. He was anything but sweet.

Signaling for Harvath to follow, Wise led him into the warehouse. They passed through a small reception area, its walls covered with pictures. In addition to noticing that Wise had traveled the world, often heavily armed and in the presence of indigenous fighters, he discerned that the man was a scuba diver, private pilot, Eagle Scout, photographer, motorcyclist, NASCAR and IndyCar fan, and a hunter with a ranch in San Saba County, Texas.

"Do you hunt?" Wise asked after noticing Harvath admiring his ranch photos.

"Strictly bipeds these days."

Wise chuckled and led him through a heavy sliding door into the main section of the building. It was a large, loftlike space with thick metal trusses and a pristine, epoxy-coated concrete floor. Parked near a wide roll-up door was a trio of perfectly restored vintage SUVs—a green 1960s Land Rover, a metallic gray 1970s International Harvester Scout, and a white 1980s Jeep Grand Wagoneer with wood paneling. Beyond them were a handful of older motorcycles in varying states of refurbishment. Harvath could make out a Triumph Bonneville as well as an Indian and what looked like a Crocker.

"Are you the force behind all of these restorations?" Harvath asked.

"I am," Wise replied. "Ever since I was a kid, I've loved taking things apart and putting them back together."

As Harvath admired the machines, the man added. "Don't ever retire. You'd be surprised how expensive 'puttering' turns out to be."

This time, Harvath chuckled. He still had no idea what Wise had done for a living, but if he was like any of the other retired spooks he'd met in his lifetime, Wise had probably done his share of consulting after leaving the Agency and had made quite a few bucks doing it.

The garage portion of the warehouse ended at an enormous floor-to-ceiling glass display case. Inside was row after row of vintage typewriters and antique sewing machines. The display delineated the beginning of Wise's living area.

There was a stainless steel kitchen, a massive library with columns of twelve-foot-high bookshelves that went all the way to the structure's rear wall, and a giant drafting table that served as the man's desk. Hanging on the wall near it were a myriad of degrees, one of them a Ph.D. in psychology, as well as several diplomas and commendations from the Army's 75th Ranger Regiment and 5th Special Forces Group. Next to those was a sleeping area, then a living room with a sectional couch, and finally a wooden bar that looked like it had been salvaged out of some small Irish pub.

"Something to drink?" Wise asked, walking around behind the bar.

"What do you have?" said Harvath, regretting the question almost as soon as he had asked it.

"Whiskey or ice tea."

"I guess I'll have an ice tea."

"Whiskey it is," said Wise, removing two glasses and setting them atop the bar. "I'm all out of ice tea."

There was a brightly colored oil painting collage of George Washington hanging behind the bar. Harvath thought he recognized the artist. "That's a Penley, isn't it?"

"It is," the man answered as he handed Harvath his drink. "Great artist and an even greater American. I stumbled onto him a few years ago and now try to get to all of his exhibits."

"A body in motion," Harvath offered.

"Tends to stay in motion. Words to live by in retirement."

"What exactly is it that you retired from?"

Wise took a sip of his drink. "The best way I ever heard it described was 'armed anthropology.' I was in the Army for a long time, predominantly the Special Operations community. The Army put me through undergrad and grad school, where I made the art of killing my focus."

"You mean how soldiers kill?"

"Not just soldiers: anyone or any organization. Soldiers, law enforcement officers, gang members, contract killers and assassins, psychopaths, nation-states, terrorists—you name them and I studied them."

"Sounds very interesting."

"Fascinating stuff and I didn't leave a stone unturned. From how our kill rate in combat skyrocketed once the Army switched from bull's-eye targets to silhouettes, all the way to how and why mass murderers select their victims and places of attack.

"What I uncovered is that there is a particular mental makeup that excels in combat. Certain aspects of that makeup could be taught, so that day-to-day soldiers are more efficient on the battlefield, but there are other aspects that can't be learned. You have to come wired a certain way. As we drilled down and began identifying what those mental markers were, our results began to shape the screening process for certain compartments within the Special Operations community."

Compartments. Harvath found the word choice interesting, as if it were something that needed to be contained. "So the military was looking to select for its most lethal killers."

"That was part of it, but as you know, Special Operations is about a lot more than just killing the enemy. In my case, we were also trying to teach the Army's SF teams what to screen for when they infiltrated foreign countries and worked with insurgent groups. Our Green Berets needed mini-Ph.D.s that would help them evaluate the potential in the combatants they were supporting. In essence, they needed to be able to rapidly assess if they were helping elevate and train the right people, or if there were better candidates for certain positions. Like I said, I found it to be fascinating work."

"The Agency must have thought so, too, at some point if you ended up over there, right?"

"They did," said Wise, taking another sip of his drink. "It was at a time when they were experimenting with a lot of *interesting* programs. They made me an offer that the Army couldn't even come close to matching, so I moved over to Langley."

"Where you continued what you had been doing for the Army?"

"But with much bigger budgets."

"Off book or on?" asked Harvath, referring to where the money had come from for these *interesting* programs.

"What do you think?"

Completely black and off the books, thought Harvath. Wise's area of expertise was not something the CIA would have likely wanted congressional input on. The politicians would have only watered it down, if not shut it down completely. Members of Congress barely understood the complexities of the military battlefield. What they knew of the intelligence battlefield you could fit in a shot glass.

"Okay, so you're Dr. Kill, armed anthropologist," Harvath continued. "Why am I here?"

Wise had been called that so many times, he'd lost count. Normally, it made him smile. This time, though, his face was dead serious. "You're here because Reed Carlton thinks I might be able to help with your case."

"Can you?"

"Maybe, but first I want to see how much you know about your victim."

"Victims," Harvath replied. "Plural."

Wise shook his head. "There may be hostages, *plural,* and a dead body, *singular,*" he said, gently chastising Harvath for correcting him, "but the object of all this is a singular victim and the sooner you understand that, the closer you'll be to solving your case."

CHAPTER 17

He had spent the afternoon taking pictures. He liked taking pictures. He took shots of King's Chapel, the Old North Church, and the Paul Revere House. In the Granary Burying Ground, near the grave of Sam Adams, he found a Gothic-inspired woman with black lipstick and nail polish who let him photograph her posing provocatively against several of the headstones. After the fourth one, she offered to take him someplace nearby and perform a sex act on him for fifty dollars.

She was a junkie who wanted to get high. He offered her ten dollars just to see what she'd say. She told him to fuck himself and flipped him the middle finger as she walked off. She came back ten minutes later as he was getting ready to leave and told him she'd do it for twenty. She didn't know it then, but she had been smart to approach him in broad daylight in an open, public space. Had this happened at night, had he been drinking or off his medication, things would have ended much differently.

He didn't know what her drug of choice was or how much it cost, but he removed a dollar bill from his wallet and extended it, telling her to get something to eat. "What? A box of Tic Tacs?" she demanded in her

Southie accent. "Go fuck yourself," she told him again, which sounded more like *go faak yaself.*

She was angry, real angry, and that made him smile. Seeing him smile made her even angrier and she tried to slap him. The speed with which he caught her wrist and twisted her arm behind her back startled her. She was going to scream, but the man sensed it and twisted her arm even tighter as he drew her against him. It was so painful all the air rushed from her lungs.

Her eyes flicked from side to side for anyone who could help her, but the few people she could see were paying attention only to the historic grave markers. He could smell the fear oozing from her pores and feel the exquisite trembling of her body. There was no telling how many diseases she carried, but he didn't care. He was interested in only one thing from her. Closing his eyes, he listened until he could hear the thumping of her terrified heart as it pounded against the wall of her chest. It sounded like a rabbit running from a wolf.

He pulled up on her arm, right to the precipice of breaking it, and then he let her go. She stood for a moment, frozen in place by fear, and then like the little rabbit she was, she ran away as fast as she could from the big bad wolf.

He smiled as he watched her run. Broad daylight, a public space and commitment to his pills: the trinity that had saved her life that late afternoon in the graveyard and which had given him an appetite.

He was wary about where he should and shouldn't go, should and shouldn't eat. Though he had taken steps to disguise his appearance, there were certain risks that were not to be taken. He walked south to the city's Chinatown neighborhood, where he ate in a small, hole-in-the-wall restaurant that couldn't afford matching chairs, much less a CCTV system.

The best thing to be said about the food was that it was edible. He gorged himself on fried rice and egg rolls, washing it all down with a syrupy sweet Asian soda he had pulled out of the cooler. Impulse control was something the medication was supposed to help, but when he overloaded on stimuli the way he had in the graveyard, he found his cravings harder to control.

In addition to his eating binge, he also had to contend with the fact that his sexual arousal hadn't dissipated. Smelling the terror on the woman as well as feeling her fluttering body pressed tightly against his was a heady combination of sensations made only more acute by the danger of it all.

He was drifting into choppy water and being pulled further and further from shore. He fingered the pillbox in his pocket as he stared over at the cooler with its beer and sodas. If he took more medication he could become dopey and slip up. But if he didn't take any, and he gave in to one of his nastier impulses, he could also slip up. He felt damned either way, which suddenly brought on an additional sensation, *anxiety*.

He decided to write his own prescription. Walking over to the cooler, he removed two Yanjings, paid the old Chinese woman with the whiskers behind the counter, and sat back down at the table.

He drank the first beer in one long swallow. With the second, he took his time and willed himself to relax. It took several minutes, but eventually the warmth of the alcohol crept into his bloodstream and he began to feel himself relax. The benefit of the anxiety, if you could call it that, was that it was an arousal killer. His erection had completely gone away.

The longer he sat in the restaurant, the more relaxed he became. The more relaxed he became, the more his mind drifted, particularly to what had happened at the graveyard and he could feel the strings of arousal starting to be tugged. He was being pulled out to sea again. What he needed was some coffee.

Finishing off his second beer, his steered his legs out onto the street and into the early evening. Rush hour was already well under way. When he finally found a café it was staffed by wrung-out baristas watching the clock, eager to close up and get home for the evening. He ordered his coffee with a "black eye," coffee-talk for two shots of espresso. As he had done in the Chinese restaurant, he paid in cash, and then exited the establishment.

He felt the caffeine hit his system faster than the beer. There was a pep in his step and he felt a buoyancy of spirit. Everything was going to be okay. He was actually looking forward to his assignment tonight. It was complicated, but not impossible. Every step had been mapped out in perfect detail. It was like making a cake. As long as you followed the recipe, you had nothing to worry about, and he *always* followed the recipe.

The vehicle and his supplies were stored in a dilapidated garage in East Boston. He spent an hour casing the neighborhood and an additional hour surveilling the garage before he approached.

The key to the padlock had been sewn into the lining of his jacket. Ripping part of the fabric, he removed it, and let himself in, closing and locking the door behind him.

He slipped a small flashlight from his backpack and cupped the head so as not to throw too much light. The white panel van was unlocked. Climbing in back, he did a quick assessment. Everything was where it was supposed to be.

Opening the lid of the large garbage can, he checked to make sure the final ingredient was in place. Squinting into the beam of his flashlight was a man, bound and gagged, with a two-day growth of beard.

He closed the lid and began to feel very excited as he laid out a blue jumpsuit and stripped off his clothes.

CHAPTER 18

General George Johnson, Director of National Intelligence, lived in a modest colonial house near D.C. with his wife, an around-the-clock protective detail, and a French bulldog named Martin. Despite nearly two years of the detail that changed shifts every eight hours, the dog still went berserk every time someone showed up at the house.

For the security-minded, this might have been viewed as a positive. General Johnson, though, saw his wife's dog as a colossal pain in the ass. Even before they had rung the bell, Lydia Ryan and Bob McGee could hear both the dog and the DNI barking from inside the house.

"Damn it, Marty! Quiet!" Johnson shouted at the bulldog. "Carol! Come get this damn dog!"

A solidly built man in a dark suit opened the door. Behind him, the DNI was trying to corral the little bulldog with his foot in order to prevent him from charging the visitors. "Sorry about this," Johnson said as he beckoned his guests. "Please come on in."

"I told you, you should have gotten a Rottweiler," McGee said as he stepped inside.

"I've got several already," he replied, gesturing at his security men standing in the foyer. "And I haven't caught them once going on the rug," he cracked before yelling for his wife again, "Carol!"

The DNI's assistant stepped out of the living room. "I'll take him upstairs, sir," he offered, bending down and scooping up the dog. Instantly, Marty's bark turned into a growl.

"Be careful, Stu."

"It'll be okay, sir."

"Sure it will," Johnson said with a smirk as his assistant began climbing the stairs. "I've got a hundred bucks that says he bites you."

"He's not going—" the assistant began just as the dog nipped him in the hand.

"Told ya," the DNI said with a laugh as he walked over to shake hands with his guests.

McGee introduced Ryan and then General Johnson invited them to follow him to his den.

"Can I offer either of you anything?" he asked, "Coffee? Soft drink?"

"Coffee would be good," said Ryan, still feeling jet-lagged from her trip. "Thank you."

"Got any bourbon?" replied McGee.

"I've got plenty. Up or neat?"

"Neat, please."

"They say consistency is the hobgoblin of small minds, Bob."

"Actually," McGee corrected, "they say *foolish* consistency is the hobgoblin of small minds. There's nothing foolish about a man loving bourbon. Unless, of course, that man starts including ice cubes in his glass. Ice is a crutch."

The DNI was a short, broad-chested fireplug of a man in his early sixties, with a bit of a paunch and thinning gray hair. It was after-hours, and he wore khakis and an oxford shirt. He laughed good-naturedly at McGee's joke as he busied himself at his wet bar pouring a cup of coffee for Ryan and a drink for himself and McGee.

By the time he was done, his assistant, Stuart, had finished taking the dog upstairs and had joined them in the den, along with a laptop, two legal pads, and a file folder. The DNI asked the security men to wait outside and had Stuart close the door behind them.

As the DNI handed his guests their drinks, he introduced them to his assistant, assured them that they could speak freely in front of him, and then asked everyone to sit down.

The den was tastefully decorated with hunting prints and wood paneling. There were brown leather couches with plaid accent pillows, two green club chairs, skirted end tables, a brass coffee table, and a large wooden desk.

Accepting a pad and pen from his assistant, the DNI took his seat and stated, "Stu needs to be home in time to watch the *Dog Whisperer*, so let's discuss why we're here."

General George Johnson had served in the United States Army with considerable distinction. His outstanding career had begun in Vietnam, where he had received multiple commendations for bravery and gallantry. He went on to lead the First Infantry Division through several conflicts, and was transferred to head the Army's Intelligence Support Activity. His pragmatic understanding of not only warfare and tactics, but also espionage and diplomatic relations, eventually secured him a spot on the Joint Chiefs of Staff, where he helped advise the Secretary of Defense, the National Security Council, and the President on all matters military. Based on his performance there, he was chosen to run the National Security Agency, before being tapped for his current position as Director of National Intelligence.

McGee had given Ryan the man's entire background on the drive from Camp Peary. He and Johnson had worked together many times in the Army and had developed a good friendship. When Ryan asked her mentor what favor the DNI owed him, McGee only said, "We both owe each other a few debts that neither of us will ever be able to repay."

The solemnity with which he spoke told her the debts very likely involved tremendous sacrifice and possibly, human life. She didn't push for more information.

"As this is Lydia's baby, so to speak, I think she is the best person to lay it all out," McGee said, leaning back and giving his protégé the floor.

Ryan gave a brief history of her background. As she did, Johnson's assistant handed him a copy of her file. But unlike most she had met in the intelligence world, the DNI didn't attempt to multitask. He set her jacket aside and gave her his undivided attention. That impressed her.

When she was done explaining everything that had happened, she handed him the file Nafi Nasiri had given her. General Johnson didn't bother to open it. There was no reason to believe it didn't contain everything the CIA operative had told him it did.

Lydia Ryan had delivered a purely clinical recitation of the facts as they were believed to be known. Now the DNI wanted to know what she *thought*. What was her gut, her experience, telling her?

"I know Nasiri. I don't think he or the Jordanians are bluffing."

"What about this former supervisor of yours back at Langley?" the DNI asked, glancing at his notes. "This Phil Durkin. Could *he* be bluffing?"

"Absolutely," McGee interjected. "The guy is a frickin' weasel."

The DNI held up his hand and turned his attention to Ryan. "What do *you* think?"

"Did Durkin shut down the program like he said he did? Maybe. But if he fired everyone else, why keep me? I didn't screw up as bad as the rest of them, but I certainly made my share of mistakes. They could have easily built a case against me, too," she stated. "But they didn't."

"Why not?"

"Maybe because Durkin was interested in me. But if that's true, why didn't he try to use it to his advantage? Why not offer to save my career in exchange for sleeping with him? I wouldn't have done it, of course."

"Of course not. But it's still a good question."

"Which doesn't have an easy answer."

The DNI looked at her. "If you had to come up with some sort of explanation for all of this, what would it be?"

"Easy. He never shut that program down. He simply moved it off the books and into the shadows. I got to keep my career with the CIA, just in a different capacity. The other members of my team got to keep their careers, too, but for that to happen, the program had to go full black."

"But why compartmentalize you off? Why not send you into the shadows with them?"

Ryan shrugged. "I've run that through my mind a thousand times.

The only thing I can come up with is that it was a pride thing with Durkin. He'd been tasked with bringing the team to heel. As a last-ditch effort, he assigned me to them as the Girl Scout who would get them in line. If I had been fired, it would have been yet another example of his bad judgment."

The DNI nodded. "Agreed. What bothers me the most, though, is Durkin's apparent lack of interest in the plot the Jordanians claim to have uncovered. While I don't like the fact that they're trying to horse-trade with us intelligence-wise, I understand it. Durkin should, too."

"Well, sir, if he did in fact shut the team down as he claims and now they have popped back up, it could be a real source of professional embarrassment for him," Ryan stated, more in an attempt to figure out Durkin's motivations than to defend him.

"You know what's even more embarrassing?" the DNI retorted. "Allowing a terrorist attack to happen on American soil because you're too proud to admit that you screwed up."

The man was right. Ryan didn't try to offer any more insights on Durkin.

The DNI tapped his pen against his legal pad. "We have a public trust to live up to. We're accountable to the American people. It's our job to keep them and the country safe. We don't have the luxury of playing chicken in our line of work, not when the stakes are as high as they are. This guy Durkin is either unqualified for his position, or he's hiding something. Both of which greatly concern me."

Ryan and McGee knew they shouldn't speak. The direction the DNI planned to take was already forming in the man's mind. At this point, he was simply trying to figure out the best way to get where he wanted to go.

"If word gets back to the CIA director about this, he's going to want *both* of your heads on a pike. He's a real stickler for chain of command. And I don't blame him," said the DNI, "but I understand why you wanted to bring it to me. There may, though, be a way around this."

Turning to his assistant, he then said, "What kind of channels do we have open with the Jordanians?"

"What are you thinking?" the assistant replied.

"I'm thinking if we can plug into Nasiri's boss, or even better the King himself, we'll not only be able to smoke out whether or not Nasiri is telling us the truth, but we'll convey back to them how seriously the United States is taking this matter."

The assistant nodded. "It would also provide you an opportunity to lean on them for more information than what Mr. Nasiri has already provided Ms. Ryan."

"Agreed," the DNI said. "Which brings us to the other issue we need to deal with."

"The destabilization team," Ryan offered.

General Johnson nodded. "Agree or disagree with the politics, the President has been abundantly clear that he supports the Arab Spring. He has also been adamant that we not influence the outcome. He sees this as an organic, democratic process that must be allowed to 'bloom,' as he says."

McGee shook his head.

"Like I said," the DNI repeated, "agree or disagree with the President's position, this is his call. That said, there appear to be two potential things happening here. Either Durkin's old team has reconstituted and is operating on behalf of someone else, or Durkin and others at the CIA are running the team in direct contradiction of the President's orders. Whatever the answer is, I want to know. And I want to know as soon as possible."

Ryan looked at him. "How do we make that happen?"

General Johnson turned back to his assistant. "Can we come up with a way to requisition Ms. Ryan away from the CIA for a little bit?"

"Probably. What do you have in mind?"

"I want her to have top cover. I don't want it to look like this has anything to do with the Jordanians. We need to tie it in with something else she is already working on and peel off some other CIA people to hide her in with. You and Ms. Ryan figure it out and get back to me."

"Won't Durkin be suspicious?" Ryan asked.

"That's a risk we'll have to run. You and Stu pull something together and I'll make it happen. Unless there's somebody else who knows about this team and their inner workings, you're the best person to move the ball forward. Now, what about extra manpower? What do you think you'll need?"

Ryan's eyes drifted to McGee, who put his palms out and said, "Don't look at me. I'm just some dumb Agency instructor. We don't get requisitioned by the DNI."

"No," Ryan replied, "but guys your age do have health issues—"

"Or marital problems," the DNI suggested.

"Or an ethics inquiry," the assistant stated.

McGee realized he was getting roped into this whether he liked it or not. "I guess I'd rather take a hit to my corpus than my character," he said. "I think I'll go with health issues."

"Good," replied General Johnson. "You two work everything out with Stu and I'll sign off on it. The tricky part will be getting you funding. We can move a little bit of money around, but we'll have to be careful."

"Thank you, sir. The fewer people who know about any of this the better."

"Understood. Anything else?"

Four sets of eyes took turns looking at each other and when no one had anything else to add, the DNI closed the meeting. "I want this kept absolutely quiet," he said. "If and when this needs to go to the President, I'll do it. Until then, we keep this locked down tight. We don't mention a word of this to anyone."

As McGee's 4Runner pulled out of General Johnson's driveway, two men in a Ford Explorer waited for him to turn right at the end of the road and begin heading toward the highway before falling in behind.

The man in the passenger seat dialed a phone number back in Virginia. "They just left," he said. "What do you want us to do?"

"Kill them."

"You want it to look like an accident?"

He had thought about this long and hard since meeting with Lydia Ryan. "No," replied Phil Durkin. "We need this to look intentional. *Absolutely* intentional."

CHAPTER 19

The Old Man had taken Harvath to task over his limited knowledge of the Federal Reserve and how it operated. Though he'd tried to hide it, Harvath knew his ignorance had also been on display for Monroe Lewis during their meeting at the Fed's headquarters. He didn't like feeling stupid and out of his depth, but he had. Talking with Bill Wise, though, was different.

"They don't want you to understand anything about what they're doing," he said. "It's purposeful obfuscation and it's *brilliant*. They weave a tapestry of BS meant to intimidate people, and it works. Very few Americans have ever really dug into what they are up to."

Wise was a polymath and Harvath was beginning to understand why the Old Man had set up their meeting. "Why do so many people not like the Federal Reserve?"

Wise took a sip of his drink, deciding where to begin. "First of all, they're not federal and they don't have any reserves whatsoever. The Federal Reserve is about as federal as Federal Express. They're a group of powerful bankers who orchestrated a phony crisis in the early 1900s to convince the American people that the country needed a strong central bank to help regulate the economy and bring Wall Street fat cats to heel. It's one of the most successful con jobs in history."

"Apparently, you're not a fan."

"I go where the facts take me," said Wise. "They took the name Federal Reserve for the sole purpose of scamming the American people and making it look like they were part of the government. They're not only *not* part of the American government; they aren't even accountable to the American people. We as citizens can't toss any of them out or tell any of them what to do. They operate in total secrecy and have never undergone a thorough audit.

"What's astounding is that since the Fed was created back in 1913, the dollar has lost ninety-six percent of its purchasing power. Because the Fed sets interest rates, we have seen massive bubbles inflated under their policies only to eventually pop and create massive downturns in the economy. In fact, America's downturns have become longer and much more severe under the Fed."

"So why do we keep the Fed? Can't we get rid of it?" Harvath asked.

"America has killed two prior central banks; it could kill this one, too, if it wanted."

"That's the key, though, Americans would have to want to. Right?"

"Exactly, and most people have no idea what it is. In fact, let me ask you something. How well do you know your American flag etiquette?"

"Very well," Harvath replied.

"Are you allowed to fly another flag above the American flag?"

"Of course not. Never."

"Do you have any cash on you?"

Harvath nodded.

"Do you have any idea what it says on top of our money? Above the words *The United States of America*?"

Harvath shook his head.

"Take your money out and look. Read to me what it says."

He removed the cash from his pocket and studied a one-dollar, five-dollar, twenty-dollar, and even one-hundred-dollar bill. "They all say *Federal Reserve Note* on top."

"Some say that's a perfect example of how the Fed sees itself, as being above the United States government. Those notes aren't even issued by the Treasury Department. They may be printed in the building, but the Treasury has absolutely no say in when they get printed or how many of them get printed. But to keep the charade going those Federal Reserve notes include both the signature of the Treasurer of the United States as well as the signature of the United States Secretary of the Treasury.

"Through its control of our currency, this unelected group of private bankers has driven the United States to the brink of bankruptcy. They're not only digitizing into existence more than one hundred fifteen million dollars an hour to cover risky loans and trades made by their pals at banks deemed too big to fail, they're—"

"Wait," said Harvath. "*One hundred and fifteen million?* They're printing that much money every hour?"

"Not printing, *digitizing* and then depositing that digitized money into the accounts of banks who turn right around and keep making the same risky loans and investments, because no matter how badly they screw up, there's no downside, no consequences. That's why the Fed was set up."

"But if there's that much more money being created, doesn't that mean that the existing money supply, the money in *my* bank account, is increasingly worth less?"

"Give yourself a gold star," said Wise. "Like I said, the dollar has lost ninety-six percent of its purchasing power since the Fed was initiated. They levy the heaviest and most corrosive taxes of all through their control of the money system, and it's all about covering the bad bets of their colleagues at the taxpayer's expense. After all, who do you think ends up with the bill?"

"We do."

"That's right. What's more, the Fed controls what the interest rate will be on your bank accounts, how much interest you'll pay on your home loan, as well as your car loan and your student loans. They use their digitized money to buy U.S. government bonds so that our government can keep spending and spending and spending, which drives us deeper and deeper into debt. And does the Fed buy those bonds directly from the

U.S. government? No, of course not. It uses brokerage firms it's friendly with in New York, so that those firms get huge commissions."

"Those firms being the same Wall Street 'fat cats' the Fed had promised to rein in, correct?" asked Harvath.

Wise nodded. "It's an incredible shell game. But what may be of particular interest for your case is that Britain wanted to place the colonies under the influence of the Bank of England. That act was considered so beyond the pale that it is said to have been the final straw that led to the Revolutionary War."

Despite Harvath's knowledge of American history, he had never heard that before. It was an amazing revelation.

"While some of the founders like Jefferson were against a central bank," said Wise, "there were others, like Alexander Hamilton, who were not only for it, but pushed hard to make it happen. In fact, to get southern lawmakers on board, Hamilton agreed to make sure America's capitol would be moved out of New York City and further south."

"Which is how we wound up with Washington, D.C.?"

"Bingo," said Wise. "All that over a central bank."

"You said two previous central banks had been killed. How did we wind up with our current central bank, the Fed?"

"Despite Jefferson's bitter opposition to central banks as being engines of speculation, manipulation, and financial corruption, President George Washington had signed the first bank's charter. But when it expired twenty years later, so many people hated it, Congress refused to renew it.

"President James Madison signed the Second Bank of the United States into existence, but when Andrew Jackson took office, he refused to renew its charter. He was a lot like Thomas Jefferson and saw the central bank as an engine for corruption. When the economy got rocky, Jackson wisely pushed for all federal land sales to be transacted in gold or silver. Many banks adopted a similar modus operandi and it started to catch on.

"Some banks, though, were so leveraged, they couldn't pay their customers when they came looking for their money. This led to waves of bank runs, some of which actually created serious imbalances in the economy. One of the worst 'bank runs' led to the creation of the Federal Reserve."

Harvath noted Wise's derogatory tone when he used the term *bank run*. "This is the phony crisis you mentioned?"

He nodded. "Are you familiar with something called the Hegelian dialectic?"

"I am. It's where a group or an individual creates a problem, knowing full well in advance how people are going to react to it. They then begin agitating for something to be done about the problem, for things to *change*. Once the masses are then worked up enough and desperate enough for something to be done, the party behind the problem unveils their solution. The people are thrilled to have a plan, any plan, and so demand that it be implemented. They never seem to realize that they've been manipulated and that they haven't really ushered in change, but actually a much worse version of what they had previously, only now in brand-new packaging."

"That's exactly what happened with the Fed. A problem was manufactured by a powerful group of people who sat on the sidelines waiting for a panicked citizenry to beg for a solution. Once people started begging loud enough, all this group had to do was set the wheels in motion and make it look like everything was unfolding naturally.

"In this case, it was a group of New York bankers colluding to set up a third central bank that would give them a monopoly over the banking system. Shortly after the New Year in 1907, an article appeared in the *New York Times* by investment banker Paul Warburg, who cautioned that Americans needed to reinstate a central bank if they wanted to avoid any more terrible bank runs.

"One of Warburg's banking partners then gave a speech to the New York Chamber of Commerce warning that if the United States didn't set up a central bank, the country was going to undergo the most severe and far-reaching crash in its history. The sky is falling. The sky is falling. All they needed then was to be proven right. Enter their pal, banker J. P. Morgan.

"Once a slew of side bets were placed that the stock market was going to fall, a run was launched on the stock of a company called United

Copper—one of J. P. Morgan's biggest competitors. Panic took over the market. It was like all of the water being sucked out to sea before a giant tsunami comes ashore. Suddenly, everyone wanted out.

"New York banks friendly to Morgan and Warburg yanked their money, the stock market dropped nearly fifty percent, and New York's third-largest trust collapsed. From there, the panic spread across the country as citizens rushed to their own banks to pull out all of their money.

"It was an all-out panic and people were screaming for something to be done. Enter once again J. P. Morgan, who pledged his own funds to help stabilize the banking system.

"Rallying other New York bankers to join him, several of whom had helped to exacerbate the panic, Morgan magically stemmed the bleeding and the panic began to subside. But as it did, panic was replaced by a nationwide outcry that something be done so that this kind of thing never happened again."

"Never let a good crisis go to waste, right?" said Harvath.

Wise smiled. "Precisely. The people blamed the bankers, but the bankers masterfully blamed 'the system,' which led to everyone clamoring for the system to be reformed. Congress instantly responded by setting up a special commission. Magically chosen to head the commission was a profiteering, multimillionaire Rhode Island senator who was friends with Morgan and Warburg, as well as being deep in the pockets of the rubber and tobacco industries. His name was Nelson Aldrich.

"As the United States was one of the last major nations without a central bank, Aldrich decided his National Monetary Commission should study the central banks of Europe—and that's exactly what he and his entourage did, spending almost two years touring Europe, wining and dining at an expense of more than three hundred thousand dollars to the American taxpayers."

Harvath shook his head. "The politicians were crooks even back then."

"It gets worse," said Wise. "After nearly two years of 'study' and over three hundred thousand dollars spent, Senator Aldrich hadn't filed a single report on what he had learned, nor had he offered any solutions for 'reforming' America's banking system."

"The guy really was a crook."

Wise held up his hand. "We haven't even gotten to the worst part yet."

"It gets worse?" said Harvath.

"Much. And I think it will give you an idea of why someone might be angry enough to want to target and kill people at the Federal Reserve."

CHAPTER 20

Wise studied Harvath for a moment before speaking. "It was a cold, windy evening in November of 1910, when a group of the most powerful bankers in the United States snuck out of New York City on a top-secret mission. In Hoboken, New Jersey, posing as a duck-hunting party, they boarded an opulent private railcar bound for an even more opulent, private resort off the Georgia coast called Jekyll Island."

"Which is where Claire Marcourt's body was found."

Wise nodded and continued. "Among the group was Abraham Piatt Andrew, who was assistant secretary of the U.S. Treasury; Frank Vanderlip, who was president of the most powerful bank in the country, the National City Bank of New York, which represented the oil interests of the Rockefellers; as well as the aforementioned investment banker who had been publicly calling for the U.S. to adopt a central bank, Paul Warburg.

"An interesting tidbit about Warburg, in addition to drawing an eye-popping salary even by today's standards of five hundred thousand dollars a year: back in Germany, his family represented the interests of one of the greatest European banking families, the Rothschilds."

"Nice work and even nicer clients if you can get them," said Harvath.

"Nothing happens by accident with these people," said Wise. "Also on board were Benjamin Strong and Henry Davison of J. P. Morgan Company, as well as Charles Norton, the president of J. P. Morgan's First National Bank of New York. There to greet them all as they boarded was the owner of the mahogany-lined railcar, our pal, Senator Nelson Aldrich. In total, there were six men who were conservatively rumored to represent one-fourth of the world's wealth.

"With the shades drawn and white-gloved staff seeing to cigars and cocktails for the men of the lustrous private car, the train steamed out of Hoboken south toward Brunswick, Georgia, where they would complete the final leg of their eight-hundred-mile journey by boat to Jekyll Island.

"Lest any of the staff figure out who their passengers were or what they were up to, the powerful men had all agreed to address each other by first names only. Vanderlip and Davison were so cocky, though, they insisted on being called not Frank and Henry, but Orville and Wilbur."

"Like the Wright brothers? Why?"

"Because," said Wise, "according to Vanderlip, he and Davison were always 'right' about everything."

Harvath shook his head.

"The last thing any of them wanted was for word to get out that they had all come together for one very sinister purpose."

"Which was?"

"To create a banking monopoly that would tilt the playing field exclusively to their advantage and crush any competition by yoking the brute force of the U.S. government completely under their control. In short, they were headed to Jekyll Island to assemble the blueprint for the Federal Reserve."

Harvath remembered being told by Jacobson, the Federal Reserve's director of security, that this was the meeting so many conspiracy theorists like to point to. He wondered what it said about Bill Wise that he was drawing attention to it as well. "I hear their visit had everything but a devil worship mass and animal sacrifice."

The man laughed heartily and caused Harvath to be even more reminded of Santa Claus. "If only that was the extent of what they were up to," he said. "They stayed on Jekyll Island for nine days, crafting a master plan for an American central bank. Warburg was the sharpest and most knowledgeable about banking so he was given the task of writing the bill that would go before Congress. Aldrich rode herd to make sure the bill was crafted in such a way that it would be passed. The others at the meeting were there to make sure their respective interests were seen to and to help remediate any problems that might pop up.

"Because of the money panics that had so devastated the country, the men at Jekyll Island knew Congress was anxious to be seen doing something bold. They also knew that the public saw bankers as the reason for the panics and hated them with a passion. That meant that they had to put a lot more than just lipstick on their pig of a central bank. They had to dress it up so it looked like a racehorse.

"Warburg was a very smart man and suggested they avoid the words 'central bank' altogether. When his cohorts asked him what it should be called, he said the 'Federal Reserve System.'

"To disguise it even more, Warburg suggested they put branches across the country, which could be helmed by prominent, and well-known locals in each region. Anything to minimize the appearance of the Federal Reserve being an operation of eastern bankers, who were a particularly detested class of bankers at that time."

It was still a lot for Harvath to take in. "By all accounts, these men were already financial successes; big-time, even by today's standards. Why go to all this trouble?" he asked.

"Simple. Self-defense. By 1910, banks in general were booming. They had more than doubled over the prior ten years and most of the new ones were out west and in the South."

"Which meant that the New York bankers were seeing an ever-shrinking market share."

Wise nodded. "The most alarming thing for the bankers, though, was that businesses at the time were doing very well and funding their own expansions out of their profits. Only thirty percent of businesses were coming to banks for loans. It was as if businesses didn't even need banks anymore. You want to talk about panic? The bankers thought their world was coming to an end."

"So what?" said Harvath. "Why shouldn't people be able to make up their own minds about how they want to finance the growth of their own businesses?"

Wise put up his hands. "I agree with you. Then again, I'm not a banker. I actually believe in free markets."

"So what happened?"

"The banks needed to change the way people thought. In particular, they needed people to adopt a 'buy now, pay later' mentality and encourage them to borrow rather than save. For that to happen, they were going to have to make it as cheap as possible to borrow money. That became one of four key items on their agenda at Jekyll Island.

"How to crush competition, how to control interest rates, how to be able to make as many loans as they wanted regardless of how much money they had in their vaults, and finally the big one.

"Everyone at that meeting knew that at some point, maybe not in twenty years, maybe not even in fifty years, but at some point all of it would come crashing down and the system would eventually collapse. When that happened, they needed a safeguard so that the bankers themselves wouldn't be held financially accountable, but rather the taxpayers would be left footing the bill."

The more Harvath learned about these people, the more they disgusted him. "Talk about morally bankrupt."

"They not only invented too big to fail, they invented too big to jail. They were brilliant propagandists. J. P. Morgan was famous for handing out shiny dimes to street urchins. Paul Warburg was the basis for the character of Daddy Warbucks in *Little Orphan Annie*. Very few realized what all of these men were up to. In fact, you're familiar with the massive hyperinflation of the Weimar Republic after World War I in Germany?"

"I am. I remember the images of people going to stores with wheelbarrows full of worthless currency just to buy a loaf of bread."

"Exactly. What most people aren't aware of is that the massive hyperinflation that crushed the German middle class, collapsed its economy, and laid the groundwork for the rise of Hitler was created by Germany's central bank, the Reichsbank, which was one of the central banks our Federal

Reserve was modeled after. But even better than that," Wise added, "was that the director of the Reichsbank was Paul Warburg's brother, Max."

Harvath stared at him. "Are you serious?"

Wise nodded.

Although Wise had given him a crash course on the Federal Reserve, Harvath didn't feel any closer to figuring out who was behind the kidnapping of the five chairmanship candidates. "So there are a lot of reasons not to like the Fed. I could say the same thing about Congress, yet we don't have people out abducting and killing their members, ostensibly trying to blackmail them into dissolution."

"Sometimes I wonder if that might not be a good thing."

Harvath looked at him. "You're joking, right?"

"Of course I am," Wise replied. "I'm just not a fan. Listen. If you did have people going after members of Congress, you'd handle it the same way, right? You'd ask yourself who would benefit from any of the attacks and then look for clues."

"True, but as far as who might benefit from shutting Congress down," Harvath said, "that's not going to narrow it down much. The entire country could benefit."

Wise smiled. "I see you're not much of a fan, either."

"Not really."

"Well, a lot of people could benefit from the Federal Reserve being shut down."

"Sounds like the entire country could, which means I'm left with just over three hundred million suspects."

"Actually, there's more if you consider the fact that the dollar is the world's reserve currency and any inflation created by the Fed is felt around the globe. Then there's the fact that the U.S. government also spends much more than it brings in, so we have to make up the difference by selling Treasury bonds. If the Fed increases the money supply, then the dollars bondholders are being paid back with are worth less."

Harvath shook his head and took another sip of his drink. Wise could tell he was frustrated. "Listen," the man said. "I know this may feel like it's not very helpful to what you are doing, but Peaches wanted to make sure you had a grasp of what the Fed was and how it operated. Are there a good number of pretty smart people out there who think the world would be better off without it? Absolutely. Are there a lot who'd be willing to murder to try to get it to go away? I don't think so."

"So how do we identify and narrow down who those people are?"

"That part's simple."

"It is?" said Harvath.

Wise nodded. "But you have to start with the actual crime itself."

CHAPTER 21

Wise stepped out from behind the bar and took the stool next to Harvath's. He offered to freshen his drink, but Harvath politely waved him off. His mind was spinning with all the information being crammed into it; he didn't need to add to the effect with additional alcohol.

Refilling his own glass and setting the bottle down, Wise said, "We've got five kidnappings and a murder, which are filled with a lot of information. What do they tell you?"

Harvath had been poring over the files ever since his meeting at the Federal Reserve that afternoon. As far as he was concerned, there wasn't much there. "I have to be honest with you, there *isn't* a lot of information. We've got next to no evidence."

"Which is evidence in itself."

"What are you talking about?"

"As far as physical clues at the crime scenes themselves, there aren't any, right?"

"So?"

"So that tells us these guys weren't just good, they were professional," stated Wise. "And to pull off five kidnappings in different cities all on the same night, there had to be—"

"Multiple teams," Harvath replied, finishing the man's sentence for him. "I already know that. That's not what I'm struggling with here."

"Just stay with me. Now, whoever orchestrated the kidnappings had to have had access to information, to the actual five names from inside the Fed itself. That's no easy feat. Couple that with professionals having been hired to actually carry out the kidnappings and now we're talking serious money. But, it gets better, or more specifically, more expensive because murder doesn't come cheap."

"You're convinced the kidnappings *and* the murder were all done for hire?"

Wise nodded. "And I'll tell you why. Per the file and the pictures, Claire Marcourt was beaten to death. Outside of self-defense or a fit of jealous rage, very few human beings are capable of taking another life like that. Then, there are her ears."

"What about them?"

"They weren't just hacked off with a pair of shears or a dull pocket-knife. The lines were clean and pretty well matched. Someone used a sharp blade, took their time, and knew what they were doing."

"But if you're going to beat someone to death, who cares if the lines are clean?" asked Harvath.

"Exactly," Wise replied. "And while we're at it, and I think your theory about the Pine Tree Riot is right on the money, why prop up the ears in the photo? Why take the time to display them like that?"

"Because whoever this guy is, he didn't want us to miss them."

"They're ears, for crying out loud. Who's not going to notice them? Why not just drop them next to that economist's quote and take the picture? Why go through all the trouble to set it up like it was some sort of an exhibit?"

"I don't know," said Harvath. "Maybe this guy's a sadist and proud of his work."

Wise tapped the tip of his nose with his index finger and then pointed it at Harvath. "Now we're getting somewhere."

Harvath waited for him to extrapolate, but Wise was suddenly lost in his own thoughts. Harvath rapped his knuckles on the bar top to get the man's attention. "Knock. Knock."

Wise shook himself out of his reverie. "Sorry, I was thinking about a Russian diplomat kidnapped in Iraq."

"What about him?"

"The FSB operatives flown in from Moscow were able to get him back within seventy-two hours."

"That's impressive. How'd they do it? I'm guessing it didn't involve *pretty please with sugar on top*."

"No, it didn't," Wise replied. "Actually, it was pretty vicious. The Russians focused on the most likely neighborhood, swept in, and started breaking hands, fingers, arms, and legs until they found somebody who knew something. From there, they were able to identify a cousin of one of the kidnappers. Once they had him, they began slicing off his body parts and had a courier drop them off one at a time at the family's house. After the man's nose and both ears had been delivered, the diplomat was returned to the embassy unharmed and the FSB agents returned to Moscow."

"That's one way of handling things. Especially in that part of the world, but do you really think we're dealing with the Russians?"

Wise shook his head. "An organization with enough expertise to penetrate the Federal Reserve? Experienced enough to pull off five simultaneous kidnappings without leaving a trace? This is something different."

"Well, if not the Russians, maybe this is some sort of a currency war. Or maybe the Fed screwed up and ran afoul of the Cosa Nostra. With the kind of money they move, anything is possible."

"But what's *probable*? What kind of group would openly invite the full ire of the United States government?"

"Who knows? Maybe they're exactly who they claim to be," Harvath stated. "Why can't this simply be a group of patriots trying to intimidate the Federal Reserve into shutting down?"

"Because that doesn't make any sense."

"None of this makes any sense."

"What I mean," Wise clarified, "is that it's nuts to think that the Fed could be bullied into doing anything, much less closing its doors."

"Then why do this?" Harvath asked. "What's the purpose?"

"Maybe the purpose isn't to get them to close their doors but to generate enough media attention to force a discussion of the Fed center stage, right into the national spotlight."

"Which is exactly what the Fed doesn't want."

"Of course not," said Wise. "The less people take an interest in them, the better. That's why you were given this assignment."

"Then let's suppose for a moment you're right. Why would someone want to force a national discussion of the Federal Reserve?"

"Maybe these patriots see the Fed as something so dangerous to the nation that it has to be dealt with. Even if that means using violence."

It was a provocative possibility, but there was something about it that just didn't feel right to Harvath. There was nothing "patriotic" about murdering other Americans in cold blood. There had to be something else.

And that something else was the pressure weighing on Harvath's shoulders, even after he had left Wise's home that night. *Would he be able to figure out what that something else was before someone else was murdered?*

CHAPTER 22

Ryan rode with McGee back to the Farm to pick up her car. She thought about stopping by the grocery store on the way home, but she was wiped out from her jet lag. All she wanted to do was throw on her robe, pour a glass of wine, and stretch out on the couch with a good book until she couldn't keep her eyes open anymore.

Of course, she hadn't told McGee any of this. He never slept, and in fact liked to joke that it was a sign of weakness. So instead, she had told him that she was going right home to start assembling a plan for how they should proceed. *Hit the ground running*, McGee had liked that.

She pulled into her complex and parked in the assigned space near her building. Any mail in her box could keep until tomorrow. Climbing the exterior steps to her second-floor apartment, she walked down the open-air hallway to her door. Opening it, she stepped inside and tossed her keys in a bowl on the kitchen counter. It had been a long day and it felt good to be home.

Her small, two-bedroom unit was tastefully decorated, particularly so for a government employee who was home so seldom she didn't even have a landline.

Ryan had painted the entire place and had installed the crown molding and baseboards herself. The walls were hung with matted prints she had razor-bladed out of old botany books picked up at a flea market. Everything had been done cleverly and on the cheap. Her only substantial investment was her stereo system. It was built around an expensive Tritium Super Analog turntable, upon which she indulged her greatest passion, a museum-quality collection of jazz and blues records she had been collecting since college.

Powering up the system, she selected a Nina Simone LP, removed it from its sleeve, placed it on the turntable, and activated the tone arm.

The chicken-and-egg battle over what would come first, the bathrobe or the wine, was over before it started. *Wine first.* Ryan walked into her kitchen and took down a bottle of OneHope petite syrah.

As Nina Simone began singing "Blue Prelude," she opened the drawer where she kept her favorite souvenir from France, a waiter's-style Laguiole snakewood-handled corkscrew. Its box was there, but the corkscrew was missing.

She opened the other drawers in the kitchen thinking maybe, after a few too many glasses of wine last time, she might have put it back in the wrong place. That wasn't like her, though. She always put it back where it belonged, but having been out of town for so long, it was hard to remember what she had done last time.

After a cursory glance through all the drawers, she gave up, and grabbed a Leatherman multi-tool from her bug-out bag.

Once the wine was opened, she fished out some cheese and crackers, and then carried everything to the coffee table. After pouring a large glass of wine, she took it with her as she went to get changed.

She came back with Nelson DeMille's latest thriller, turned off her cell phone, and made herself comfortable on the couch.

Two glasses and nine chapters later, her eyelids started getting heavy. She laid the book on the table and intended to close her eyes for just a second, but before the final notes of "Solitaire" had been played she was asleep.

• • •

Bang, bang, bang! It sounded like gunshots; close gunshots. The earsplitting cracks nearly caused her to leap off the couch. *What the hell was going on?*

Ryan tried to shake the cobwebs from her head as the banging came again. *Someone was pounding on the door.* "I'm coming," she said loudly, hoping to quiet down whoever was outside before they woke her entire complex. *Who the hell could this be?*

Tightening the belt of her robe, she approached the door and looked out the peephole. A young blond girl in her early twenties stood glassy-eyed and swaying. She raised her fist to pound again, but Ryan unlocked the door and pulled it open before she could make contact.

"I don't know who you're looking for," Ryan stated, "but you've got the wrong apartment."

The girl stood dazed for a moment, as if unsure what to say, but then collected herself and asked, "Do you drive a black Nissan Altima?"

"Oh crap. What happened?"

"It wasn't my fault," the girl said, quickly adding, "And it wasn't my boyfriend's fault. Someone cut us off."

"Cut you off? What are you talking about? Better yet, who the hell are you and what happened to my car?"

"I'm Chrissie," she replied with an inebriated smile and a look of misplaced expectation as if the mere mention of her name should be cause for fireworks or a parade. "I live in the building next door."

She extended her hand, but Ryan ignored it. Clutching the lapels of her robe, she looked out into the hall and then said to Chrissie, "What happened to my car?"

"Like I said. It wasn't our fault."

"I got that part, Chrissie. Did you and your boyfriend hit my car? Is it damaged?"

Chrissie tried to raise her thumb and forefinger to indicate that there might be a little damage, but suddenly had trouble raising her arm while keeping her balance. The woman was smashed, and so too, Ryan worried, was her car.

She grabbed her keys from the bowl on the kitchen counter, slipped on a pair of flip-flops kept near the door, and said, "Why don't you and I go take a look."

"Sure," slurred Chrissie as if she had just been invited shopping. "Do you want me to show you where it is?"

"No," replied Ryan. "I think I can remember where I parked my car."

As they started toward the stairs, Chrissie said, "Remember, you promised you wouldn't be mad."

She had promised no such thing, but there was no reason to argue. The girl was so wasted it probably wouldn't even get through.

They walked down to the parking lot and over to Ryan's Nissan. The right rear quarter panel was crushed. Idling perpendicular was a piece-of-shit white panel van with a dinged up push-bumper that must have belonged to Chrissie's boyfriend. Ryan needed this kind of trouble like she needed a hole in the head.

As she walked over to inspect the damage, the boyfriend got out of the van. "Is that your car?" he asked. He sounded a lot more sober than his girlfriend. Ryan should have taken that as a warning, but her concern over what had happened to her car, coupled with her anger over the repeated problems with so many of the young residents in the complex, caused her to let her guard down.

His headlights perfectly illuminated the damage. This was going to cost at least a thousand dollars to repair, and judging by the looks of these two, they didn't even have a hundred dollars between them. They probably didn't have insurance, either. Ryan was growing angrier by the second.

"How did this happen?" she asked, vaguely aware of the young man's approach on her left side as she bent down to examine the damage. "Do you have any idea how much it's going to cost to fix this? I want to see your license and insurance card right now."

The man's right hand was in his jacket pocket and it didn't come out until he had reached Ryan's car and he was close enough to touch her.

It wasn't until that moment that she processed the unmistakable shape of the Taser in his hand. The cartridge had been removed, which meant he didn't want to leave a shower of micro-stamped aphids behind as evidence. It also meant he wasn't afraid to get up close, press the device against her, and deliver its jolt of electricity via a technique known as a "stun drive."

Either this guy was really good when it came to hand-to-hand, or he had no idea whom he was dealing with. Ryan didn't wait to find out.

Pivoting on the ball of her left foot, she bladed herself to her attacker and snapped her left arm out in a wide arc. She crashed her forearm into the man's wrist, knocking the Taser from his hand. She followed with a blow to his sternum, which knocked him backward two steps.

Before he could regain his balance, she charged, throwing a rapid combination of punches and elbows. It was happening so fast that all the man could do was cover up as Ryan rained down the pain.

The jabs, the crosses, all of it had been drilled into her through years of training. All of it came naturally. There was only one thing she neglected to do—sweep the area around her with her eyes.

Had she done that, she might have seen Chrissie coming up from behind. She might have been able to whip her head back and catch Chrissie on the bridge of her nose. Maybe she could have knocked her unconscious. Maybe she could have connected hard enough to render her temporarily dazed. At the very least, she might have been able to buy herself a couple of extra seconds to prevent Chrissie from getting close enough to her, placing another Taser against the side of her neck, and activating the trigger.

CHAPTER 23

Before the effects of the Taser had worn off, Ryan was tossed inside the back of the van, where her hands, feet, and mouth were duct-taped and a black hood was yanked down over her head. As soon as the vehicle started moving, she had her wits about her enough to try to interpret their speed and direction. Every piece of information was vital. Even the smallest data point could mean the difference between life and death.

How could she have been so stupid? She wanted to blame the wine or her jet lag, but she knew that *she* was ultimately responsible for her predicament right now. She should have never let her guard down.

The only silver lining she could find was that she wasn't dead, yet. If they had wanted to kill her, they could have put a gun to the base of her skull and pulled the trigger rather than using a Taser on her. But while she saw breathing as a silver lining, she knew that at some point tonight she could end up wishing they had killed her in the parking lot.

She ran through her mind the long list of people around the world she had pissed off badly enough to want to come get her. The fact that the attack had been carried out by two young Caucasians worried the hell out of her, as it could very well be an Islamic operation. As box-of-rocks stupid as so many Muslim foot soldiers were, the men in the organizational structures of the more aggressive terror organizations tended to be rather intelligent. If one of those groups had the wherewithal to track her down like this, they'd never be dumb enough to send a Muslim man, or even a Muslim woman to lure her out of her apartment. The minute she saw either on her doorstep, her antennae would be up. The tipsy blonde with the fender-bender story was the perfect ploy.

Was this about one of the countless harsh interrogations she had conducted? Because if so, there wasn't a single one that she would go back and change. She believed in the methods the CIA used, including the ones that members of Congress would never know about. They had no idea the type of determined enemy the United States faced. And while she believed in harsh interrogation methods, most of them were tactics that she would never want to be submitted to.

What worried her even more was that boastful lies and one-upmanship were the Muslim terrorist's stock-in-trade. This went double for stories of capture and interrogation at the hands of the Americans. No matter what had happened in an interrogation, there'd always be one of them quick to jump up and claim they had a worse one. It led to a very perverse view of what Americans actually did in their interrogations.

It was why the thought of being kidnapped by Al-Qaeda or a similar group was something that kept some CIA personnel up at night. They knew that if they ever were grabbed, the interrogation wouldn't be "harsh," it would be brutal, and it would definitely be torture.

There was no way Ryan was ever going to submit to that, even if avoiding it meant throwing herself out of a moving vehicle. While she tried to keep track of the movement of the van, she also tried to keep calm as she sought a way to get free. But she was on her stomach, her naked body half exposed beneath her open robe, with her hands and feet bound up hog-tie style. She remembered watching a video once of someone actually getting out of being duct-taped. It involved twisting the hands down and out with a quick pop. It also required that your hands be bound in front, something professionals never did.

Rolling onto her right side, she inched in that direction praying that she'd find a screw or an exposed piece of metal, anything that could be used to cut through the tape and get herself free. There was nothing, so she rolled onto her opposite side and slowly felt her way along the filthy floor in that direction. It was just as fruitless. But then she felt something.

It was a small, narrow strip of metal banding, the kind used to secure loads to a wooden pallet. It was about half an inch wide and only an inch long. It wasn't exactly sharp, but it had been cut on an angle and therefore had a point. Gripping it as best she could, Ryan ignored the pounding in her chest and went to work on her restraints.

About fifteen minutes later, she felt the van make another turn. Based on the speed and lack of stoplights, she figured they had been on Route 123 headed out of Fairfax. Now they were headed in a new direction. *Toward what? A safe house? The forest?* She worked harder on the duct tape. It had been wrapped around so many times, Ryan couldn't tell if she was making any progress at all.

A few minutes later, the vehicle began to slow as if the driver was looking for something, an address or a road sign, maybe. *No,* she said half to herself, half in prayer. *Don't stop yet. I need more time. Please, I need more time.* Frantically, she rubbed and stabbed at the tape with the little piece of banding. She could feel the time on her clock running out.

Whatever the driver was looking for, he must have found it, because he made another turn, this time onto a rough, uneven surface. Ryan thought it might be a dirt road of some sort, but after several hundred yards she felt the van make a sharp cut and come to a stop. *Was it a turnout or were they in a driveway of some sort?*

For several minutes, nothing happened. The van just idled. As best she could tell, no one had gotten out. They were just sitting there. *Why? What was going on?* Were they waiting for something or *someone?*

Through the hood, she could hear voices coming from the cab, Chrissie and the boyfriend. It sounded like they were arguing. There was a crescendo as Chrissie, who must have been driving, punctuated her words by throwing the van into reverse and stepping on the accelerator.

The tires spun wildly, before finally biting into the dirt and finding purchase. And that's when it happened.

Just as the van was beginning to back up, something slammed into it from behind. *Hard*.

CHAPTER 24

As soon as he saw the van's reverse lights come on, Bob McGee knew he was going to get blown. He'd never be able to reverse his own vehicle fast enough, much less turn around and find a place to hide. There was only one way he could hope to turn this to his advantage and he took it. Slamming the gas pedal to the floor, he aimed right for it.

The force of the impact sent the van skidding sideways. Before its occupants knew what had happened, McGee was out of his 4Runner, 1911 pistol in hand, rushing the cab.

In the less than three seconds it took him to get there, both the male passenger and female driver had scrambled for their weapons and were about to bring them up high enough to fire at him. *Big mistake.*

McGee killed them both with two .45-caliber rounds to the chest and one to the head fired in rapid succession. The shots from his 1911 echoed through the wooded area like thunder.

After inserting a fresh magazine he took better cover and yelled, "Lydia! Can you hear me? Lydia!" There was no response. Cautiously, he crept forward and, grasping the handle, slid the door back.

He found her, still hog-tied and up against the side of the van. Taking off her hood, he peeled back the tape from across her mouth as gently as he could.

"Are you okay?" he asked as he pulled out his knife and cut her hands and feet free.

Ryan covered herself with her robe as McGee helped roll her into a sitting position. "I'm okay," she said, pulling at the tape around her wrists. "What happened? Are they dead?"

"Yeah, they're dead. Both of them."

"How'd you find me?"

"They sent a team to my house, too. It's a good thing I get up every two hours to piss or they might have gotten me also. I tried to call your cell."

Ryan shook her head. "I needed some sleep. It was turned off."

"Well, when you didn't answer I rushed to your place. Got there just as they were loading you into the van."

"Why didn't you do something?"

McGee put up his hands. "I needed to make sure there wasn't a tail-gunner or some sort of support team in a follow car."

"Why didn't you PIT them to get them to spin out or run them off the road?"

"And have the van flip over? Something told me they probably didn't take the time to put a seat belt on you. Listen, I picked my moment. They're dead and you and I are both alive."

He was right. "Who the hell are they?"

McGee held up his index finger indicating he'd be right back. Stepping out of the cargo area, he moved back to the cab, and after making sure both of the occupants were dead, he conducted a quick search. He returned to the cargo area with a black duffle bag, which he set on the floor and opened up.

"Two H&K MP5s, two Glock 19s, a couple of Tasers, duct tape, power bars, some water bottles, a cell phone, which is probably a burner and won't lead anywhere, and enough ammo to take on a small Latin American army."

"But no ID?" asked Ryan.

"No."

"So they're pros."

McGee nodded.

Ockham's razor. The simplest explanation was usually correct. They had come after both of them. But before today, there wasn't anything that she and McGee shared that somebody could want to kill them over. All of that had changed since she had confronted Durkin. This wasn't a co-incidence. This *had* to be tied to him. She could feel it. "Did you see any books?" she asked.

"*Books?*"

"A paperback of some sort."

"Now that you mention it," said McGee, as he returned to the front of the van.

Ryan could hear him open the cab. "Durkin liked to use them for codes," she said, loud enough for him to hear. "French lit translated into English. Rousseau or some author like that."

McGee returned and tossed an aged paperback to her. "Balzac."

"Damn it. It *is* Durkin, then."

"Or," McGee said, his voice trailing off.

"*Or* what?"

"Or this is bigger than either of us thought and Johnson is involved, too."

Ryan looked at him. "The DNI? You've got to be joking. I thought he was someone you trusted."

"At this point, you're the only one I trust. And until we get to the bottom of this, that's the way it's going to stay."

She winced as she pulled the last piece of duct tape from her arm. "Why'd they drive me all the way out here?"

"It's as good a place as any to dump a body. Or maybe even two bodies. When I rolled up, they were trying to signal someone with their head-lights but I never saw anyone signal back. They waited a while and either got spooked or decided to move to Plan B."

"Who do you think they were signaling?"

"I don't know; maybe this was a rendezvous with the team who came gunning for me."

"Did the men at your house have guns," Ryan asked, "or Tasers?"

"Both. Why?"

"Because if they'd wanted to kill us, they would've. Why bother giving Tasers to a wet-work team?"

"Lots of reasons."

"No," she disagreed. "This *has* to be about the Jordanians. It's the only reason we'd *both* be targeted. And I told Durkin everything. There's nothing he could gain from interrogating me. He knows all of it already."

"What if he wanted to know who else you might have told about the Jordanians?"

"Then he could have asked me. Listen, the only reason Durkin could possibly have to snatch me alive is that he wanted to kill me someplace else other than my apartment. And apparently, he didn't want me to die alone, which means he had something cooked up to explain why you and I died out here together in the middle of nowhere."

"Did you tell Durkin you were going to talk to me?" asked McGee.

"No."

"Then that would mean he had a tail on you. So, he not only knows that you talked to me, but that we talked to Johnson. How could he hope to get away with killing us?"

"I hate to say it, but either you're right and Johnson's involved, or Durkin came up with something so airtight, he was convinced our deaths could be explained away without even the DNI asking any questions. Either way, I don't think you and I were supposed to walk out of here tonight."

"I think you're right. So now what?"

"Now we get the hell out of here," replied Ryan as she grabbed one of the MP5s from the bag and moved toward the door.

McGee extended her his hand to help her exit, and then gathered up the duffle. "What should we do about the van and the bodies?" he asked.

Ryan looked inside the cab. In addition to the two corpses slumped over in their seats, the cab was splattered with blood and pieces of brain. "If we had enough time to clean it up and make it look like we took their people hostage, I'd say let's opt for that. But all we've got time to do now is burn it. Let's burn the entire thing."

McGee nodded and after throwing the duffle in his 4Runner, he backed it a safe distance away. While he got to work on the van and prepared to set it on fire, Ryan walked over to the spot from where he had been shooting. With a flashlight from his glove box, she began looking along the dirt road for the shell casings from his 1911.

It took several minutes, but she was able to locate all six. "Got 'em," she said as she pocketed the last one. "You ready?"

"Good to go," he said, flashing her the thumbs-up.

They drove out of the woods and toward the highway just as the van exploded in a billowing fireball. When they arrived at the junction where the dirt road ended and the pavement began, he stopped and asked, "Okay. Which way? South or north?"

They both knew that neither of them could go home. They had to go to ground, someplace safe; someplace where they could assess and plan their next move.

Ryan removed the atlas wedged next to her seat and studied it for a moment. Finally she said, "South."

McGee accelerated and turned onto the pavement. "Where are we headed?"

"How long will it take us to get to Fort Belvoir from here?"

"About twenty minutes, why? What's at Belvoir?"

Ryan looked over at him and replied, "For the moment, sanctuary."

"What do you mean, *sanctuary*?"

"I mean, Belvoir has one of the last rocks in the world Durkin would ever think of looking under."

"Knowing Durkin," McGee countered, "he's going to be looking under *every* rock."

"Not this one," Ryan said. "Trust me."

CHAPTER 25

The four-story redbrick office building was a block east of Boston Common at the corner of Washington and Essex streets. On its ground floor was an entrance to the subway station and a smattering of retail space, including a Dunkin' Donuts. On the fourth floor was the killer's destination, a Massachusetts Registry of Motor Vehicles office.

Keys, as well as the building's layout and the RMV's alarm code, had already been provided for him. He kept a silenced semi-automatic beneath his coveralls, but it had not proved necessary. It was the middle of the night and the building was vacant. No one would have any idea he was there. All he needed to focus on was his assignment.

Using the service elevator, he brought all of his equipment, including the man inside the commercial-grade rolling trash can whom he had drugged with the same paralytic he had used on the woman in Georgia, to the fourth floor. Once he had ascertained where he needed to set up, he positioned all of his gear and began to unpack.

He wasn't a fan of the coarse hemp rope. It was thick and difficult to deal with. He would have preferred to use a modern climbing rope, but the instructions had been explicit.

Cautious not to be seen from the street, he used his small flashlight sparingly and never near the windows. Even at this hour, there were still people on the street stopping and looking up at the building's façade. Most would be armed with cell phone cameras and some might even be disposed to take a picture or two. He couldn't afford to be caught in anyone's casual photos. Within a few hours, everyone was going to be talking about this building and anyone who had passed by and snapped a picture was going to be reviewing their footage to see if they unknowingly caught anything that might have warned of what was to come.

With everything staged, he attached the hoses together and ran the end with the rubber faucet adapter to the restroom. Even though the trash can had wheels, it would be difficult to move. He preferred to position it and then fill it in place. Things would be much easier that way.

As the water sloshed into the trash can, he looked at his watch and measured the rate of flow. He had planned for every eventuality: a late office worker, a random security patrol, being accosted by another cleaning company, anything that might have delayed his assignment. For every possible contingency, he knew how much water he would need.

He doubted his figures were absolutely precise, but they didn't have to be. All that mattered was that his work be done before the first person entered the Registry of Motor Vehicles in the morning. If anyone came in before, everything would be ruined.

He had been told not to get violent with the prisoner unless absolutely necessary. Of course, being told he couldn't do it had only made him want to do it even more. It was yet another wave added to the tumultuous sea of whitecaps roiling inside him. He tried to focus on the minutiae of his assignment; the importance of completing the job properly and not leaving behind any clues.

The distraction worked at first, but its force soon began to wane. He was tempted, so tempted, to abuse the man; to break him mentally and emotionally, to have him weep and beg for his life. He positioned himself so that the man could watch him knotting the heavy rope and made sure he could also see the backboard that had been prepared specially for him.

He wanted to ask the man if he had ever heard of an engineer named

Reuben Garrett Lucius Goldberg, or simply Rube Goldberg for short. He wanted to share how Mr. Goldberg had inspired the contraption he had built and lay everything out for the man so he could watch the already intense fear in his eyes build to an even greater degree. He knew, though, that if he toyed with the mouse, he might very well end up eating it and that was strictly forbidden. Everything had to be done according to the instructions. Any deviation and everything would be ruined.

He tried to take his mind off the man in front of him. His thoughts wandered to the woman he had taken from Sea Island, how powerful he had felt with her life in his hands, and what it was like extinguishing her. It was like the final wisp of smoke rising from a candlewick. One moment there was pain and fear and death in her eyes, then release as everything just slipped away. But he hadn't been able to savor it. He had wanted to take more time, especially with her ears, but his schedule meant that he had to keep moving.

That woman, and the one in the cemetery, made two back to back now who had gotten him significantly aroused without his being able to do anything about it. Tonight, after his work here was complete, he would find a way to change that. He deserved a reward. The mere thought of taking a woman shortly sent a pulse of excitement racing through his body. He now had the perfect goal to get him through what he had to finish and he focused on his task like a laser.

He finished his knots, placed everything just so, and even went back and rechecked his calculations for a fifth time. Once he was confident he had everything all set up exactly as it needed to be, he removed his cordless drill and selected a drill bit.

The prisoner's eyes widened as the killer attached the bit and then gave the power tool's trigger a quick press to make sure it worked. *It did.*

Satisfied, the killer closed the box of bits and began walking toward his victim. Before he even reached him, the man started to scream from behind his gag. The killer wasn't listening. Raising the spinning drill in front of him, he reveled in the high-pitched whine and watched the bit as it was transformed into a blur of sharp gray metal. It was so ingenious, easily one of the cleverest ways ever devised to kill.

CHAPTER 26

Bill Wise had sent Harvath home with a stack of books. The two he wanted him to focus on were *The Creature from Jekyll Island* and *Economics in One Lesson*.

The Jekyll Island book, all about the secrets behind the Federal Reserve, was thick enough to be a doorstop. Thankfully, its author encouraged readers to skip around in it and not read it from cover to cover. Harvath loved to read and if he'd had the time, he might have tackled it from front to back. Instead, he followed the author's advice and read the summaries at the end of each chapter and then dipped into the chapters that interested him the most.

Economics in One Lesson was a sliver of a book in comparison. Like *The Creature from Jekyll Island* it was well written and easy to read. He was halfway through it before finishing his first cup of coffee. The slim volume had originally caught his eye because its author was the same Henry Hazlitt whose economics quote had been hung around Claire Marcourt's neck. He was plowing through the book not only in hopes of better understanding the killer's, or killers', mind-set, but also because of how interesting it was and how much he was learning.

Despite not having hit the sack until well past midnight, he awoke at 5 A.M. feeling rested and decided to go for a run. Four miles in, he could feel his IT band tightening up. He hadn't stretched as well as he should have and now his body was punishing him for it.

He pushed himself to his five-mile marker and then turned back toward home. It was a cloudy, overcast morning with lots of humidity that hinted at a good rain at some point during the day. It was a good thing he was getting his run in now. As he ran, lots of things passed through his mind, predominantly about the case. He made a mental note to call Bill Wise after breakfast to see if he had made any progress.

Arriving back home, Harvath showered, shaved, and was downstairs with the TV on cooking breakfast when the Old Man called. "You need to get to Boston," he said without so much as a good morning.

Harvath muted his TV. "What's going on? What happened?"

"There's been a second victim."

"Who?"

"Herman Penning. Boston. I want you to get up there as soon as possible. Lewis says you can use the Fed's plane. He has it standing by."

Harvath looked at his watch. "I can be out the door in fifteen minutes."

"Be out the door in five. I want you there before the trail goes cold or the Boston cops muck it all up. I'll send what I've got to your phone. You can read it on the plane."

After shoveling his half-cooked eggs into the garbage, he ran upstairs to get dressed. Flying private, he didn't have to worry about carrying weapons, so he gunned up and grabbed a bunch of extra magazines. He also grabbed his knife, flashlight, a handful of EZ Cuff restraints, his cell phone, charger, and a small digital camera, then laid everything out on the bed.

Studying the items as he hastily tied his tie, he guessed there were probably a bunch of things he was forgetting and would later wish he'd thought to bring, but that was too bad. He had to get moving.

He pulled his ScotteVest trench coat out of the closet, slipped his gear into its multiple pockets, and then, grabbing the overnight bag he always kept ready, headed for the door.

The traffic on the George Washington Memorial Parkway was lighter than usual. Had he left home even a minute later, he had no doubt that he'd be sitting still right now instead of proceeding apace to Reagan National. He allowed himself to believe that somewhere up there, he was being watched out for. Then four miles from the airport, the rain began to fall and right on cue, the traffic slowed to almost a stop.

He decided to suffer the honks and explosion of one-fingered rush hour salutes by driving up the shoulder. In an attempt to at least make himself look somewhat official in his black Chevy Tahoe, he kept flashing his brights. No one bought it. He could hear people honking and, looking in his rearview mirror, he saw the phalanx of left hands with middle fingers extended pop out of one car window after another. The only good part was that nobody seemed to notice him and what he was doing until he'd already passed. In other words, nobody had been able to move halfway onto the shoulder in front of him in a preemptive block.

The world, unfortunately, was filled with people who felt the rules didn't apply to them. They were folks who felt entitled to do whatever they wanted and Harvath had no doubt that several of them, late for a flight at Reagan National, likely had attempted this same up-the-shoulder maneuver before. What was even more certain was that a vehicle speeding toward the airport disobeying traffic laws was going to be seen by law enforcement as a threat.

Harvath stayed on the shoulder for as long as he could and then, to an almost choreographed opera of additional horns and middle fingers, he muscled his way back into the creeping flow of traffic and over to the far right lane so he could exit. He parked at the Signature Flight Support FBO, checked in, and was escorted out to the Aerion SBJ. The crew was assembled at the bottom of the air-stairs waiting for him and while he was slightly disappointed that the flight attendant wasn't Natalie, it was probably a blessing in disguise. He needed to focus on the task at hand.

The crew, as one would expect on such an expensive private aircraft, was exceedingly professional. Harvath, while trying his best to be polite, encouraged them to dispense with the formalities and get off the ground as quickly as possible. He needed to be there *yesterday*. They all understood.

With the preflight check already complete and the tower ready to bump them to the head of the list as soon as they were ready, Harvath was encouraged to take his seat and buckle up, which he did. Less than fifteen minutes later, they were airborne.

The flight to Boston's Logan airport was faster than any shuttle flight he had ever experienced from D.C. No sooner had they climbed up and out over the Atlantic, than they had passed New York City and were making their descent and landing. The flight attendant had apologized for not being able to offer him anything more than coffee and Dunkin' Donuts. They hadn't received much heads up, either, and there'd been no time to alert the airport catering company.

Harvath told her not to worry. While he wasn't a donut guy, he did enjoy their coffee and had been glad to have at least gotten something in his system. As he scrolled through the information the Old Man had sent to his phone, Anna the flight attendant kept his cup topped off.

When the sleek Supersonic Business Jet landed at Logan, Harvath was as up-to-speed as he expected to be until he reached the crime scene. Carlton had texted that travel into the city had already been arranged. Harvath assumed that meant someone, though likely not as attractive as Sloane Ashby, was going to meet him at the Logan FBO and drive him in.

After opening the main cabin door and lowering the air-stairs, the flight attendant apologized again for the lack of breakfast. She offered Harvath a couple of donuts for the road if he wanted, but he smiled and said, "No thank you," as he disembarked.

Stepping onto the tarmac, he noticed a clean-cut man in a navy suit standing next to a plain sedan talking on his cell phone. *That must be my ride.*

As his passenger approached, the man pulled the phone away from his ear for a moment and asked, "Harvath?"

Harvath nodded and the man ended his call. After sliding the phone back into his pocket, he extended his hand. "I'm Special Agent Montgomery. Boston field office."

"Short straw, huh?" he said as they shook hands. "Thanks for coming to pick me up."

"No problem. I was on my way in to work anyway. Besides, this'll be the first time I've used lights and sirens in Boston. Do you need a pit stop before we get on the road?"

He shook his head. "Good to go."

Montgomery threw his bag in back, and once Harvath was in the passenger seat and buckled up, the agent activated his lights and siren and raced out of the airport, headed for downtown.

CHAPTER 27

Despite the crush of morning traffic, they finally arrived at their destination, 630 Washington Street.

Looking up, Harvath wasn't surprised to see that the body had been removed. A host of gruesome photos taken by passersby was already making the rounds of the Internet. Interestingly enough, many of the amateur photographers had failed to capture the enormous plaque embedded in the building's redbrick façade, commemorating the structure's significance.

Known as the "Liberty Tree" building, it marked the location of a famous elm tree from which an effigy was hung in protest in 1765. The effigy represented Andrew Oliver, the man Mad King George had appointed to carry out the Stamp Act tax on the American colonies, and it drew a very large crowd—the first of its kind in public against the king. It was considered a seminal moment leading up to the Revolutionary War and the men who had hung Oliver in effigy would go on to call themselves the *Sons of Liberty*. Harvath wasn't surprised at all that this location had been chosen for another symbolic murder.

A Boston PD patrolman was blocking the main entrance. As Harvath grabbed his bag out of the back, Montgomery stepped up to the officer and flashed his FBI credentials and told him to let Harvath pass. The young FBI agent had already explained he was working another case and was only functioning as his driver.

Harvath thanked him for the ride as the patrolman said, "Fourth floor," and waved him inside.

Harvath rode the elevator upstairs and stepped out into a hive of activity. There were crime scene technicians, uniformed police officers, detectives, and FBI agents. They all had short hair, and while the FBI agents were all trim and in good shape, the cops looked like cops everywhere and represented a wide range of physical fitness levels.

The patrolman downstairs had already radioed up to the officer controlling the inner perimeter of the crime scene and had told him to let Harvath pass. The officer directed Harvath down the hall to where a pair of technicians, who had ostensibly photographed everything, was beginning to disassemble a very odd contraption. There were old-fashioned wooden pulleys, hooks, and lengths of rough, fibrous rope that looked like they were twisted from hemp.

"Can you hold off for a second please, fellas?" he asked the CSTs. "I'd like to take a look at all this."

"Just what this investigation needs," one of them said derisively, "another Fed."

"You picking up the overtime?" his colleague asked.

Apparently, there wasn't a lot of love lost between the Boston PD and the FBI. Harvath wasn't surprised. The Boston Homicide Unit had some excellent detectives, but overall a terrible and unfortunately long-standing record when it came to their ability to actually solve murders. On multiple cases, the FBI had been forced to come in and bat cleanup. It was a source of embarrassment for the city and they had been working hard to turn things around. Nevertheless, it didn't excuse the attitude Harvath was getting.

"No, I'm not picking up your overtime," he replied. "In fact, I'd be happy to recommend you both for a permanent vacation."

"And just who the hell are you anyway?" the first CST demanded.

"Wyatt Earp," Harvath replied, shooting him a very serious, don't-fuck-with-me look that backed the man down. Smiling, he suggested, "Why don't you two take a break and get a cup of coffee? I'll only be a few minutes."

"Fine by me, pal," the short-tempered tech said as he stopped what he was working on, stood up, and gestured for his partner to follow.

Harvath was glad to be able to have a few minutes to work in peace. Stepping back, he took the entire contraption in piece by piece.

From an engineering standpoint, it was ingenious. Everything had been assembled facing the broken window. The ropes and pulleys were suspended from the sprinkler pipes and helped balance a polished plank of wood atop a modified fulcrum. The plank actually comprised three pieces of wood fitted together, which likely had made it easier to transport. Holes were drilled on each side to accommodate the ropes.

At first, Harvath had thought that all of the water had come from a broken sprinkler pipe. The problem was that only the floor was wet. No other surface areas were—not the desks, not the file cabinets, not even the windowsills.

Looking around, he noticed the large plastic industrial garbage can on wheels again. Originally, he hadn't paid much attention to it, figuring the can belonged to a cleaning crew or something. Now his interest was piqued.

Removing his flashlight, he walked over to the can and shined some light inside. It was streaked with moisture and there was a small puddle of what looked to be water in the bottom. There was also something else.

Returning his flashlight to his pocket, he bent down and examined the exterior of the can. Near the very bottom, he found it. It appeared that the can had been filled with water, but that someone had drilled a hole at the bottom to let the water out. *Why?*

Harvath stood and went back over to the plank and reexamined everything. That's when it hit him. The killer, or killers, had probably left long before Herman Penning was even dead.

It was all making sense now and what he had originally seen as ingenious was quickly reaching the brilliance level.

The sixty-year-old man had been fitted with a noose and was then placed onto the plank, which would function like a chute. When the appointed moment arrived, the chute tipped forward and gravity jettisoned the father of two and grandfather of four through the window. The man then fell, but only until he reached the literal end of his rope, at which point his neck was snapped.

Judging by the size of the garbage can and how much water it could hold, it had functioned like a timer. Secured to the plank, it would have acted as a counterbalance, holding it horizontal for as long as its weight was greater than the victim's. As soon as that ratio changed, gravity would take over.

After taking several pictures of everything, Harvath grabbed a chair in order to better examine the pulleys. He'd only been up on it for a few moments when he heard a throat being cleared behind him.

He turned around to see a man and a woman, shields on their belts and their hands very near their weapons.

"Agent Wyatt Earp, is it?" the woman said. "I'm Detective Annie Oakley and this is my partner, Buffalo Bill. Why don't you step down. We'd like to have a word with you, please."

CHAPTER 28

"Annie Oakley" turned out to be Boston Police Homicide Detective Lara Cordero. Her partner's name sounded like Sabatelli or Sabatano, but Harvath didn't catch it. He wasn't really paying attention at that point. He was trying to not appear as if he was staring at Cordero while he was, in fact, staring at Cordero.

She was a very exotic-looking woman and quite attractive—a knockout, actually. If Harvath had to guess, he would have pegged her as maybe Spanish with something else. It was hard to discern. She was in her early thirties, tall, tan, and took *very* good care of herself. She had green eyes and long brown hair that was streaked blond by the sun.

Harvath introduced himself and presented each of them with a crisp white business card embossed with his company's name and a phone number, nothing else.

"So you're the kidnap and ransom specialist," said Cordero. "I wasn't aware that the kidnappers had made any demands."

"They haven't," Harvath replied. "Not yet."

"Maybe it got lost in the mail," her partner said.

While Cordero's Boston accent was almost nonexistent, this guy's was over-the-top. It had an edge to it, too, that Harvath didn't care for.

"Who's the client?" Cordero asked.

The Old Man had warned him to be ready for this question. The FBI was being circumspect with the details it was sharing with the Boston PD. Monroe Lewis had told him to do the same. "The deceased has some very powerful friends in Washington."

"Had," Cordero's partner corrected him. "Past tense."

Harvath studied him for a moment. He was dressed in a halfway decent suit. Other than that, there wasn't anything particularly impressive about him. He wasn't short, he wasn't tall, and his features were unremarkable. He looked to be in decent shape compared to a lot of the other cops in the room, but that wasn't saying much. It was obvious that the man didn't like him, and that was fine by Harvath, who was about to thank him for the English lesson when Cordero asked another question.

"So what's your background?"

"Why do you ask?" Harvath replied.

"You don't strike me as the law enforcement type."

"Is that so?"

"Yeah. You've got more of a military vibe to me. They hire a lot of ex Special Forces types for Kidnap and Ransom companies, right? What, are you an Army Ranger, or maybe a Navy SEAL?"

It was either an incredibly good guess or she was intentionally flirting with him. He couldn't tell. Either way, he didn't really want to get into what his background was and laughed it off. "A SEAL? They only take smart guys," he replied. "Plus, I can't swim."

Cordero smiled. "I think you may be downplaying the smarts part."

"Why's that?"

"Because I was watching the way you examined the pulleys and the rest of the crime scene."

"I did that good of a job, huh? How about we trade places and I'll watch you this time. Maybe I can learn something."

"How about we go swimming instead?" the partner interjected.

Good one, but this guy was getting on Harvath's nerves. He ignored him and said to Cordero, "Who found the victim?"

"About half of Boston," she replied. "We're right downtown. We've got lots of people on their way to work. Our 911 center was flooded with calls. A patrol unit responded within about four minutes. Within fifteen minutes of arriving on scene, they had accessed the building and retrieved Penning's body. They'd hoped that he was still alive and one of the officers even tried to resuscitate him, but we're confident his neck was broken instantly. There's nothing they could have done."

"Where's the body now?"

"On its way to the ME."

Harvath leaned and looked out the window to the street below. "Any CCTV footage, traffic cams, that sort of thing you can pull from the area?"

"Why didn't we think of that?" the male detective snarked.

"What I meant to say—" Harvath began, but Cordero interrupted him.

"I know what you meant and yes, we've got a few cameras we've already requested footage from. We're not holding out much hope, though."

"Why not?"

"Because we've already checked the security cameras here in this building. As far as that footage is concerned, no one ever entered."

"The footage was looped," said Harvath.

Cordero nodded. "With that level of sophistication, plus getting around the alarm system and no signs of forced entry into the building, we think the chances are slim that we'll get him on any of the cameras, but you never know. They got the Son of Sam with parking tickets, right?"

"Have you uncovered anything else unusual?"

The woman's partner rolled his eyes. "Nah, we see murder scenes with ropes and pulleys and little dolls every day."

"*Dolls?*" Harvath repeated.

"Yeah, it was shoved into the boot Penning was wearing."

"He was wearing only one?"

"We think the other one fell off and maybe some homeless person picked it up or something. We're looking into it."

"No doubt," replied Harvath. "Let me ask you about the victim's boot. Was the sole painted green?"

"Yeah, it was."

"And the doll. Does it look like a little devil?"

"Yeah," the man answered, his eyes narrowing. "How'd you know that?"

Harvath plowed forward. "It's grinning and holding a scroll, too, right?"

"What the fuck? How do you know all this?"

Harvath held up his hands and looked around as if it were obvious. "This is the Liberty Tree Building, right?"

The male detective mimicked Harvath's gesture and replied, "It obviously ain't Fenway Park. So what?"

"It's not important. Never mind."

Cordero, to her credit, knew that it *was* important and that Harvath understood much more than he was letting on. "Sal, can you give us a few minutes, please?" she asked.

Her partner looked at Harvath and then back at her. He didn't like being asked to leave. It made him feel as if he were some sort of impediment and that hurt his pride. He paused just long enough to suggest that he was trying to come up with something clever to say, but nothing materialized.

Finally, he replied, "No problem. I need to talk with the uniforms anyway and see how the canvass of the neighborhood is going."

"Thanks, Sal," Cordero replied. "I'll be down shortly."

"Mr. Harvath," he said, drawing out the word *mister* as if to highlight Harvath's non-law-enforcement status before turning on his cheap shoes and walking away.

"Interesting guy," Harvath said once the man was out of earshot.

"He means well."

"You two been together long?"

"Partners for six years. Best cop I've ever known. Loyal and nobody knows the streets better than him."

"I don't think he likes me."

"I can see it's breaking your heart."

"I'm insecure like that."

Cordero stifled a laugh. "Yeah, you've got insecurity written all over you. That was the first thing I noticed when you came in."

"What was the second?"

Ignoring his question, she said. "Follow me. I want to show you something."

As they walked, Cordero asked, "How did you know about the boot and the doll and all that?"

"I paid attention in class."

"And what class would that be?"

"American history," said Harvath. "Boston colonists hung an effigy of Andrew Oliver, the man chosen by King George to impose the Stamp Act. They hung it from an elm tree right on this spot that became known as the 'Liberty Tree.' Along with it, they also hung a British cavalry jackboot with its sole painted green. It was meant as an 'up yours' to two British prime ministers tied to the Stamp Act. One was named Grenville and the other Bute. Grinning from inside the boot was a devil doll holding a scroll with the words *Stamp Act* written on it."

The female detective nodded as she turned the information in her mind. "I guess I really didn't pay enough attention in class."

"You walk by history every day in Boston."

"But nobody's ever a tourist in their own hometown, are they?"

That was true. "Did you grow up here?" he asked.

"We moved here when I was a little girl. I was born in another country."

"Is Cordero Spanish?"

"No, Portuguese, but via—"

"Brazil," Harvath replied, everything about her falling into place.

She stopped and smiled. "Very good," she said. "You know your geography."

"My parents felt bad that they couldn't afford swimming lessons, so they gave me a globe instead. I got rather good with it."

"Your insecurity is showing again."

"Is it?" Harvath asked, glancing over his shoulder. "I'm going to have to get a better tailor."

Cordero started walking again. "Been there recently?"

"Brazil? Yes, a few years ago, but only a quick in-and-out for business."

"Kidnap and ransom business?"

"You could call it that," he replied as he remembered traveling there to track down a man he believed to be involved with the torture and killing of several friends and family of his.

The female detective appraised him once more, this time with a bit more appreciation. "Maybe you actually could be Navy SEAL material."

"Except for the swimming and the smarts stuff."

"Except for those," she agreed with a smile as they arrived at a long counter where the evidence technicians had arrayed everything that had been bagged, tagged, and would soon be dragged to headquarters once the rope, plank, and pulley apparatus was disassembled and packed up.

"Here," she said, tossing Harvath a pair of latex gloves. "Anything you see and want to touch, please just ask my permission first."

There were only a million responses that rushed to the front of Harvath's brain at that point, but being the consummate professional that he was, he refrained from all of them. "Why don't we start with the doll?"

Cordero nodded at her evidence tech, who presented a log and asked Harvath to print and sign his name before allowing him to examine the item.

Harvath didn't need to remove the grinning demon from its clear plastic bag. He only wanted to see what was on its little scroll. "Does anyone have a magnifying glass or something that I can use on this?"

The evidence tech borrowed one from a crime scene technician and handed it to him. Harvath held up the bag so he could get as much light on it as possible. Upon the scroll had been drawn the same skull and crossbones with a hovering crown that he had seen in the Claire Marcourt crime scene photos. Beneath it were written the words *Death to Tyranny*. And beneath that were the initials *S.O.L.*

Harvath thanked the evidence tech and handed back the doll and the magnifying glass.

"Any idea what any of the writing stands for?" Cordero asked.

She wasn't asking for state secrets. A few minutes on a Web browser and she'd be able to figure it out for herself. "*Death to Tyranny* and the skull-and-bones motif with the crown summarized popular anti-British sentiments in the colonies leading up to the Revolutionary War," he said. "We think *S.O.L* may be shorthand for *Sons of Liberty*. They were an organized resistance group back then and were believed to have been responsible for hanging the Oliver effigy in the Liberty Tree."

Cordero jotted a couple of notes in a notebook, then asked, "What's the connection to our victim, Mr. Penning?"

Now she was drifting into state secrets. "What do you mean?"

"Why so heavy on the symbolism?"

"Maybe somebody thought he was a tyrant."

"What do you think?"

"I barely know anything about the man, certainly not enough to have an opinion."

Glancing back at the ropes and pulleys, then returning her gaze to Harvath, the detective said, "This all looks pretty personal."

"The killer definitely wanted to send a message."

"*Death to tyranny?* Pretty nonspecific, if you ask me," she replied. Making a final mark in her notebook, she looked up and asked, "What else would you like to take a look at?"

Harvath scanned the table. There wasn't really anything else of interest, nothing that screamed *lead*. "I think we're good."

"Okay," she replied, adding her own signature to the evidence log and letting the tech know he could take everything down to the lab. "Now let's talk about why you're really here."

"I told you, Detective, the victim has—excuse me, *had*—some very powerful friends in D.C."

"First the FBI pretends all it knows is that Penning was kidnapped. Then we find out there were four others grabbed the same night, but the FBI won't tell us what they have in common. You don't have to be a detective to pick up on the fact that they're probably holding something back. Now, a wisecracking James Blond type in the K-and-R business shows up at my murder scene knowing a bit too much about American history and won't tell me who the client is. You'll forgive me if my BS meter is drifting into the red zone."

James Blond. He'd have to remember that one. "I imagine your job requires you to be a little suspicious about everything."

"And *everyone*," she added.

Harvath smiled and tried to change the subject. "What can you tell me about the circumstances surrounding Penning's kidnapping?"

"Nothing."

"Nothing?"

"That's right," she replied, her right forearm resting on the butt of her holstered pistol. "I think you know a lot more than you're telling me. Can we help each other? Maybe. Maybe not. But I'm not giving you anything else until you come clean with me."

"I could call back to Washington and have some of Mr. Penning's friends call your chief."

Cordero nodded. "You could do that. But the chief would only kick it down to my commander, who would end up assigning Sal to be your liaison. *Mama mia*, can that guy be slow in handling requests, especially if he doesn't like you. Which he doesn't. So why not just cooperate and make it easy on yourself?"

"I bet you use that line on all the guys you meet at murder scenes."

"Only if it's the right guys and I haven't already put a bullet in them."

Harvath thought about her offer. When it came to investigating a murder, you wanted to be as close to the streets as possible and that meant lashing up with the cops. No matter what happened, it was much more likely that the Boston PD would hear about it before the FBI. In the end, he needed her cooperation.

"Okay, I'll tell you what," he said. "Take me someplace for breakfast, I'll tell you anything you want to know."

"Anything?"

"Anything within reason."

Cordero didn't like the qualifier, but it left the door open. "I know a place not far from here," she replied. "We'll take my car."

CHAPTER 29

Since Cordero and her partner had both arrived at the Liberty Tree Building in separate vehicles, she told him she would catch up with him at headquarters later and drove Harvath to the city's Beacon Hill neighborhood.

The Paramount was a local institution known for its breakfast by generations of Bostonians. That was her primary reason for taking Harvath there. There was also a secondary reason. She wanted to prove she wasn't completely illiterate when it came to Boston history. She waited until he had ordered and they'd both been served coffee to fill him in.

"Really?" Harvath said. "It happened here?"

Cordero nodded. "Right upstairs. Her name was Mary Sullivan. She was nineteen years old and the Boston Strangler's final victim."

"I saw a documentary about him. He was a sick guy."

"I've seen the crime scene photos. You have no idea."

Harvath took a sip of his coffee and set the cup back down on the table. "They caught the guy, though, didn't they?"

"They caught *a* guy, a rapist named Albert DeSalvo. He allegedly confessed while being held in jail for a rape he committed nine months after the rape and murder of Mary Sullivan. There still remain a lot of doubts as to whether or not DeSalvo was the actual Strangler, or if there may have been more than one killer."

"What do you think?"

"I think DeSalvo knew too many details about the crime scenes not to have been involved," she replied. "Either he was the killer, or he knew the killers. Either way, it was good to get him off the streets."

"That was when, exactly? Early 1960s?" Harvath asked.

"Yup. The murders started in June 1962 with the last one occurring upstairs with Mary Sullivan on January fourth, 1964. There were four-teen women, all between the ages of nineteen and eighty-five, murdered."

"DeSalvo got life in prison, right?"

"Yes, but it was for the long string of robberies and sexual offenses he had committed before the Strangler murders. The police couldn't find any physical evidence tying him to the murder scenes. Did he know some pretty impressive details that hadn't been released to the public? Yes, but that wasn't enough to charge him with."

Harvath shook his head. "Plus he had O. J. Simpson's lawyer, didn't he?"

"He did. F. Lee Bailey. Bailey was representing the jailhouse snitch whom DeSalvo originally admitted being the Strangler to. When Bailey heard that, he scooped DeSalvo up. He tried to get a not-guilty on every-thing by reason of insanity, but the court didn't buy it."

"But he did get life in prison."

"He did. He also escaped that same year, only to turn himself back in the next day. Six years later, though, he was jumped in the prison infir-mary and stabbed to death. The killer or killers were never caught."

"At least justice was finally done and the people of Massachusetts didn't have to foot his bill anymore."

Cordero nodded just as Harvath's Spanish omelet showed up.

"You sure you don't want anything?" he asked.

"I'm good," she said. "I ate before I left the house this morning. Most important meal of the day, you know?"

Harvath smiled. "That's exactly what I was thinking this morning as I was cooking my eggs and the call came in telling me to get up here."

"Why'd you know so much about the whole Liberty Tree thing?" she asked, changing the subject. "And please save me the whole *I paid attention in class* response again, okay?"

She was a very perceptive woman, an important trait for a homicide detective, or any detective, for that matter. You'd have to get up pretty early in the morning to put one over on her and even then Harvath was not sure how successful he'd be. That being the case, there wasn't any reason to lie to her. He just needed to refrain from telling her the entire truth. It was something that was on a need-to-know basis and she didn't need to know.

"You said that the FBI told you that Penning was one in a string of kidnappings, right?"

"Right."

"Well, what they didn't tell you was that he wasn't the first victim to be killed."

Cordero looked to make sure no one was listening to their conversation and then leaned in closer. "Another murder? When? Where did it happen?"

Finishing what was in his mouth, he said, "Sunday night. A small island off the coast of Georgia."

"Same MO?"

He had no idea how hungry he had been until he began eating and nodded as he took another bite. "The killer left a note there, too."

"What did it say?"

"It was about the tree of liberty needing to be refreshed with the blood of patriots and tyrants."

"Another death-to-tyranny reference?"

Harvath nodded again as he set his fork down and reached to take a sip of water. "Same skull and crossbones with the crown, too."

"The FBI wouldn't say how the victims are related. Is it family? Personal relationship? Business? What are we talking about?"

"I'm not at liberty to discuss that specifically."

"What is it? Above my pay grade?"

"Mine, too."

Cordero studied him. "I think you're lying."

"Can you pass the pepper, please?"

"Is this a joke? Because I can tell you right now, this is not a joke to me. And when you go back to D.C., this is still going to be the Boston PD's case and the people of Boston are going to want resolution. They're funny like that. Do you remember the marathon bombing? They expect us to do our job."

Harvath picked his fork back up and cut another piece of omelet. "I've seen a lot of bad things over my career, Detective, and I bet you have, too. I think you understand graveyard humor. I also think you understand having to answer to a command structure. I do what I'm told."

"And right now you're being told to withhold information that may be critical to solving a murder."

She was frustrated and rightly so. "Listen, Lara. Can I call you, Lara?"

"You can call me Detective Cordero."

"Fine, *Detective* Cordero, I'll level with you. At least as much as I can."

"This ought to be good," she replied, leaning back and folding her arms across her chest.

There was no mistaking her body language. Any rapport he might have built with her was melting away. In any other situation, he would have let it go. Was she attractive? Exceedingly so, but he wasn't in Boston looking for a girlfriend; he was here to find a killer and until he did, he was going to need all the help he could get, especially from the Boston Homicide Unit.

The ball was in his court. He needed to make a significant overture to her. And against his better judgment, that's exactly what he decided to do. Leaning forward, he gestured for her to come closer so no one could overhear.

"This goes no further than us," he said as she met him halfway over the table. "It doesn't go into your report. You cannot tell your superiors. You can't even mention it to your partner."

Flicking him away with her hand, she leaned back and looked at him like he was nuts. "Not going to happen. Sorry."

"Fine by me," Harvath replied as he too leaned back and shoveled in another mouthful of eggs.

They sat for several minutes in silence. She sipped her coffee as he ate his omelet. The waitress came over and, after warming up their cups, asked if they wanted anything else. Harvath said, "No thank you," and asked to be brought the bill.

As the waitress walked off, he looked at Cordero and said, "Is stubbornness a Brazilian trait?"

"If you think just because I'm a woman you can come into my town and mess around with my investigation, you've got another thing coming."

Harvath grinned. "And whose insecurity is showing now?"

Instead of voicing the foul remark she had in mind, she let one of her fingers do the talking for her.

"That's pretty good," said Harvath. "If you can now count to two, I'll let you have my toast."

Cordero stood up from the table. "I hope you enjoy the rest of your time in Boston."

Before Harvath could respond, she had turned and was walking toward the door.

He pulled a wedge of cash from his pocket, peeled off what he thought would be enough to cover everything, and dropped it on the table. He looked at his half-eaten omelet and decided reluctantly to leave it. Grabbing his coat from the back of his chair, he went off after her.

"Lara," he said as he tried to catch up with her outside. "Lara. Damn it, Detective Cordero!"

With that, she turned around on the pavement and stopped, both hands on her hips. "Quid pro quo, Mr. Harvath. That's all I want. Quid pro quo. None of this mysterious cloak-and-dagger BS. Maybe that works with the Georgetown coeds, but it doesn't work here, not with me."

Good God, she was frustrating, and *obstinate*. He wanted to bring her a little bit further into the light of what was going on, but she insisted on fighting him. She wanted everything on her terms. She acted just like . . . *him*.

"Come over here," he said, trying to steer her into the doorway of the building next door.

"That's not a very good idea," she stated, taking his hand from her arm. "If you have something to tell me, you can tell me right here."

The street was too crowded. "I'm going to tell you what you want to know, but come on. We can't do it standing on a busy sidewalk. Not here. Not like this."

She looked at her watch, "I have something I have to do. If you want to come along, we can talk."

Harvath agreed and they headed back toward her car. As they approached, he figured they could talk as they drove, but she walked past the vehicle and kept going.

"Detective Cordero," he asked. "Where are we going?"

"I'm killing two birds with one stone," she replied, and that was all she said.

They crossed Mount Vernon Street and took a left down the tree-lined, red and black bricked sidewalk. A block later, Harvath zeroed in on their destination.

"I have an aunt who's not well," Cordero offered as they stepped inside.

Having been sent to Catholic school as a child, Harvath had been inside plenty of Catholic churches. Boston's Church of the Advent was an amazing structure. Unlike the churches he was used to, this one was built predominantly from brick, a feature its architects didn't try to hide, but rather drew attention to by offsetting the brickwork with stone. It was actually a very beautiful combination.

They had timed their visit well. The church was between masses and there was no one there except for an unseen organist practicing a song Harvath had not heard since grade school, Gibbons's "Almighty and Everlasting God." There was only one way to describe the notes as they floated through the church—*mesmerizing*.

He had always been amazed at how religious composers could so perfectly create music that was absolutely brilliant for both the organ and church acoustics. Then, between high school and college, Harvath had met a very cool church organist—the elusive figure whom people always hear, but never seem to see. The pair had a discussion about music composed for church and the organist invited Harvath to come visit her at work, which Harvath did.

The organist played Handel's *Messiah,* César Franck's setting to music of St. Thomas Aquinas's "Panis Angelicus," and then she surprised Harvath with an amazing performance of "America the Beautiful." It was the first time Harvath had ever heard nonreligious music in a church and he was dumbstruck by how incredible it sounded.

The woman played other songs for him as well, but the one that had stuck, besides "America the Beautiful," was a song from the organist's generation, "Whiter Shade of Pale." She drew out all the notes with such soul and such feeling. After making sure no one else was in the building, she then transitioned into funk music. It was a genre that Harvath had heard of but knew very little about. The organist was a pious woman, and played only snippets of two songs she felt were appropriate. She did, though, mention several of the classics and encouraged Harvath to look into them, which he did. Funk ended up becoming one of his favorite styles.

While Detective Cordero lit a candle for her aunt, Harvath continued into the church. He thought of Mukami, the Kenyan engineer who had been killed in Somalia, and decided to light a candle for him.

After he was done, he walked in and sat down in one of the pews. Closing his eyes, he let the music wash over him.

A few minutes later, he sensed that Cordero had joined him, but she was respectful and didn't say anything while he continued to enjoy the music. When it stopped, he opened his eyes.

"I wouldn't have figured you for a guy who appreciates music," she said.

"You'd be surprised what I appreciate."

Cordero smiled and then looked at her watch. "My whole schedule has been turned upside down today. I need to get to the office, so what is it you want to tell me?"

Harvath took a deep breath and quietly let it out. "You asked me what the victims had in common."

"Besides the notes from the killer?"

He nodded. "Yes, besides those."

Cordero waited as patiently as she could for him to respond. Eventually, she said, "Mr. Harvath?"

Harvath had made peace with the fact that he couldn't hold back any longer. "Both of the victims were nominees for a government position."

It was a half-truth, because the Federal Reserve wasn't really a government organization, but he didn't want to get into all of that with her.

"What kind of position?"

"Management at an economic agency."

"Which agency?"

"One that doesn't want the publicity," Harvath replied.

"Is that who hired you?"

Harvath nodded. "And they hired me because I'm serious about client confidentiality. If I could tell you, I would. But I can't and I'm sorry. I hope you understand."

Cordero was silent.

"Two of the kidnappings have turned into murders. That's why I'm here," he said. "I need your help. I don't want there to be another one."

She was about to respond when her phone vibrated with a text message.

Harvath watched her as she read. Slowly, her facial expression changed. "What is it?" he asked.

"Another murder."

"Is it a bad one?"

She looked at him. "Is there actually such a thing as a good one?"

Depends who's on the receiving end, he thought to himself, but he didn't say it. Instead, he said, "Something about that text got to you. I can tell. What is it?"

"The victim's a prostitute. They just pulled her out of the Charles River."

"And?"

"*And* whoever killed her cut off her ears before dumping her in the water."

CHAPTER 30

C ordero had no intention of allowing Harvath to tag along to an unrelated murder scene, but that changed as soon as he explained how Claire Marcourt's body had been found with her ears removed.

With her wigwags flashing and siren blaring, she raced through traffic toward the river. The Community Boating Inc. boathouse was located on the Esplanade, right in between the Hatch concert shell and the Longfellow Bridge.

When they arrived, there were already multiple officers on the scene, including Cordero's partner, Sal whatever-his-name-was.

"What'd you bring him along for?" he asked upon seeing Harvath. "They don't give swimming lessons here. This is a sailing school."

Harvath looked out over all the boats. "I always wanted a sailboat as a kid. I used to pray every night for one."

"Is that so? I'm all broken up."

"I was, too, until I learned God doesn't work that way. So I went out and stole one and asked for forgiveness instead."

Cordero's partner was a prick, but now that Harvath had had a little something to eat, he didn't feel like riding the guy as hard. Besides, he always heard that the shortest distance between two people was either a good laugh or a smooth trigger pull. He figured he'd try the laugh route first. He watched pointlessly for any hint of a sense of humor in the man until Cordero jumped back in and changed the subject.

"I brought him along," she replied, "because we think there may be a connection to our other homicide."

"So the two of you are partners now?" he asked.

"Lighten up, Sal. Where's the body?"

"This way," he relented, waving them toward the water.

The dock formed a long, narrow U shape large enough to pen about fifty sailboats, all of which appeared to Harvath to be small, Cape Cod Mercurys. There were at least fifteen officers present, including members of the Boston Police Rescue/Recovery Dive Team.

Detective what's-his-face stopped at a blue plastic tarp and lifted it up so they could see the body of the prostitute, along with the rope and anchors that had been used to weigh her down. As Cordero's text message had read, both of her ears had been sliced off.

Harvath examined the work. Though he was no expert, the cuts looked clean, similar to Claire Marcourt's. "Where was the body found?" he asked.

"Just on the other side of the corral. One of the staff had come down to open up and get the boats ready for the day. He was carrying a bunch of stuff and apparently dinking around on his iPhone at the same time. iPhone goes in the water, staffer goes after iPhone, staffer meets Kelly Davis and the rest is 911 history."

"Any idea how long she's been in the water?"

"Less than twelve hours."

"Was she dumped here or did she drift from another spot?" Harvath asked.

"With those anchors tied around her like that? She didn't move more than a couple of feet, if at all. Whoever dumped her, dumped her right here."

Harvath looked at the ropes that had been wrapped around her. Removing his camera, he took several photos. The killer had done a good job of tying her up. "Where did the anchors and all this line come from?"

"The staffer says someone broke into a utility shed they have up at the boathouse. We're pretty sure that's where they came from."

"Anybody have any gloves?" Harvath asked, as he put his camera away.

An evidence tech handed him a pair and he examined the body. When he was finished, Cordero remarked, "I take back what I said about you not looking like law enforcement. Spent some time around dead bodies in your past?"

"One or two. I'm sure you'll want to take a look."

"Why don't you tell me first what you see?"

"From what I can tell, it looks like she's been strangled. I don't see any trauma to the head, other than the ears, of course, so I'd be willing to say strangulation's the most likely cause of death."

"You think she was dead before she went in the water?" Cordero asked.

"I do, though an autopsy will look for water in her lungs, which would tell us if she was still alive when she went in."

"If there's no water in the lungs, would that rule out death by drowning?"

"Not necessarily," Harvath replied.

"Why not?"

"Because the minute water enters your airway, your larynx seizes up. It doesn't matter if you are conscious or unconscious at the time. It's a self-preservation mechanism. The vocal cords slam shut and stop any more water from going down your windpipe. It's called a *laryngospasm*.

"In most people the spasm recedes after they lose consciousness, at which point water pours into the lungs as the body struggles for air and tries to breathe. In layman's terms that's a *wet* drowning. In about ten to fifteen percent of cases, though, the spasm continues until the person dies from cardiac arrest and no further water gets in. That's a *dry* drowning. Even if there's no water in the lungs, a good ME will look for water in the stomach."

"Why's that?"

"A laryngospasm may prevent water from getting into a person's lungs, but it doesn't stop water from getting into the stomach. It goes down a different pipe that isn't closed off as the drowning person sucks in water. Conscious or unconscious, it doesn't matter. If you go in the water alive, you're going to end up with water in your stomach."

Cordero was impressed. "Pretty good. Where'd you learn all that?"

"It was part of my drownproofing as a SEAL."

Cordero's partner, who was still holding the tarp up said, "Stick with the sailboat jokes."

"Why's that?"

"They're more believable than you being a SEAL."

"You know a lot about the military?"

"I know enough," the man said.

Harvath shook his head and peeled off his gloves.

Cordero didn't know what to believe at this point, but whoever Harvath was, he was starting to grow on her. And the way he was growing on her was something she wasn't comfortable with. Widowed with a two-year-old son, her life was complicated enough.

She decided to chill what she was feeling by embarrassing him. If she could shake his confidence, maybe he'd seem a little less attractive. "Let's have you move a little further south and examine the body for any signs of sexual assault."

Harvath held up his hands and smiled. "Already took my gloves off, sorry."

"We can get you another pair," she said, waving one of the techs back over.

Harvath took a step back from the body. "Gynecology isn't really my strong suit."

Cordero's partner lowered the tarp back down and as he did, Harvath heard him say beneath his breath, *"Pussy."* The man had said it just loud enough for Harvath to hear.

What was this guy, in fifth grade? "Hey, Sal," he said, examining a cloth one of the evidence techs had been using and tossing it to the detective. "Does this smell like chloroform to you?"

The man looked at Harvath like he was crazy.

"Go ahead," said Harvath. "Take a deep breath. It can be a tough odor to detect. Let's just be one hundred percent sure before we rule it out."

The man threw it back at him. "Blow me."

"She can't hear you," Harvath said, pointing down at the tarp. "She has no ears. Plus, she's kind of dead."

Cordero could see her partner's blood pressure rising just by watching his face. He was overprotective and had a short fuse. She'd seen him get rough with suspects and even occasionally other officers. Harvath, on the other hand, seemed eerily patient and willing to goad his opponent into making an emotional mistake. Either way, she didn't need these two bulls going at it, especially over her. It was becoming clear that if they couldn't play nice, they'd need to be separated.

She was just about to suggest a few minutes to cool off when one of the patrol officers came down the dock talking over his radio. A few feet from the tarp, he stopped. Cordero recognized him and waited until he was done speaking.

"Officer Kaczynski, isn't it?" she asked.

"Yes, ma'am. It's good to see you again, Detective."

Cordero turned to Harvath and said, "Officer Kaczynski was first on scene. When the dive team brought up the body, he made the tentative ID." Looking at the patrolman, she stated, "Isn't that correct?"

"I've arrested her multiple times; twice last month. Her name is Kelly Davis."

"All for prostitution?" Harvath asked.

"Prostitution, drugs, petty theft. It's all tied together."

"Is there anyone who may have seen her with our potential killer last night?"

The young officer nodded. "That's the call I just took on the radio. Ms. Davis ran with a couple of other girls. They like to work the tourist areas downtown, but all three of them live in the Old Colony public houses on East Ninth Street. Southie."

"*Southie?*" said Harvath.

"South Boston," Cordero explained. "It's a working-class neighborhood."

"These girls are meth heads, you know, tweakers. They stay up for days at a time," Kaczynski continued. "When I saw that Kelly was the victim, I radioed a couple of guys on patrol and asked them to keep a lookout for her pals."

"And they found them?" Harvath asked.

"Yes, sir. One admits she even saw Kelly with a john last night."

"How about the other one?"

"That's the thing. The other one was giving both officers a hard time. *I know my rights. I don't have to talk to you.* She was a real piss-and-vinegar type—right up until her friend started describing the john that Kelly was last seen with. Suddenly, Ms. Piss and Vinegar was as quiet as a church mouse and as white as a sheet. The officers think she definitely knows the guy. I figured you detectives would want to hear this right away."

"He's not a detective," Cordero's partner piped up, glaring at Harvath.

"Leave it alone, Sal," Cordero replied, and then asked the patrolman, "Are the two officers still with the ladies right now?"

"Yes, ma'am," said Kaczynski. "Over by Park Street Church near the Granary Burying Ground."

"Tell them to hold on to them until we get there."

"Yes, ma'am. Will do."

As the patrolman walked away, Cordero turned to her partner. But before she could say anything, he offered, "I'll process the scene here. I want Popeye the Sailor out of my sight anyway. Take him with you to visit the Southie lasses."

"Are you sure?"

"Go," he replied. "Before I change my mind."

CHAPTER 31

"When we get there," said Cordero as they approached Park Street Church, "let me do the talking. Unless, of course, you also have interrogation experience."

Harvath held up his thumb and forefinger close together. "One or two. But I'm lost without jumper cables and a bucket of water. Why don't you do the talking when we get there."

She was starting to believe there might be more truth to the remarks he made than he let on.

They parked in front of the Orpheum Theatre and played dodge-car crossing Tremont Street. Harvath had never seen a tweaker in person before. In fact, the only reason he was familiar with the term was because a buddy of his at Taser had told him about them. Before the company learned to lock their dumpsters up, local tweakers used to dumpster-dive behind their facility and scavenge parts.

Twitching for days on end with tons of energy and fine-motor skills, they had figured out how to, sort of, rebuild Tasers from the broken and discarded parts they had found in order to resell them on the street for drug money.

The Frankenstein devices they created were not only incredibly unreliable, but also incredibly dangerous. Nevertheless, it was a fascinating, albeit scary accomplishment.

Harvath had seen pictures of the ravages meth could visit upon people. Some of the before-and-after photos of young women were particularly heartbreaking. Not only did the drug rob them of their good looks, but it rapidly aged them, with some looking like they were seniors when they were only in their twenties and thirties. It was described as a high so irresistible that it hooked nearly everyone on the first try.

Despite being exposed to them all the time growing up in Southern California, Harvath had never been a drug guy. The only better-living-through-chemistry he allowed himself was from the three B's—beer, bourbon, or the occasional Bordeaux. You always knew what came out of a bottle. Not many alcohol companies got nailed for "stepping" on their product.

Walking up to the two ladies from South Boston, Harvath immediately noticed their overabundance of nervous energy. It had been drilled into him to look at people's hands and they were both doing oddball things. If he had been working a rope line as a Secret Service agent, he would have bounced both of these two. One was scratching her thighs raw while the other touched the tips of the fingers of her right hand to her thumb and then reversed the process and did it again.

The closer he got, the more makeup he noticed they were wearing. Skin lesions were a nasty side effect of the drug and they were both covering up some big problems. You'd have to be out of your mind to pay either one of these women for sex. He could only imagine what their teeth looked like. "Meth mouth," as it was known, was a rapid decay of tooth and gum and a hallmark of crystal meth abuse.

Cordero introduced herself to the two officers and then to the two young women. They appeared to be in their mid-twenties. One was tall, but skinny as a rail, with stringy blond hair. Her name was Agnes. She looked like a local college girl who gone away on spring break, partied every night with no sleep, and was now home looking for the party to continue.

The other girl, Brittany, was shorter and still had a little bit of meat on her. Now that Harvath could see her up close, he realized her skin wasn't that bad. She just wore a lot of makeup because that was her style. She had hair blacker than Cordero's—undoubtedly made possible only by some very serious dye. She complemented it with black nail polish, black lipstick, and lots of eyeliner and mascara. It was the full-on Goth look and she had a short black miniskirt, tight black top, and vintage flea market jewelry to match.

Right away, it was obvious that Agnes was the talker. She was so loquacious Cordero almost couldn't get a word in edgewise. Normally, standard procedure with witnesses was to split them up so they didn't pollute each other's stories. Agnes, though, was the only one who had seen the deceased with her customer last night. Brittany hadn't seen anything and Harvath favored keeping them together. Cordero had explained what she was going to ask and he wanted to study how Ms. Piss and Vinegar reacted.

Cordero was amazing. Not only was she an excellent interrogator, she was also a pro at understanding the Southie dialect, much of which was like a foreign language to Harvath's ear—all except the F-word, which this young woman dropped with abandon. She used it as a verb, a noun, an adverb, and an adjective. Not even in the military had Harvath heard someone's speech so peppered with it. Cordero was old-school and didn't care for it and warned the young woman to clean it up. To her credit, she did, though it was obviously difficult for her and she still slipped up from time to time.

Eventually, Cordero brought the conversation around to a description of the john.

"He was average," said Agnes. "Not too short, not too tall. You know. *Average*."

For her part during the interview, Brittany kept her mouth clamped tight as she ground her teeth back and forth. Harvath couldn't tell if it was from nervousness or the meth. Considering her eyes were dilated, he figured she'd recently used, which only made her harder to read.

He had been trained in the Secret Service to watch for microexpressions: small, almost imperceptible facial cues that indicated when a person was lying or under a tremendous amount of stress because they were concealing the truth or intent upon doing harm. It was a great tool to use in interrogation, but considering the condition of their current subjects, it might just be a waste of time.

That changed, though, when Cordero asked about the man's hair. "He was wearing a skally," Agnes replied, "but you could still see his whiffle."

Harvath had no idea what a *skally* or a *whiffle* was, but Brittany did, and even in the midst of her drug-induced fidgeting, he saw her shudder.

"Hold on a second. What the hell is a whiffle and what does it have to do with whatever a skally is?" he asked the detective.

"A skally is a type of cap," she replied.

"Like a baseball cap?"

"No. More like a driving cap."

"And a whiffle?"

"It's a tight haircut with clippers. Kind of like a military crew cut."

The revelation took Harvath aback and his silence encouraged Cordero to continue the interview.

He waited until Cordero was done and then suggested they speak with Brittany alone. Agnes, of course, was keen to keep on talking. The patrol officers humored her and moved her toward the street so Harvath and Cordero could talk with Brittany.

Cordero went from good cop to bad cop so fast that Harvath almost got whiplash. She'd been downright congenial with Agnes, but then again Agnes was cooperative. The moment Brittany refused to engage, Cordero went nuclear and it scared the hell out of the young woman.

"You want to see what he did to your friend Kelly?" she pushed. "Let's go now. C'mon. They just fished her out of the Charles. She's still lying on the dock under a plastic tarp. He's got a special signature, this guy. You haven't eaten breakfast, have you?"

Brittany shook her head.

"Good, 'cause I don't want you puking all over your shoes. We'll take my car. You're okay with that, right? Kelly was your friend. You want to say goodbye, right? Even if somebody comes up with the money, it's going to have to be a closed casket service. This'll be more personal for you. Friends should say goodbye, right? Face-to-face, as it were."

Brittany continued to shake her head and Harvath saw her jaw tighten as she ground her teeth harder.

Cordero moved closer, deeper into her personal space. "If you think Kelly's going to be this guy's only victim, you're wrong, sweetheart. She's not even his first. You want Agnes to be next? Better yet, how about if it's you?"

The young woman said nothing.

"See this man next to me?" the detective asked, nodding at Harvath. "He came to Boston to stop this guy. But that's not going to happen unless you cooperate."

Brittany's gaze shifted to Harvath.

"Nobody needs to know you told us anything," he said. "You're not in any trouble here. You've got a chance to do something right. You can help us catch the person who killed your friend."

"I don't want you to catch him," the young woman stated.

Harvath tilted his head to hear her better. "You don't?"

"No. I want you to kill the motherfucker."

"What did I tell your friend about that language?" Cordero interjected.

Brittany shot her daggers, while Harvath held up his hand for the detective to back off. "I understand how you feel," he told Brittany. "There are quite a few people who'd agree with you, but we need to focus on finding this guy. Anything you can tell us, no matter how small, will help."

The woman shifted nervously from her left foot to her right, looking back and forth between Harvath and Cordero. Finally, she settled her eyes on him and began to tell her story about the man who had photographed her yesterday in the cemetery.

Cordero took copious notes while Brittany recounted her tale. The F-bomb got dropped multiple times, but the detective was smart enough to let it go. Now that the young woman was cooperating, interrupting her narrative would have been a mistake.

It was obvious that Brittany cared not only about what had happened to Kelly Davis, but about stopping Kelly's killer. She hadn't seen the john who picked her up that night, but the man described by Agnes sounded exactly like the man who had assaulted her. Neither Harvath nor Cordero had reason to doubt the young woman. She had been incredibly forthright, even admitting to having solicited the would-be killer.

Cordero asked her several follow-up questions. When she was done, Brittany asked, "You're not going to bag me for the solicitation, are you?"

"No," the detective replied. "I'm not. I appreciate your cooperation. Is there anything else you can think of, anything at all?"

The young woman was quiet for a moment and then responded. "That's pretty much it."

Cordero looked at Harvath. "Anything you want to add? Any questions I missed?"

Harvath's eyes had drifted down to Brittany's hands again. "I do have one question." Looking up at the young woman, he asked, "You're right-handed, correct?"

The young woman nodded.

"So when you tried to slap him, you did it with your right hand, which is when he caught you by the wrist and twisted your *right* arm behind your back?"

"Yes," she replied.

Harvath removed a wedge of cash from the pocket of his trousers and peeled off two hundred-dollar bills. Brittany's eyes widened at the sight of the money. Pointing at the tarnished metal cuff on her right wrist, he said, "Detective Cordero could seize that as evidence, but I'd like to rent it from you. I only have one condition."

The young woman looked at the cuff and then back up at Harvath. "What is it?"

He peeled off two more hundreds and held all four bills out for her. "You and Agnes stay off the street until Detective Cordero and I catch this guy. Deal?"

The wheels were turning in the young woman's head. She was undoubtedly doing some sort of calculation and it wasn't about how many holy candles she and her pal could purchase with that kind of money. Finally, she replied, "Deal."

After tucking the money away, Brittany removed the cuff and placed it into the handkerchief Harvath had retrieved from his jacket.

He then let her rejoin her friend, while Cordero phoned her department to make sure they had the young woman's complete arrest record in the system.

Satisfied, Cordero asked the ladies for a few more details, including contact information, and then gave each of them her business card along with her cell phone number on the back. With that, the patrol officers were asked to drive the women back to South Boston.

"You're definitely not a cop," the detective said to Harvath, as they watched the cruiser pull away from the curb and head toward Southie.

"Why's that?"

"Because outside of a drug buy, no one hands over that kind of cash for something the law empowers them to take."

Harvath shrugged. "Just because something is legal, doesn't always mean it's the right thing to do. Trying to keep those kids off the street for a couple of days was the right thing to do."

Cordero shook her head. "They're junkies. They're going to burn through your four hundred dollars in the blink of an eye. But hey, if it buys you a good night's sleep."

Having seen what he had of this killer, Harvath doubted he was going to be able to sleep well anytime soon. Even if the money kept Brittany and Agnes off the street for only one night, it would be worth it.

Though he didn't yet have physical proof that the woman pulled from the Charles River had been killed by the same person as Claire Marcourt and Herman Penning, his gut told him that he was right on the money. It also told him something else. The killer was losing control.

CHAPTER 32

B ob McGee had spent the better part of his career engaging in risky operations, but the minute Lydia Ryan explained her plan, he told her it was off-the-charts stupid. It was one thing to screw up and have Phil Durkin triangulate on them that way; it was something entirely different to openly invite him to come kill them, and that's what he had felt Ryan was doing.

Just as the porch light came on, and just in case she hadn't internalized it the last one hundred times he had said it, he stated, "This is going to go down as the mother of all bad ideas."

"You're overestimating your prowess in this category," she replied as someone inside unlocked the door.

"Like hell I am" was the last remark McGee made before the door opened. He had decided to stand behind Ryan not so much because he didn't want to appear imposing, but because if the person on the other side was armed and the rounds began flying, Ryan would suffer the fate she so rightly deserved for this idea and function as his bullet sponge while he took off running. He turned out to be wrong, but not about the being armed part.

Colonel Brenda Durkin had opened the door with her Beretta M9 pistol just out of view. One of the last people she ever expected to see on her doorstep, much less in the middle of the night in a bathrobe, was Lydia Ryan. "What in God's name are you doing here?"

"We're in trouble. Can we come in?"

The woman looked at the man standing behind Ryan as if deciding what to do, and then stood back and opened the door the rest of the way. "Of course you can."

They sat in the kitchen, where the closest thing to coffee Durkin had to offer her guests was Diet Coke. Both Ryan and McGee accepted. Grabbing three bottles out of the fridge, she brought them over to the table and sat down.

"When I told you if there was anything I could ever do for you," said Durkin, "I didn't actually think you'd show up at the house. I figured maybe you'd call or send an email."

"I know," Ryan replied, opening her Coke. "I would never have come like this if it wasn't serious."

"Wait a second," McGee interrupted. "You two actually know each other?"

Durkin looked at Ryan before responding. "I needed to make sense of my marriage, or what was left of it at the time. The only way I could do that was to meet Lydia and have her tell me, face-to-face, that nothing had happened between her and Phil. She was kind enough to do so."

"But you still left him."

"Our marriage had been over for a long time. Would it have been easier to end it if Phil had been having an affair? Probably. That's why I had wanted to meet Lydia. As soon as I saw her, I was convinced they'd been having an affair. I mean, *look* at her."

"Yeah," Ryan replied, extending a clump of her ruffled hair and tugging on the lapel of her dirty robe. "Look at me."

Durkin smiled. "Then we sat down and started talking. I wanted to believe she was sleeping with Phil because then I could blame him for everything, walk away, and never have to acknowledge my role in the fact that our marriage collapsed."

"I threw a wrench in that plan, though, didn't I?"

"You did. In fact, you caused me to take a deep, hard look not only at my marriage, but myself. Getting divorced was one of the hardest things I have ever had to do, but it was the right thing. Phil Durkin is a colossal asshole. Had Dante known that son of a bitch he would have invented a whole other circle of hell for him."

"So what you're saying," McGee replied with a grin, "is that you've moved on. It's all behind you at this point."

Brenda Durkin laughed. "I guess that's the Scottish in me. We can hold a grudge like nobody's business."

"If it's any consolation, I agree with you. Not about the grudge, but about your ex being a colossal asshole. I told Lydia she should have dumped him in a shallow grave. In fact, I even offered to dig it."

"I came close to digging one for him many times myself, but in the end, he dug his own. That's the way it should be."

McGee and Ryan nodded. Brenda Durkin was right.

"So why don't you tell me why you're here," the Colonel said, and with that, Ryan filled her in on their story.

They talked until just before dawn. It was agreed that if they were going to hole up in her house, Brenda Durkin needed to act as if nothing had changed. That meant not missing her morning group run and not calling in sick to her position at the U.S. Army Intelligence and Security Command. The one thing she decided to do differently was to park her car in the driveway so that McGee's 4Runner could be kept out of sight in her garage.

Ryan tried to grab a couple of hours of sleep, but it came in fits and starts. When she finally gave up and came downstairs to the kitchen, she found McGee had had about as much luck as she had. He was sitting at the table with a Diet Coke, a café-au-lait mug full of Lucky Charms, and the television tuned to some Animal Planet program.

"Just once, I'd like to see the little guy at the back of the herd kick the lion's teeth in," he said as Ryan got a Diet Coke for herself and sat down next to him.

"Any word about what happened last night?"

McGee picked up the remote and clicked back over to one of the local news channels. "Not really. There was a brief mention of a car fire, but that was it. My guess is that local law enforcement kept the press from getting too close and didn't give them much in the way of details."

"Which means they probably don't have much themselves."

"Or they've been told not to talk."

She took a sip of her drink and set the bottle back on the table. "What about the men you shot at your place?"

"I don't think that's going to make the news."

"Why not?"

"Because I live alone. If my neighbors had heard any shots, they would have already called the cops."

"But somebody is going to be looking for those men."

McGee took another bite of cereal and wiped the milk from his mustache. "Of course. You know the game. When they fail to report in, a team will be sent out to check on them. They'll show up at my place dressed like exterminators, utility workers, or some sort of contractor. They'll have a big van with a name and backstopped phone number emblazoned along the side of it, so the neighbors won't get suspicious.

"They'll walk the perimeter and peek in the windows. At some point, they'll muster up the courage to break and enter. That's when they'll find the bodies and will have to decide what to do."

"Meaning, sanitize your place like it never happened or try to use the scene against you."

McGee nodded and through another mouthful of cereal said, "I hope they sanitize it. I haven't had a cleaning lady through that place since Reagan was in office."

Ryan studied the crawl along the bottom of the TV screen, trying to pick up any updated information. "So what do you think? No news, then, is good news?"

"I don't know. Maybe this thing doesn't reach as high as we feared."

"Meaning up to the DNI, General Johnson?"

McGee nodded. "But the flip side could be that, thanks to the Jordanians and you asking questions about your old team, you've surprised them and now they're scrambling to pull their act together."

"In order to do what?"

"If they're willing to try to kill you, then they'd be willing to do anything, including framing you."

"Framing me for what?"

McGee shrugged. "Depending on how high up this thing goes, you could wind up as the shooter on the grassy knoll."

"Except for the fact that I wasn't even born."

"They'd find away around it, believe me. They think of everything."

"But what about you and me? What were they going to do, kill us and just dump our bodies out there in the woods?"

He sucked the milk off his spoon and set it down on the table. "I patted down all the hitters I splashed at my place. One of them had a key fob. After I tossed my go-bag and a couple of other items in my truck, I went outside to make sure there wasn't another team waiting for me. As soon as I felt it was safe, I kept pressing the unlock button on the fob. I finally found their vehicle parked not far from my place."

"Was there anything inside?"

"Anything that could ID them? No. Just some picnic crap."

Lydia looked at him. "What do you mean, *picnic crap*?"

"A blanket and a basket with a couple of glasses and a bottle of wine."

"So no ID, but tons of firepower *and* a picnic basket? Doesn't that seem odd?"

"All of this seems odd to me. Why? What are you thinking?"

"I'm thinking that could be part of a cover story. Maybe they were going to make it look like you and I were having a picnic out in the middle of the woods and got shot."

He thought about that for a moment. "Or better yet," he replied, "how about a murder-suicide? You kill me and then turn the gun on yourself. Not only would Phil Durkin's problems be solved, but he'd be able to play the I-told-you-Lydia-Ryan-was-crazy card all the way to the Agency bank."

She shook her head. "I wouldn't put it past that son of a bitch."

"I'm just speculating, of course."

"No," Ryan replied. "You're *right* on the money. That's exactly what he would do."

"I don't think either of us can be sure. Maybe the stupid picnic basket was some part of their cover."

Her eyes narrowed as a question came to her mind. "You said there was a blanket and two wineglasses. What else was there?"

"I don't know. I was in a bit of a hurry to get out of there, but I guess there was some food and a couple of bottles of wine."

"What about an opener?"

"Yeah," McGee recalled. "It wasn't the type with the arms, though. It was a fancy, pocketknife style. Expensive-looking, you know, with that brass bee on there from that French knife-making company."

"Laguiole."

"That's it."

"Did it have a wooden handle?" she asked.

He nodded. "It did. Why?"

"Because that was *my* corkscrew. That son of a bitch took it, or had someone take it out of my apartment. That way, even if the police did a half-assed investigation, they'd find the empty box I normally keep it in back in a drawer in my kitchen."

"That would make it look a lot less like the picnic was staged."

"And more like we had undertaken it willingly," she said, finishing his statement for him. "What kind of wine was it?"

"Give me a break, Lydia. I don't know the first thing about wine. That's always been your thing. I'm a bourbon guy. You think I stood there and read the labels?"

"Keep it simple. Was it red? Was it white?"

"It was *dark*," McGee responded. "All I saw was black bottles with black frickin' labels."

She didn't need to ask him anything more about the wine. She knew what it was. "OneHope red," she stated. "It's the same wine I drink at home."

"There you go. Killing, framing or both, they're not above anything."

"Which means we're racing against two clocks—whatever plot the Jordanians have uncovered, as well as whatever Phil Durkin has planned for us."

"All the more reason for us to figure out what he's up to and put his balls in a nice little box with a big pink bow."

"The question, though, is going to be who do we deliver the box to?"

"It all depends on what he's doing and what we can make stick," McGee replied as he picked up the remote and turned back to Animal Planet.

There was a new program on. It was showing home videos of people who got too close to animal enclosures at foreign zoos. Suddenly, Ryan got an idea.

"How much cash do you have?" she asked.

"I have five grand in my go-bag. Why?"

"Because we can't use credit cards and you need a new suit."

McGee looked at her. "I do?"

Ryan nodded. "We're going to go rattle a very big cage, but before we do, I want to see who's throwing the meat into it."

CHAPTER 33

The only thing McGee disliked more than having to cut his hair was being forced to shave his mustache. Ryan, though, had insisted. And in order to set the example, she had cut her hair first.

They stood in Brenda Durkin's master bath with their feet in plastic lawn and leaf bags to help catch as much of the hair as possible. Ryan did a halfway decent job cutting her hair into a short, spiky cut. McGee's spin as a coiffeur was horrible and Ryan had to step in to rescue him and clean it up.

McGee did his mustache on his own and when he was finished, they both looked in the mirror together. The transformation was remarkable.

With the Colonel's blessing, Ryan selected clothes and a pair of shoes from her closet. She was fortunate they were so similar in size. McGee had changed into some of the extra clothes he had fled his home with.

The operatives were well aware of the amount of domestic surveillance technology that could be arrayed against them and had already ditched their cell phones. That one move would go a long way toward blinding the monster that would be tracking them. The other move that would keep them hidden was abandoning their credit cards. From this point forward, everything would be paid for in cash.

The last thing they agreed upon was very selective use of the Internet. Social media platforms were a godsend to the intelligence community. They recorded in stark detail almost everyone, everywhere, and everything you were connected to. Along with cell phone and credit card activity, social media and email accounts were one of the first places Phil Durkin would be looking for them.

Because people's digital exhaust gave so many clues about them, they had to break with all of their old habits. They also needed to break with any friends, family, or colleagues they normally communicated with. That was another pond Durkin would be skimming as he tried to determine their whereabouts.

In essence, they were dropping completely off the grid. For her part, Ryan considered them blessed that the Colonel had made her home available to them. If not, they would have been forced to break into a vacant house or leapfrog from cheap hotel to cheap hotel, and both strategies were fraught with a myriad of problems.

The other thing Brenda Durkin had graciously made available to them was use of her 1990 Ford Mustang LX. Not only was it a nondescript vehicle, it also was built before the explosion in GPS technology. It was perfect for their new, under-the-radar personas.

Leaving Fort Belvoir, their first stop was an office supply store. While Ryan purchased what they needed inside, McGee walked around back. After making sure there were no security cameras or personnel present, he checked all three dumpsters until he found what he was looking for. By the time he returned to the Mustang, Ryan was already waiting for him.

Their next stop was a midrange men's clothing store that specialized in business attire. Against McGee's more flamboyant taste, Ryan picked out a cheap, off-the-rack gray suit, along with a plain white shirt, a boring tie, a belt, shoes, and a pair of dress socks.

"You got me everything but the pocket protector," he said as she directed him toward a dressing room to put it all on.

When he stepped back out and the salesman complimented him on the fit, Ryan had him remove the jacket. Because of his physique, it was too tight. That was not going to do for her purposes. "This isn't a casting call for a mob movie," she stated as she sent the salesperson to find him a bigger size.

Twenty minutes later, and with McGee costumed for his part, they paid cash for the clothing and left the store. At a coffee shop a couple of blocks away, they assembled their props and quietly went over the plan one last time.

"What if I get asked a question I can't answer?" said McGee.

"You're there strictly for intimidation. You don't answer questions, you *ask* them. By the time we leave, I expect this guy to be admitting to things he did all the way back in grade school. The object of our visit is simple. We scare the hell out of him and then we give him an out."

"But what if he talks? What if the minute we leave, he picks up the phone?"

"When you see his credenza, you'll understand why that won't happen."

The small community bank was an hour's drive northwest of the Central Intelligence Agency headquarters. Ryan parked a couple of blocks away, rather than in the bank's parking lot, just in case anyone got suspicious and wanted to take down a description of their vehicle along with its license plate number.

It was a pleasant enough bedroom community with broad sidewalks and thick-trunked, stately trees. It looked like it was probably a nice place to raise a family.

As they walked toward the bank, Ryan wished she had brought along an umbrella. It was warm and the cloud cover was thickening. They were going to get a heck of a thunderstorm at some point. *Probably as soon as we're ready to leave the bank*.

The air-conditioning hit them full blast as soon as they stepped into the lobby and was a welcome relief from the heavy humidity outside. With McGee in tow, Ryan approached the receptionist.

"Good morning. We're here to see Erick Stevenson, please."

"Do you have an appointment?"

"No, but please tell him Lydia Ryan is here to see him."

The receptionist smiled and picked up her phone. "If you'd like to take a seat right over there, I'll see if he's available."

Ryan had eyeballed Stevenson's vehicle in the parking lot, so she had no doubt that he was in. She also had no doubt that he would see her. Durkin had chosen well when he had recruited the small-town banker. Erick Stevenson loved feeling like he was a part of the CIA. No matter what any members of the team had ever needed, he had always dropped everything to take care of them.

Within seconds of the receptionist hanging up her phone and telling them that Mr. Stevenson would be out shortly, they could see him coming down the hallway. He was a middle-aged man with a round, ruddy face and a stomach that hung well over his belt buckle. He was wearing a tie but no jacket and had a grin on his face that stretched from ear to ear. He was obviously very pleased to see Ryan. That wouldn't last long.

"Lydia," he exclaimed as he crossed the reception area. "How wonderful to see you again. How have you been?"

Ryan set the tone immediately. "Erick, this is Robert McGee. I wonder if we could go back to your office where we can talk."

McGee neither smiled, nor offered his hand, but simply stood there with a stack of bulging file folders under his arm.

Stevenson looked him up and down and sensing something was wrong turned back to Ryan and said, "Sure. Of course. Please follow me."

After they had been seated and he had offered his visitors coffee, the banker closed his office door and sat down behind his desk. "Wow. It really has been a while. And you cut your hair. It looks great."

"Erick, I don't mean to be rude, but we have some pretty serious business to discuss with you."

"I understand," he said, somewhat deflated. "What is it I can do for you?"

Ryan looked at McGee and then at the banker. "If you decide at any time during this process that you would like to have counsel present, we'll of course understand, but that means everything will stop and we will have to set a time for you and your attorney to come to CIA headquarters."

Stevenson's eyes turned into a pair of saucers. "My *attorney*? Why would I need an attorney? What the hell is this all about?"

"What this is about, Mr. Stevenson," McGee lied, "is a substantial sum of money that has gone missing."

"Erick, if you come clean and return the money, this will go a lot easier on you," Ryan offered.

The banker couldn't tell which of them to focus on and his eyes swept back and forth between them as he tried to decide whom to address. "I have no idea what you're talking about. What money?"

McGee glanced past Stevenson to the credenza filled with family photos. There were pictures from the beach, fishing trips, camping, sailing, even shots from Cub Scouts with Stevenson, apparently a den leader or scoutmaster of some sort, in uniform.

"There's money missing from the Caring International account, Mr. Stevenson."

"I'm sorry," said the banker. "Who are you again?"

"Mr. McGee," Ryan stated, "is on loan to the Agency from the attorney general's office."

"But I didn't do anything. Why are you here asking me questions?"

McGee pulled out a manila file folder stuffed with printouts he had fished out of the dumpster behind the office supply store. Across the outside of the folder in capital letters he had written CONFIDENTIAL CASE FILE: STEVENSON, ERICK along with the name of his position and the name of the bank. He held it up so that Stevenson could see the writing, but not the documents he was flipping through inside.

Care International was the name of the NGO front organization that Ryan's political destabilization team had operated under. Knowing the CIA in general and Phil Durkin in particular, if the program had been moved to the dark side, she doubted they would have built a whole new cover for it. They would have changed passwords and authorizations, but probably not much of anything else. She had come to see Stevenson in order to put that assumption to the test. If the funds were still flowing, that would jump their investigation to an entirely new level.

"Erick, listen," said Ryan. "If you haven't done anything wrong, you don't have anything to worry about."

"Of course I haven't done anything wrong," he insisted. "I'm a patriot. I don't steal from you guys. I'm here because I want to help you. I want to help my country."

Although she didn't let it show, that remark was like having a little knife slipped between her ribs and up into her heart. Stevenson was a good man. She didn't like doing this to him, but people's lives were on the line, including her own.

"Then the sooner you cooperate with us, the sooner we can get out of here," she replied.

"I am cooperating."

"Then tell me why funds are missing from the Caring International account."

"Because I was told to bring that account down to a certain level."

Ryan looked at him. "Told by whom?"

"Durkin."

"Why would he tell you to do that?"

Stevenson put up his hands. "I provide the accounts and I move the money as directed. That's it. Everything else is on your end. Speaking of which, something's not making sense about all of this."

"What's not making sense?" she asked.

"You," the banker replied. "Your name was removed from everything. Durkin called me himself and told me to scrub you from all of it. He said you were moving on to a new position or something. Said he wasn't going to be working with you anymore. That's why I was so surprised to see you. If there's a problem with the money, why didn't I get a call from Durkin?"

Ryan, who had come up with the ruse of misappropriated funds, had thought the banker might take this road, but McGee was way ahead of her.

"Ah, yes. Mr. Durkin," McGee said, cocking an eyebrow as he removed another file, this time with DURKIN, PHILLIP written across the front of it. "Mr. Stevenson, how long have you been conducting transactions with Mr. Durkin?"

The banker was thrown off balance and was suddenly nervous again. "I don't know. About six years?"

"Are you asking me, Mr. Stevenson," McGee stated. "Or are you telling me?"

"I guess I'm telling you. That is to say, I *am* telling you."

"During those six years, did you ever assist Mr. Durkin in setting up a personal offshore account for his own use in Grand Cayman?"

"No, of course not."

"Zurich?"

"No."

"Andorra?"

"I never did any private, personal banking for him."

McGee ran his finger down an imaginary list in his Durkin file. "So no accounts then in Gibraltar, Grenada, Belize, or Vanuatu, either?"

"My God, he's got that many personal accounts?"

"There's a lot of money missing, Mr. Stevenson."

The banker turned to Ryan and implored her. "Lydia, you have to trust me. Whatever money is missing, I had nothing to do with it. The Caring International account was drawn down and a new account was started."

"New account for whom?" she asked.

"The same team. The only name I left off was yours."

Bingo. "Did it ever occur to you that Durkin might not have been authorized to ask you to do that?"

Stevenson gaped at her. "Lydia, you guys came to *me*. I didn't come to *you*. I manage a small community bank. One day a couple of CIA agents walk in, I think they're here for a small business loan, and suddenly I'm being asked to serve my country all without leaving my office." He paused for a moment. "My wife warned me something like this might happen. What have I gotten myself into?"

"Big trouble. That's what," McGee replied.

"Hold on," Ryan said, intervening. "If what Erick is telling us is true, then the investigation should focus on Durkin."

"It is true. It is," the banker stated emphatically.

McGee looked skeptical and remained silent.

"What name is the new account under?" she asked.

Stevenson turned to his computer and brought it up. "They kept the same NGO structure, just changed the name to Hands of Peace International."

"When did the account last receive funding?"

"Two weeks ago."

"Credit cards, wire transfers, it's all feeding into that account?"

The banker punched a couple more keys. "Through a series of branch accounts, yes."

Ryan looked at McGee. It was now time to give Stevenson a way out. "I think we know now how Durkin has been hiding the money," she said.

"That doesn't change Mr. Stevenson's involvement," he replied.

The banker started to protest, but Ryan held up her hand to quiet him. Turning to her partner, she said, "Bob, I think Erick has proven he's willing to cooperate with us."

McGee tapped the Durkin file against his thigh as he pretended to mull it over. "That might not be good enough."

"Not be good enough?" Stevenson exclaimed. "What else do you want from me?"

"My biggest problem, Mr. Stevenson," he responded, "is your safety."

"My safety?"

"And your family's."

The banker's eyes had gone wide again. "Why would we be in any danger?"

"Suffice it to say that since we began our investigation, banking in some parts of the world has become particularly dangerous. Especially if Phil Durkin is your client."

"Oh my God. What am I supposed to do? What about my wife and my children? What if Durkin calls me? What do I tell him?"

"If Durkin calls you," Ryan instructed, "just act natural. Handle whatever he asks for and that's all. Be professional and be polite."

"He'll know I know something."

"No, he won't. Relax."

"And my family? How are you going to protect us?"

"The only way we can help you," said McGee, "is if you help us."

The banker opened his arms. "I'll give you anything you want. What is it?"

An hour later, they walked out of the bank with a cardboard banker's box, which contained a paper trail a mile long.

"Now what?" McGee asked as they climbed into the Mustang and the first drops of rain began to fall on the windshield.

"Now that we know who's putting the meat in the cage," Ryan said as she put the key in the ignition and fired up the car, "it's time to rattle it."

Off in the distance, there was a low growl of thunder. It was matched by the throaty growl of the Mustang as Ryan pulled away from the curb and pointed the car back toward Fort Belvoir. She had already decided what they would do next. McGee was going to like it even less than he had her idea that they shelter in place at Brenda Durkin's house. But as dangerous as this next step was, they had been left with no other option.

CHAPTER 34

Patience had never been Harvath's strong suit, but the SEALs had taught him well. He'd gone from a toe-tapping, I-want-it-all-to-happen-now immature kid, to a thoughtful, risk-assessing, mission-focused young man who could wait in the tiniest of hide sites or lie prone for days on end until the absolute right moment to hit his target. None of it was easy, and it often sucked, but he'd learned how to put the mission above himself and that had marked a watershed moment in his life. Never had he been prouder than when he had finally become a United States Navy SEAL.

On his first mission, it was immediately apparent why his SEAL instructors had been so incredibly hard on him and his teammates. When you were dropped far behind enemy lines and it seemed like one thing after another was going wrong and one piece of equipment after another was failing, you knew you would still accomplish your mission. Failure was not an option. And as the SEALs were famous for saying, the only easy day was yesterday.

At this point, there was nothing Harvath could do but wait. Cordero had submitted the wrist cuff to the Crime Lab Unit to have it fingerprinted and had asked them to get it done ASAP. They understood that Cordero was investigating a possible serial killer and promised they would get it done as quickly as they could.

In the meantime, patrol officers and FBI agents were canvassing and re-canvassing all of downtown, including the area around the Liberty Tree Building, Boston Common, and the Granary Burying Ground. Additional officers had been assigned to review all of the CCTV footage that they could get their hands on from the last forty-eight hours, including footage from the airport and train and bus stations.

Marcourt had been killed the same night she was taken. Based on her ears being removed, as well as those of Kelly Davis here in Boston, Harvath was certain it was the same person. He had to have gotten from Georgia to Boston somehow.

With Brittany's description of the man who had assaulted her, as well as Agnes's description of the man Kelly Davis had last been seen with, Harvath was hoping that they'd stumble across something—either on camera, or in the minds of people who might have seen him.

To their credit, the Boston PD and the FBI were keeping a lid on the details surrounding Penning's murder, which Harvath was grateful for. Kelly Davis's murder had been reported as a potential homicide of a young woman from South Boston. None of the details, other than her body being found in the Charles, had been released to the press.

The monotony of having been inside the Homicide Unit at police headquarters most of the day was wearing on Harvath. One of the detectives had made a run to Potbelly for lunch, but that had been hours ago. He needed a break. He needed to get outside, take a walk, and get some fresh air.

It had started raining, but Harvath didn't care. He traded Cordero his cell number for an umbrella. When his phone rang four blocks later and the caller ID showed a blocked number, he thought it might be her with a breakthrough on the case. It turned out to be Bill Wise from D.C.

"What's all that noise in the background?" he asked.

"It's raining," replied Harvath, "and I'm out on the street. Hold on a second. There's a doorway up ahead. I'm going to duck in there."

When Harvath had reached it, he stepped in and said, "Okay, this should be better. Go ahead."

"I've done some digging since you were here last night and I think I may have found something interesting. When can you get over here?"

"I'm not sure. I'm up in Boston right now."

"What are you doing in Boston?" Wise asked.

"Long story. You tell me your news first."

There was the sound of pages flipping, as if Wise was going through a notebook or something. Finally, he said, "Remember how I told you that when I joined the Agency they were doing lots of *interesting* programs?"

"Yes, I do remember."

"Well, there were rumors that one of those programs was running parallel to mine. Instead of taking operatives and making them more capable killers, it was taking killers and trying to make them into capable operatives."

Harvath was taken aback for a moment. "Like psychopaths?"

"Psychopaths, sociopaths; antisocial personalities, you name it. The program's pendulum swept the full spectrum of psychological dysfunction."

"Why?"

"They wanted a stable of operatives who would kill on command without any hesitation, without any resistance, remorse, or moral hangover. The Agency wanted to be able to wield a scalpel that never blunted from use nor ever questioned why it was being used. In essence, they were trying to create the ultimate assassin."

Harvath was confused. "Isn't that the kind of crackpot stuff they were toying around with back in the 1960s?"

"*Nineteen sixties?* They've been throwing millions of dollars down rat holes since the 1950s trying to figure out how to pharmacologically and surgically unplug people from their moral compasses. But it wasn't until the success of the human genome project and huge leaps forward in neuroscience in the 2000s that the Agency discovered their path forward."

"And with the tidal wave of money that flooded into the intelligence community after 9/11," Harvath stated, "I assume they were able to fund almost any bizarre programs they wanted."

"That's right," said Wise. "A lot of the money that flowed in did so via black accounts with no accountability and no congressional oversight. The only thing requested was that the money be used to 'make America safer.'"

"You can hang a lot of ornaments on that kind of Christmas tree."

"Don't misunderstand. There were some excellent programs the Agency pursued. There were also, unfortunately, some less than excellent programs."

Harvath thought about Claire Marcourt and everything that had now happened in Boston. "Did the program you're talking about have a name?"

"It's code name was *Swim Club*. Rumor had it that it came from the CIA's desire to see how deep the psychological pool was for these types of candidates. They had begun by trolling state mental facilities, but then realized they needed a much bigger net. They created one of the first electronic medical record software companies, which allowed them to sift through reams of patient information, but even that wasn't enough.

"They couldn't monopolize the EMR industry, so they simply hacked into medical databases from insurance companies, psychiatry and psychology practices, addiction and recovery centers, even hospital CT scan departments.

"They hit a thick vein in the criminal justice system, but the real pay dirt came when they conned the military via a phony counseling organization to deal with not only psychologically unbalanced applicants, but also existing service members who snapped or suddenly became psychologically unfit for service."

Whiffle, a military-style crew cut. Harvath could feel himself gripping the phone tighter. "Are you saying vets who needed counseling were purposely not getting it?"

"On the contrary, if you made it into the Agency's program, you'd be getting exceptional counseling. The problem was that you'd also be getting sized up for membership in Swim Club."

Harvath wasn't sure he had heard the man correctly. "You think the Agency is behind the attacks on the Fed?"

"Why not? The CIA may be overflowing with bureaucrats, but it still has plenty of Americans concerned with the survival of the country."

While there were lots of bureaucrats in the intelligence community whom Harvath didn't care for, there were also many exceptional Americans who risked everything day in and day out for their love of the United States. But to kill otherwise innocent people just because they disagreed with what the Federal Reserve was doing? That didn't make sense.

But what if Wise was correct? What if it was elements within the CIA that were behind the attacks on the Fed? "You said these were rumors. Can they be substantiated? Is Swim Club legit? Is it a live program?"

"As of last year, yes, it was a live, black program, but then the new CIA director allegedly caught wind of it. He not only didn't like it, he also didn't like its potential for disastrous PR fallout if word ever leaked, and had it shut down. Staff were either moved to other projects or dismissed entirely," said Wise.

"How did you find all of this out?"

"I made a couple of phone calls and ended up getting plugged back into an old colleague of mine named James Gage. Jim's a Ph.D. who had worked on my project for a while before being transferred. I didn't see him much after that, but guess where it turns out he was transferred to?"

"Swim Club," said Harvath.

"Yup. When they let him go, he was pretty bitter. He probably talks more than he should, but old friends do that, right?"

While Harvath was careful about discussing classified operations, Wise had a point. There were more than a few people who talked out of school. He'd seen it in the military and intelligence worlds and had no reason to doubt that scientists or researchers were any different. Old friends, especially those expected to keep similar secrets, did talk.

"Jim filled in several blanks for me," Wise continued. "The ones he didn't were easy enough to figure out. A couple of times, it was nothing more than the look on his face. His silence on some of the information spoke volumes."

"Wait a second. You met with Gage in person?" Harvath asked.

"Of course. Why not?"

"Did anyone see you? Does anyone else know you were with him?"

Wise could tell something was very wrong. "No, no one saw us. No one knows. But something is bothering you. What is it? What's going on up there?"

"Our killer struck again overnight," Harvath replied. "Twice."

CHAPTER 35

Harvath gave Wise a full rundown of everything that had happened. The man took copious notes on the other end of the phone. When Harvath was done filling him in, Wise was in full clinical mode.

"So what does all of this tell us?" he asked rhetorically. "Our man is professional, at least when it comes to his work. As far as we know, there were no clues left at the Marcourt murder scene on Jekyll Island, or at the Penning murder at the Liberty Tree Building. But in what we'll call his personal life, he's appearing impulsive, *less* careful. Perhaps he is even losing control."

Harvath let out a long breath.

"What is it?" said Wise. "You disagree?"

"Not necessarily. I'm just trying to process all of this. Listen, I don't like to underestimate anyone, especially someone this dangerous, but I also don't like to overestimate them, either."

"You think I'm giving him too much credit?"

"What I *think* is that the guy screwed up. Whether he is a sociopath or a psychopath or whatever, I'm not a doctor and I don't care. What I know is that as good as he's been, he's finally made a mistake. Is he losing control? Maybe, but when he grabbed that girl's wrist in the Granary Burying Ground, I don't think he could have known that he would go on to kill that night, that he'd kill a friend of the girl he grabbed, or that we'd tie it all together."

Wise agreed. "That makes sense, but keep in mind that not only are we potentially dealing with someone who is not rational and who does not make sense, but he's now killed three people. If I'm right and he is losing control, he may become more dangerous."

"He may also make another mistake," Harvath replied. "Speaking of which, what do you make of how the body of the young girl was left in the Charles River? Does that tell you anything?"

"It tells me several things. The first is that this was likely an impulsive crime of opportunity. The woman made herself available to him and he struck. Once he did, though, he had a decision to make. Presumably, he could have left her right where he killed her. But instead, he risked the added time to steal the things he needed, weigh her down, and then drop her in the water."

"Which means what?"

Wise took a few moments to reflect before answering. "Whoever this girl was, I think we can safely assume he hadn't come to Boston to kill her."

"But he cut her ears off like he had with Claire Marcourt. Why?"

"Without interviewing him, it's hard to say for sure. He may have simply enjoyed it and wanted to relive it, or he may have rushed Marcourt's murder and wanted to take his time with the prostitute. Remember, for a lot of these killers, the act is all about the power they wield over their victims."

"And weighing the body down in the Charles?" Harvath asked.

"Perhaps he was ashamed of what he had done and wanted, symbolically, to be rid of it, or maybe he realized on some level that this impulsive act was a mistake that could not only jeopardize him, but also his operation. Therefore, he had worked to cover it up as quickly as possible."

Processing information from Bill Wise was like drinking from a fire hose. Harvath was still trying to wrap his mind around the fact that there could be even a remote CIA component to the attacks. Circumventing alarm systems like the one at the Registry of Motor Vehicles, as well as looping CCTV footage, though, was straight out of the Agency's playbook.

"Could the killer have weighted the body down simply because he needed to buy time?" Harvath asked.

"For what?"

"He killed Marcourt in Georgia then came up here for Penning. Maybe he's traveling by air and didn't want the body to be found until after he had made it safely away to wherever he was going next."

As he waited for the man to respond, Harvath ran the list of remaining kidnap victims through his mind: *Betsy Mitchell—Seattle, Jonathan Renner—San Francisco*, and *Peter Whalen—Chicago*. Since getting the call to come to Boston, he had been racking his brain trying to zero in on locations in the remaining kidnap cities that would be symbolic for the group behind the killings. The only thing he could come up with was that they all had Federal Reserve branches. But would the killer be that obvious, especially after the choices of Jekyll Island and the Liberty Tree site?

"There is another possibility," Wise said, interrupting Harvath's train of thought. "What if you're right? What if the killer was trying to buy more time, not to get out of Boston, but rather because his work in Boston wasn't complete?"

Harvath was about to comment when his other line rang. "Bill, I have another call. Stand by for second."

"Will do."

Harvath clicked over to the other line. It was Cordero back at police headquarters.

"The crime lab just called," she said. "They finished processing the wrist cuff."

"Did we get any prints?"

"We did. It looks like a thumb and a partial that may be an index finger. They're working up the report now. How soon can you get back here?"

"I'm only a couple of blocks away," he said. "I'll be there in less than five minutes."

"Ten-four. Hurry up. As soon as we get the prints, we're going to start running them through the databases." With that, she said goodbye and hung up.

Cordero and the FBI could run every database she had access to, but he doubted she was going to get a single hit. If this guy was who Harvath was beginning to think he might be, there was only one place that would have a record of him and even then it would be guarded like Fort Knox.

He clicked back over to Wise. "We got a hit on the wrist cuff from the girl accosted at the Granary Burying Ground. We believe it's a thumb and a partial index finger."

"That's terrific."

"Do you think your Swim Club pal, Gage, can do anything with it?" asked Harvath. He could sense Wise's hesitation before he even responded.

"At the CIA when you're gone, you're gone. They watch you clean out your desk, and then they go through everything, and I mean *everything*, before you're escorted off the property. All of your access is canceled and the only information you're leaving with is what's between your ears. He's not going to be sitting on reams of data, much less the jackets of the people Swim Club was spinning up to place in the field. There were a bunch of them and most were freelancers with lives entirely separate from the Agency. They just got called up when Langley needed them."

"Wait," said Harvath. "You're telling me they can lead *normal* lives? How the hell is that even possible?"

"Think of them like alcoholics. Some were exceptional at hiding their illness. With treatment, they were quite functional."

"And the others?"

"With time, the others lost the fight and fell over the edge."

It was a chilling analogy. Harvath wanted as much information as he could get. "Reach out to Gage," he said, "and lean on him as hard as you can for whatever he can give you."

"How much are you comfortable with me revealing to him?"

"Right now, limit it just to the killer," Harvath replied. "You can use the partial description we have and feel free to talk about his MO as much as you want, but keep the names of the victims and any mention of the Fed out of it."

"Understood," said Wise. "Email me the prints and I'll let you know if I find out anything."

"Sounds good. There's just one last thing."

"What's that?"

"Be very careful who else you talk with beyond this Gage fellow. And make sure to keep a pair of eyes in the back of your head."

"Same goes for you," Wise said. "Our killer isn't done yet. Not by a long shot. He not only likes to kill, he's compelled to. And if he did come out of Swim Club, he's very, very good at it."

"So am I," said Harvath, ending the call and slipping the phone back into his pocket.

Stepping out into the rain, he opened his umbrella and headed back toward 1 Schroeder Plaza and Cordero's office. As he walked, he was haunted by several of the things Bill Wise had said, not the least of which was that their killer might still have work left to do in Boston.

CHAPTER 36

Detective Cordero was on the phone trying to make child-care arrangements when Harvath hung up his coat and set the umbrella she had lent him in the corner.

"Okay, I understand. Thank you," she said and then hung up. Looking at Harvath she stated, "I'm definitely in the wrong business."

"Why?"

"The day-care center where I have my son charges a dollar a minute for every minute after five that you're not there to pick him up."

"That's pretty steep."

"It is, but I understand. Too many parents are irresponsible these days. If they didn't have some sort of penalty, people would be leaving their kids there until midnight. What about you?"

"What about me?" asked Harvath.

"Are you married? Do you have any kids?"

He smiled. "No."

"Divorced?"

"No."

"I knew it," she said. "The haircut and suit were a dead giveaway."

"A dead giveaway to what?"

"Don't be so defensive. Boston's a very progressive city. We've got a few gay cops on the force here."

Harvath laughed. "I'm not gay. And by the way, this is a Brooks Brothers suit and I've had the same haircut since college."

Cordero looked at him for several seconds.

"What are you looking at?" said Harvath.

"You've gotta be *what*, in your mid, maybe late thirties?"

That was a heck of a compliment and one he had no intention of correcting her on. "Give or take," he replied.

"So what's your problem? Never grew up? Peter Pan syndrome?"

Boy, is she direct. "Just never met the right girl."

"Your first mistake," said Cordero, "was looking for a *girl* instead of a *woman*."

Brutal, too. "And my second mistake?"

"Allowing yourself to get to this age without realizing you're the problem."

"Wow. This is turning into a heck of a beating. I hope your paramedics respond faster than your crime lab."

Cordero smiled. "What? No defense of your lifestyle? Isn't right about now the time you're supposed to stand up for confirmed bachelorhood? You know, trot out that old *don't hate the player, hate the game* line?"

"My bad," Harvath replied. "I didn't know there was protocol for this sort of guy-bashing. Speaking of which, why isn't *Mr. Cordero* helping you figure out picking up your son?"

The smile faded from her. "Because he's deceased. He died shortly before Marco was born."

Harvath felt like a total asshole and winced at her response. "I'm sorry. I didn't know."

"It's not your fault," she replied, attempting to bring back a small smile in order to take the sting out of the exchange. "How could you?"

"Was he a cop?"

"No, stockbroker. We'd known each other since grade school."

"So Cordero is your married name?"

"It's my maiden name. He had this long Eastern European name with a billion consonants that nobody could ever pronounce. I decided to keep my name."

"Marriage is all about give-and-take. That's what they say, right?" said Harvath.

Cordero rolled her eyes. "I know nothing about you, yet I get this sense—and I hope I don't hurt your feelings, but—you're a real idiot. You either have yourself convinced that it's easier to just drift from one casual thing to the next in a state of perpetual adolescence, or you're looking for that perfect ten. That sort of thing doesn't exist. If you're hitting on five out of six cylinders, or even four out of six with someone who truly cares about you, you should run, don't walk, all the way to the bank with it."

"If it's that easy, how come you're not remarried?"

"I never said it was easy," she corrected him. "It's hard work, but along with raising a child, it's the most rewarding hard work you'll ever do. Even better than being a SEAL, if only you knew how to swim."

"And if I was—"

Cordero rolled her eyes again. "And if you were *smart* enough. I got that part the first time, too."

"Any chance we can talk about something other than my love life?"

The detective slid the crime lab report across her desk.

Harvath skimmed it and eventually said, "So based on the elimination prints they used from Brittany Doyle's arrest record, the crime lab is certain this other full and partial print belongs to our killer?"

"No. That's not what they do. That's our job. All they can tell us is the two prints we have been given do not belong to Ms. Brittany Doyle of Southie. The additional prints belong to someone else."

"So what's the next step?" he asked, knowing already what her answer was.

"We begin searching the databases. We already sent a copy of the prints to the FBI, so we'll start with state and local. If we don't come up with anything, we'll go international. Sound like a plan?"

"I think I'd rather go back to getting lectured about my love life."

"Don't worry. I can walk and chew gum at the same time. We'll do both."

"Why doesn't that surprise me?" Harvath replied. "Listen, as much as

I enjoy discussing my shortcomings with people I've just met, why don't we bifurcate our work? You take the state and local databases, and if you give me a computer, I'll work on the international. That way, we'll be twice as fast and hopefully get you to your little boy by five o'clock. Make sense?"

Cordero smiled. Whatever his problem was, a healthy sense of humor and what appeared to be a decent sense of compassion weren't part of it.

Once again, she found herself attracted to him. More unsettling, though, was her growing feeling that whatever was wrong with him relationship-wise, she could fix it. But then there was her rational side. Through years of counseling brokenhearted girlfriends over countless glasses of wine, she knew what a dangerous proposition that was. You couldn't fix something that was intent upon staying broken.

After showing Harvath to an available computer, she pushed her romantic notions from her mind and returned to her desk so she could begin scouring the databases.

In any other circumstance, Harvath would have smiled and watched a woman like Lara Cordero as she walked away. Not now, though. Now all he was focused on was catching a killer, and catching him before he could kill again.

CHAPTER 37

Harvath went through the motions of searching all the databases he had access to, but he knew he wasn't going to find anything. Even if their killer had a prior record, it would have been scrubbed clean. An operation this sophisticated, regardless of who was behind it, would not roll the dice on everything falling apart because their lead hitter had his prints on file in a law enforcement database somewhere.

That didn't mean, though, that his prints didn't exist somewhere. If the man was indeed part of some black-ops program, the Agency was going to have a full dossier on him. Accessing that dossier, though, was going to be very difficult, particularly if the powers-that-be at Langley were trying to keep the program secret. Based on what he had heard about Swim Club, if the guy they were looking for was a part of it, Harvath would have a better chance locating Jimmy Hoffa than the man's personal information. He decided to turn it over to the Old Man. Monroe Lewis wanted regular updates and he owed Reed Carlton a situation report anyway.

Typing up a brief synopsis, Harvath transmitted it to Carlton via a secure server they used. Attached to the email were photos from the crime scenes as well as scans of the prints the Boston PD crime lab had isolated from Brittany Doyle's wrist cuff. He asked him to please forward the materials along to Bill Wise. With the two of them working on the prints, there was nothing else he could do in that arena and he logged off the computer.

Pushing his chair out from the desk, he stood and walked back to Cordero. "Any luck?" he asked.

"Nothing. You?"

Harvath shook his head.

"You knew we weren't going to find anything, didn't you?"

"I had a pretty good feeling," he replied. "Whoever this guy is, he's a pro."

"A professional psychopath," Cordero replied. Looking at her watch, she said, "I've got to pick up my son. Are you staying in Boston tonight?"

Harvath hadn't thought that far ahead. "I'm not sure. It depends."

"On whether or not the killer is still here?"

He nodded.

"Five victims from five different cities," she said. "For all we know, the killer has already left Boston and is on his way to the next."

"That's the problem. He could be anywhere. I've got no idea."

"Any reason at all to think he may still be here?" she asked.

Harvath thought back to what Wise had said. "There may be a slim chance. A *very* slim chance."

"Based on what?"

"I spoke with an expert back in D.C. Call him a profiler. He thinks one of the reasons the killer weighted Kelly Davis down and sunk her in the river, rather than leave her body wherever he killed her, was that he needed to buy himself more time."

"You don't seem convinced," said Cordero.

"My question is what would he be buying more time for? To get out of town and get to one of those other cities? Or is it something else?"

"What does your profiler think?"

"He thinks maybe the killer still has unfinished business here."

"You're the guy who paid attention in history class," she stated. "If this guy was going to stage another murder in Boston, where would he do it?"

Harvath had already thought about that and had been doing a little research online. It could be any number of locations. But there was no reason, apart from Wise's speculation, to believe that the killer hadn't already left.

Cordero glanced at her watch once more.

"Go pick up your son," said Harvath.

"What about you?"

"I'll be fine. I'll probably hang around here a little bit longer to see if anything breaks. Maybe the FBI will get lucky. If not, I'll head back to D.C."

"And what if the killer *is* still here?" she asked.

"Then I guess you and I'll see each other again."

Cordero and Harvath shook hands, holding on a fraction of a second longer than they should have.

"Stay safe, Annie Oakley," he said as she let go of his hand and brushed past him to pick up her umbrella and a small plastic bag with a box in it.

"You, too," the detective replied.

As she reached the door, the answer to the question she had asked him popped into his mind and he said, "Fort Hill."

Cordero stopped and turned around. "What?"

"You asked me where I thought the killer would stage another Boston murder if he was still here and the answer is Fort Hill."

"The water tower in Roxbury?" she replied as her partner entered the office and walked past her.

"Water *tank*," the male detective corrected her, drawing out the words in his heavy Boston accent as he sat down at his desk.

"Excuse me, water *tank*."

"No," said Harvath. "We're talking about two different things. It's a fort."

"It *was* a fort," Cordero's partner said. "When the town of Roxbury was annexed by Boston in the 1800s, they put a water tank on Fort Hill made to look like some fairy princess tower and renamed the area Highland Park."

Cordero looked at her partner. "Where the hell did that come from?"

"What are you talking about?"

"Other than arcane Red Sox trivia, I've never heard you mention one historical thing about Boston."

"I guess you just don't know me."

She stared at him, half in disbelief and half with the conviction that he was not telling her the full truth.

The male detective looked at Harvath and said, "Do you want to tell her why Fort Hill is significant, or should I?"

Though Harvath didn't know the man from Adam, he was equally stunned by his sudden fluency in Boston history and chose to let him keep the floor.

"By all means," Harvath said. "Please."

The male detective looked at his partner and said, "After Penning's murder this morning, I decided to do a little research."

Cordero was going to be late picking up her son, but this was more than worth a dollar a minute. "Do tell, Sal."

"I'm a smart guy, with an even smarter smartphone," he said with a smirk. "So I researched what happened after they hung Andrew Oliver's effigy from the Liberty Tree."

"And?"

"The mob ginned itself up and ended up tearing down the dockside warehouse Oliver owned. Probably because that's where he was storing all the stamps from King George."

"What does that have to do with Fort Hill?"

"Oliver lived at the foot of Fort Hill. The mob set the effigy up in front of his house, chopped its head off, and set it on fire.

"When local law enforcement showed up and tried to calm things down, they got showered with rocks. The crowd then looted Oliver's house and set *it* on fire. The next day, Oliver resigned his commission from King George, but the colonists weren't done with him. They made him march down and publicly renounce his office beneath the Liberty Tree."

Cordero's partner shifted his gaze to Harvath and said, "Correct?"

Harvath hated to hand it to the guy, but he had done his homework. "That's right," he replied.

"So, let's pass that along to the FBI and beef up patrols around High-land Park and the water tank just in case. We'll see what happens."

"Sounds like a plan," said Cordero, who then looked at Harvath and asked, "How about dinner?"

"What about your son?"

"My parents live in the apartment above mine. They're older. They don't drive anymore. But they can babysit after I get Marco put to bed. If the killer is still here, you want a crack at him, right?"

"Of course," Harvath replied.

"Good," she said, as she turned to walk out the door. "So do I. I'll text you in an hour and we'll pick a place to meet. In the meantime, have Sal help you find a hotel. If you're lucky, he'll put in the good word with his sister. She's one of the assistant managers at the Four Seasons."

As he watched her leave, Harvath looked at the male detective and realized that he probably had a better chance of having the killer walk right into the police station than he did of having Cordero's partner put in the good word for him anywhere, much less with his sister at the Four Seasons hotel.

CHAPTER 38

After purchasing groceries and a few extra items of clothing, McGee and Ryan returned to Brenda Durkin's. With coffee brewed, they made sandwiches and turned the Colonel's dining room into their makeshift operations center.

The name of each member of Ryan's former destabilization team was written on a three-by-five card and taped to the wall. Under those, cards were added based on what Ryan could remember about her teammates including physical descriptions, training and experience levels, where they lived, what their marital status was, if they had children, and what their weaknesses and potential pressure points were, among other things. They were attempting to create the best 30,000-foot picture possible and from there they would zoom in on their target.

Stevenson, the community bank manager, had been very helpful. The reams of banking information he provided included credit histories, ATM transactions, and credit card statements. Two team members had even set up their mortgages through Stevenson's bank. The guy Ryan ultimately wanted, though, had been much more careful. His personal financial presence in the data was almost nonexistent. There was only the corporate stuff. He had been smarter than the rest of the team members and had established follow-on bank accounts for his money to wash through. Even if somebody pierced the community bank, they'd have a lot more work to do to track down where he lived.

That was fine by her. They'd catch up with Tom Cushing, the team's leader, eventually. They weren't looking for the head of the pack now anyway. They were looking to pick off someone a little bit further back.

As far as Ryan was concerned, they had taken a significant leap forward. The team had not been disbanded; it had just been pushed further into the shadows. The question that she didn't want to wrestle with, but which was still there, was why had she been cut loose? Why did they not bring her along with them? She had thought she had been a pretty good fit, even when she was acting as her teammates' conscience.

Was that it? Was that why she had been let go? Had her morality been that inflexible? Granted, she'd been fairly rigid when she joined the team, but once she'd been tossed in the deep end and saw not only how much was at stake but how ruthless the enemies of the country were, she had begun to quickly play ball.

Maybe her being added to the team had only ever been window dressing. Maybe someone on the seventh floor had leaned on Phil Durkin and he had assigned her to the team in order to appear like he was at least trying to make things right. *Who the hell knew what was real and what was fiction when it came to anything anymore at the CIA?*

Ryan forced the question from her mind. It was a rabbit hole that went absolutely nowhere. There were bigger things she needed to focus on at the moment.

The Eclipse team still existed and they were still being funded via the Central Intelligence Agency. That was a big part of the puzzle that had now fallen into place. The next question she needed answered was what they were up to. Were they destabilizing Islamic countries so that their current governments could be overthrown and replaced? If so, was Jordan on their list? And if it was, how far along were they and who else beside the Muslim Brotherhood figures that had been photographed meeting with them in Cyprus were they involved with? Nafi would want all the details. Of that, she was sure.

She was also sure of what their next move should be, but McGee didn't agree. He liked the idea of isolating one of the team members; he just didn't like the person she had picked. McGee had his own feelings when it came to whom they could double back against Phil Durkin and the team.

"There is no way you'll get Tara to crack," Ryan had told him.

"The hell I won't," the man replied. "Everyone cracks. Drag their kids in and they crack so fast your head'll spin."

"We're not bringing anyone's children into this."

"That's a mistake."

"Jesus, Bob. We're talking about little kids."

"What kind of monster do you think I am?" McGee retorted. "Nothing's going to happen to them. We're just going to use them for leverage."

Ryan fixed him with a withering look. "No, we're not."

"So then what? We go with your guy? Florence of Arabia?"

"Cut it out. Florentino makes more sense than Tara at this point. He's the weakest one on the team, he's the person I had the strongest rapport with, and based on his credit card history, we know what bar he spends every Tuesday night in when he's in town."

"The only reason you two had such strong rapport is because he didn't try to put the make on you."

"He actually had reservations about many of the things Cushing was pushing the team to do."

The older operative stood looking at the names on the wall and took a sip of coffee. "Just because your Arabist had his moral compass set a little truer north than the rest of them," he said, lowering the mug, "doesn't mean he's going to cooperate with us."

"We'll see what happens."

"I'm telling you, it's a mistake. We should go after the Tara woman. We use her kids, she talks, and bang. We're golden."

"No kids. No bang."

"I didn't mean *bang* as in—"

"I know what you meant, but we're done discussing leveraging anybody's children. I'm not doing that. Understood?"

McGee was silent and Ryan shot him another look. *"Understood?"*

"Fine," he finally replied. "We'll do it your way. No kids."

"And you'll let me handle Florentino? You promise to stay out of my way?"

"What are we, suddenly in a negotiation?"

"No," she said. "This isn't a negotiation, it's an operation, and I want to make sure that there is no confusion as to chain of command. This was my team, I know these people, this is my op. Easy enough?"

"Fine," McGee relented again. "But let's just be clear on one thing."

"What's that?"

"The minute any guns come out, this becomes my op and we do things my way."

CHAPTER 39

Florentino Marche had been born in Brooklyn, New York, and was the only child of an Italian father and a Puerto Rican mother. He had attended Columbia University, where he showed considerable aptitude for languages, particularly Arabic. From there he had gone on to Georgetown and a master's degree from the Center for Contemporary Arab Studies. The Central Intelligence Agency made their approach shortly thereafter.

He was a tall, thin man with dark features and curly hair. With his black-framed eyeglasses and retro fashion sense, he came off as more geek than chic.

There were at least a hundred other hipster men in the crowded bar dressed just like him. Waitresses shuttled to and fro with pitchers of beer and trays laden with rings and wings. Televisions mounted on every wall broadcast a myriad of current as well as classic sporting events. It was difficult for Ryan to move through the crowd unimpeded. Table after table of young men invited her to join them, some less sober and more insistent than others. Finally, she spotted Florentino.

He was sitting with a group of friends in a booth. Instead of talking to each other, they were all looking down at their phones, texting. Occasionally, some team on one of the TVs would score, the crowd would cheer, and Florentino's booth full of hipsters would look up and react. She needed to get his attention.

Tipping a waitress to slide him a cocktail napkin with a cryptic message had occurred to her but Florentino was too smart and too paranoid to bite on something like that. Guys like him didn't get sent notes on cocktail napkins.

She was trying to come up with another option when she saw him tuck his phone in his pocket, say something to his friends, and get up from the table. As he walked toward the restrooms, she fell in step behind him and followed.

Her question now was whether she was going to present herself before or after he used the men's room. *Probably better to wait till after.*

Slowing her pace, she picked a spot where she could wait and watch for him to come back out. He didn't go into the men's room, though. He kept walking toward the back of the building.

He hip-checked the crash bar on a fire exit and stepped outside. *Smoke break?*

She needed him isolated anyway. Behind the building was just as good as anyplace else. Besides, it was too noisy inside. She could barely hear herself think.

Catching the door before it closed, she slipped outside behind him.

The rain had recently stopped and a mixture of young men and women stood in the puddled alley smoking and carrying on conversations. Florentino stood near a dumpster with his back to her. He never was very good at tradecraft. He was more academic than true field operative and no matter how many times she had tried to impress upon him the need for situational awareness, he had never seemed to get it. It was obvious by the ease with which she was able to approach him that he still didn't.

"Hello, Florentino," she said.

The young man looked over his shoulder and then turned to face her. "Lydia," he said. "What the hell are you doing here?"

"I'm supposed to meet a friend for drinks. I thought she might be back here having a smoke. What are you doing here?"

"Out with friends, too. Drinking. You know."

"Yeah."

"You got your haircut," he said. "It looks good. Cool."

"Thanks. So what have you been up to?"

The young man paused, reluctant to answer. "Not much. You know. A little bit of this, a little bit of that."

"Florentino, you don't have to lie to me," Ryan replied. "I know what you've been doing."

"What are you talking about? What have I been doing?"

"From what I've been told, lots and lots of travel. How was the food in Cyprus?"

"Cyprus?" he said, stalling. "That's in Greece, right?"

"Or Turkey. It depends."

"Yeah, right. You mind if I?" he said, fishing out a pack of smokes from his pocket and holding them up.

"No, go ahead. You know how bad those things are for you, right?"

He smiled, tapped one out, and pulled it from the pack with his mouth. "You sound like my mom."

"Your mom's right," said Ryan, as she watched him remove his lighter and fire up his smoke. His hand appeared to have a slight tremble.

"How are you doing?" he asked after a deep drag. "I heard you're still with the company, huh? How's that been going?"

"I don't have a lot of time. How about we talk about Cyprus instead?"

It sounded like a question, but it wasn't. "Uh, okay," he replied, his eyes flicking to the left.

Ryan glanced over her shoulder. "Are you expecting someone, Florentino?"

"Me? No. I mean, one of my friends was supposed to come out for a smoke, too."

"In the meantime, tell me about Cyprus. Better yet," she said, growing uncomfortable, "why don't we step back inside?"

He pulled the cigarette from between his lips and held it up as he exhaled a cloud of smoke. "Can't smoke in there."

"Well, when we're done talking, you can come back outside."

"I don't think that's a good idea."

Ryan was going to ask *why* that wasn't a good idea when she saw his eyes shift once again. This time, though, there was something different about the way he did it and the blood in her veins turned to ice.

Dropping to the ground, she spun and was just about to pull her Glock when a volley of shots rang through the alley.

CHAPTER 40

Ryan had pulled Florentino to the ground and was trying to maneuver them to cover behind the dumpster. There was chaos as the smokers ran in multiple directions screaming.

"You knew!" she wanted to yell at Florentino, but then she noticed he wasn't moving. He had a gunshot wound to the chest and another at the base of his throat. Blood ran from his mouth as he lay on the wet pavement. As she reached out to feel for a pulse, two more shots skipped off the side of the dumpster and Ryan leapt back. She knew better than that. The only aid you gave in a gunfight was putting rounds on the enemy.

Two shots rang out, both in rapid succession. They were followed by two more. She had no idea how many attackers were in the alley, but she did know that someone was using a suppressor and someone wasn't.

With her weapon up and ready, she was about to snatch a quick peek around the edge of the dumpster when she heard McGee's voice.

"Tangos down. I'm coming to you. Don't shoot. Be ready to move. Copy?"

"Affirmative," Ryan replied. Her weapon was in tight, close to her chest, but ready to be fired.

McGee approached soundlessly and then scuffed the ground with his shoes the last couple of feet, so she would know where he was. He nudged Florentino with his foot to see if he would move. He didn't. He was probably dead.

Stepping around the dumpster, he held his free hand out to Ryan and helped her up.

"Is he dead?" she asked, looking down at her former teammate.

McGee nodded. "I think so."

Ryan bent over and felt for his pulse as she surveyed the scene. "What the hell happened?"

"At least three shooters," McGee replied, pointing with his 1911 to the bodies on the ground. The baying of police Klaxons could be heard only a few blocks away. "We need to get going."

"Go through their pockets," she told him, jerking her head toward the shooters. "I'll do Florentino."

"Waste of time. We need to get moving."

"Bob, please," said Ryan.

Shaking his head, McGee disengaged and moved quickly over to the three dead men. By the time he was done patting them down, Ryan had joined him. She had Florentino's iPhone.

"That's not coming with us," the former Delta Force operator said as he pointed at the phone. "They can track us with it."

She knew he was right. "I just want to see what he has on it and then we'll toss it."

"Fine. Right now, let's just get the hell out of here."

Ryan nodded and followed McGee as he headed quickly down the alley. Just before they emerged at the sidewalk, he stopped and listened.

"Damn it," he said.

"What is it?"

"The police are getting close. We're going to have to go the long way around to get the car."

They had debated whether to park far from the bar or to park closer. Ryan had wanted to be closer in case they needed to get out of there fast. McGee had wanted to be farther away for exactly that same reason. There were good arguments to be made for both and in the end they had split the difference.

They moved perpendicular to the sound of the approaching police cars and made sure not to be seen. As keyed-up as police officers would be racing to a shooting, they were still taught to keep their eyes open and look for any potential suspects leaving the scene of a crime. While Ryan doubted the cops had anything more to go on than an address and "shots fired" in the alley, she didn't want to risk getting rolled up. The only way they were going to get to the bottom of what was going on was to stay as many steps ahead of Phil Durkin as possible. They couldn't do that if they were sitting in jail.

They also couldn't do that if they were dead. Even though Ryan had a bunch of questions she wanted to ask, she kept quiet. It wasn't only the police they had to watch out for. There could be more shooters looking for them right now. Both she and McGee needed to move quickly and quietly.

As they neared the car, Ryan removed Florentino's iPhone and rapidly scrolled through his texts, emails, and browsing history.

"Anything?" McGee asked.

"Personal stuff, but nothing we can really use," she replied as she stepped over to a storm drain and tossed it in.

"For what it's worth, the stiffs in the alley were clean, too. No ID, no pocket litter, nothing."

"More pros."

McGee nodded. A block away, they could hear another police car and they both climbed quickly into the Mustang.

Once they had put enough distance between them and the scene, Ryan asked, "How the hell did they find us?"

"I think maybe we found them."

"Meaning there was a team on Florentino?"

McGee nodded and made another turn in order to see if anyone was following them. "I'll bet they have teams on all of them."

"But why kill Florentino?"

"I don't think they meant to kill him. I think they meant to kill you."

Ryan was quiet for a moment as that sank in.

"They nailed him in the upper chest and base of his throat," McGee continued. "Right where—"

"My head would have been had I not dropped," she said, finishing his sentence for him.

"With that kind of luck, we ought to stop off and have you buy a lottery ticket."

"It wasn't luck," she replied pensively. "It was instinct. Florentino knew they were there. His eyes gave them away. For some reason, something inside me just told me to react."

"Call it whatever you want, but you were smart to listen to it. Between you and that Florentino guy, I'm glad it was him and not you that bought it."

Ryan didn't respond.

McGee accelerated to make it through the light that was changing up ahead. Once he had cleared the intersection, he asked, "Do you think he knew what they were intending to do to you?"

Ryan shook her head. "No. We were friends once. If he knew, I think he would have found a way to warn me."

"Maybe he did."

She fell silent again and McGee didn't push the conversation. After several minutes, Ryan said, "I'm glad you followed me outside. Thank you."

"You would have been fine," he replied. "You've got great *instincts*."

"No, you were right. I got lucky. Very lucky."

"Don't start second-guessing everything now and overanalyzing it. It's done." Changing the subject, he asked, "Did you recognize who was shooting at us?"

"No. I've never seen them before."

"I don't know what kind of pies Durkin has his dirty little fingers into, but he has access to a lot of manpower. Two hitters at my place, two at yours, and now two more on Florentino."

"If you're right," said Ryan, "and he's got people watching the other team members, we're not going to be able to get close to them, much less get them to talk to us."

"There is still one way," McGee reminded her.

"Bob, I told you no. No children."

"That was when they'd only used a Taser on you. I thought being shot at might change your mind."

"It hasn't. We'll have to come up with another way."

"Well, the McGee idea factory is closed for renovations. You're going to have to come up with something on your own."

Ryan turned in her seat to face him. "Are you telling me you won't help?"

"I'm telling you that you got my best idea. Hell, you got my *only* idea. I'm fresh out. That's it."

She didn't believe him. "We just need to think harder."

"If I try to think this thing through any harder, there's going to be smoke coming out of my ears. Listen, you know me. I'm a simple guy. I made a career out of tracking down bad guys, kicking in their doors, and shooting them in the head. Sometimes I delayed that last part long enough to have a chat with them, but not often. I'm not a schemer. I don't construct intricate plots and ruses. I'm a door kicker. It's in my blood and I'm not ashamed of that.

"As far as I'm concerned the shortest distance between two points really is a straight line. Often the simplest answer is the best."

"Wait," she interjected. "Say that again."

"What? About the simplest answer being the best?"

"No, the other part."

McGee took his eyes off the road and looked at her. "About the shortest distance between two points being a straight line?"

"That's *it*," Ryan admitted with a look of satisfaction.

"What's *it*?"

"It's something Tom Cushing, our team leader always said. The shortest distance between two points isn't a straight line, it's an *angle*."

"Meaning?"

"*Meaning*," said Ryan as she opened the Mustang's glove box to see if it had a map, "I think I know how we're going to beat Phil Durkin at his own game."

CHAPTER 41

She had lied to him. She had told him her name was Chloe. He knew it wasn't, but it didn't matter. Prostitutes lied. Drug addicts lied. Runaways lied. They all lied. He had lied, too. When her instincts kicked in and the fear began to consume her, he told her he wasn't going to hurt her. She knew he was lying, but at that point there was nothing she could do about it except die.

The doctors had lied, too. They had told him that as long as he continued diligently with the medication, he would be able to keep things under control. And by *things,* they meant his urges, his impulses, that primal part of himself that delighted in power and the taking of life. He saw himself as a lion on the savannah; free to eat whatever he wanted whenever he was hungry. Of course, that's what the meds were for. They were supposed to curb his "appetite."

It didn't mean he stopped killing, though. They brought him out from time to time, sent him hither and yon. One of the doctors asked him once if he expected any explanation as to why he was asked to kill. It was a very frank session, but then again it was a very frank subject. Nevertheless, he merely shrugged in response. He didn't need an explanation or a justification. It was all about balance. Without some form of equilibrium, all living things on the savannah, even the lion, would perish from the earth. Taking a kudu or a water buffalo or even a giraffe or elephant from time to time was simply nature's way of maintaining harmony. He was the lion. It was what lions did.

Tonight, the lion was preparing to kill again. It would be dramatic, as befitted his stature. The young woman he had left in the Charles was because he had been hungry. When a lion is hungry it eats. This is the way of the world. This was the way of his world. For the moment, he was satiated. Having cleansed himself of his need, he could focus on the task at hand.

Another key, another garage, another vehicle, another neighborhood. Everything was waiting for him, just as before. Locking the garage door behind him, he removed his flashlight and surveyed the van. Upon it was the name of a plumbing company. It had a Boston address and a Boston telephone number as well. It wouldn't strike anyone as unusual that such a vehicle might be out at night conducting a plumbing repair. Plumbing problems happened and they happened at all hours.

Sliding open the cargo area door, he found coveralls with the name *Mickey* embroidered on the left chest and the company name on the back, worn work boots, a tool belt, a pillow, and a clipboard loaded with invoices and the other accumulated receipts and pieces of paper a person of his assumed identity would amass in the course of doing his job. There were lengths of copper and PVC pipe, blowtorches, cylindrical tanks, a padded moving blanket, various pieces of plumbing equipment including grates, drain snakes, and rods of all sizes, heavy metal buckets with lids, plungers, spare parts, multiple service manuals, old plumbing catalogs, a few cinder blocks, and a small stack of bricks that looked like they might have been reclaimed from a job site. The monotony of it all would bore even the most inquisitive of police officers. For his part, though, he had no intention of dealing with law enforcement. They merely appeared after the fact to admire the lion's work.

In the back of the van was a large metal "gang box" on casters used for organizing and locking up tools or other pieces of equipment. Removing another key from his pocket, he placed his flashlight between his teeth and stepped into the van. He walked back to the gang box and tapped its lid with the key. He knew there was a little mouse inside but the mouse was being very quiet.

He tapped again, and then again once more. Fear radiated out from the box like steam from a pile of hot rocks doused with water in a sauna. He felt a chill run through his body. Getting a purchase on the gang box, he shook it violently and then pounded the lid near one of the airholes with his fist. He pressed his ear up against the side and strained to listen. *Was the little mouse cowering?* He certainly hoped so. A mouse should cower in the presence of a lion.

He rested on his haunches for a full five minutes without moving. Then, without warning, he lashed out and gave the appliance a kick. He enjoyed torturing his victim this way. It made him feel powerful and in control, which of course he was. Looking at his watch, he ran though all of the steps on his agenda for the evening. It was going to be a long night, but he was looking forward to it.

Reaching into his backpack, he removed the dinner he had prepared and laid everything out on a piece of newspaper. He turned off his flashlight and allowed himself to be consumed by the darkness. It was not something that frightened him anymore. It had become part of him and he a part of it.

The darkness had been when his grandfather would come for him. The man's enormous, gnarled hands trafficked in unspeakable terror. On a shelf overlooking his bed, as those hands did what they did, sat a small plastic lion, watching. It never attacked, never pounced and went for the man's throat, though night after night the boy wordlessly willed it so. No matter how horribly he suffered, or how strenuously he entreated the lion with his eyes, it never moved, it never so much as even twitched.

How he had admired the lion. How he had admired its supernatural reserve and its lack of concern for anything but itself. It didn't fear the darkness. It didn't fear the old man and his gnarled hands. It feared nothing and everything feared it. When he committed his first kill, he had made sure the lion was there to savor the moment with him. He wanted the lion to see that he was no longer afraid. Just as important, he wanted the lion to see that he could strike fear into others.

Sitting back in the van, the killer steadied his breathing, slowed his heart rate, and became one with the darkness. From inside the stainless steel box, he caught a fresh scent of fear, heavy with the inevitability of what the night would bring, and the certainty that there was nothing and no one who could ever stop the lion.

CHAPTER 42

Cordero had chosen a small Italian restaurant in Boston's North End, not far from the Paul Revere House and the Old North Church. The neighborhood's narrow, European-style streets had been washed clean by the rain and might have added to the ambiance if Harvath didn't have so much on his mind. Even Cordero, who had changed into an attractive outfit for dinner, couldn't shake him from the mood he had slipped into.

"I heard from Sal," she said after the waiter had set down their drinks and went to take care of another table. "The FBI came up bust on the prints as well."

Harvath wasn't surprised, but he still shook his head. "I feel like we're missing something."

"We're not."

"How can you be so sure?"

"Because this is what I do for a living," Cordero replied. "Building a homicide case is like assembling a watch. It takes time. Every single piece is important and has to be put in the right place. They're very labor-intensive.

In fact, you know what one of the most important qualities is for a homicide investigator?"

"Attention to detail?" he asked.

"*Patience.*" Picking up her wineglass, she switched gears. "What did you do before getting into K-and-R?"

She had a knack for asking him questions that required careful answers. "I actually worked for the Secret Service."

"So you *were* in law enforcement."

"Not really," he replied. "I did protective work."

"Why the change?"

"There were great people there, but I came to the conclusion that I didn't like being on defense. Too often, it felt like I was just sitting around waiting for something to happen."

"Kind of like now."

"Ironic, huh?"

"But that's what's bothering you, isn't it? Without some major breakthrough, there's probably going to be another victim. Maybe even more than one."

He nodded.

She looked at him. "It bothers me, too."

"So what do we do about it?"

Cordero took a sip of her wine. "We hope for a major breakthrough."

"I'd settle for even a minor breakthrough," Harvath replied as he picked up his menu.

"Patience is the companion of wisdom."

"I've heard that before. Who said that?"

"St. Augustine."

Harvath smiled knowingly.

"What?" she asked.

"I had a commanding officer a long time ago who liked to quote St. Augustine. His favorite line was *no eulogy is due to a man who simply does his duty and nothing more.*

"Apparently, it stuck with you."

Harvath nodded. It was his turn now to switch gears. "Why did you ask me to dinner?"

"I wanted to get you drunk."

He laughed. "And then what?"

"And then I'm going to pry every secret I can out of you."

"Well, that's a relief. For a minute there, I was worried you were going to take advantage of me."

"You don't strike me as the kind of person who gets taken advantage of."

"Are you kidding? I'm the softest touch on the planet. Anything having to do with kids or animals—"

"Right," she said, interrupting him. "For your information, I'm not the kind of person who gets taken advantage of, either."

"You think I'm kidding?" he asked as he pulled his phone from his pocket and unlocked it. Scrolling through some pictures, he found the one he wanted and showed it to her.

Cordero's eyes widened. "What kind of horse is that?"

"That's not a horse," he laughed. "That's my dog."

"What breed?"

"He's a Russian Ovcharka."

"A what?" she asked with a grin, trying to pronounce the name, but not doing very well.

"Ovcharka," Harvath replied, drawing the word out slowly. "They're also known as Caucasian sheepdogs. The Russian military and the East German border patrol loved these dogs. They're very fast, very loyal, and let's just say you wouldn't want to make one angry."

"I'll take your word for it. He's *huge*. What's his name?"

"Bullet."

"You named your dog *Bullet*?"

"He's named after a pal of mine whose nickname was Bullet Bob."

"Was?"

"Bob was a counterterrorism operative. He died doing what he loved."

"I'm sorry," she said.

'It's okay."

"How do you keep a dog that big in D.C.?"

"He doesn't live with me. I travel too much."

"Where's he live, then?"

"With an old girlfriend."

"You share custody of your dog with an ex? You really are a soft touch," said Cordero.

"Do you have a picture of your son?"

"I do," she said, reaching into her purse and removing her phone.

It was taken at the beach on a beautiful sunny day. He was a handsome little boy with a big smile.

"He's very cute," Harvath replied. "He looks a lot like you."

The detective smiled. "He actually looks a lot like his father."

"Do you mind if I ask how he died?"

Taking the phone back, she looked at her son's picture for a moment and then placed it in her purse. "No. I don't mind you asking. He drowned. It was at that same stretch of beach in the photo I just showed you. We used to go there every summer with friends. It was the middle of the day. It was hot, sunny. We were all swimming, having a good time. One moment he was there and the next he was just . . . gone."

"Is that why your partner took over the scene at the Charles River this morning? Is that kind of thing hard for you?"

"Not usually. I guess it depends."

"Well, you seemed like you had it together. You were pretty tough on me."

Cordero smiled. "I enjoyed being tough on you."

"I could tell. Both of you did."

"Sal can be a bit overprotective."

"No kidding," replied Harvath.

"As far as kicking me loose to go interview those girls with you, I'll fill you in on a little secret. Sal's also a bit of a snob. He's from Southie, you know."

"Really?"

"Yup. Joined the Army to escape his old neighborhood. Ended up coming home and becoming a cop. He helped me out a lot after my husband died."

"Again, I'm very sorry for your loss."

"Me, too, but mostly for Marco. Children need fathers."

"You know, I lost my dad the same way," said Harvath.

"He drowned?"

"He did. Not too long after I graduated from high school."

"I'm sorry to hear that. At least you knew him. You were lucky to have had the time that you did."

"I know that now. My father was a good man."

"The apple doesn't fall far from the tree."

Harvath grinned. "You don't know anything about me."

"I'm very intuitive."

She was flirting with him and he definitely felt attracted to her, but business and pleasure were often a bad mix. "I think we'd better order dinner," he said, raising his hand to get the waiter's attention.

They polished off a bottle of wine together and Harvath wondered if maybe she really was trying to get him drunk when she asked if he wanted to order another one. He declined, but did say yes to some grappa.

They talked about many things: how Cordero became a cop, what it was like balancing her career with being a mom, what they both did to stay in shape, how Cordero's partner had not helped him at all regarding the Four Seasons, and how Harvath had subsequently checked into the W hotel on points.

They spent the majority of their time discussing the case, and they did so in detail. Harvath admitted that even though he'd offered up Fort Hill as a likely site for the killer, it was still a long shot. He'd been trying to think outside the box. The fact was, though, that if the killer had remained in Boston, he could end up striking anywhere. For all Harvath knew, the killer was gone. He was growing more and more certain that the next time his phone rang, it would be with news of the killer having struck in Chicago, San Francisco, or Seattle. He'd hop back on the plane, fly to wherever it had happened, and start another murder investigation from square one. It was not only frustrating, it made him angry.

But there was also something else. On top of his professional reasons for not wanting to leave Boston, he also had a personal one. The more time he spent with Cordero, the more he liked being around her.

It was a beautiful night and still early, so they decided to walk for a while. They passed several historic sites, like Faneuil Hall, the Old Corner Bookstore, and the Old South Meeting House, where they stopped to read their weathered bronze plaques. Harvath showed off his knowledge of Boston's role in the American Revolution and teased her good-naturedly from time to time, but she took it all in stride with a smile.

By the time they reached Boston Common and his hotel, neither wanted their evening to end. He invited her in for a nightcap, but she demurred. It was already later than she had intended to be out. She joked that the one thing you could count on with children and criminals was that neither class cared how little sleep or how much to drink you'd had the night before; both would try to turn your weakness to their advantage.

He waited with her while the hotel doorman flagged a cab and then helped her climb in. "I had a very nice evening, Lara," he said. "Thank you."

"I had a nice time, too. And it's still Detective Cordero," she replied with a mischievous grin as she closed the door and gave the driver her address.

Harvath smiled and stood back as the taxi pulled away. Her sense of humor was one of the many things that were growing on him.

He stopped in the bar and ordered a cup of coffee to take up to his room. He needed to check his email, and undoubtedly the Old Man, who was a night owl, would be up and would want to talk. He might even have some good news for him. At least that was what Harvath told himself as he stepped into the elevator and pressed the button for his floor. In his gut, though, he had a very bad feeling that something evil was hovering on the horizon and would make itself known sooner, rather than later.

CHAPTER 43

Garden Court in Boston's North End was a one-way street that only allowed parking along one side. It being Boston, parking was always at a premium and there were no spaces available. The killer hadn't expected there to be any. Pulling his van up as far as he could onto the sidewalk, he made sure there was enough space for traffic to get by and placed a placard on his dashboard that read EMERGENCY PLUMBING REPAIR IN PROGRESS. It wouldn't stop a cop determined to give him a hard time, but he hoped not to be here long enough to draw much attention. In the meantime, the sign might prevent an angry local from calling the police because of how the van was parked.

He parked as close as he could to 5 Garden Court Street in order to use the van to obscure the entrance. Stepping into the cargo area, he opened the sliding door from inside and had unfettered access to the building's front door.

With his pick gun, he made quick work of the cheap lock. In the blink of an eye, the door to the empty, unoccupied ground-floor apartment was open. Stepping inside, he did a quick check to make sure no squatters had taken up residence since his last reconnaissance. It was clear.

He used a collapsible aluminum loading ramp to wheel the gang box out of the van and into the squalid apartment. As soon as it was in, he quickly offloaded the rest of his equipment, including the van's spare tire.

The window facing the street had been covered over with newspaper and he had no idea if the apartment even had functioning electricity. Not that it mattered. He wouldn't risk any light from inside spilling out and drawing attention. Snapping a series of glow sticks, he tossed them into corners of the tiny apartment and then used a staple gun to hang the padded moving blanket over the inside of the window.

With that complete, he focused on getting the buckets cooking. Using his knife, he pried off their lids and with the cinder blocks and bricks, he created a series of raised platforms for each, in order to get them up off the cracked linoleum floor.

Next, he ignited the torches and placed them around the metal buckets in order to start heating their contents. The trick was getting them close enough to bring the ingredients to a boil without rupturing the buckets themselves and having them spill their contents all over the floor. It had taken him some practice in the days leading up to this moment to get it just right, but he had been able to perfect his technique and was confident that he could reproduce the results once he arrived in the apartment.

Very soon the air was filled with the liquid's pungent odor. He knew that it wouldn't take long to spread farther up into the three-story building. As he had at the Liberty Tree Building, he kept a silenced pistol at hand while he worked. If anyone came to investigate the source of the smell, they'd be immediately dispatched. The lion would not be deterred from his kill.

He used a professional-grade infrared thermometer to monitor the temperature in each of the buckets. As they started climbing closer to their boiling points, he assembled the rolling winch system that would allow him to move each of the buckets to where he needed them without risk of spilling any of the liquid on himself.

When the winch system was assembled, he rolled the spare tire into the bathroom, placed it in the tub, unscrewed the lid of a large jug, and poured the contents over it. He then placed the timing mechanism and rapidly made his way back to the living room and extinguished all the blowtorches.

Unlocking the lid of the gang box, he lifted it up and looked inside. The man inside had been stripped of all his clothing and his head had been shaved. His hands, feet, and neck were shackled to eyehooks welded to the bottom of the box. He had also been gagged. The gag was necessary not only for quietly transporting him, but to silence the screaming he was about to do.

The killer knew he was deviating from his instructions, but nevertheless he had chosen not to administer the paralytic this time. He wanted his victim to thrash and spasm. When they later examined the body, he wanted all involved to see the signs of the man's struggle and to envision how painful his death must have been.

Making sure that the casters beneath the gang box were locked, so that it would stay in place and not begin moving across the floor, he used the rolling winch system to pick up the first boiling bucket and bring it to the box.

It took a moment to get it to the correct height, just above the rim of the box, but once he had it where he wanted it he hooked two claw hammers underneath and splashed the boiling liquid inside.

The naked man writhed and screamed in agony as the hot substance boiled off his flesh. Quickly, the killer fetched the next bucket and poured it in.

The gang box was made of thick metal panels, which helped retain the liquid's intense heat, while its welded seams prevented even one drop from leaking.

It took him exactly eight and a half more minutes to empty the remaining buckets and then five more minutes to clean up and make sure he hadn't left any clues. His hair and clothing reeked, as did the rest of the apartment, but it was nothing compared to what it was going to smell like soon enough.

Confident that the scene was exactly as he wanted it, he retreated outside, pulled the apartment door shut behind him, and climbed into the van. He looked at his watch and reached into his backpack for a small handheld scanner. Turning it on, he set it on the seat next to him and turned the key in the ignition. As he drove off the curb and headed away, he smiled. Sleepy Garden Court Street was about to get very, very active.

CHAPTER 44

The bald-headed CIA operative watching the house had a thick neck, broad shoulders, and meaty hands that looked like a bunch of sausages sewn together. His were not the hands of a surgeon or a pianist, but they nevertheless conducted very skilled labor. If this were not so, he never would have risen to the level he had.

When he picked up the phone vibrating on the armrest next to him, it looked like a child's toy being held in a baseball mitt. He activated the call. "Samuel speaking," he said.

"You're being retasked. Priority one," a voice said on the other end.

"Same targets?" Samuel asked, his eyes never leaving the house.

"No."

"What is my new target, please?"

"It's all in the file. You know where to find it."

"When?"

"Now," said the voice. "I'm sending someone to relieve you. They should be arriving any moment."

"Understood," Samuel replied and disconnected the call. Less than ten minutes later, another black Lincoln Town Car pulled up across the street and turned off its lights. The parking lights came on momentarily before being extinguished. The relief shift had arrived. Samuel started his car, checked for traffic, and pulled away.

As he did, there was a third car just up the street whose occupants had watched the changing of the guard transpire.

"Did you see that?" McGee asked. "No *Hello Igor how are you? How is Natasha and little Boris?* No *nothing*. That's not how these limo drivers are. They're all tight, they all come from the same part of the world, and they all clump at the same companies. That was way too fast."

Ryan agreed. "You're right," she replied. "He wasn't here for some late-night airport run. They've got all the team members under surveillance. He was watching Tara's building to see if we'd show up."

"Or to follow her if she left," McGee said as he looked at the clock on the dash. "It's your call. What do you want to do?"

She didn't need to think about it. She knew exactly what she wanted to do. "Follow him."

"Roger that," he replied.

After letting two cars pass, McGee pulled into the street and began tailing the black Town Car.

It was the only move they could make at this point; the only move that Phil Durkin wouldn't see coming.

The comparison of the espionage world to chess was quite apt, except that to be the best, your mind had to be trained to see the board in all three dimensions. Of all the former teammates Ryan could have reached out to, Florentino was the most obvious. They had not only anticipated that she would do it, they had been ready for her. Hindsight was always twenty-twenty and she and McGee both now realized what a mistake it had been.

For his part, though, McGee didn't seem to have fully learned the lesson. He wanted to go after another team member, this time being "more careful." As far as Ryan was concerned, being "more careful" was not a clever enough plan. They needed to be more cunning. There was no use trying to grab another gazelle from the back of the herd if there was a predator hiding in the bushes waiting to spring once you made your move.

Ryan's plan was to wait until the predator had left the safety of the bushes and then spring her own trap. Was the man driving the Town Car their predator? She couldn't be one hundred percent sure yet, but her gut told her that they were right on the money, and her gut was seldom, if ever, wrong.

As they followed him, the driver conducted multiple SDRs to ascertain if he had anyone on his tail.

"This guy appears to have had a little bit of training," said McGee.

"Which means we were right to follow him," Ryan replied. "Whatever you do, don't lose him."

They came close to doing just that, three times. The driver of the Town Car was good, but McGee and Ryan were better.

He led them to a neighborhood alive with nightlife in the northwest part of the city, known as Adams Morgan. After circling the block, he parked illegally on Eighteenth Street near a twenty-four-hour restaurant called "the DINER" and left his vehicle with its flashers on.

"What's he up to now?" McGee asked as he eased the Mustang into a no-parking zone at the end of the block. "He can't be here for the coffee."

Ryan turned in her seat and watched out the rear window. "Why not?"

"Because I've eaten here before. The coffee's good, but it's not worth driving halfway across town and risking a parking ticket over."

By her count, they had passed at least three places where the driver could have gotten coffee and been able to legally park. "Maybe he's getting something to eat."

"Maybe. Or maybe there's another reason he left his surveillance post and had to hightail it over here."

A few minutes later, the man reemerged with a Styrofoam cup and climbed back in his Town Car.

"I call bullshit," said McGee.

"You can call it whatever you want," Ryan stated, as she continued to watch him, "but get ready because he's going to pull a U-turn."

"Where's he going now?" he asked as he checked the approaching traffic and tried to figure out how he was going to execute the same maneuver without the driver of the Town Car seeing him.

"I don't know, but something tells me he didn't know either until he went into that diner."

Samuel placed his hot tea in a cup holder before gauging the traffic and executing his U-turn. No sooner had he done so than his cell phone rang.

"Samuel speaking," he said after activating the call.

"You retrieved the envelope?" the voice on the other side asked.

"I did."

"You read the contents?"

"I did."

"I understand there are personal reasons why this assignment could be problematic," the voice said. "But you are not going to allow any personal reasons to make this assignment problematic. Is that correct?"

"That is correct," replied Samuel. He had removed the envelope from its hiding place in the bathroom, read, and then memorized its contents. All of it was printed on a water-soluble paper, which he destroyed by dropping it in a toilet and flushing.

The target was indeed known to him. They had a history together. But that history would not stop him from carrying out his assignment. His job was to act, not to ask questions. This would be like any other assignment. A job was just that, a job.

Once the call was finished, he placed his cell phone down on the seat and picked back up his tea. Peeling back the plastic lid, he blew into the cup and gauged the temperature by how much steam rose from the surface. It was much too hot to drink now, but by the time he got to Bill Wise's house, it should be just about perfect.

CHAPTER 45

Samuel did an inconspicuous drive-by of Bill Wise's property. It was an older building that appeared to have been a warehouse at some point. This was both good and bad.

It was good in that Wise didn't have neighbors right on top of him that would see or hear things, but it was bad in that commercial buildings presented their own special challenges for surreptitious entry.

Whenever possible, Samuel liked to surveil his own targets. Tonight, though, this wasn't possible. The job needed to be taken care of right away.

The building had a front entrance, a side roll-up garage door, and an alley entrance. The alley looked like it was going to be his best bet. Getting in wouldn't be a problem, as long as Wise cooperated.

Samuel noted that Wise had a security system. That was going to need to be turned off. He felt confident he could get the man to do that for him. With a plan beginning to form in his mind, he set off in search of the items he would need to accomplish his mission. Forty-five minutes later, everything was ready to launch.

• • •

When the weather was nice, Bill Wise liked to sleep with his skylights vented. Staggered sensors were one of the easiest and smartest inventions alarm companies had ever come up with. The breeze was free to come in, but if anyone tried to raise the skylight beyond where it was right now, the alarm immediately sounded.

Living in the city, he'd learned to sleep through a lot. Helicopters, emergency vehicles, rap music thumping out of passing cars, none of it bothered him. He knew physiologically that all of those sound waves were penetrating his ear canals. For its part, his brain didn't process any of those things as a threat, and therefore allowed him to continue sleeping. The sound of a breaking bottle right outside, though, was something different.

While you could walk down any street on any given day and see shards of broken glass, it was rare for most people to ever hear bottles being broken. That sound normally meant alcohol had been consumed in excess. It also meant that violence to persons or property might be imminent. Wise's brain passed along the message: *Bottle broken. Outside. Close.*

He went from being fully asleep to fully awake in a fraction of a second. As he lay in bed, eyes open, he wasn't waiting for confirmation. He knew what he had heard. He was attempting to gather additional information. *Had the bottle been thrown out of a car? Had it come from the front of the building, or in the alley? Had the person or persons moved on?*

Almost instantly, he had his answer as another bottle broke and voices were raised. There was at least one adult male, in front, and he was arguing with someone else. Once the neighborhood was fully gentrified and real estate prices went even higher, Wise was going to make a fortune from selling his property. Until then, he had to put up with crap like this.

Grabbing the remote, he flipped on his TV and clicked over to his security camera feeds. He was greeted by the sight of two local crackheads, one male and one female, engaged in urban couple's counseling only a few feet in front of his building. He watched as the woman reached into the plastic bag at her feet, pulled out a third bottle, and launched it at the man. As it sailed past its intended target and shattered against the front door, Wise had had enough. It was time for the crackheads to pack it in and move their party someplace else.

He quickly pulled on jeans and a T-shirt and slipped his large feet into a pair of boots. After tucking the Beretta from the nightstand in his waistband, he grabbed his SureFire flashlight and headed for the front door.

From a closet off the reception area, he retrieved an aluminum baseball bat and deactivated the alarm system. He left the lights off so as not to silhouette himself when he opened the front door. By the time he got it unlocked, two more bottles had smashed against the front of the building and Bill Wise was fit to be tied.

"What the fuck's wrong with you?" he roared, as he threw the door open and stepped outside.

"This ain't none of your damn business!" the woman yelled as she fished in her bag for another bottle.

"Like hell it isn't. There's broken glass all over my fucking property."

"She's crazy, man," the male crackhead replied as he tried to hide behind Wise.

"Whoa, whoa, whoa," Wise replied, extending the bat like a traffic control arm at a border crossing. "You stay right in front of me where I can keep my eye on you."

"You don't want to mind your own business?" the woman challenged. "Then you gonna get some pain, too!"

Wise thought about pulling his Beretta, but instead whipped out his SureFire and aimed the bright beam in the woman's eyes. "Put that bottle down right now," he ordered.

"Fuck you!"

"Put it down, or you're both going to jail. Do it now."

"You heard the man," the male crackhead said. "Put the damn bottle down."

"You zip it," Wise commanded. "I'm the one giving orders."

"Whatever you say."

"Last chance," Wise said to the woman. "Put the bottle down, *right* now."

Slowly, the woman lowered the bottle and set it on the ground. Wise released the tailcap switch on his flashlight and the beam extinguished.

"Man, I can't see shit now. I oughtta sue your ass for giving me blindness," she spat.

"Yeah, I *gave* you blindness," Wise replied. "And the next thing I'm going to *give* you is a taste of old school. I'm getting a broom and a dustpan and then you two are going to sweep up all of this glass."

"I ain't sweeping up shit."

"You bet your ass you're sweeping, honey," Wise replied. "If you don't, I'm having you two arrested. I know you live in the neighborhood and I'm guessing several of my cop friends know who you are. The choice is up to you."

The woman relented. She exhaled a drawn-out and dejected "Shit."

Wise shook his head. Careful not to turn his back on the pair, he retreated inside for a broom, a dustpan, and a small garbage can. Stepping outside, he half expected them to be gone, but they were still there and had even begun to argue again.

"Pipe down," he barked. "You two lovebirds can coo all you want once this is all cleaned up and you've flown off someplace else."

As they were going to be cleaning up around his entrance, the last thing Wise wanted was for them to be able to have a clear look inside. Not that his foyer area was all that fancy, but the less these two pillars of the community knew about his domicile, the better, and so he closed the door behind him.

Wise stood on the sidewalk and watched. It was pathetic. You'd have thought neither had ever handled a broom or a dustpan before. They were completely useless. He let it go on for about five minutes before finally throwing in the towel. They were so drug- or alcohol-addled that they could barely stand up straight, much less bend over to sweep and pick up broken glass. At some point, one of them was going to get hurt and that wasn't something he wanted.

"That's enough," he said, taking the broom and dustpan away from them. "Go on. Get out of here. Get lost."

Wise watched as they looked at each other, then looked at him and began to walk away. The woman stopped to pick up her plastic bag until

Wise shook his head and clucked his tongue. It was bad enough they had woken him up. The least he could do was make sure they didn't roust anyone else in the neighborhood.

The one-man community watch strikes again. He half laughed and half sighed as he picked up the woman's bag, dropped it in the trash can, and then made quick work of the broken glass.

He had no idea whether being forced to clean up some of the mess would have any impact on the pair. It likely wouldn't, but Wise felt he had done the right thing. Too many people didn't stand up for what was right anymore.

Picking up the trash can, he stepped back inside and set it down along with the broom, the bat, and the dustpan.

He sensed the man's presence just before the figure stepped from the darkness and with his gun pointed right at him said, "Good evening, Dr. Wise."

Wise knew better than to go for his Beretta. He'd be dead before he could pull it from his waistband. Instead he calmly and politely replied, "It's good to see you again, Samuel."

CHAPTER 46

"All the way down to my shorts? Seriously?" Wise asked after he had carefully, albeit reluctantly, already surrendered his firearm, as well as his flashlight.

"Please see it as a token of my respect," Samuel replied as he stood still partially concealed and a safe distance away.

"If you intend to show me proper respect, Samuel, why don't you tell me why you are here."

"We'll have plenty of time to talk, Dr. Wise. Right now, I'd appreciate your cooperation."

Wise did as his captor asked. After removing his boots, jeans, and T-shirt, he did a 360-degree turn for Samuel with his hands above his head. The hit man then had him face away from him, sweep his arms behind him like a sandpiper with his palms up. Samuel told him to look up at the ceiling as he bent over at the waist. He instructed him to spread his legs so far apart that Wise was forced up onto the balls of his feet and having trouble keeping his balance. That was when Samuel struck.

The first handcuff was on him so fast and was converted into a steel wristlock so quickly, that even if Wise had wanted to react, he couldn't have. The pain was exquisite. Samuel delivered so much precise and practiced pressure that Wise's knees simply buckled and he dropped to the ground. Even the most veteran of street cops would have been blown away with how rapidly Samuel had subdued his prisoner and applied the handcuffs.

Wise was told which knee to bend and then on the count of three, used momentum to bring him back up to standing. An amateur would have simply grabbed him by the chain of the cuffs and lifted, risking tearing the prisoner's shoulders out. Samuel was no amateur.

He took great care in guiding Wise back to the building's living area. He knew all too well that a man like Wise would have all sorts of weapons hidden all around. Near the machinist's bay where Wise worked on his cars and motorcycles, Samuel had placed a chair. He asked Wise to sit there now. Wise complied.

"Now we talk?"

Samuel nodded. "Yes, doctor. Now we talk."

"I assume that you have a list of specific questions you would like answered?"

"I do."

Wise pursed his lips. "And what will I get in return?"

"Out of respect and professional courtesy," he said, unrolling a suede tool bag with multiple stainless steel instruments and a handful of zip ties that had been rubber-banded together, "I will not cause you any pain."

"That is very thoughtful, Samuel. Pain is something neither of us likes, is it?"

"No, doctor. It is not."

"Will I be free to go afterward?" Wise asked.

The CIA operative shook his head as he pulled the rubber band from around the zip ties. "I'm sorry."

"So am I."

Samuel stepped forward and in a move that belied his thick, lumbering appearance, grabbed a handful of Wise's hair and snapped his head backward, banging it against the back of the chair.

It was a move meant to stun and disorient, which was exactly what it did. Before Wise knew what had happened, Samuel had attached his handcuffs to the chair with several of the zip ties. His legs would be next.

Samuel came around front and looked at Wise. The man's eyelids fluttered like a pair of shades that had just been drawn too tight and his head lolled to one side. Grabbing his left ankle, he slammed it up against the left leg of the chair and had just gotten the first zip tie halfway around both when a shot rang out and piercing and painful darkness overtook him.

For a moment, he had no idea what had happened. Then the excruciating pain came rushing in and he realized that Wise had head-butted him. Then, still cuffed to the chair, he had run.

Samuel reached up and touched the bridge of his nose. It was broken and bleeding. "I understand why you had to do that, Dr. Wise," he called out as he stood and pulled his pistol. "I even forgive you for it, as I hope you will forgive me for what I have to do."

The CIA operative looked around as his mind whirled through multiple calculations. It was a large space, but not so large that a man Wise's size could disappear, especially not when attached to a chair. He would try to find concealment first and then he would avail himself of a weapon. That was, of course, only if he could free his hands.

Samuel settled on Wise's library and its rows of metal bookcases. They provided the closest and most logical place to hide. He approached the stacks with caution, pausing every couple of steps to listen. All he needed was the squeak of the chair beneath Wise's weight or the scrape of its legs on the floor to give the man away. *Step. Step. Pause. Step. Step. Pause.* Suddenly, he heard something else.

At the end of the next aisle, a book had been knocked from its place and lay on the floor. He had him now.

Samuel rushed along the row of books and no sooner had he made it to the halfway point than he heard the groan of metal on metal and a wall of books began to rain down on him. *Wise was trying to tip the bookcase over from the other side and crush him!*

The bald-headed man ran for all he was worth as the tidal wave of books poured over him. With the case only centimeters from his head, he dove to get out of the way.

He landed hard, his chin slamming into the ground and his pistol clattering out of his hand. He saw stars once more, but he also saw something else, *Wise*.

The man was doing everything he could to break the chair and free himself. Their eyes locked and then both men's gaze snapped to the gun. Wise was closer and though he was still attached to the chair, it had splintered and he was close to being free.

Samuel pushed himself up to standing and put his head down, his shoulder forward, and ran for all he was worth. This wasn't about getting to the gun first; this was about stopping Wise from getting to it at all.

The CIA operative built up such an amazing head of steam that when he collided with Wise, it was like a locomotive hitting a fruit truck stalled at the crossing.

As the thick-necked bull of a man barreled into him, Wise's chair shattered and he was sent tumbling backward. His head cracked against the floor and his vision dimmed. The pain was off the charts and he teetered on the verge of unconsciousness. He couldn't allow himself to slip into that dark, cold void. He had to fight. He wouldn't get another chance.

Flipping onto his left side, he planned to lash out with a kick, either to push the gun farther away or to incapacitate his attacker. As he looked up, though, he saw he was too late. Samuel had already retrieved the weapon. He had also wisely taken two steps back, once he was able to stand. He was too far away for Wise to make contact. He had had one chance and he had blown it. Samuel was back in control.

Neither man spoke. Both stood or lay where they were catching their breaths and trying to overcome the pain of their injuries. Wise could see that he had opened up a pretty good gash at the top of Samuel's nose. It was going to require stitches. At least there was that.

Out of habit, Wise started analyzing his own injuries and then almost laughed at the absurdity of it all. He wasn't going to live to see another hour, much less anyone who could give him medical attention.

Samuel, who must have sensed something in his expression, said, "What's so funny?"

Just then a man stepped from behind Samuel, pressed a Taser against his jugular, and said, "This."

CHAPTER 47

Harvath and the Old Man spoke for more than two hours. He had gone through everything that had happened since he had arrived in Boston and then the Old Man had asked him to repeat it, twice. He asked question after question and expected Harvath to drill down to even the minutest details.

When they were done talking, Harvath not only needed aspirin, he also needed a drink, and he helped himself to a glass, some ice, and two bottles of bourbon from the minibar.

Even that, though, wasn't enough to help him unwind. He thought about turning on the TV, but he knew it would only keep him up for hours. He also knew that pouring another drink wasn't the right path. He might get a couple of hours of sleep, but it wouldn't be quality sleep. Instead, he fished out one of the books Bill Wise had given to him and which he had tossed in his overnight bag on the way out of his house yesterday.

The reading did the trick and he soon found his eyes growing heavy. As soon as he couldn't keep them open any longer, he tossed the book aside, turned out the light, and fell asleep.

Much like the night before, he felt like he had just drifted off when his cell phone rang. He snatched his Kobold off the nightstand and looked at the time. It was just after 3 A.M.

It was Cordero. "The killer struck again," she said.

"Wait. What?" Harvath replied, as he tried to shake off the cobwebs. "Where? Boston?"

"North End. Close to where we ate dinner. I'm already in the car. Be downstairs in fifteen minutes."

Harvath was downstairs in ten and Cordero showed up a minute and a half later.

"Tell me what happened," he said as he got into the car and Cordero sped away from the hotel.

"Apparently, another elaborate scene like the Liberty Tree Building."

"Who was it?"

"We don't have an ID on the victim yet," said Cordero as she weaved through the sparse traffic, her lights blazing and Klaxon blaring. "They're saying it could take a while."

"Why?"

"A lot of his flesh is missing. It sounds like he was boiled to death."

"Boiled to death?" Harvath replied.

"That's what Sal said. He told me I'd see for myself once I got there."

"Who found him?"

"Fire department, apparently. The killer used a timer of some sort to start a controlled fire with lots of smoke. It didn't do any real damage, but it scared a lot of folks. The guy lit a tire in the bathtub or something."

If you want to get someone's attention, that is the way to do it. Tires burned with thick, acrid black smoke. Harvath had seen more than his share of tire fires across third-world countries. It was a smell you never forgot and one he absolutely hated.

"The ME is going to need dental records from the two males on your missing persons list," said Cordero.

"Being boiled to death is pretty unusual, so is a timed tire fire, but how can you be sure this is our killer?"

"Because," she replied as she swerved and narrowly missed a car that had slammed on its brakes, rather than pulling over to allow her to pass, "the killer left a note, along with a picture."

"Of a skull and bones with the crown floating above."

"Yup."

"Do you know anything about the address we're going to? Any reason why it might be significant?"

Cordero shook her head. "No. It's not one of the ones we passed last night, I know that."

"Do you know anything about the area at all?"

"It's near the intersection of Fleet Street and Garden Court. I think that's the neighborhood where JFK's mother was born or grew up or something."

Or something . . . If that was the case, it didn't make any sense. What would Rose Kennedy have to do with a vendetta against the Fed? And why would the killer switch tactics like that all of a sudden? It had to be something else.

When they arrived, narrow Garden Court was blocked off at each end by police cruisers and all of the buildings up and down the street were awash in the glow of emergency vehicle lights.

"We'll end up getting blocked in if I try to get any closer," Cordero said. "Let's park here."

Harvath agreed and after parking her car, they got out to walk the rest of the way.

"Did you get any sleep?" he asked as they made their way to the scene.

"A little. How about you?"

"Not nearly enough, but I'll be okay."

"We'll get coffee after," she promised.

Because it was a one-way street with parking only on one side, most of the responding vehicles had parked on the west side, many of them all the way up on the sidewalks so as not to block through traffic for the fire trucks.

Harvath and Cordero walked on the opposite side. As they drew parallel with their destination, Harvath noticed a plastic plaque on the building next to Cordero.

"You were right," he said. "Look."

The female detective skimmed the historical marker. "How about that? I know some Boston history after all. Four Garden Court Street. Home of John J. 'Honey Fitz' Fitzgerald, Boston mayor, and birthplace of daughter Rose Fitzgerald, mother of American president John F. Kennedy."

As they slipped between two parked cars and around a fire truck idling in the middle of the street, Harvath tried to process what the Kennedy connection could be.

That train of thought, though, came to an immediate halt when they arrived in front of 5 Garden Court Street, which had an even more dramatic plaque, this one from weathered bronze, announcing the building's, or more appropriately the site's, historical significance.

"Here stood the mansion of Governor Thomas Hutchinson," Harvath read aloud as he typed the man's name into the web browser on his phone.

"Who was he?" Cordero asked.

"Apparently, one of Boston's most hated citizens. Brother-in-law to Andrew Oliver, the man they hung in effigy from the Liberty Tree. Hutchinson was also the last royal governor of Massachusetts before the Revolutionary War. It says here that Sam Adams couldn't stand him. For many of the colonists, Hutchinson represented everything that that they believed was wrong with Britain. He was greedy, arrogant, and a pretty big snob. A couple weeks after the Liberty Tree incident, angry Bostonians looted and tore Hutchinson's house apart."

"Didn't Hutchinson have something to do with the Boston Tea Party?"

Harvath scrolled further down on his screen and nodded. "When the colonists wanted to send a large shipment of tea back to England to protest the tea tax, Hutchinson intervened. When word leaked that he was the secret distributor for the tea, people went berserk. There were citywide protests, which grew in scope and anger until culminating in—"

"The Boston Tea Party."

"Bingo," said Harvath. "He left not long after and died in exile in England."

"So he wasn't killed in Boston? Never boiled to death?"

"No, not according to this," he said, as he slid the phone back into his pocket. "But that doesn't mean there isn't some sort of connection to whatever it is we're about to see."

"Are you ready to go in?" she asked.

Harvath wasn't even near the front door and already he could smell the horrible odor of burnt tire. Taking a last breath of semi-fresh air, he nodded and followed her inside.

CHAPTER 48

The smell of a burnt tire was worse than driving behind a bubbling asphalt truck. The smoke had left black streaks up the front of the building from where it had escaped out the front door and where the firemen had smashed the front windows.

Inside, you could trace the smoke's path along the upper walls and ceiling straight back to the bathroom. Unless there was something terribly interesting he had to see in there, he'd put off ground zero for the tire burning for as long as he could. What he was most interested in was the victim. He followed Cordero into the living room.

Her partner was there waiting, smug as usual and looking fresh as a daisy with his perfect hair, face shaved, and shoes shined. He'd probably gotten a great night's sleep as well.

"Looks like you were wrong about the killer's next stop being Fort Hill," he said.

"Let's not start, Sal," said Cordero. "Okay?"

"I'm just saying, our golden boy here isn't right about everything."

"Why don't you sit down and give your mind a rest, Sal," Harvath said as he brushed past him.

Cordero joined him in the living room. "Can we not do this, please?" she asked quietly.

"Without looking at the body, how do you expect to figure anything out?"

She cut him a look and tilted her head toward her partner in the entry hall. "You know what I'm talking about."

"I'll try," Harvath replied as he approached the gang box. As he got closer, he began to pick up another scent.

Cordero could smell it, too. "What is that?"

"Pine."

"Like Pine-Sol?"

Harvath shook his head as he noticed a couple of stray feathers near the gang box. "Pine tar."

"What is—" she began, but stopped when she looked into the box and saw the horrific state of the body.

Harvath stood next to her and looked at the corpse as well. For several seconds neither said anything. Then, he stated, "Pine tar was used in the colonies to preserve wood on sailing ships and to weatherize rope. It was also used for a form of physically and emotionally painful public humiliation called tarring and feathering."

As seasoned as she was to death and murder, this one was particularly rough to look at. "Do you think he died from the tarring and feathering? Or from having his head shackled to the bottom of the box and having it filled up with pine tar? Feel it," she said, reaching her hand out to touch the metal. "It's still warm."

Harvath didn't need to feel it. He would take her word for it. What he was interested in was the message painted in red on the underside of the lid. In addition to the crossed bones with the skull and crown hovering above was a sentence, which read *How strangely will the Tools of a Tyrant pervert the plain Meaning of Words!* Beneath it were the letters *S.O.L.*

"Any idea what that phrase means?" she asked.

Harvath was unaware of its historical context, but he had a pretty good idea of why it had been chosen by the killer. Bill Wise had mentioned something about how the Fed purposefully obfuscated what they did in order to divert attention. If he had to bet, that was what he'd put his money on. As far as who said it, he had no idea.

"Sam Adams," said Cordero's partner, who had come into the living room to join them. He held out his smartphone and read, "From a letter to John Pitts. January twenty-first, 1776."

She couldn't tell if Harvath was warming up another jibe or not, but she decided to circumvent it and keep the conversation focused. "What do we know about the victim?" she asked.

Harvath had already identified him, but he wasn't about to spill that information to anyone but Cordero. And it would be done in private.

"Right now," replied the male detective, "we don't have anything. He's a John Doe. We'll see what the ME gets prints-wise and if they turn up anything. If there's nothing on file for this guy, we'll have to attempt dental records, and maybe facial reconstruction."

"How about the fire?" asked Harvath. "Any clues there?"

The man shrugged. "Go ask the arson investigators. They're back in the bathroom."

Harvath figured Sal had already gleaned a preliminary report from them and could have easily filled him in, but he had promised Cordero he'd try to go easy on him.

Walking to the bathroom, he stopped just short of the doorway. The lingering odor was terrible.

"What do you guys have?" he asked.

"Who are you?" one of the investigators asked tersely.

"Emily Dickinson," he replied just as tersely, sensing that was about the only thing this guy was going to respect. "Now tell me what you've got."

His partner held up a plastic evidence bag with what looked like a charred and half-melted circuit board. "Pretty simple setup. A timer and an igniter. Left it sitting on top of the tire. Tire was soaked with gasoline or kerosene. Consensus right now is that he wanted to send a smoke signal, not burn the building down."

"Think you'll be able to trace those parts?"

"Maybe, but they look rather basic. Could have come from anywhere. I wouldn't hold my breath if I were you."

That was exactly what Harvath was doing, and he needed some fresh air. Passing through the apartment, he signaled for Cordero to join him.

Outside, he stepped away from the building and took in a couple of deep breaths.

"You all right?" she asked.

"I'm fine. I just hate that smell."

She wrinkled up her nose. "It *is* pretty awful. Why'd you want me to follow you out here?"

"I think I know who the victim is."

"You do? How? A huge part of the poor guy's face was melted off and he's covered in feathers."

"It's Peter Whalen from Chicago," said Harvath. "In the file I have on him, it describes him as being five foot five. The other missing man, Renner, is six foot two. You wouldn't have been able to fit a six foot two man in that box unless you sawed him in half. Make sure to tell the ME to look for scars on the victim's knees once they get all the tar and feathers cleaned off. Whalen was a skier. He'd blown both his knees and had to have them repaired back before the surgery got a lot less invasive. The scars should be pretty obvious."

"I'll let them know."

He took a breath and said, "This means there's only two left now."

Cordero nodded. "Do you think the killer plans to do them both here in Boston?"

Leaning against the side of a police cruiser that had been parked up on the sidewalk, he tried to think. "I honestly don't know," he said.

"Whalen went missing in Chicago, right?"

"Right."

"Well, if the killer brought Whalen here, why not the others?"

It was a good question, except for the fact that all five missing candidates had been grabbed on the same night, which meant there had to have been teams involved. At least one of those teams had brought Peter Whalen from Chicago to Boston. Had the others been brought here, too? *Anything was possible.*

"The remaining two *could* be here," said Harvath. "I suppose."

"You've had one murder in Georgia and two now, unfortunately, in Boston. I'd say just numbers-wise Boston is your best bet."

"So what do you suggest?"

"First, coffee," said Cordero.

"And then what?"

"And then we try to figure out where the killer is keeping the remaining two and get to them before he can kill again."

CHAPTER 49

"Go easy on him," said Wise, as he watched them secure the CIA operative. "You don't have to hurt him."

Bob McGee looked up at the man like he was nuts. "In case you missed what just happened, Mahatma, this guy wasn't here for yoga class. He came to kill you. In fact, he came here to torture you *and then* kill you. Why are you so bent out of shape about how tight I put the cuffs on him?"

"Because I know Samuel, and I want you to treat him with respect."

McGee shook his head. "This is a big boy. We're trussing him up tight. After that you can show him all the respect you want. Fair enough?"

Wise knew there was no point in arguing. In fact, he wanted McGee to restrain Samuel as tightly as possible. If he didn't, and the man got loose, they'd all be in trouble. What's more, by petitioning for kind treatment, Wise was already conditioning Samuel for interrogation. The gruffer and more inconsiderate of Samuel that McGee was, the more it played into Wise's plan.

"There," said McGee, as he stood back and admired his handiwork. "This fella ain't going anywhere anytime soon, are you?"

Samuel did not reply.

Wise looked at Ryan and said, "You can lower your weapon now."

Ryan looked at McGee, who nodded, at which point she aimed the muzzle of her weapon down, but didn't put it away.

Samuel had been secured to a support column and was facing away from the living area. Wise brought over a pair of shooting muffs.

Showing them to Samuel, he said, "This is only going to be for a few minutes while we discuss what we're going to do. May I?"

Samuel nodded and Wise slipped the muffs over the man's large head. They almost didn't fit. When he had them in place, he laid his hand on Samuel's shoulder for a moment and then walked away to join the others.

They gathered on the other side of the glass display case with the sewing machines and the typewriters. It was not only an additional sound barrier; it also allowed them to keep Samuel in their sight. McGee was the first one to speak.

"Why are you so deferential to that guy? Do you have any idea who he is? What he does?"

"Of course I do. I trained him."

"Wait. What?"

"Maybe *trained* is the wrong word," said Wise. "Samuel was under my tutelage for a time."

McGee looked at Ryan. "I told you I knew who this guy was." Looking back at Wise he stated, "You're that guy from the Agency they called Dr. Kill. Some of our people in the Special Activities Division worked with you on a couple of your projects."

"Can we back up for a second? Can you please better explain who you both are and what you're doing here?"

In the chaos of taking down Samuel, getting him secure, and helping a dazed Bill Wise to his feet, there hadn't been time for introductions. Ryan stepped forward and did so now.

It was a bit of an intellectual standoff. Ryan and McGee wanted more information about why Wise had been made a target, while Wise felt he was owed the same explanation from Ryan and McGee. "You are in my house" battled against "If it wasn't for us, he would have killed you." In the end, it was Wise who finally conceded. To his credit, though, he didn't give them everything. A good operative always kept a little bit in reserve. Just in case.

"I've heard of Swim Club," said McGee. "Past tense, though. I thought it had been shut down."

"Seems like there's been a lot of that going on at Langley," Ryan stated.

That piqued Wise's interest and he raised his eyebrows in response, but McGee had a couple more questions first.

"So Samuel passed from your program into Swim Club?"

"That's my assumption. I think he'll tell me if I ask."

"Why?"

"Because I know him and he sees himself as a good man. Honor is important to him."

McGee shook his head. "A psychopath with honor. That's a first for me."

"Samuel may possess a certain moral flexibility, but he is not a psychopathic personality. He's actually quite gentle most of the time. In fact that's why they took to calling him 'the Lamb.'"

"That's the Lamb? Samuel? He's *that* Lamb?"

"You've heard of him?" asked Ryan.

"Yeah, I've heard of him. I'd never met him, but some of our people have used him. The guy's a legend and not in a good way. In a Hannibal Lecter sort of way."

"He eats people?"

"No, he's just a stone-cold killer," said McGee. "Somebody you send in to do very difficult or very disagreeable wet work. There was another guy we used whose nickname was the Axe Murderer and there were things even he wouldn't do. The Lamb, though, came through every time. No matter what."

"So imagine," said Wise, "how interested I must be to find out why you followed Samuel here."

The ball was now in their court and Ryan did the talking. While she was generous with her information, she wasn't completely generous. Like Wise, she understood that it was smart to keep a little bit in reserve.

She walked him through everything, beginning with her surprise meeting with a foreign intelligence official all the way up to how they had found Samuel and decided to follow him when he engaged in a sudden shift change.

When she was done, Wise had almost the same question for her that she had asked upon her rescue by McGee. "What took you so long to step in? Why didn't you intervene sooner?"

"We were trying to pick the right moment," Ryan replied.

"*She* was trying to pick the right moment," McGee offered. "I was trying to decide which of you I was going to shoot."

"And I assume you wanted to hear some of my interrogation," said Wise.

"That, too."

"Speaking of which," interjected Ryan. "I'd like to take a crack at Samuel. I have a lot of questions I want answered."

"It sounds like we both do."

McGee cleared his throat. "Make that three."

Wise nodded. "You'll find Samuel much different than what you are used to. He's highly intelligent, and if he can play you, he will. He also appreciates being treated with courtesy. Respect is a significant issue with him. He only has one true loyalty and it trumps anything at the Agency, so we should attempt to leverage that to our advantage."

"Why don't I take second chair and let you run the show," said Ryan.

"I think that would be best. If we handle this properly, it can be quick and smooth."

"And if we don't handle it properly?" asked McGee.

"Then you may wish you had your friend the Axe Murderer here instead."

CHAPTER 50

"I'm sorry if wearing these was uncomfortable at all, Samuel," Wise said as he removed the shooting muffs from the man's head and sat across from him. He was relaxed and spoke calmly, almost soothingly.

"It wasn't uncomfortable, Dr. Wise, but thank you for saying so."

"Samuel, do you recognize this gentleman and this lady?" he asked, gesturing to Ryan and McGee.

"Yes, doctor. The lady is Ms. Lydia Ryan and the gentleman is Mr. Robert McGee. Both are employees of the Central Intelligence Agency."

"As are you, correct?"

"No, sir."

"Excuse me?"

"It is not correct that I work for the Central Intelligence Agency."

Wise looked at him for a moment and then rephrased. "You work for a black program funded by the Central Intelligence Agency, which allows them to disavow you if you are caught or captured."

"That is correct."

"Samuel, do you recognize the position you are now in?"

"I have been restrained by you, Dr. Wise—a former CIA employee, as well as Ms. Ryan and Mr. McGee—current CIA employees."

"Correct. And do you recognize that what happens to you going forward will be entirely based upon the degree to which you cooperate with us?"

"I have been cooperative," Samuel said.

Wise got back to his original question. "Please tell me how it is that you were able to identify Ms. Ryan and Mr. McGee to me."

"They were both targets I was tasked with terminating."

"And who gave you that tasking?"

The man was silent and didn't respond.

"Samuel?" Wise prodded. "That is a direct question and I expect an answer, please."

The man remained quiet.

"Samuel, this is very serious, and it goes far beyond you targeting fellow agents, or even coming after me."

Nothing.

Wise removed his phone. "I'm sorry to have to do this."

The bald-headed man was suddenly agitated. "Who are you calling, Dr. Wise?"

"You know who I'm calling, Samuel."

"Dr. Wise, I strongly recommend you stop. *Now*."

"I'm sorry, Samuel. This is beyond my control."

"Stop!" he shouted, but as quickly as he had lost his temper, he brought it back under control. "Please hang up the phone, Dr. Wise."

Wise looked at him as he put down the phone. "Your sister still doesn't know, does she?"

Samuel's face reddened, though whether from anger or shame, it was not immediately clear.

Wise looked at Ryan and McGee. "Samuel was raised by his older sister, who nurtured and protected him. She saw to his spiritual and moral upbringing as well. She explained away and helped hide some of his more antisocial behavior until it couldn't be hidden anymore.

"Samuel and I met shortly after I arrived at the Agency. Isn't that true, Samuel?"

"Yes, doctor."

"But eventually, they asked you to leave my program and be part of another. Isn't that correct?"

"Yes."

"It had an interesting, almost benign-sounding name. Do you recall what it was?"

Samuel went mute.

Wise pretended to rack his brain. Finally, he said, "I remember now. Swim Club. That's what they called it. That's the group you were asked to join. The group your sister knows nothing about."

Silence.

"She sacrificed so much to raise you, to protect you. She gave up any hope of a life of her own. But she believes you turned out to be a successful man. You take care of her now that she's had her stroke. You, the—what was it she believed you did for a living? It was something that sounded boring but allowed you to travel."

"I facilitate mining contracts."

Wise snapped his fingers. "That was it. She's very proud of you, isn't she? You are the only family each of you has. If she knew what you really did for a living, she would be devastated, wouldn't she? She would be incredibly disappointed not only in you, but in herself for allowing you to become what you have become. Do you think she would see you as a monster, Samuel?"

The man's face reddened again. He was angry. "Dr. Wise, please stop speaking about my sister. She has nothing to do with this."

"I think you're wrong, Samuel. She has everything to do with this. She raised you. She lied and covered up for you. She knows what you are capable of. She knows she didn't get you the treatment you should have had a long, long time ago. Why do you think that is? Did she think you would get better? Or had she covered up so many unspeakable things that she was tainted as well, an accomplice? Did you poison her chances at happiness, Samuel, her chances for a normal life? Is that what caused her stroke, holding all of those unspeakable things inside until something finally snapped in her as well?"

The man leaned forward, every ropy fiber in his wide, muscular torso straining as the steel handcuffs dug into his wrists. "If you do not stop, Dr. Wise . . ." he threatened, his voice trailing off.

"If I don't stop, what, Samuel? You'll *retire* me?"

Samuel's eyes snapped up to meet his and there was a flash of evil. He was completely changed, consumed with rage. A battle had been kicked off inside him and he was quickly losing control. Wise could read it in his face and over every square inch of his taut, coiled body, waiting to spring.

"It would hurt your sister to know what you do. It would cause her great pain, wouldn't it?"

The man's eyes shifted to the floor.

"Like it or not, Samuel, she is a factor in this equation. But how she factors depends on you. *Everything* depends on you."

When his body went almost limp and tears began to form at the corners of his eyes, Wise put his hand back on the man's shoulder to comfort him. "It's going to be okay," he said, and at that moment he knew he was going to get everything he needed out of the killer known to so many as the Lamb, but whom he knew as a deeply disturbed, very sick man named Samuel who was fighting to keep a spark of decency alive within the hurricane of his severely tortured soul.

CHAPTER 51

It was going to be a long day and Harvath had no intention of fueling it with police coffee, so Cordero took him to Caffé Vittoria on Hanover Street. Billed as the first Italian café in Boston, they were not yet open at this early hour, but there were signs of life and Cordero told him not to worry. She tapped on the glass with her car key and caught the attention of an older man setting up inside.

He smiled when he saw her and came over, unlocked the door, and let them in. "The lovely Lara. So nice to see you," he said as he welcomed them in.

"*The lovely Lara?*" Harvath repeated quietly.

"I've been here once or twice before."

"Okay," the man said as he stepped behind the counter, "what can I do for you, officers?"

"He's not an off—" Cordero began, but then decided to let it go. "What do you have that's hot and ready to go?"

With its tin ceiling, vintage espresso machines, antique grinders, and old black-and-white photographs, it was one of the most charming cafés

Harvath had ever visited. If the character and ambiance were any indication, he was in for some pretty good coffee.

"Okay if I order for us?" Cordero asked.

Harvath nodded, and she placed the order. While the man behind the
counter worked he asked about what had happened a couple of blocks
away over on Garden Court. To her credit, she played it vague while still
making the man feel like he had an inside connection with an important
Boston homicide detective.

When the coffee was ready and paid for, the man told her to wait a
minute and he slipped several pastries into a paper bag and handed them
to her.

"You don't have to do that," she said.

"For your partner."

Harvath began to put his hands up to say no thank you, but the man
behind the counter said, "Your other partner. The Italiano."

"You mean Sal," Cordero said with a smile.

"He only eats small children," Harvath interjected.

The female detective shook her head and removed a ten-dollar bill.
"I'm sure he'll appreciate these. How much do I owe you?"

"Nothing. Free. Free," the man said.

"You were sweet to let us in early. Thank you, but I don't need a discount, or anything for free. That's not how we do things."

The man didn't know how to respond. Finally, he said, "Okay, eight
dollars."

Cordero handed him the ten and told him to keep the rest as a tip.
He thanked her and showed them outside, then locked the door behind
them and got back to setting up for the day.

"Thanks for the coffee," Harvath said.

"You're welcome."

"I'm a little bit disappointed, though."

"You haven't even tried the coffee yet."

He smiled at her. "Yesterday, you took me for breakfast where
the Boston Strangler killed his last victim, and today it's just a coffee
bar."

"*Just* a coffee bar," she replied, shaking her head. "Shows what you know about Boston history, Mr. Expert. Trust me, you don't want to know about this one."

"I knew it," said Harvath as he peeled the lid off his to-go cup and blew on his coffee. "You homicide cops can't help yourselves. Like moths to a flame."

"I'm telling you, we're here for the coffee. Trust me."

"That's the second time you've asked me to trust you. Why?"

"Because there is a story attached to this building and it's horrible."

"I'm a big boy," he said, turning around to study the building's brick façade. "What's the story?"

"Just remember," she said, relenting. "You asked."

"I take full responsibility."

"Okay. Do you know what a baby farm is?"

He'd heard of a *baby factory* before, but something told him this was different. "No," he replied. "I don't think I know what that is. What are we talking about?"

"Back in the 1800s, women who got pregnant out of wedlock and who wanted to avoid the social stigma that came along with it would often place their infants in what was pejoratively called a baby farm. These baby farms could provide wet nurses and would take the child off the mother's hands for a limited time or 'adopt' the child altogether if the price was right. The understanding was that the child would be cared for."

"I'm guessing that wasn't the case in this instance."

"There was a notorious baby farm right here in the late 1800s. The woman who ran it was named Mrs. Elwood and she abused many of the children quite severely and even murdered several of them."

Harvath grimaced. The idea of babies being given up by their mothers was bad enough, but to think they were abused and even killed at the hands of people entrusted with their care turned his stomach. There was nothing lower in his book than someone who abused children or animals.

"The café's owners," she continued, "opened a cigar bar in the basement that everyone said was haunted. They brought in some paranormal researchers who found a disgusting syringe from the 1870s that one of the ghosts allegedly drew their attention to. Once the syringe was taken out of the building, the haunting stopped."

"Do you believe in all that stuff?" Harvath asked, taking a sip of his coffee.

"Spirits? Ghosts? I don't know. I've seen some absolutely horrific crime scenes in my time, the last two days included. I suppose I can understand why some souls are unable to cross over. I'd like to think that if I got murdered, I'd be pissed-off enough to stay around until the case got solved. But I'm stubborn like that. What about you?"

"If anyone tried to murder me, it wouldn't be unsolved because I'd take them with me."

"Tough guy, huh?" she said.

"No," he replied. "Just stubborn like that. You know."

Cordero smiled, and suggested that they get going. As they walked, she said, "It all makes me wonder."

"Wonder what?"

"What people will say a hundred years from now when they pass the murder scenes we're working."

It was a good question. "Let's hope they say it was a tough case, but you and I figured it out as quickly as we could and we stopped anyone else from being killed."

"Agreed," she said as they reached her car and she looked at her watch. "Let me tell you what I think we need to do."

CHAPTER 52

"Damn right I'm not happy!" Reed Carlton shouted into the phone at Harvath. "I don't care what kind of contacts Monroe Lewis and the Federal Reserve have. Part of what they are paying us for is to be their eyes and ears in this case. They should have heard about this from me and I should have heard it right away from you. You were at the scene before the FBI, for Chrissake."

"Sir, let me—" Harvath attempted, but he was cut off.

"Be quiet and listen to me. I don't care if it's three in the morning, three in the afternoon, midnight, twilight, firelight, whatever frigging time it is! If there's a development in a case we're working on, especially a murder, I expect you to call me. Whether or not you're going to wake me up should never factor into it. Do you understand?"

The boss was fired up and Harvath knew better than to respond in any fashion other than completely professional. "Yes, sir," he said. "It's my fault. It won't happen again."

Harvath's phone had rung just as Cordero was dropping him back at his hotel. He had planned to shower and change while she went home to pick up her son and drop him off at day care. They were going to meet back at her office. In between then, Harvath was going to call the Old Man and give him an update, but apparently Monroe Lewis had heard from the FBI first.

There wasn't much Harvath could add to what the Old Man had been told, only his belief that the victim was Peter Whalen, the missing Fed chair candidate from Chicago.

The information didn't make the Old Man happy. Not that Harvath had expected it to. He wasn't happy, either. Quite the contrary. They had been hired to try to help save four people and half of them were now dead.

"So besides another dinner and maybe some dancing with this female detective you're playing footsy with," the Old Man stated, "do you have any plans to actually solve this case, or should I expect to read about it when you get around to sending me a postcard?"

Carlton was one of the most brilliant people Harvath knew, but he could be a real curmudgeon when he was pissed-off. In those instances it was a free-fire zone for his acerbic tongue. The only thing he could do was bite his own tongue and wait for the storm to pass.

"The Bureau guys at the scene are proceeding on the assumption that the remaining two missing Fed candidates are here in Boston," said Harvath. "And we agree."

"We?"

"Detective Cordero and I."

"So what are they planning on doing about it?"

"They're going to go public with the names and photos of the last two missing persons. Their hope is that maybe somebody in Boston has seen something and will provide actionable intelligence."

"Are they going to publicize the Fed connection as well?"

"No," Harvath replied. "It sounds like they're going to do a straight missing persons, believed to be in the Boston area approach."

"That should keep it out of the national media for a bit longer," said Carlton. "But not much."

"Lewis and the Fed have been on borrowed time anyway. The only reason all the missing persons haven't been linked together is that nobody really knows who they are."

"And the newest murder?"

"Boston PD has the scene locked down pretty tight. Because of the smoke and the fire trucks, they're going to allow people to assume there was a fire. They're not taking the body out in a body bag. They're going to drain the gang box and transport it with the corpse down to the ME's office."

"How are they planning on putting the word out regarding the last two missing candidates?"

"If they hustle, they can get it included in the morning police roll call briefings. All the detectives and all the patrol officers will be given the names and photos, along with a brief description and as much of the story as the FBI decides they want put out there. I think they're going to connect it to the other murders."

"Then you can speed up the timetable of the national press getting hold of the story," said the Old Man. "Police departments leak like sieves."

"Hopefully, they'll keep it under wraps."

"What about beyond the PD?"

"Names and photographs of Betsy Mitchell and Jonathan Renner to run on local television news along with the FBI's one-eight-hundred number for tips. The names and photographs are also going to the local papers."

"Better late than never," Carlton said.

"With detectives and patrol officers out there beating the bushes, along with the public keeping their eyes open, we may get lucky."

"I hope it works."

"Me, too," said Harvath. "I'm going to get cleaned up and then get back down to police headquarters. Is there anything else you need?"

"Yeah. The client wants to speak with you."

"Monroe Lewis? What for?"

"He wants an update from the field."

"I just gave you one."

"I know," said the Old Man, "and even though he just spoke with the FBI, he wants to hear from you, too. He asked me for your cell phone number and I told him I'd give it to him after you and I spoke. Keep it short and keep it limited to the facts. Understood?"

"Yes, sir."

CHAPTER 53

The call with Monroe Lewis turned out to be a call not only with Lewis, but also with William Jacobson, the Fed's head of security.

While Lewis wanted Harvath's overall thoughts and impressions of where the case was going and why they hadn't developed any leads, Jacobson grilled Harvath for exacting and excruciatingly specific details. They were getting ready for the media firestorm they knew was on its way.

Finally, Lewis resignedly asked, "There's not going to be any ransom demand, is there?"

"No," Harvath replied. "I don't think there will be. Not unless going public spooks whoever's involved."

Lewis knew the Fed better than anyone else. He had risen to his position by dedicating his life to the organization. He had no family, no significant other. He could be found there nights and weekends. He knew that many saw him as cold and distant. He also knew that when he tried to be more convivial, it often came off as phony. Chairman Sawyer had been the first person to take a deep, personal interest in him. Sawyer had become his mentor and had helped orchestrate his promotion to where he was now. He had confided many things in Lewis, and it had been a particular shock when Sawyer suddenly died. Lewis had been forced to come to grips very quickly with what was important not only for the Fed, but also for his own career. None of it was easy, and the course they were charting was fraught with peril.

"You think it's possible to spook these people?" asked Jacobson. "After what they've done?"

"I don't know."

"What do you think the odds are of catching them?"

"I have to be honest with you," said Harvath, knowing full well the Old Man would hate him for saying this, "I don't think the odds are very good. Not unless we catch some sort of a break. But that's exactly what you hope for in a case like this."

"You're right," said Lewis. "We have to remain positive. We've got to do everything we can to solve this thing."

"As far as we know, the last two are still alive."

"Jon and Betsy," he said, distraught.

"I'm going to do everything I can to find them."

"Please do, Mr. Harvath. And make sure to keep us abreast of everything that's happening."

"We will."

After hanging up, Harvath showered, changed, and then picked up another coffee in the lobby. It was just under two miles to 1 Schroeder Plaza and police headquarters. Rush hour was in full swing and there were already several people lined up for taxis, so he decided to walk it. The fresh air and uninterrupted time to think would both do him good.

He was bothered by how little he'd been able to develop in the way of actionable leads. Granted, he had been on the case less than forty-eight hours, but so much had happened. He had never believed in the perfect crime. There was no such thing. Criminals always left clues, always.

That said, even the prints they'd been able to recover had been a bust. Their killer was a ghost. What was worse, Harvath was relegated to playing catch-up. He wasn't even on defense, fending off an attack. It was like being blindfolded and shoved in a dark room with fifty people wielding bats. You knew you were going to be hit, you just had no idea where the next blow was going to come from.

As he walked, he tried to sort through the facts of the case. The Federal Reserve chairman had died from heart failure just over a week ago. Days later, the top five candidates to replace him had been abducted. That was Sunday, today was Wednesday, and in between a woman named Claire Marcourt, a man named Herman Penning, and another man named Peter Whalen had all been brutally murdered.

Despite knowing the approximate times of day and the areas he had passed through, neither the police nor the FBI had been able to catch the killer on a single CCTV camera. It was as if cameras couldn't capture his image, like he was some sort of vampire whose reflection was never cast in a mirror. Whoever the killer was, he was exceptionally skilled.

Which brought Harvath to Bill Wise and the idea that the man they were looking for was highly trained, possibly even created by the CIA. He certainly wasn't operating alone, but the idea that Agency personnel could be behind something like this was almost too much for Harvath to swallow. There was, though, more than one person at work here, and whoever they were, they felt justified in committing murder. It was all Harvath needed to know about them. It helped frame how he would deal with them, *if* he got the chance.

When Harvath arrived at police headquarters, Cordero was already upstairs in her office.

"This just went out," she said, handing him the police bulletin on their last two missing persons.

Harvath read it over and handed it back.

"The Federal Reserve," she said. "That's what they were all being considered to head, isn't it?"

He nodded. "How'd you figure it out?"

"If you hadn't told me about Claire Marcourt, I might not have. But when you combine her background in economics and banking with the death of the recent Fed chairman and what I learned from a five-minute Web search about Jekyll Island, it doesn't take a detective to put it all together."

"I didn't tell you about Jekyll specifically, though."

"No, you said an *island* off the coast of Georgia. One of the FBI agents mentioned it by name this morning." Changing tack, she said, "You could have told me that this was about the Fed."

"I know. I'm sorry. Orders." Looking at his watch, he asked, "Did the bulletin on Renner and Mitchell make it in time to be included in the morning roll calls?"

"It did. What do you think our next move should be?"

"Well, short of going back to church and lighting a candle, there's only one thing I can think of to do."

"What's that?"

Harvath took a deep breath and exhaled. "We map out every major historical location in Boston and try to figure out where he's going to strike next."

CHAPTER 54

B etsy Mitchell had tried all the tricks she knew in order to stay calm. The conditions under which she had been kept were terrible. She didn't remember much from her abduction. She had been on her way back home from having dinner with friends. There'd been an accident. She had stopped to help. The rest was a blur. Whoever had kidnapped her must have drugged her, too.

She had been kept in some sort of a crate, like a large dog kennel. It was dark most of the time and she was wearing restraints. Every once in a while, a small panel opened in the top and a water bottle and power bars were thrown in. She had not been allowed out to exercise or use the facilities. She figured out fairly quickly that was why the plastic bags had been left in the crate. Despite having double- and triple-bagged her waste, the crate smelled putrid. She could only imagine what she smelled and looked like at this point.

Though she'd been drugged, she remembered the splitting pain in her ears. She had never done well equalizing pressure when flying and normally wore custom earplugs that helped her avoid barotraumas. Wherever they had transported her, they had made multiple stops along the way. When they had reached their destination, the crate had been placed inside some sort of a truck. It had been a diesel vehicle. She could tell by the sound of the engine and the smell of the fumes. The truck had driven for some time until it finally ended up where she was now.

Without a watch or any natural light with which to mark the passage of time, she had no idea what day it was or how long she had been gone. Surely people were looking for her by now. Hopefully they had started looking when she didn't show up for work Monday morning. The CEO of a successful hedge fund didn't just go missing without people noticing.

More than once during her ordeal she had chastised herself for not taking her board up on its suggestion that she have bodyguards. She'd always thought the idea ridiculous. If she were a Bill Gates or a Warren Buffett, she might have considered it, but she was Betsy Mitchell. She was an approachable, popular-cause-promoting finance guru. People didn't want to harm her; they wanted to hug her. Besides, she used to joke, when was the last time you ever heard of an American executive being kidnapped in the United States? When knowledgeable people ran the stats down for her, she'd laugh them off. Betsy Mitchell was all about budgets and bottom lines, not bodyguards. Until, that is, she was taken.

As little as she knew about being kidnapped, she did know that if your kidnappers hid their faces that was a good sign. It meant that you would be free at some point and they didn't want you to be able to identify them.

When the door to her crate was opened, she found the sight of the powerfully built man, crouched on his haunches with a green glow stick, jarring. He wore coveralls and a smiling Guy Fawkes mask, the kind popular in anticapitalist movements.

Though the mask was unsettling, its choice told her something about the people who had taken her. If they had done their homework into who she was, which they very likely had, they would know that she supported many popular causes likely aligned with theirs. Whatever their beef, she was not their enemy. She had simply been chosen because her company would pay to get her back. It was an easy score. In desperate economic times, people turned to desperate measures. She hoped that they understood that she appreciated their struggle. Under different circumstances, she might have even freely contributed to whatever their cause was.

That made little difference now. She was their prisoner. And while the tough businesswoman in her wanted to see if she could talk them into letting her go, there was something about the eyes behind the mask that shook her self-preservation instinct to the core and told her to keep her mouth shut and do what she was told.

He beckoned her out of the cage with his gloved hand. She did as she was instructed.

In the corners of the room, he had placed other chemical lights, which cast the space in an eerie, green pall. It was difficult to tell where she was. The space was dirty and industrial, constructed of brick and concrete.

As she neared the front of the cage, he grabbed a fistful of her thick brown hair and twisted so hard she could hear her scalp begin to pop as it tore away. She screamed and he struck her across the face with the glow stick.

He slammed her face against the floor and then slid something underneath her neck. She had no idea what it was until he let go of her hair and she could feel him fumbling with a buckle of some sort. She was being fitted with a collar. *Why? Was he trying to humiliate her? Were they going to make some sort of a video to send with their ransom demand?* There were a million questions flying through her mind, not one of which she dared to ask. The side of her face where she had been struck with the glow stick still hurt. She had no desire to incur the man's wrath any further. For right now, she would keep her questions to herself. Whoever this man was, he meant business.

Inside the cage, she had been free to move around, but now, once the collar was attached, the man jerked her the rest of the way out and restrained her hands behind her back again. Her legs, though, were left alone. This brought even more questions to her mind, most too hideous even to contemplate, and she tried to block all of them out. She would know the man's intent soon enough.

After being cooped up in the cramped cage, her legs were sore and her joints stiff. She had trouble walking, and this angered the man in the Guy

Fawkes mask, who had to half drag her to the far side of the room, where a metal ring had been bolted into the wall.

There was a length of chain hanging from it, which he then affixed to her collar. With her hands secured behind her back, there was no possible way she could free herself. She was able to at least stand and move around a little bit, and it felt good to be on her feet again once more and no longer folded up inside the fetid metal box.

The man in the mask stood back and stared at her, assessing her. Slowly, he put his hands out in front of himself and began to do calisthenics. He started with squats and he motioned for her to follow suit. He was encouraging her to limber up. *Why? Were they letting her go?* The thought was too good to be true, but instead of banishing it from her mind, she embraced it. *They are going to let me go!* She repeated the thought over and over again in her mind.

Once she had gone through the series of exercises, the man in the mask removed what looked like a small digital audio recorder. He held it out so she could see it clearly and he activated its PLAY button.

The male voice that came from the speaker was upbeat and dramatic as it overaccentuated its words. "Please repeat after me," it said. "Lucy Lockett lost her pocket, Sally Fisher found it. Not a penny was there in it, just a ribbon 'round it."

She had no idea what bizarre game the man in the mask was playing at. Her silence aggravated him. Rewinding the message, he forcefully extended the recorder out to her and played it again.

"Please repeat after me," the digital voice said. "Lucy Lockett lost her pocket, Sally Fisher found it. Not a penny was there in it, just a ribbon 'round it."

She was understandably scared and her mind wasn't working as well as it normally did. "Sally Fisher lost her locket," she stammered.

Drawing his free hand back, the man in the mask struck her across the face again. He rewound the message and thrust the recorder at her once more.

"Please repeat after me," the digital voice said. "Lucy Lockett lost her pocket, Sally Fisher found it. Not a penny was there in it, just a ribbon 'round it."

She could taste blood in her mouth this time. The man's violence terrified her. She now knew what she had seen in his eyes that was so unsettling. The man was a killer and as sure as she was standing there, if he felt her life needed to be ended, he would do it.

Please let me get this right. Please, God, let me get it right. I just want to leave. I just want to go home.

"Lucy Lockett lost her pocket, Sally Fisher found it. Not a penny was there in it, just a ribbon 'round it," she said, picking up speed right at the end as she knew she had it.

The man in the mask gestured for her to do it again.

She did and with more confidence. "Lucy Lockett lost her pocket, Sally Fisher found it. Not a penny was there in it, just a ribbon 'round it."

The man in the mask tucked the digital recorder into the pocket of his coveralls, brought his gloved hands together, and politely clapped. The muffled sound echoed in the hard, cold space.

He stood there looking at her, almost appraising her. Then, he slowly extended his left hand and placed it gently on her shoulder.

No sooner had her mind formed the words *He's trying to reassure me, they're going to let me go,* than his hand drew back with an explosion of force that took her blouse with it.

CHAPTER 55

Without access to the books in his home library, Harvath had to make do with what was available on the Internet. Hanging a map of Boston on the wall in Cordero's office, they used colored pushpins and thumbtacks to mark every location of interest to them. Seeing everything displayed on the wall helped them take in the big picture.

The only outlier was the murder of Claire Marcourt on Jekyll Island, Georgia. A photo of Jekyll Island was printed out on an 8.5x11 piece of paper and taped to the wall next to the lower right-hand corner of the Boston map. This way they had visual access to everything.

Not only was their map awash in pins marking the sites of historic events, they had no idea which direction in time the killer was going to move in next. On a whiteboard set up on an easel, Harvath drew a time line and walked Cordero through it as much for his own thought process as for hers.

"The first murder happened Sunday night on Jekyll Island and incorporated elements of the Pine Tree Riot, from New Hampshire in 1772," he said, sticking a pin above the map to represent New Hampshire. Coming back to the easel, he continued. "The second murder then took place in Boston late Monday night, early Tuesday morning at the Liberty Tree site and mimicked the hanging of Andrew Oliver in effigy in 1765. So we moved backward in time.

"The third murder then took place in Boston's North End last night, at the site where then–lieutenant governor Thomas Hutchinson had his house sacked and destroyed, also in 1765. Just shy of two weeks, in fact, after his brother-in-law, Andrew Oliver, was hung in effigy."

"Let's assume for a moment," said Cordero, studying everything, "that whoever the Sons of Liberty are, they wanted their first murder to be big, symbolic, and aimed unmistakably at the Fed. That's why it happened on Jekyll. If they had wanted to kill Claire Marcourt in Boston, they could have brought her here the same way they did Peter Whalen from Chicago, right?"

Harvath nodded. "Sure."

"So let's assume Jekyll Island as a location, as well as the elements of the murder were all meant for shock and awe."

"Okay."

"If that's the case, it's the exception, and what we've seen in Boston becomes more of the rule. The Liberty Tree to the site of the Hutchinson mansion shows the killer moving chronologically."

"You're not wrong," Harvath said, "it just isn't enough to build a foundation on."

"We have no choice. The absence of additional corroborative data doesn't mean the data we have is incorrect. It's like I told you, we're building a watch. Right now, I have two gears that fit together. It's illogical to sit here and not pair those gears up and try to go to the next step."

It took a special mind to do this kind of work. As much as Harvath prided himself on his patience and self-control, he realized that Cordero had a unique talent for this kind of work. It was an area in which he was definitely at a deficit.

"All right," he replied. "Let's marry up our two gears. Let's assume for a moment that our killer is now moving forward chronologically. What kind of thing are we looking for next? Is it a big historical headline, or still significant, but more nuanced?"

Now Cordero was out of her depth. "You're asking me?" she said.

"I thought we already established my less than stellar aptitude in all things historically Boston."

"What's your gut tell you?"

"My underinformed gut?"

Harvath shook his head. "No, your homicide cop gut. Whoever is behind this, they've got two more potential victims. Do they go big symbolism-wise, or do they play small ball?"

"If we literally let history be our guide, what do they have available to them?"

It was a good question. Taking a different color dry-erase marker, Harvath referred back to the American history website he had pulled up and drew a new time line.

"In 1767," he said, "the British Parliament passes the Townshend Acts, essentially a tax on tea, paper, glass, and lead in the colonies. It creates more cries of no taxation without representation in the colonies and the colonists boycott British goods. One of the real rubs, though, is that Townshend allows for the quartering of British troops in colonial homes and businesses, which brings us to 1768.

"In 1768, the Sons of Liberty issue a very serious threat of armed resistance if any British troops show up. Shortly thereafter two regiments appear in Boston to 'help collect taxes.' Many colonists see this as the beginning of the British occupation of Boston."

"Do we know where they were housed?" Cordero asked.

Harvath had been working on her computer and had multiple windows open. It took him a minute or two to find the information he was looking for. "Here it is," he said. "One regiment set up camp in Boston Common, the other at Faneuil Hall."

"Which we passed last night after dinner."

He remembered. It had been a marketplace and meeting hall where Sam Adams and others gave fiery speeches encouraging the colonies to break away from Great Britain.

"Seeing as how it has been called the 'Cradle of Liberty' by some," said Harvath, "I can see where it might make an attractive backdrop for our killer."

"Let's put it on our list," she replied. "What else do we have?"

Before Harvath could reply, Cordero's commander hastily stuck his head in the office. "We just got word that we may have gotten a hit on the missing persons bulletin from this morning."

"Someone spotted Renner and Mitchell?" said Harvath.

"Not specifically."

"What do you mean?"

"We got a report of suspicious activity at an old warehouse near Cabot Yard."

Harvath looked at Cordero. "Where's that?"

"Southie," she replied. "What kind of suspicious activity?"

"Two patrol officers pinched a metal thief. He'd been stripping abandoned buildings in the area. He's got felonies on his sheet and they caught him in possession of a weapon. That means he's looking at going away for a long time. No surprise, once they dragged him down to the station, he wanted to make a deal. They asked him what he had to trade and he offered up a lot of low-level bullshit. Mixed in there, though, was something interesting.

"He says he was casing an empty warehouse over the weekend and had planned to come back and hit it. The only problem was that when he did, it wasn't empty anymore. This time it was occupied."

"Occupied by whom?" asked Harvath.

"According to the metal thief, a handful of white guys with guns. But not just any guns, small automatic weapons that looked to the thief like submachine guns. He says there were also four metal boxes, like kennel crates. He thought maybe these guys were into dog fighting or smuggling exotic animals or something, but then he caught a glimpse of what was inside one of the boxes."

"People," said Harvath.

"Correct. We think this could be it. SWAT and FBI are already being scrambled. Where's Sal?"

"He's still at the Garden Court scene," replied Cordero.

"Call him. I want you both at the warehouse when this goes down. It could end up being a real feather in our cap. I don't want it screwed up. Understood?"

"Yes, sir."

CHAPTER 56

Cordero's partner arrived at the staging area about ten minutes after she and Harvath got there. The SWAT team already had surveillance on the warehouse and were putting together their entry plan in consultation with the FBI. A restaurant supply company had been kind enough to allow them to pull their vehicles inside its building in order to avoid detection.

Mixed in with the uniformed SWAT team members were a handful of plainclothes operatives. With their short haircuts and muscled builds, none of these guys looked like run-of-the-mill folks from the neighborhood. None of them would be able to walk up to the warehouse. They'd have to hit it fast and hard before anyone inside knew what was happening.

If the men inside were the caliber of professional that Harvath suspected they might be, they were going to put up one hell of a fight. The SWAT team needed to know what they were potentially going up against.

Harvath took advantage of a break in their briefing to pull the team commander aside and share his concerns. The man listened to what he had to say, thanked him, and then updated his officers.

As they continued with their planning, one of their spotters radioed in. So far, the warehouse was dead. They had even managed to get an operator up on the roof near the skylights where the metal thief had allegedly seen everything, and there was still no sign of activity inside. It was too quiet. Either the thief had lied, or somehow the men inside knew they were coming.

The SWAT team's greatest concern was the safety of the hostages. Not knowing where they were being held made the officers' job incredibly difficult. The moment the team made entry into the warehouse, if they didn't move fast enough, it was a very real possibility that the kidnappers would kill the hostages. Balancing officer safety against the two innocent lives they believed might be inside was like dancing on a knife blade. There was only one good outcome and no shortage of bad ones.

The commander was meticulous and refused to rush anything. He called in additional assets and did everything he could to maximize their surveillance. Finally, he made the call. It was time to hit the warehouse.

After one last check of their radios, weapons, and equipment, the SWAT team mounted up.

The owner of the restaurant supply company offered the plainclothesmen use of one of his vans. The fact that it belonged to a local business so close by would hopefully divert any suspicion away from it. This of course was based on a dangerous assumption—that the men inside the warehouse hadn't already noticed they were under surveillance and were not waiting to engage any threat, plainclothes or otherwise, foolish enough to enter the structure.

Harvath had been on enough building takedowns to know that while time would slow down for the men on the team, for everyone else things were going to happen very rapidly. He told Cordero and her partner to get ready to move.

They exited the restaurant supply company and decided to drive Sal's Crown Victoria to the warehouse. He had two Rubbermaid bins on the backseat filled with gear, one of which he moved onto the floor to give Harvath a place to sit. Cordero climbed in front. As soon as the FBI agents were in place and the SWAT team had departed the restaurant supply company, they followed.

Sal turned up his radio so they could listen to the takedown in real time. When he was half a block away from the warehouse and had it in sight, he pulled to the curb. This was close enough. If bullets started flying, they'd be sitting ducks out front.

"Keep it running," said Harvath, as he noticed the man reaching for his ignition.

Sal nodded and they stayed glued to the radio.

The team practiced excellent communications discipline. Messages were transmitted via predetermined brevity codes. Finally, the warehouse doors and windows were breached, flash-bangs were tossed inside, and the SWAT team members made their rapid entry.

Harvath's entire body was keyed up. *Was this it? Had they tracked down the Sons of Liberty?*

He hated being outside in a car, half a block away. He wished he was on the entry team, hell, he wished he was *leading* the entry team into the warehouse.

After what seemed like an eternity, more thorough communications started crackling across the radio as room after room of the warehouse was searched and found to be empty.

With the raid and then the secondary sweep of the warehouse complete, the team leader relayed the message "The building is secure."

Sal put his vehicle in gear and they drove up to the front of the warehouse as a handful of SWAT operatives came out the front door. The FBI agents on scene had already begun going in.

Harvath looked at one of the SWAT team members as he passed and the officer shook his head. "No HUTS," he said, which Harvath knew stood for no hostages, no unknowns, no tangos, and no shooters. The raid had been a bust.

The team leader met them inside. "The crates are here," he stated, "but that's it."

"Where are the crates?" Cordero asked. The man pointed the trio to the back of the building.

The crates had been collapsed and leaned against the wall, as if someone was considering taking them along but then had second thoughts. In another room, where a length of chain hung from the wall, one of the

FBI agents had found a woman's blouse. It smelled terrible and was spattered with blood.

"Do you have Betsy Mitchell's blood type in your file?" the female detective asked.

"If it's not," said Harvath, "they should be able to get it pretty quickly."

She turned to her partner. "Where's your camera?"

"Out in the car."

"I don't want to wait for the CSTs to get here. I want to get pictures, I want to do our drawings, and then let's start bagging things up for analysis. Okay?"

"Fine by me," said Sal. "We'll need to coordinate the Bureau folks and set up a canvass in case anyone else around here saw anything, plus we should see if we can get a better description of the men the metal thief says he saw."

"What can I do?" asked Harvath.

"Do you have any forensics experience?"

He shook his head. "Not much."

"Then I have the perfect job for you," she replied. "Go out to the car and bring those two Rubbermaid bins in."

"Then what?"

"Then you're really going to prove your worth to this investigation."

"How?" he asked.

"You're going to find us coffee somewhere in this neighborhood."

CHAPTER 57

To his credit, Harvath not only didn't mind going out for coffee, he actually found some and it wasn't half bad. He returned with three cups in a cardboard tray.

The evidence techs still hadn't arrived yet, but Cordero had made a significant find.

"Check this out," she said, holding up a clear plastic bag. Inside, there was a piece of black card stock the size of a business card. On one side, printed in blood red, was a skull and bones with a floating crown. On the other side were the words *I glory in publicly avowing my eternal enmity to tyranny.*

It was followed by the letters *S.O.L.*

"I think that's a line from John Hancock," said Harvath.

Sal held up his smartphone. "Correct. Part of the speech he gave on the fourth anniversary of the Boston Massacre."

"Why is it printed on a card? And why leave it here?"

"Maybe it was left by accident," said Cordero.

"Where'd you find it?"

"Behind where the crates were stacked up against the wall."

She had a point. Maybe it had been left by accident. One thing was for certain, though: finding this warehouse was a huge breakthrough. At least he hoped it would be.

"What else have you been able to find?" he asked.

"Other than that card and the blouse," replied the female detective, "nothing."

"There's got to be something more here. We just haven't found it yet."

"You're welcome to look around," said the male detective. "If you find anything, just don't touch it. Call one of us or one of the FBI agents."

Harvath nodded and went to the other end of the warehouse. He was used to hitting terrorist safe houses where the kind of evidence he was expected to collect were things like thumb drives, CDs, and written documents, not hair and fiber samples.

Finding the card with the Hancock quote, though, had been huge. They were definitely in the right spot. The only question was, had any other clues been left behind?

Once the crime scene techs arrived, they would go through the laborious process of dusting for prints. Undoubtedly, they'd find a ton and he didn't envy the person or persons who would be charged with having to run all of them down. Considering a building of this size with this many surfaces, the question wasn't what to dust, but what not to?

He figured they'd do the obvious items like the crates, the chain attached to the wall near where the blouse was found, the door handles, the light switches, and any bathroom surfaces. Other than that, it was anybody's guess, though he knew there was a strict procedure both the police and FBI followed.

What he was looking for as he walked through was something out of the ordinary, something that didn't belong or something that was conspicuous because it wasn't there.

Whoever had been using this location had probably been here since the early hours of Monday morning. That was only two days ago. If they were careless enough to leave one of those cards behind, where else had they screwed up? *Was the blouse a mistake? Or was it left on purpose? Or did they simply not care about it?*

The fact that the metal thief had seen multiple males in the warehouse backed up the theory that they were dealing with a team. The fact that they were carrying what looked like submachine guns bolstered the hypothesis that they were well trained, possibly even aligned with a military or intelligence organization. Add to that the way in which the victims had been killed, particularly the ear removal of Claire Marcourt and Kelly Davis, and it looked like Bill Wise's Swim Club was a real potential factor in this entire thing.

As Harvath continued to walk the building, his mind was drawn to the passage on the back of the card from John Hancock. As he had been laying out the time line for Cordero, the Boston Massacre was the next big event he was going to mention before her commander had interrupted them.

What if the killer's next murder scene wasn't going to be Boston Common or Faneuil Hall, where the two regiments of British troops had stayed, but the actual site of the Boston Massacre?

The more he thought about it, the more the idea began to crowd out all other possibilities. The line from Hancock had to be tied to where the killer was going to strike next. *It had to be.*

The only question that remained was whether they should spend any more time at all in the warehouse or turn it over to the evidence techs and try to get a jump on the next location. Actually, there wasn't any question at all.

Giving up his search, Harvath turned around and walked quickly back to find Cordero. If they did this right, they might be able to set up a trap and have the killer walk right into it.

CHAPTER 58

A circle of cobblestones with a star carved into the center was all that marked the location of the Boston Massacre. It sat embedded in a downtown sidewalk, almost directly beneath the east balcony of the Old State House. It was one of the least glamorous but most important stops along Boston's "Freedom Trail," a two-and-a-half-mile-long red stripe that runs through the city and connects sixteen historically significant sites in the run-up to the Revolutionary War. On that spot, five Bostonians became the first to give up their lives for the cause of American liberty.

Waiting for a group of tourists to pass, he looked at Cordero and her partner and said, "The symbolism here is pitch perfect. Right up their alley. This has got to be where the next one is going to happen."

"What do you think, Sal?" Cordero asked.

"My smartphone isn't so smart when it comes to predicting what people are *going* to do. I don't know."

She looked back at Harvath. "Do you think they'd stage something from inside the Old State House? Another hanging maybe? Have the body come out over the balcony?"

Harvath looked up and considered it. "We know they like to operate late at night. It gives them cover. They also like to limit their exposure. That's why the Liberty Tree and Hutchinson sites were done inside. It's pretty hard to kill somebody out in public."

Cordero's partner looked up at all the office buildings surrounding them. "Maybe not. What if they used a sniper?"

It was a good point. Harvath hadn't thought of that and now looked up as well. There were plenty of places a sniper could be positioned. It would be dramatic and draw a lot of attention. It also felt like something the people he believed they were dealing with would be capable of.

Playing devil's advocate, he said, "If they did use a sniper, how would they get the victim to walk right up to where they wanted?"

"If it were me," Cordero mused, "I'd put a cop there."

"You would?"

She nodded. "I'd call something into 911, wait until the cop was right where I wanted him, and then I'd turn the victim loose."

Harvath thought about that. "Make the victim think you were setting him free?"

"Or *her* free," she clarified. "Remember, we've got one man and one woman who are still missing."

"That's correct. So you'd let him or her think they're being set free, you'd dump them on the street someplace close, and then tell them to run for the cop."

"Then when they get to the cop," Sal said, mimicking a sniper with an invisible rifle, "end of story."

It was an excellent theory, but just that—a theory. He looked up again at the buildings. It was a base worth covering. "How much of a SWAT presence could we get?"

"We can reach out to the state guys to augment what we already have," said Cordero as her eyes scanned the area. "But not knowing precisely what these people have planned, we also need to flood this entire zone with plainclothes cops. If the victim makes it to that historical marker, it could be too late."

Harvath agreed. "The Boston Massacre was all about British soldiers mowing innocent people down with muskets, so if they do go the sniper route, they'll have the victim in the crosshairs the entire time. Nevertheless, we need to cover our other bases."

"Such as?"

"We definitely want to have officers positioned inside the Old State House," he said, as his mind sifted through the countless possibilities. When you had a location, particularly one out in the open, you learned how to defend it by envisioning how the bad guys would likely attack it. Looking down at the historical marker, he added, "Is there anything running underneath here? Sewers? The subway system?"

"Probably. Why?"

"Just in case this historical marker isn't really *on* the site of the Boston Massacre, but actually *above* it, we'll need cops down there covering it as well."

"That shouldn't be too hard to find out," Cordero replied. "What else do we need?"

It was odd to have her suddenly defer to him, and it took a moment for him to realize that the shift had happened. Maybe it was because she knew that he had been a Secret Service agent, though she had no idea it was on the President's detail, but somehow she sensed that this was in his wheelhouse and was something he was good at.

He thought through all the other things he would like to have, knowing they'd never get there in time, and settled on the one thing they needed more than anything else. "If you can find us a whole busload of luck, that'd be all I'd ask for," he said, forcing an optimistic laugh.

Harvath heard Cordero's partner laugh, but as he looked up, he couldn't tell if the man was laughing with him, or at him.

CHAPTER 59

Betsy Mitchell felt the vehicle, probably a van of some sort based on the sliding sound the door had made once they had gotten into it, bump and jostle along through traffic. She had no idea where they were. Based on the drugs she had been given and all of the takeoffs and landings of the plane she had been on after her abduction, she had no idea if she was even in the United States anymore. She could hear car horns outside, but she couldn't see anything. A hood had been placed over her head.

Despite a split lip and an eye that felt painfully swollen from the blows she had suffered, the rape Betsy had feared back at the warehouse never happened. After tearing away her blouse, the man in the mask had left the room. He came back with a small camera and microphone combination, a third the size of a lipstick tube, and showed it to her. He then taped it to her chest, and that was when he had placed the hood over her head.

As he removed the collar from around her neck and began to dress her, he used the digital recorder to relay a message explaining what was about to happen.

Her ransom had been agreed on. Within a matter of hours she would be free, if she did everything she was supposed to do. That was the purpose of the video camera and microphone. Though she couldn't see it with the hood over her head, she could feel him adjusting her clothes around it. He explained that he would be able to see and hear everything she did. He also explained what would happen if she veered even one inch from her instructions. Her blood froze in her veins. Once she found her voice again, she swore she would do exactly as he asked. She promised them that in no condition would she waver from what she had been told to do.

When the voice on the digital recorder asked her to repeat the rhyme she had been taught, she did, repeating it perfectly, word for word. Once he was satisfied that she was ready, he had loaded her into the vehicle and they departed.

She lost track of how long they had been driving. It could have been an hour. It could have been ten. All she could think about was doing everything he demanded, exactly as he had demanded it. All she wanted was her freedom. All she wanted to do was go home.

The vehicle turned for the umpteenth time, but began to slow and then eventually pulled over to the side and stopped. The man with the mask joined her in the back of the van and removed her hood. His eyes bored into hers for several moments before he produced the digital recorder and pressed PLAY. The words she had first heard it speak poured forth again.

"Please repeat after me. Lucy Lockett lost her pocket, Sally Fisher found it. Not a penny was there in it, just a ribbon 'round it."

Betsy dutifully complied. The man then rewound the recording and played it again. Betsy repeated the phrase again. In fact, she kept repeating it. It was her mantra. If she said it enough times, she would be free.

The man in the mask produced a knife and cut the nylon EZ Cuffs from her wrists and ankles. Then tapping her chest to remind her of the camera, he slid open the door and gestured for her to step out onto the sidewalk.

Wherever in the world she was, it was evening. That was all she knew. Her instructions had been quite specific. With her hand first in the right pocket of her coat and then the left, she began walking away from the van.

As she walked, she continued to repeat the rhyme over and over again, hoping the man in the mask hadn't lied to her.

"Lucy Lockett lost her pocket, Sally Fisher found it. Not a penny was there in it, just a ribbon 'round it."

"Here you go," Cordero said, handing Harvath a bottle of water she had just purchased for him. "See anything new?"

Harvath took the water from her and screwed off the cap. "Nothing yet. What did the SWAT commander say?"

"He asked the same thing he did an hour ago. How much longer do we think this is going to go on."

"What did you tell him?"

"I told him not to worry. His team will be home for Christmas."

Harvath smiled. At least she still had her sense of humor, but it was fading. It had taken all day to set the operation up, most of it with the FBI going back and forth with their headquarters in Washington as to how everything should be handled. A lot of time, in Harvath's opinion, had been wasted on where everyone should be placed, how many Boston PD versus FBI agents should be in plainclothes, et cetera. By the time everything was settled, it was already late afternoon.

"These kinds of ops aren't easy," he said, referring to Cordero's interaction with the SWAT team leader. "Scanning rooftops and windows is mind-numbing work. You can burn out fast and lose your edge. The commander is just looking out for his guys."

"Like I said, they'll all be home for Christmas."

Harvath nodded. Everyone was on edge, their nerves a bit frayed. They were anxious for something to happen. And unlike other types of stakeouts, they had to keep moving.

Cordero's partner had helped coordinate changes of clothes so she and Harvath could rotate in and out of the area with different appearances. He was also coordinating the plainclothes cops and FBI agents.

There had already been a couple of false alarms as people bearing a similar resemblance to Jonathan Renner or Betsy Mitchell had passed by. It had sent everyone into high-alert mode, only to turn out that it wasn't the people they were looking for.

As the evening wore on, Harvath could see the fatigue begin to eat away at the corners of Cordero's mind.

"What if somehow we tipped our hand?" she asked. "What if they figured out we're here?"

Harvath looked at his watch. "It's still way too early for you to be going soft on me."

"I'm not going soft. But what if I'm right?"

"You know, I once lay in a hole, not much bigger than the trunk of a car, for four days waiting for the right guy to go past. I didn't have a café half a block away with cold sodas and a bathroom so clean, people from the third world would think they were at the Ritz-Carlton."

"I guess it could be worse," she admitted.

"Yeah. There could be snakes and truckloads of guys shooting at you."

Cordero looked at him. "At some point, you and I are going to have a long talk about who you actually are."

Harvath took a sip of his water and screwed the cap back on. "We'll have to do it over coffee. You'll need it to keep you awake."

"Somehow, I doubt that."

Harvath was just about to change the subject when a voice crackled over their earpieces. It was Sal.

"We just got a heads-up from a patrol officer in the area," he said.

"What is it?" Cordero asked.

"Seems he found a couple of cards like the one you found in the warehouse."

"Where is he?"

"Hold on," said Sal. "I'll get him on this frequency."

A moment later, the male detective said, "You're on with Detective Cordero. Go ahead."

"Detective Cordero?" a voice said. "This is Officer Kaczynski."

"What have you got, Kaczynski?"

"We were told to keep our eyes peeled for anything with a skull and crossbones on it with a crown on top. I've found several black cards with the skull and bones on one side and the sentence *I glory in publicly avowing my eternal enmity to tyranny,* followed by the letters *S.O.L.*"

Harvath tucked his water bottle into his pocket and looked at Cordero.

"What's your location?" she asked the patrolman.

"I'm headed north on Devonshire, almost at Quaker Lane."

She looked at Harvath and said, "He's about half a block south."

"There's a whole bunch of these things, like a trail of bread crumbs. I've been picking them up in case your guys can get a print off one of them."

"Officer Kaczynski," Harvath interrupted. "Leave the rest of them. We need to know who is dropping them."

"Okay, stand by. Let me see what I can do."

Cordero started to move in Kaczynski's direction, but Harvath gently grabbed hold of her arm. "Somebody may be trying to smoke us out. Let's wait a second."

"We may not have a second," she said as she radioed the other teams and told them what was going on and to be ready.

Seconds later, one of the SWAT officers came over the radio and said, "I think we've got it. Looks like some kind of a homeless person, possibly female. Brown hair, heavy brown coat, dark pants. She's dropping something from her pockets."

"Can you see patrol officer Kaczynski?" Cordero asked.

"Roger that," the SWAT officer replied. "He's approximately ten meters behind her."

"Kaczynski," Cordero said over her radio. "Do you see a female homeless woman approximately ten meters ahead of you? Brown hair, brown coat?"

"That's affirmative," Kaczynski replied. "Not only can I see her, I can smell her. Sweet Jesus, it's terrible."

"Do not engage. I repeat. Do not engage. They may be trying to smoke us out," the female detective ordered as she looked at Harvath. "What the hell is going on?"

"I've got no idea," he said, "but I don't like it. Something feels very wrong about this."

Cordero radioed the other team members. "Everybody on your toes.

The woman in the coat might be a decoy. Keep your eyes peeled on our other ingress points. If one of our targets is being sent in, we don't want to miss him or her."

Harvath's eyes continued to scan the area. He paid particular attention to the historical marker and kept looking toward Devonshire Street. Suddenly, he saw the woman in the brown coat.

Kaczynski's voice came back over their earpieces. "This woman is crackers. I can hear her repeating some rhyme about someone called Lucy Lockett or something."

"Officer Kaczynski," Cordero warned. "Do not engage her. Is that clear?"

"Ten-four."

"She's headed our way," said Harvath.

The female detective could see her now. The woman's hair was a rat's nest. She walked with her head down. Like many homeless people, she was overdressed for the warm weather in a winter coat.

"She's almost to you," said Kaczynski.

"We see her," Cordero replied.

Both she and Harvath could now clearly see her reaching into her pockets, pulling out the black cards and dropping them in her wake.

Harvath's feelings of unease were continuing to build. His gut was telling him *something*. He just couldn't put his finger on it.

The woman walked like she was in a dream, mumbling as she moved forward, placing one foot in front of the next. Harvath had seen this before. *Where? Why was it so familiar?* The alarm bells were going off full force in his head now.

Cordero took a step in the direction of the woman. Harvath reached out and grabbed her arm again.

They watched as the woman stepped out into the street. As she did, a car speeding through the intersection slammed on its brakes. The woman looked up.

One of the SWAT team members watching through a spotting scope identified her first. "Target A. Target A. The woman in the brown coat is Betsy Mitchell. All teams, the woman in the brown coat is Betsy Mitchell."

Cordero shook off Harvath's hand and began running. So did Officer Kaczynski.

Kaczynski got to Betsy Mitchell first, knocking her to the ground and throwing himself on top of her.

Harvath got to Detective Cordero just as the suicide vest Betsy Mitchell was wearing was remotely detonated.

CHAPTER 60

"What the hell was that?" Bill Wise asked as Ryan and McGee rushed to the hotel room window.

Ryan got there first. "It sounded like an explosion."

"It sure as hell felt like one," McGee added.

They could see an enormous, roiling fireball climbing up into the night sky. The shock wave had been so powerful, it had almost blown out their windows, and as best they could tell, they were a good four or five blocks away. Moments later, the sound of emergency vehicles racing to the scene began to fill the air.

"I hope that wasn't a bomb," said Wise. "That's the last thing Boston needs. We should check it out."

"No way," replied McGee. "If it was a bomb, there could be a secondary waiting to go off as first responders get there. Besides, it's not our problem."

"Give it time," Ryan stated as they stood looking out the window. "You'd be surprised how fast problems metastasize when Tom Cushing is around."

"Speaking of Cushing," Wise replied, "can we finalize everything now that we're here?"

After interrogating Samuel, Wise had contacted Reed Carlton, who showed up with two rather large men and a female operative named Sloane. Samuel had admitted that he had a second target—a former Swim Club doctor named Jim Gage. While Sloane and one of the men were dispatched to take Gage into protective custody, Wise warned Carlton about Samuel and provided detailed instructions for where and how he should be held. He then shared what they had learned from the interrogation.

One of the most significant elements, but hardly the most surprising, was that Phil Durkin had held on to several covert programs after the Agency had ordered them shut down. He would go through the steps of firing everyone and closing up shop, but then he'd go back out and rehire the personnel he wanted while he shoved each operation further into the shadows, taking them all full black.

Through some untraceable funding source, he had managed to keep everything afloat and operational. Those who didn't know anything figured Durkin was providing plausible deniability for his superiors. No one knew exactly how many programs he was overseeing, but the whisper on the black-ops side was that he had cobbled together his own shadow agency.

Bill Wise didn't know how much of what Samuel shared was actual fact and how much was office gossip. Nevertheless, RUMINT, or rumor intelligence, was something any good operative was expected to be attuned to.

Another significant piece of intelligence was that Ryan's old team was still active and still being led by a man named Tom Cushing. Samuel admitted to having conducted a handful of operations for them.

According to Samuel, Phil Durkin liked the way Cushing operated and had elevated his status in the black-ops community, feeding him more and more assignments and entrusting him with more and more responsibilities.

Cushing, though, wasn't Bill Wise's concern, at least he hadn't thought so until he asked Samuel if he knew anything about what was going on in Boston. That was when Ryan had stiffened.

When the interrogation was complete, Wise had asked to speak to her privately. When he confronted her, Ryan admitted that she and McGee had traced Cushing, along with two other team members, there. Now that they had arrived in Boston, Wise wanted to know how they were going to nail them.

Ryan stepped away from the window and pulled a large envelope from her bag. "We're going to nail them with this."

Wise looked at her. "I don't follow."

"You know the old line, how do you eat an elephant?"

"One bite at a time."

"Correct," Ryan replied. "One of the last bites of our elephant is going to be Phil Durkin. Before we get to Durkin, we have to go through Tom Cushing."

Wise interrupted her. "At this point, though, I want Cushing more than I do Durkin. If Cushing is behind these murders and he's using a killer from Swim Club to do it, we need them stopped ASAP."

"As long as we take Cushing alive, that's all I care about. I need answers out of him to take to the Jordanians."

"My team is going to want answers out of him, too," said Wise, referring to Carlton, Harvath, and their client, the Federal Reserve. "I don't think it's an accident that our paths have crossed."

McGee chuckled as he turned away from the window. "It's lucky for you that they did. If we hadn't shown up, Samuel would be picking his teeth with your bones right about now."

"For which I am eternally grateful. Now, how are we going to handle Cushing?"

"That's where the banking records come in," said Ryan as she walked over to the couch with her envelope and sat down. "I don't know what it was like when you were there, but the CIA is terrible when it comes to funding their people in the field. They're always months in arrears and it can really screw things up. You learn early on that robbing Peter to pay Paul is the only way to keep your sources funded. Some intel people have been forced into fronting their own personal money just to make sure things get paid on time and they don't lose assets."

"So?"

"So, this thinking gets pretty ingrained. Once you have a steady flow of funds, particularly if it comes through a front organization, there's this kind of *fuck the Agency* mentality that surfaces. You never stick your hand in your own pocket again. In fact, you may even start putting your hand in the Agency's pocket.

"Cushing was very strict about stealing. It wasn't allowed. Setting up hotel and airline mileage accounts, though, was considered an acceptable perk. The idea being that throughout the year, they could build up enough points with which to take personal trips in their off time."

"Assuming they travel under their real names."

Ryan smiled. "They do. And not only that, but two of Cushing's team, Vaccaro and Stark, checked into their hotel here in Boston using their Hands for Peace corporate credit cards."

"What about Cushing himself?"

"He's there, too. Trust me. He's just more compulsive about covering his trail."

"You were talking about eating the elephant one bite at a time. I assume that means you want to start with Vaccaro and Stark, then?"

"Yup," she said, holding up the envelope. "And you're going to help."

CHAPTER 61

The Renaissance Boston Waterfront Hotel was exactly the hotel Ryan would have expected her old team to pick. They always chose Marriott properties when they traveled, and one of their requirements was that the hotel have its own workout facility. If the property was just off a major thoroughfare that connected directly with the airport, that was another plus. Finally, if a city offered a higher-end experience like a Renaissance property, and it didn't chafe their NGO cover status too badly, Cushing and company usually opted for it. Some things never changed. Never changing, no matter how skilled you might be, was a bad trait in the espionage game.

With its large, aquatic-themed lobby, the Renaissance provided lots of good places from which to see, while not being seen. Ryan had already checked the bar, the restaurant, the hotel Starbucks, and the fitness center without any luck. It was now time to try their rooms.

Picking up a house phone, she gave Vaccaro's full name and asked to be connected to his room. There was no answer. She then asked to be connected to Stark. He answered on the second ring.

"Good evening, Mr. Stark," Ryan said. "This is Julie with guest services. An envelope was just dropped off for you. Would you like me to send it up, or should we hold it downstairs?"

Before Stark could answer, she added, "And I see here in my files that we made a mistake when you checked in. You're one of our most valued Marriott Rewards customers and should have received a much more significant welcome gift. I apologize for that. Can I have both brought up to your room for you?"

Stark agreed, Ryan thanked him, and after hanging up the phone she flashed McGee the peace sign.

Walking toward the bell stand, McGee cornered an older bellman standing nearby and asked to borrow a pen. He wrote Stark's name across the front of the envelope and, producing a fifty-dollar bill, said, "I need to get this to my colleague's room ASAP. He's on a big conference call, so please don't knock, just slide it under, okay?"

"The last name is Stark?" the bellman asked.

"That's right," McGee replied, and quickly changed the subject. "I'm already late for dinner with a new client. Where can I get a cab? Right out front here?"

The man nodded and was pointing toward the front doors, but McGee had already walked away. The bellman stepped behind the stand, checked his computer for the room number he needed, and then told his colleague he was going to make a delivery.

With the envelope in hand, he strode over to the elevators, and after holding the doors open and waiting for a group to step out, he stepped in. The doors had almost shut when he heard a woman ask for the elevator to be held and a man's hand reached in to stop the doors from closing all the way.

The doors slid back to reveal a man who looked like Santa Claus carrying a gray duffle bag and a very attractive woman in her mid-thirties with a black rolling suitcase. "What floor do you need?" the bellman asked Ryan.

"Nine, please," said Wise.

The bellman looked at him as if to say *I was asking the lady first,* when Ryan responded, "Seven, please."

The bellman, who had already punched seven for his delivery, smiled back at Ryan and then pushed the button for the ninth floor. "All set."

The man made polite hotel chitchat on the ride up and wished them both a nice stay as the doors opened on the seventh floor and he stood back to allow Ryan to exit first. As she did, she removed a cell phone Wise had given her and rolled her eyes.

"It wouldn't be a business trip for Mom if I didn't get called six times before I got to the room," she said.

The bellman smiled and left her standing at the elevator bank, chastising a pair of imaginary children.

She had already marked the location of the nearest stairwell in case the bellman forgot his instructions and knocked on Stark's door and she needed to beat a hasty retreat.

The bellman, though, did as he had been told. Ryan marked the location of the room and began walking in the other direction. Knowing how abundantly helpful bellmen can be, or any man for that reason when presented with an attractive woman, she kept up the intensity of her conversation in order to keep him from offering to help her find her room and get situated.

The combination of body language and tone did the trick. The bellman returned to the elevators. Once she had heard the doors close and was sure that he had gone, she radioed McGee and Wise and told them which stairwell to meet her in.

"Now for the fun part," Wise said as he fished the can of aerosolized pepper spray from his bag.

McGee looked at it. The label said Guardian Protective Devices, and attached to the nozzle was a narrow piece of flexible, clear plastic tubing about eighteen inches long. "You're like Felix the Cat with that bag. You got that bicycle I wanted for Christmas all those years ago, too?"

"This is going to be better than Christmas. Just watch."

"We're not going to get a flashover with that stuff, are we? I don't want to light this guy Stark up like a Christmas tree unless we absolutely have to."

Wise shook his head. "This is the best stuff the military has ever fielded. Burns like a mother, but it's not flammable."

"Whose idea was the hose? Yours?"

"It was actually their idea. Believe it or not, the inspiration was hotels. Some asshole bangs on your door at three in the morning, you slip the hose under the door, spray this into the hallway, and suddenly it's filled with pepper mist and a very inhospitable place to be. We, though, are going to do the opposite."

McGee smiled. "Smoke him out of his room into the hall. I like it."

Wise looked up at Ryan. "You good to go?"

She nodded.

"Okay, let's go."

The contents of the envelope would only keep Stark busy for so long. It was a page from the *Wall Street Journal* with three letters crossed out in pencil. Whether or not the team still used the same code, it didn't matter. It would take Stark fifteen minutes at least to figure the message out and to check the online dead drop where further instructions would be waiting.

It had been one of the team's emergency protocols, intended to be used only when their primary and alternate codes had been compromised, and for that reason she had hoped it would work. The one thing that was for certain was that Stark would be in a hypervigilant state of alert. That's why it was so important that Wise's plan worked.

Readying their gear, they gave everything one last quick check and stepped out of the stairwell. The coast was clear. They moved rapidly down the carpeted hallway and took their positions outside Stark's door.

When Ryan and McGee returned his thumbs up, Wise worked the tube underneath the door and then depressed the button, releasing the mist of pepper spray into the room.

Stark started coughing in less than a minute. Within two minutes he had opened the window, which was when Wise pumped an even thicker mist into the room. Stark was really hacking now.

They heard him tear a towel from the bar in the bathroom and begin running the water in the sink. Moments later, they noticed a shadow pass across the peephole. Even if the man could focus, he wouldn't have seen anything in the hall. Wise, McGee, and Ryan were all crouching down, off to the sides, out of sight.

Used covertly, pepper spray was very disorienting. If you weren't standing in the middle of a riot or had someone aiming a can at you, its effects were very unsettling and hard to attribute. Your mucous membranes dumped, your eyes drained buckets of water, and your throat, lungs, and eyes burned like crazy.

With the wet towel pressed against his face, Stark unlocked his door and leaned out to see what the hell was going on.

That was when McGee nailed him with the Taser.

CHAPTER 62

The first person Harvath saw as he came to was Cordero's partner. The man's lips were moving but no sound was coming out. Harvath could hear what he thought was the rustle of the detective's Boston PD nylon windbreaker. He soon realized that it was the rush of blood pounding in and out of his ears.

As the detective's voice became discernible, it was accompanied by a loud ringing.

"Are you okay?" Sal yelled.

The man might as well have been yelling across the Charles River. Harvath could barely make out what he was saying, but he got the gist of it. He nodded and waved him off as he sat up and looked for Cordero.

It smelled like gasoline and burnt flesh. There were fires burning everywhere. The ground was littered with bodies and broken glass.

Sal was about to leave him and Harvath reached out and grabbed his arm. "Is she okay?" he asked. "Where's Lara?"

A triage area had been set up near a row of ambulances. EMTs were working their way through the dead and wounded, assessing who needed immediate care, who needed immediate transport, and who was beyond being helped. Through his blurred vision, he could just make out Cordero, who was being examined.

The male detective waved over one of the other EMTs, who gave Harvath a quick assessment and then helped him to his feet and walked him over to where Cordero was sitting.

"Are you okay?" he asked as he was helped into a sitting position next to her.

"Sir," the EMT said to Harvath, "I need to ask you some questions."

"I'm fine. Go take care of everyone else."

"Sir, I understand you were unconscious. I'd like you to follow this light with your eyes."

Harvath took out his credentials. "I'm fine. Please go help someone else."

The EMT treating Cordero looked at his colleague and said, "I got this. Don't worry."

The man nodded and went off to treat the next victim of the blast.

Cordero looked over at Harvath. "You saved my life."

"Are you okay?"

"I'm alive. A little bit beaten up, but alive. You, though, look terrible."

Harvath reached up and touched his forehead. When he drew his fingers away, they were slick with blood.

"I'm good," Cordero said to the EMT. "Why don't you see to my partner for a minute here."

Partner. It hurt his sides to laugh, but Harvath did anyway. "What the hell happened?" he said. It was a rhetorical question.

"Our guys have cross-trained with the Israeli police and military for years. We always wondered when we'd see our first suicide bomber. I guess we don't need to wonder anymore."

Harvath looked at the EMT. "Do you have a pair of forceps by any chance?"

The man looked at him askance for a moment and then removed a pair and handed them to him. He placed his hand gently on Cordero's arm and had her tilt a little bit to her right. Using the forceps, he managed to extract a deformed metallic object from the wall behind her.

"Ball bearing?" she asked.

Harvath shook his head. "It looks like lead. I think it's supposed to be a musket ball."

Cordero closed her eyes and shook her head. "How many dead?"

"Ten? Twenty? I can't tell. Whatever it is, there's scores more wounded. Are you okay, though?"

She looked at the EMT, who nodded and said, "She's going to be fine."

Cordero then looked at Harvath. "All the macho bullshit aside, are you sure *you're* okay?"

Harvath looked at the EMT, who shrugged and said, "You got your lights turned out. You should let us transport you to the hospital so you can get a full workup."

"Not really a big fan of hospitals," he replied.

"You took a good blow to your head," the EMT stated. "I'm not kidding. You really should let us take you in."

"Not going to happen."

"Sir, how many fingers am I holding up?"

Harvath forced a smile and held up his fist. "Now how many fingers am I holding up?"

Cordero shook her head.

"It's up to you," the EMT said. "I can't force you to go."

Harvath looked around. The devastation was amazing. "And here we were so sure it was going to be a sniper."

"We were half right," she replied, picking up the forceps with the deformed lead ball. "How many of these things do you think were packed in that suicide vest? Hundreds? Thousands?"

Harvath had no idea. "Almost done?" he asked the EMT.

"Just about," the man responded as he affixed the gauze over Harvath's left eyebrow and taped it in place. "Now we're done."

He thanked the man, and after he and Cordero signed off on paperwork refusing to be transported to the hospital for further evaluation, the EMT stood up and moved on to treat other people.

"Now what?" Cordero asked.

"Pretty serious crime scene. Multiple homicides. I'd imagine you want to investigate."

"No," she said, looking at how filthy she was. "You know what I want? I want to change my clothes, hug my son, and have a drink."

He understood how she felt. They were both in shock.

"You want company?" he asked.

Cordero looked at him.

"For the *have a drink* part."

He didn't need to clarify his remark. She knew what he meant.

"I'd like that," she replied.

Harvath helped her to her feet, and they leaned against each other for a moment. It felt good. It also felt wrong. They shouldn't be going for a drink. They should be working this crime scene, trying to find clues, something that would lead them to who had done this so that they could prevent any further deaths.

He also knew that this entire investigation had gone to a completely new level. This was beyond a homicide investigation now. This was going to be classified as terrorism. Boston PD, the FBI, ATF, DHS, all the alphabets in the soup were going to be involved. They would comb every square millimeter of space looking for clues, and they would bring to bear the most sophisticated technology available.

This wasn't the place for them now. If something broke, they'd be notified. Besides, after what they had just been through, cheating death like that, they needed some downtime. Nevertheless, Harvath felt guilty about leaving.

Cordero seemed to be able to read his thoughts.

"This wasn't our fault," she said.

She was right, but it didn't change the way he felt. This was the first time that they had been ahead of the killers, but it hadn't made any difference. It hadn't stopped anything. There were even more people dead now.

They walked in silence, showing their credentials when they had to duck under crime scene tape to get out of the blast area.

Just past where Betsy Mitchell had been detonated, they stopped at one of the corpses. It had been covered with a plastic tarp. Cordero leaned over and pulled it back. It was a mass of cloth and bloody flesh. There was no human form to it all. The man had been so close when the explosion happened. The only possible means of identifying him was the half-melted nameplate that still read KACZYNSKI.

Cordero lowered the tarp. "He was a good cop," she said, her voice heavy with emotion. "A *really* good cop."

"We're going to get the people who did this. I promise you."

She turned and faced him. "How can you promise something like that?"

"You wanted to know what I do? What I *really* do? That's what I do. I *get* people. And I promise you, I *will* get the people who did this."

CHAPTER 63

Harvath's clothes were filthy. There were bits and pieces of things on them that neither he nor Cordero wanted to identify. They spent twenty minutes looking for Sal, hoping they could grab some of the extra clothing he had in his vehicle. His cell phone was off and he wasn't responding to any calls over the radio. They figured he was either with the head of the homicide unit, or more than likely debriefing with the FBI. It wasn't a big deal. At least Cordero knew he was okay. His had been the first face she had seen after the explosion. In the chaos, he had helped her to her feet and then helped get her to a safe area. He had even found the EMT for her before she had sent him back to find Harvath.

When they got to her car, Harvath asked her if she was okay to drive. She nodded.

"I guess if you want to drop me at my hotel," he said, "I'll change into my old clothes there."

"I have clothes I think will fit you," she replied. "That is, if you don't think it's too weird."

"No, I don't think it would be too weird at all."

At any other time, Harvath would have turned her invitation into a joke about an offer to wear her clothing, but he knew that wasn't what she was inviting him to do. It was an incredibly vulnerable moment for her, and he treated it and her with all the respect that it deserved.

They drove through the Boston streets in silence. There wasn't much to say. Not after what had just happened.

It was a goofy analogy, but as they got closer and closer to her house, Cordero was like a knight letting one piece of armor fall away at a time. You could almost hear them clanking onto the asphalt and receding behind them as they drove.

As each piece fell, she softened, and Harvath saw a different side of her, something he hadn't even noticed over wine at dinner. The take-no-prisoners cop was sexy, but the woman beneath was even more so. It was like watching her turn into a completely different person. Which was exactly what was happening. She was shifting into becoming a mother, a daughter, and simply a person. The transformation was captivating. It was a depth he had never really appreciated in the women he had known before.

They arrived at her home and she parked her car in the garage. It was an attractive three-flat made from heavy blocks of stone.

"Is the whole place yours?" he asked.

Cordero nodded. "The whole building's mine. I rent out the ground floor unit, Marco and I are on the second floor, and then my parents have the top."

"Whose watching Marco now?"

"I'm guessing it's my mom. Dad has probably already gone to bed."

She checked the mail on her way in and then led Harvath up to the second floor. Just inside the front door, there was a closet with a small gun safe. Unloading her primary and backup weapons, she tucked them inside along with her cuffs, her badge, and her credentials.

"You don't keep something next to the bed?" he asked.

"I absolutely do," the detective replied. "Just not this one. Racking a twelve-gauge shotgun sounds a lot more intimidating than racking a Glock."

Harvath smiled. He liked her, more than just a little bit. The female detective smiled back and led him into the living room, where her mother was watching TV.

She made the introductions in English and then spoke to her mother for a few moments in Portuguese. He had no idea what they were talking about but assumed, by the look on the older woman's face, that she was giving her a quick rundown on everything that had happened. She seemed like the type who would try to spare her mother any unnecessary worry and had probably watered down a lot of what had transpired. At the end, both women had looked at Harvath and the mother had appeared impressed. He couldn't tell why. He figured Cordero had told her how he had knocked her to the ground and thrown himself on top of her to protect her from the blast.

The female detective showed him down the hallway to the guest room.

"The guest bathroom is through that door," she said. "There's fresh towels in there. You can help yourself to anything you need. I'll grab some clothes and leave them here on the bed for you."

"Thank you," said Harvath.

She lingered in the doorway. "You're welcome."

He smiled again. "I saw that look on your mother's face."

"What look?"

"At the end, when you were telling her what happened with the explosion and everything, how I knocked you to the ground. You didn't have to tell her that."

Cordero laughed. "Don't flatter yourself. I didn't."

"What?"

"She asked me where you grew up. I told her Southern California. She said you look like a surfer. I told her that was impossible."

"Why is that impossible?"

"Because you never learned how to swim."

She was playing with him, and he liked it.

"There's a neighborhood place around the corner that stays open late," she added. "We can get a drink and something to eat there."

"What about Marco?" he asked.

"My mother will stay. Now hurry up and take a shower. I'm getting hungry."

Cordero really put the "guest" in guest bathroom. There were razors, mouthwash, combs, everything he could possibly need. After taking a quick shower and grabbing a shave, he stepped out of the bathroom to find she had left clothes on the bed for him as promised. For the most part, it all fit pretty well.

After getting dressed, he threaded his holster through his belt, double-checked his weapon, and then put on the jacket she had picked for him. He looked at himself in the bathroom mirror. He thought his pistol would print through the material, but it didn't. All in all, she had done very well.

He transferred the contents of his pockets into the clothes he was now wearing, exited the guestroom, and walked up to the front of the apartment.

He made small talk with the detective's mother until Lara emerged from her room wearing jeans, boots, and a very flattering top. Her hair was pulled back in a ponytail and she had gone light on the makeup, focusing mostly on a shade of lipstick that drew attention to her attractive, full lips.

"It all fits," she said. "You look good."

"Thank you. So do you."

"Are we ready to go?"

"What about that hug for your son?"

Cordero smiled. "I gave him one while you were in the shower, but I do want to kiss him goodbye. Why don't you come with me?"

"Sure. I'd love to."

Harvath followed her down the hall, past the guest room to a small room off the master bedroom. With enormous stuffed bears, airplanes suspended from the ceiling, and bright blue walls, it was the perfect little boy's room. And asleep in his race car bed, complete with rails that made sure he didn't fall out, was the perfect little boy.

Marco had sandy blond hair and was tan like his mother. He had cheeks that probably got pinched, a lot. He looked so peaceful, so unaware of what had happened in the world tonight. It was the way it should be. Harvath was immediately taken by the little guy. He was even cuter than the photo Cordero had shown him.

As she walked in to kiss her son, Harvath's eyes scanned the shelves above the little boy's bed. There were lots of great children's books, a bunch of stuffed animals, several Fisher Price vehicles, and something that stopped Harvath's heart cold.

Cordero spotted the look on his face instantly. "What is it?" she asked. "What's wrong?"

Harvath leaned over the bed and grabbed the object off the shelf. "Where did you get this?"

"It's just an airplane. Why?"

"Lara, where did this come from?" he demanded, as his other hand began to reach for his gun.

"It was a gift from Sal. What's this all about?"

Placing the detailed display model of the Aerion Supersonic Business Jet back on the shelf, Harvath said. "I'll explain in the car, but we need to move. *Now.*"

CHAPTER 64

They had argued the entire above-the-speed-limit drive to Sal Sabatini's home. No matter how strenuously she defended him, though, Harvath knew she was entertaining the possibility. Over their years together, she had seen something, perhaps even several things that either she had chosen to ignore or that hadn't made sense until this evening. The bottom line was that she was cooperating and that was the most important thing at this point. Coming to grips with it was something he could help her with later.

As he stood in the backyard and peered through the kitchen window, he could hear the phone ringing inside. After dialing the number a second time and letting it ring, Harvath signaled for Cordero to put her phone away. Sal was home and waiting for this to happen, in which case Harvath regretted showing up without the SWAT team, or he'd already offed himself, or maybe was someplace else entirely, preparing to kill the remaining hostage. Having looked in the garage and finding it empty, he figured Sal was dead or someplace else.

That said, he had fooled a lot of people for a long time and had been exceptionally well trained. For all Harvath knew, he could have parked his car around the corner to give anyone considering entry a false sense of security. Harvath's mind was doing flips trying to sort out all the possibilities. There was only one way to approach this—prepare for the worst and hope for the best.

With his weapon out and ready, he said to Cordero, "Good to go?"

She nodded, and removed her picks from the lock. He hadn't seen any signs that the house had an alarm system. That was the funny thing about cops. Some were extremely security conscious, while there were others who were incredibly lax. Sal Sabatini, though, was also nuts, so who knew what his deal was.

Harvath counted in a whisper, backward. "Three, two, one."

On one, she turned the handle and quietly pushed the door open so Harvath could slip inside. The kitchen was thirty years out of date, but clean and smelled faintly of spices. There was a door to the basement and Harvath made a quick command decision. They'd save that for last.

Grabbing one of the vinyl-backed, lime-green kitchen chairs, he tucked it under the knob and made sure the door was securely closed. If Sal or anyone else was hiding down there and tried to come back up, they were going to make quite a ruckus trying to get out.

With Cordero covering his six o'clock, Harvath swept in and cleared the dining room, living room, and the front hall closet. Next were the bedrooms, which he hated almost as much as basements. The tiny bungalow-style dwelling only had two bedrooms, which were clear. There was no one in the closets or under the beds. The bathrooms were also clear, as was a tiny attic space above that they accessed from a set of pull-down stairs. That just left the basement. Lord how he hated basements.

Weighing the odds that there might be a teachable, I-told-you-so-moment in the kitchen, he opened the freezer, but it was devoid of severed heads or any other body parts. Time to face the real music.

Cordero put her hand on his arm this time. "I'll do it," she said.

Harvath shook his head.

"He might not shoot me, but if this is all true, he'll *definitely* shoot you. I'm doing this, so get out of my way."

Removing the chair from underneath the doorknob, she flicked on the lights and waited. *Nothing*. She then did something Harvath hadn't thought of. Noticing there were no risers, she lay down on her stomach and peered between the first and second stair. After that, she used her flashlight to illuminate the far corners.

Satisfied, she stood up and went down to clear the basement. Two minutes later she was back in the kitchen.

"Nothing," she said. "Nothing at all. Everything must have taken place via that warehouse."

"I'll bet he's the one that tipped them to clear out before we hit it."

Cordero didn't comment. She was still having trouble wrapping her mind around everything. She felt guilty and disloyal, doubly so by agreeing to accompany Harvath and break into her partner's home.

"Why don't we see what else is here," he said, heading back toward the living room, a small corner of which had been set up with a desk and appeared to function as the man's home office.

Sal was meticulous. There were records and receipts for everything, just nothing attaching him to anything illegal. While Harvath had hoped against hope that there would be something here, he wasn't surprised. A detective would hopefully be much too smart to leave anything directly tying himself to a crime.

Harvath powered on the computer and waited for it to boot up. Once it did, he was greeted with a password screen.

"Try *REDSOXFAN7*," Cordero said from behind him. "All caps. All one word. That's what he uses at the office."

Harvath entered the password and was granted access.

"It worked," he said.

"I'm sure after all these years he knows mine, too."

"What is it?"

"None of your business," she replied.

"All caps? All one word?" he said as he tried to pull up Sal Sabatini's recent Web browsing history. There was nothing there. It had all been scrubbed. There was nothing in his email history, either, though he doubted that was how Sal conducted clandestine communications. He would have received better training than that.

Harvath looked at his Word documents as well as his iTunes folders.

It was all very pedestrian and boring, right down to the wallpaper on his desktop. It looked like Sal had chosen the factory default, which was a little odd, as Harvath didn't know anyone who didn't monkey around with their desktop at least a little bit to try to make it more personal.

Going into the settings area, he opened the folder that held sample photos for the desktop. They were typical stock landscape shots. He then clicked over to the screen saver folder, and that's when he saw it.

Cordero was looking through some of Sal's books on the other side of the living room.

"You're going to want to see this," Harvath said. "Recognize this young lady?"

There were a series of shots of a Goth-type woman posing around headstones at the Granary Burying Ground. "That's Brittany Doyle. The one you paid four hundred dollars to for her bracelet cuff."

"From which we got a full and a partial print."

"But if those were Sal's prints, why didn't we get a hit on them?"

"Because whatever prints the Boston PD has on file for Detective Sal Sabatini, they don't belong to Sal Sabatini."

She was about to ask who was capable of making prints disappear from the Boston PD database when her cell phone vibrated in her back pocket. Looking at the caller ID, she froze.

"Who is it?" Harvath asked.

Cordero held the phone up so Harvath could see. "It's him. Sal."

CHAPTER 65

Cordero activated the call and waited. She didn't know what to say. How do you greet the man you've just learned is a cold-blooded killer? As it turned out, she didn't have to say anything. He started the conversation himself.

"I'm sorry to have to do this over the phone," he said.

"What are you talking about, Sal? Where are you?" she asked. In the background, she could hear what sounded like noises from the harbor.

"I wanted to say goodbye to you and Marco in person."

"Goodbye? Why? Where are you going, Sal?"

"Lara, I know you're in my house. That means you must know everything."

Cordero covered the phone's mic and quickly whispered to Harvath, "He knows we're here."

"We need to get out. There could be a bomb. Keep him talking."

"Tell me why you did it, Sal," she said as they moved out of the living room and through the dining room. "Why did you kill all those people?"

"You weren't supposed to be hurt," the man replied. "I love you and

Marco very much and I'm very angry about what happened tonight. You could have been killed."

"You act like you didn't know it was going to happen, Sal."

"I didn't. Betsy Mitchell was not my responsibility."

"Whose responsibility was she, then, Sal?"

"Don't worry. I'll take care of it."

"Sal," Cordero said firmly. "What do you mean, you'll take care of it? What are you taking care of?"

The man was silent on the other end of the phone as Harvath and Cordero rushed out the kitchen door and into the backyard.

"Sal," she demanded, "where's the last hostage? Tell me. You can still make this right. Where's Jonathan Renner?"

Finally, Cordero removed the phone from her ear.

"Where's Renner?" Harvath asked. "Did he tell you?"

"No. He just hung up."

"Damn it."

"He said he was angry about what happened tonight, that I could have been hurt. He wanted me to know that Betsy Mitchell had not been his responsibility."

"What does that mean?"

"I think somebody else was responsible for killing her," she replied.

"Maybe suicide vests are someone else's job. He didn't deny killing the other victims, though, did he?"

"No, he didn't."

"We've got to find him. Where would he go for safety? Where do you think he'd try to hide?"

"I could hear ambient noise behind him," she said. "I think he was at the harbor."

"Is he running? Was he catching the ferry for Logan Airport?"

"He said he was going to 'take care' of the danger I was put in tonight. It sounded to me like he was going to take care of the person who put me in danger."

"Did he say anything else?"

"I don't know," Cordero replied. "After that, he hung up."

"He must have had some sort of monitoring system on his house or his computer that alerted his phone when we came in. He's blown and he knows it. We need to get to the harbor as fast as possible."

"He could be anywhere."

"I don't think so," Harvath stated as he led her down the driveway and back toward where they had parked her car. "I think they're out of time and they're pulling out all the stops. They're going to kill Renner tonight, too."

"But where?"

"What's the last significant historical event that also happens to take place at the harbor?"

Cordero stopped as she realized what it was. "The Boston Tea Party."

The pieces were all coming together for her and made so much sense now. How the killer had been able to avoid being picked up on any CCTV cameras, how he'd not left any clues behind at the crime scenes, even the crazy contraption at the Liberty Tree site, as Sal had studied engineering in school before switching to criminology and had remained fascinated by it.

But for every piece that fell into place, it came attached to a thousand questions. Harvath had explained what Swim Club was and even how they may have recruited Sal, but Cordero still didn't understand why they would be kidnapping and killing people. It didn't make any sense. And as much as she wanted it to, she knew she had to focus her energies elsewhere. Sal and the people he was working with needed to be stopped.

When she got in her car and the Bluetooth synched with her phone, she pulled into the street and activated the speaker. There was no way they could risk using the police radio or their mobile data terminals. Sal had access to those and she and Harvath didn't want to tip their hand.

She called her commander and filled him in on everything as she raced toward the harbor. She then told him what they needed and reminded him again to keep everything off the police network. They absolutely had to assume that Sal was listening.

Harvath listened to the conversation, and no sooner had she disconnected the call than his phone rang. It was Bill Wise. He was calling on his cell phone, rather than his blocked landline from D.C.

"Bill," he said, answering the call. "It's not a very good time right now."

"We've got a positive ID on the killer. He's definitely from Swim Club. His name is Salvatore—"

"Sabatini," Harvath said, finishing the man's sentence for him. "I know. We just left his house."

"How did you—"

He cut him off again. "It's a long story. Listen, where are you? Carlton said you were on your way up here to help us catch these guys."

"We're here now. And we've already caught one of them."

Harvath looked at Cordero and said, "They've already caught one of them." Turning his attention back to his phone, he said, "Bill, I'm putting you on speaker with me and Boston PD detective Lara Cordero. She was Sabatini's partner. You can trust her."

"Who did you capture?" Cordero asked as Harvath pressed the button and held the phone out between them.

"A CIA operative named Stark," said Wise. "We've been interrogating him, and apparently there are two more operatives with him in Boston somewhere. A man named Vaccaro, and another, the team leader named Tom Cushing."

"I've got news for you, Bill," Harvath interjected, as he reflected on the model plane in Marco's room. It was the same model he'd been given after his first flight on the Fed's Aerion SBJ. "I don't think these guys are working *against* the Federal Reserve. I think they're working *for* them."

"You're right, and wait'll you hear why. Someone at the CIA named Phil Durkin put all of this together with the previous Federal Reserve chairman."

"Chairman Sawyer? The one who just died?"

"Yes," Wise replied. "It's a long story, but the Saudis blackmailed Sawyer into doing something for them. The only way Sawyer could pull it off was to hire Durkin for the job. Durkin agreed, but only as long as Sawyer would fund several of his black-ops projects. It worked until Sawyer started having second thoughts and, with his tenure at the Fed coming to a close, crafted a list of potential replacements he thought might be able to make things right."

"Which was the last thing Durkin probably wanted if 'making things right' meant he was going to get his funding cut off."

"Exactly. And before he could get his own candidate installed as the new Fed chair, he needed to get rid of the five others who were actively being considered."

"Where are you?" Harvath asked.

"We've got Stark at a hotel near the harbor."

"That's where we think Sabatini is. We're headed there now."

"Scot, you've got to hurry," Wise insisted. "Stark says they have the last hostage and they're going to kill him, now."

CHAPTER 66

When Cordero's vehicle screamed to a stop at the edge of the harbor in full lights and sirens mode, the head of the Boston PD's Rescue/Recovery Dive Team rushed up from the dock to meet them.

"The rest of the team is inbound," the man said. "Five minutes we'll be on the water."

"We don't have five minutes, Sergeant," Harvath replied. "We have to get going now. Where's your boat?"

The dive team commander led Harvath and Cordero down a gangplank to a thirty-foot-long rigid inflatable boat that belonged to the Boston Fire Department. A bunch of dive gear was already loaded on board. It would have to do. Spinning his finger in the air, he gave the boat's pilot the signal to get the craft's twin, 225-horsepower Evinrude E-TEC engines fired up.

As the sergeant untied the boat, Harvath helped Cordero on board, stepped into the pilothouse, and told the man captaining the vessel what they were looking for. He also reasserted that they were to maintain strict radio silence, as the men they were chasing had access to police communications. Thirty seconds later, they were away from the dock and roaring into Boston Harbor.

The dive team leader unpacked two scopes, one thermal, the other night vision, and offered Harvath his choice. Harvath took the night vision device, and both men moved forward as the boat slammed through the water.

There was a ton of traffic in the harbor. Any one of the boats they were seeing could be the one they were looking for. The CIA man whom Wise had been interrogating supposedly had no idea what the boat's name was or what kind it was. He was never intended to be part of what was happening in the harbor. His job had been to prep Betsy Mitchell to look and sound like a mentally disturbed homeless person, track her progress via the remote camera she'd been outfitted with, and get her to the site of the Boston Massacre and remotely detonate the suicide vest she had been forced to wear.

When Harvath asked how Wise had been so successful in getting so much information out of the man so quickly, he explained that it had been Reed Carlton's idea. Apparently, the Old Man had his own Swim Club assassin in custody back in D.C. The man's name was Samuel. Carlton had Samuel driven to Stark's home and then a phone call was placed. When Samuel got done describing the exterior of Stark's home and what he could see his family doing inside, Stark had completely caved and told them everything.

Harvath's mind was still reeling from what Wise had told him about the former Fed chairman being blackmailed by the Saudis. When he asked how Sawyer had ever crossed paths with Durkin, Wise explained that the relationship had been facilitated through the chairman's security chief, William Jacobson.

What bothered Harvath the most was the way it all fit together; how much sense it made. Actually, that wasn't what bothered him the most. What bothered him the most was that by doing the right thing, he might end up actually hastening his own country's collapse.

There had to be a way around it. There had to be a way to prevent it all from happening and using their own plan against them.

If there was, it wasn't coming to mind at the moment, which was just as well, because through the night vision scope, he picked up something floating off their starboard bow, a hundred meters out. He quickly relayed the information to the crewman in the pilothouse, who adjusted course and headed right for it.

Harvath handed the night vision scope to the sergeant, told him to relay the information on the vessel that was speeding away, and then rushed to the back of the boat, where Cordero was.

"What are you doing?" she said as she watched him rapidly get undressed.

"They've already dumped the body."

The sergeant, upon seeing what Harvath was doing, yelled, "Hey, you can't do that! You're not qualified."

He already had the weight belt around his waist, had tested the regulator, and had swung the tank onto his back. He lowered the mask over his face and grabbed a knife and flashlight just as the fire department boat coasted to a stop. A large wooden box, made to look like a crate of British tea, was bobbing on the surface. As Harvath switched on his light and went over the side into the water, the last thing he noticed was the skull, bones, and crown that had been painted on its side.

The water was cold, but Harvath had been in much worse and didn't pay any attention. It was also dark. There was no light at all except for the beam from his underwater flashlight.

The crate on the surface was meant as a marker and he followed the rope attached to it deeper and deeper into the water. There were no air bubbles rising up to meet the beam of his flashlight. All he could think was *Please don't let Jonathan Renner be dead. Let us have at least saved one of the victims.* Soon thereafter a form began to take shape at the end of the line.

As he got closer, he saw it was some sort of bag or a sack made of canvas and big enough to hold a body and be weighted down with rocks or cannonballs, as was historically seen with burials at sea.

Harvath reached out and touched the bag. He could feel Renner inside it. Placing the tip of his knife at the top of the canvas, he plunged the blade through and ripped open the biggest hole he could.

He saw the man's hair in the beam of flashlight and pulled furiously at the fabric until he could access his face. Removing the regulator from his mouth, he moved it toward the man and hit the purge button, preparing to deliver lifesaving air.

That's when he noticed two things—that the man was dead, and that he was also *not* Jonathan Renner.

CHAPTER 67

Bill Wise had no intention of leaving Stark alone in the hotel room. Ryan and McGee, though, wanted to be part of taking down Cushing and his people, so Wise had asked Harvath to take them along. Harvath had agreed, provided they made it to the dock by the time he got there. He had been crystal clear that he wouldn't wait for them, and he didn't. He and Cordero had hopped onto the Boston FD boat and taken off immediately.

Ryan and McGee got there just in time to see the boat speeding away into the harbor. They weren't the only ones left behind. Several members of the dive team showed up minutes later and were without a boat.

Maintaining their operations security, one of the divers got on his phone and made a call. Minutes later, a Boston PD Harbor Patrol boat raced up to the dock; the divers loaded their gear and sped back out after their teammates.

By the time they caught up with the thirty-foot Boston FD boat, Harvath had just surfaced. As the Harbor Patrol boat pulled up alongside, they shined a powerful spotlight on him.

"It's not Renner," he yelled after removing his regulator. "It's somebody else. Shot point-blank."

Climbing back into the boat, he told Cordero and the dive team leader what he had seen. The sergeant barked a series of rapid orders, and once they had cleared off the Harbor Patrol boat, Harvath and Cordero hopped on. They introduced themselves quickly to Ryan and McGee.

Cordero flashed her credentials to the two Boston PD officers operating the boat and told them the last known direction of the vessel they needed to catch.

"It's all over the radio now," one of the men said.

"There's not supposed to be any radio traffic."

"The way these guys were moving through the harbor, they caught the Coast Guard's attention. They're now in pursuit. If you'll sit down and hold on, we'll see if we can get you close. It sounds like they're going to cross our path about a mile from here."

Cordero nodded, everyone held on, and the Harbor Patrol officers threw the throttles all the way forward.

Their boat was even faster than the fire department's and it sliced through the choppy harbor. Cordero leaned in close so Harvath could hear her above the roar of the engines and the wind rushing by them.

"If it wasn't Renner's," she said, "whose body did you find down there?"

"I have no idea," Harvath said. "But I have a feeling Sal made good on his promise."

"What promise was that?" Ryan yelled.

"Sabatini said he didn't have anything to do with the bombing tonight. Said it made him angry. He claimed he was going to settle up with who was responsible."

"Fat chance of that," McGee replied. "The guy responsible is cinched up back at the hotel with an MP5 pointed at his chest."

"Then who's bouncing along the bottom of Boston Harbor right now?"

Ryan had an idea and was about to respond, when a deafening roar overtook them like a tidal wave from behind.

They all spun at once to see a giant Sikorsky MH-60T Coast Guard

"JayHawk" helicopter race right above them, headed in the same direction.

"They've already got eyes on the target," one of the Harbor Patrol officers shouted from the pilothouse. "Suspect is wearing a Boston PD raid jacket."

Ryan got Harvath's attention and yelled over the engines, "Sabatini?"

Harvath nodded.

When the large, oceangoing cabin cruiser came into view, they counted five other boats in hot pursuit—three from the Boston PD and two from the U.S. Coast Guard, all of which were keeping it lit up with their spotlights. Up on the fly bridge, Harvath could just make out Sal's Boston PD jacket.

The Sikorsky banked to come around and Harvath saw that its door was open and its interior blacked out. The Coast Guard didn't goof around and that door hadn't been left open for the breeze. Though he couldn't see him, Harvath knew there was a sniper in there.

As soon as the helicopter was in place another round of commands were issued over one of the Coast Guard vessel's PA systems for the driver of the cabin cruiser to bring his boat to a full and immediate halt.

When the cabin cruiser didn't respond, two earsplitting cracks that sounded like thunder erupted from the Sikorsky and two heavy .50-caliber rounds were loosed to pierce the boat's engine blocks.

Within seconds, smoke began to billow from the stern and the boat lost power. It eventually came to an eerie stop and just bobbed up and down on the water. No matter how many commands were given over the PA system to the man on the fly bridge, he refused to move. The boarding teams on their respective vessels made ready while the helicopter with its sniper hovered nearby.

McGee tapped one of the harbor patrolmen on the shoulder and said, "Make sure they know that in addition to the rogue Boston PD detective, we believe there are two accomplices and a hostage on board. The accomplices are very well trained and will be well armed."

The officer nodded and relayed the information to the other units. For Harvath, Cordero, Ryan, and McGee, it was now a waiting game.

The Coast Guard relayed one last series of instructions to the man on the fly bridge, and when he didn't respond, the boarding teams were given the green light to launch their assault.

As Harvath watched the teams work, something out of place at the stern caught his eye. Suddenly there was activity over the radio, which the Harbor Patrol officers had turned up the volume on so that Cordero and everyone else could listen in on what was happening.

The man on the fly bridge was dead.

"Dead?" Cordero repeated. "How the hell is that possible?"

The patrolman started to shrug when another message was received. *The boarding team had located a survivor. The rest of the vessel was clear.*

Harvath stepped into the pilothouse and said to the copilot, "Radio the Coast Guard that we're coming aboard." To the officer piloting the boat, he said, "Bring us alongside, now."

When it was explained that Cordero was not only Boston PD but the partner of the rogue cop, they were granted permission to board.

The first person they saw was the survivor, Jonathan Renner. He was sitting in the boat's salon, wrapped in a blanket.

Harvath approached the man and asked, "Mr. Renner?"

The man looked up and nodded.

"I'm very glad to see you alive, sir. We're going to get you back to shore and to your family as quickly as possible, okay?"

Renner nodded again, and Harvath walked out of the salon and back onto the deck.

Climbing up to the fly bridge, he joined Cordero along with Ryan and McGee, who were already there.

"It's not Sal," the female detective said.

"Who is it, then?" he asked.

"Tom Cushing," Ryan replied.

"Whoever killed him," said McGee, "used fishing line to keep him in a seated position. The boat has an autopilot."

Harvath studied all the blood pooled in the man's lap and running down his legs. "Somebody gutshot him. Not many more painful ways to go than that."

"I think we can make an educated guess as to who pulled the trigger," Cordero stated.

"And with Renner safe downstairs, I think we also can make a pretty well educated guess who I found underwater."

"Vaccaro," said Ryan.

Harvath nodded.

"Then where's Sabatini?"

Harvath led the group down the stairs to the stern of the cabin cruiser. Two of the Coast Guardsmen had already vented the engine compartment and made sure there was no threat of fire.

Leaning over the back of the boat, he pointed at the swim platform, where two nylon tie-down straps were dangling.

"How much do you want to bet that until just a little while ago, there used to be a WaveRunner or a Jet-Ski there?"

Ryan looked at McGee. "We need to warn Wise."

The knock on the hotel door was loud and unsettling. In fact it wasn't even a knock. It was a pounding.

"Boston Police! Open up!" the voice commanded. "Police! Open the door!"

Not only did Bill Wise have a prisoner secured to a chair and gagged, but the room was also awash in Class 3 weapons and other assorted items like Tasers and recording devices. Without credentials, there was no way he'd be able to explain his way out of this. Police involvement was something they absolutely didn't need.

What they needed was to get Stark to D.C. as quickly and as quietly as possible so he could tell his story there. That step, though, was now suddenly in jeopardy.

One of the guests or hotel security must have seen or heard something.

As he approached the door, his cell phone back on the desk began ringing, and another thought suddenly gripped him.

"Police!" the voice shouted as the pounding recommenced. "Open up!"

Bill Wise raised his MP5 ready to fire just as the door was kicked in from the outside.

He stumbled backward and landed on his ass in the bathroom. A fraction of a second later, something was tossed into the room and was followed by a blindingly bright light and an overpowering explosion.

CHAPTER 68

Ryan's cell phone rang just before the Harbor Patrol unit boat reached the dock.

"It's Wise," she exclaimed, as she activated the call. "Bill, we've been trying to reach you. We think Sabatini may be on his way to you."

Wise interrupted her and she listened as he relayed what happened. She then told him to hold on while she shared it with the others.

"Bill's okay, but Stark's dead. Sabatini pitched a flash-bang into the hotel room, and while Bill was down he put a round into each of Stark's kneecaps and then a round through the base of his throat. There was nothing Bill could do for him. Bill says it was pretty obvious that Sabatini wanted Stark to die as painful a death as possible."

"Where is Bill now?" Harvath asked.

Ryan asked him and then replied, "He sanitized the room as quickly as he could and barely made it out of the hotel. He's about four blocks away now. Says there are police cars everywhere."

McGee, who had been listening to the radio, nodded. "Boston PD has confirmed a gunshot fatality at the Renaissance."

Harvath looked at Cordero. "Anyone answering?"

As Ryan's call had come in, Cordero had checked her own phone. She had missed a call from home.

This was the second time she had tried calling back. Pulling the cell phone away from her ear, she shook her head. "That's not like them. My parents always pick up."

Whether it was the mother in her or the detective, she decided to call her tenants in the downstairs apartment just to make sure everything was okay.

As the boat pulled up to the dock, Harvath addressed Ryan and McGee. "You know where the rally point is, so pick Wise up, or have him meet you there. But hurry."

Hopping out onto the dock, he offered his hand to Cordero and helped her out of the boat. No sooner had her feet touched the pier than all the color drained from her face.

"What is it?" Harvath asked.

"One of the neighbors saw Sal going into my building. We need to get back there. Now!" she ordered.

They both took off running and found her car right where she had left it. Leaping in, they made as much noise leaving the harbor as they had when they had arrived.

In any other city, Harvath would have wanted to be the one doing the driving, but with Boston's nightmare of one-way streets, he was glad to have her behind the wheel.

As they entered her neighborhood, she killed the siren but kept the wigwags flashing. Then, a block before her home, she killed those, too.

The gradual falling away of her mental armor and police persona that Harvath had so admired earlier in the evening wasn't happening this time. There'd be no stand-down until she knew her family was safe.

They parked around the corner and Cordero laid out how she wanted to handle it.

"Promise me," she insisted.

Harvath didn't like what she was proposing. Sal Sabatini was a killer. It didn't matter how many years they had worked together.

"Promise me," she repeated.

There was no way he was going to talk her out of it. She had made up her mind. Reluctantly, he agreed and gave her his word.

Standing there as she walked away, he was certain that they had both just made the biggest mistake of their lives.

Opening the downstairs door, Cordero crept up to her second-floor apartment as quietly as she could. The stairs were more than a hundred years old, and even in places you thought were safe to put your weight, they still creaked. It was almost as bad as having a little dog yapping the alarm that someone was coming. Not that it mattered, because when she reached the landing, she saw that her front door was wide open and knew that Sal Sabatini was already waiting for her.

Stepping into her apartment, she saw her mother first, tears rolling down her cheeks. Next to her was her father, his face a mixture of fear and anger. Finally, as she stepped all the way inside, she saw Sal, holding them at gunpoint.

"Please close the door behind you," he said.

Cordero did as she was told.

"Good. Now please, slowly, remove both of your weapons and slide them across the floor to me."

"Where's Marco?" she asked as she slid both of the guns to him.

Sliding the weapons into the new jacket he was wearing, he replied, "He's safe."

"Where *is* he, Sal? *Tell me*."

"He's in his room, asleep. You don't have to worry."

"Why did you come here?"

"I wanted to tell you that I took care of everything."

"Meaning, what? That you killed those men?" she said. "Cushing? Vaccaro? Stark? Along with all the other people you've killed? That's why you came here?"

Sabatini held his finger to his lips. "Shhh, be quiet. You don't want to wake Marco."

"Sal, this needs to end. You're sick. You need help."

The man smiled at her. "It is going to end. Trust me. By the way, where's your new partner?"

"I don't have a new partner, Sal. You're my partner."

The killer's smile faded, replaced by anger. "What do you think I am? Stupid? You don't think I see how he looks at you?"

"Sal, he doesn't—"

"Shut up!" he roared. "Shut up!"

"Sal, I want to get you help."

"I don't need any help. I help *you*. Remember? When your husband died?"

"I remember, Sal. You helped us a lot."

"You don't remember shit. All you care about is yourself, you selfish bitch!"

Cordero's father attempted to stand, but Sabatini shoved him back down.

The female detective tried to deescalate things and spoke calmly to her father in Portuguese.

"That's right," Sabatini sneered. "You tell him that if he does that again, he's a dead man."

Cordero said a few more words and then turned back to the killer. "Sal, if you came to say goodbye, let's say goodbye. Please, before anyone gets hurt."

His face went from enraged to an odd smile. "I didn't come to say goodbye. I came to take you with me."

"I'm sorry, Sal. My place is here, with my son."

"Marco will be with us."

The way he said it sent shivers down her spine.

"I'm not going to hurt anyone. I'm done hurting people. I'm done hurting myself. No one is going to feel any pain anymore."

"Sal, please—" she began, hoping she could talk him into laying down his weapon and not harming anyone else.

"Fuck *please*!" he shouted. "I'm *the lion*. You don't tell the lion what to do. Not now. Not ever. You do what I say, when I say it. You *obey* me. Do you understand me?"

Cordero nodded. The man was coming completely unspooled.

"Now, where's your fucking boyfriend? And don't you lie to me."

"I don't have a boyfriend, Sal."

"Liar!" he screamed, reaching out with his free hand and striking her across the face.

Cordero's father leapt up to challenge him and Sabatini struck him across the side of his face with his pistol. The older man's knees buckled and he fell back onto the couch.

Cordero spoke to him rapidly in Portuguese once more and then turned her attention to the killer.

"Sal, stop this."

"Sal, stop this," he replied, mocking her. "No more games. It's time to go."

Grabbing her by the hair, he pulled her head down so she had to walk with it sideways. Looking at her angry father and terrified mother, Sabatini said, "If you move, everyone dies. The boy dies. Do you understand?"

Cordero spoke again in Portuguese to her parents, who sat frozen in place on the couch, and they nodded.

Sabatini smiled. "Good. Let's move," he commanded as he dragged her over to the base station for her cordless phone, ripped it out of the wall, and then dragged her down the hall toward Marco's room.

"Sal, you don't have to do—"

"Shhh," he whispered, cutting her off. "It's all going to be very quiet, very soon. You'll see. We're going to be happy."

They reached Marco's room and Sabatini used the toe of his boot to push the door open. He looked down into the bed, but the little boy was gone.

Sabatini flipped right back into rage mode.

"Where is he?" he shouted. "Where the fuck is he?"

Cordero didn't reply.

Pulling her with him, he stepped into the room and flipped over the race car bed. He then threw open the closet doors but the little boy wasn't there either.

He then dragged Cordero back down the hall and threw her like a piece of trash onto the living room floor. He pointed his weapon at her and was about to threaten to kill her in order to get her parents to tell him where the little boy was hiding when he noticed her parents were gone, too.

"What the fuck is going on here?" he screamed. "Where the fuck are they?"

"Out stealing me a new sailboat, asshole," said a voice from behind.

Before Sabatini could even react, Harvath depressed his trigger twice, the shots perfectly aimed and placed exactly where the killer deserved them.

CHAPTER 69

With its money and powerful reach, the Federal Reserve, or more precisely Monroe Lewis acting under the auspices of the Federal Reserve, was able to make the impossible possible, including establishing phony flight plans for its Aerion Supersonic Business Jet.

As Reed Carlton, Lydia Ryan, and Bob McGee huddled with General George Johnson and his team at the Directorate of National Intelligence, Harvath had been able to cut through all the red tape and trace the plane with one phone call.

"Buenos Aires," said Natalie, the Swedish flight attendant. "Additional passengers boarded, we flew further south to Tierra del Fuego and then everyone disembarked when we landed at the airport at Ushuaia."

Harvath thanked her and gave the information to Johnson's people. Within an hour, they had CCTV footage from Argentina. It didn't take long to ID the men Phil Durkin had picked up in Argentina. They were a cross section of thugs and hired killers the Agency had used from time to time for assignments in South America.

When they had identified his destination, Ryan called her ex to see if she might know why he had selected it. Had he ever mentioned any assignments or did he have any contacts all the way down there? Brenda Durkin had laughed.

"Phil had plenty of contacts in Patagonia," she said. "And they were all slippery, but not in the way you think."

Brenda explained that her husband was an avid fly fisherman and had taken multiple trips to Tierra del Fuego. His favorite place was the Kau Tapen Lodge on the banks of the Rio Grande River. The river flowed from the Andes down to the Atlantic and boasted the best sea trout fishing in the world. Before their marriage had turned sour, he had talked of retiring there. Though she could never prove it, she half suspected he had been building a house down there.

That was all Harvath and the rest of the people gathered with General Johnson had needed to hear. They were convinced they knew where Phil Durkin was. At that point, it was only a matter of how to deal with him.

Argentina was a politically sensitive country for the United States to deal with. They could be helpful in some areas and downright obstructionist in others. It was decided that the less they knew about what was happening the better.

The weapons arrived in Tierra del Fuego via the Falklands and a contact the Old Man maintained in the British SAS. They offered shooters as well, but Carlton had politely declined. What he did take them up on, though, was surveillance. The SAS had an excellent stable of covert operatives on Tierra del Fuego and they were happy to help out. By the time Harvath and his team arrived, Durkin's house had been located and everything was in place. Back in Northern Virginia, General Johnson and the Old Man were watching everything unfold via satellite.

Lydia Ryan had insisted on coming along for the operation. From everything Harvath had heard about her, she was more than up to the task and he had no objection. The Old Man wanted Sloane Ashby there, too, and Harvath was glad to have her. Her record spoke for itself.

He had also roped in Matt Sanchez, who had performed so well in Somalia. General Johnson had recommended the team's final member.

Chase Palmer of Odessa, Texas, had the distinction of being the youngest operator ever to have been admitted to the ranks of the U.S.

Army's elite Delta Force unit. He was smart, battle-tested, and an exceptionally talented killer of the enemy. The Department of Defense had file cabinets stuffed full with accounts of his exploits. His teammates had nicknamed him "AK" for *Ass Kicker*, but the nickname took on a whole new meaning when he was caught with an empty AK-47 and was able to bluff six heavily armed Taliban into surrender.

Some of his superiors resented not only his talent and meteoric rise, but also his above-average intelligence. When they called him AK, it stood for *Asshole Kid*. General Johnson, though, saw him for what he was—a tremendous asset to the United States—and had taken him under his wing. Though still technically a member of Combat Applications Group, or CAG (the name given to Delta Force to allow the Army to deny the existence of Delta Force), Palmer was assigned to General Johnson and served at his pleasure. Right now, the general's pleasure was to see to it that *Operation Sierra*, the code name given to the capture of Phil Durkin, was successful.

"Targets have all been ranged. Command Six is good to go," Sanchez replied over his microphone as Harvath asked his team members one by one for their SITREPs.

The terrain was barren and windswept; more rock and loose shale than anything else. It was cold and misty. Everyone would rather have been someplace else, but you wouldn't have heard a complaint from a single one of them. This is who they were and what they did. Each of them consoled themselves with the knowledge that no matter how damp and how cold it was, it easily could have been worse, and that what they did, they did for their country. They all knew that there were people who would never know their names and would never know what they were doing this night, but that their way of life hung in the balance.

Lowering his night vision binoculars, Harvath looked at Ryan and said, "Are you ready for this?"

She nodded.

He pointed in the direction of the lodge and said, "We're on, then."

Ryan didn't need the binoculars. She could see the pair of headlights as they drove out of the Kau Tapen and began bouncing along the rutted, partially washed-out road.

"This is Command One," Harvath said into his microphone as he opened the door of his vehicle and stepped into the rain. "Park Place. Repeat. Park Place."

Ryan exited as well and, opening her umbrella, stood near the back bumper of their 4x4 with a flashlight. While Harvath pretended to work on a tire, she watched the vehicle from the Kau Tapen Lodge as it wound its way up the ribbon of road, getting closer and closer.

When it reached the right distance, Ryan began to flag the driver down with her flashlight. As the green Land Rover neared, it began to slow, coming to a stop behind their SUV.

The driver was a handsome young man dressed in Helly Hansen foul weather gear. Putting his Land Rover in park, he immediately stepped out to see if he could help.

"Can I help you?" he asked in Spanish.

"I think we may have broken our axle," Ryan replied in English.

The polite young man switched into English as he approached. "Would you like me to take a look?"

"You're from the Kau Tapen Lodge?" she asked, pointing at the logo on the side of the man's vehicle.

The young man nodded. The lodge participated in a hotel management program that brought in international hotelier students throughout the year, many from Canada, the United Kingdom, and the United States. They were always polished and attractive, which added to the establishment's world-class feel.

"You probably have guests you need to get to the airport. We don't want to keep you."

"I'm by myself. I'm just delivering food. It's no problem for me to take a look. My cousin is a mechanic in town."

"I apologize," Ryan said.

Whether it was her statement, or the gun she produced, it didn't matter. The effect was what was desired. The young man stopped and froze in place.

"Turn around," Ryan ordered. "Hands on your head."

"You're robbing me?" he asked, as he turned and did as she had instructed.

"Not exactly."

As Ryan kept him covered, Harvath rushed forward, cuffed his hands, and placed him in their vehicle. Waiting inside were Sloane Ashby and Chase Palmer. They listened carefully as Harvath asked the young man a quick series of questions regarding Phil Durkin's home and security measures. The young man was frightened and answered as best he could. Ryan tried to calm him down.

"Just answer our questions and everything will be okay. No one will hurt you."

The young man gave descriptions of everything he was asked until Harvath was satisfied that they had everything they needed.

"Let's roll," he said.

Nodding, Ashby and Palmer climbed out of the 4x4 and jogged back to the Land Rover. It was time to go to the next phase.

As they got the Kau Tapen Lodge's Land Rover back on the road, Harvath alerted the rest of the team.

"Boardwalk," he said over the radio. "All teams, Boardwalk."

CHAPTER 70

As Ashby drove, Palmer sat in the backseat and organized the trays of hot food. If it had been him, he would have hired a local to do his cooking for him instead of having his dinners catered from the lodge. It didn't matter that Durkin could afford to do it; it just didn't seem tactically wise.

Durkin, though, must have seen things differently. The hired help liked to talk. That was a potential liability he couldn't afford. Not when he was on the run and knew people would be looking for him. Having the food prepared and brought over, while expensive, did have several advantages, not the least of which was that access with the outside world was limited.

As they closed in on Durkin's small ranch, Ashby gave a SITREP over her radio and then asked for radio silence, as she didn't want any distractions at the gate.

Pulling up to the wooden doors, she brought the vehicle to a stop and waited. Two burly men in ponchos stepped out of a stone guardhouse and motioned for the windows to be rolled down as they approached. Palmer had peeled back the lids on several of the trays so that the odor of food would permeate the Land Rover.

Even standing outside the vehicle in the rain, the men smelled like coffee and cigarettes.

The man on the driver's side asked where the other delivery boy was. Ashby answered that he had the "Chilean flu" and pantomimed drinking a large glass of booze. The man chuckled and asked her where she was from. He wanted to flirt a little bit with her. His buddy, on the other hand, wanted to eat.

"She's from the lodge, via the kitchen," the other guard said. "Go see her when your shift is over. The food's getting cold."

Palmer laughed, though he shouldn't have. The line was not meant for him to hear. He was a servant and should have remained invisible. It was good-natured ribbing between two comrades. His interjecting himself had made it about the man's machismo.

"You think something is funny?" the first man asked.

"No, señor," he replied.

"Why are you laughing, then?"

Shit, Palmer thought to himself. *This guy is bored and itching for a fight.* He needed to come up with something quick.

"I laughed because she doesn't work in the kitchen, she works in the bar. And it's her fault our colleague has such a bad hangover."

The man on the passenger side laughed himself. "See? There you go."

Palmer looked at the man on the driver's side. "There are two things you can never trust a woman with: alcohol and guns."

The gruff man seemed to like this joke and smiled. Reaching his hand in the window, he touched Ashby a little too close to her breast and said, "And what would a little girl like you do with a gun?"

Ashby pumped the gas as she took her foot off the clutch, which caused the Land Rover to leap forward a couple of feet. It also caused the overly friendly gate guard to snatch his hand back out of the window. The man on the other side of the vehicle found this quite amusing and laughed even louder.

"Okay," the first man growled as he caught back up to the Land Rover, "you can go in. Make sure you tell them to bring us our food." He added, pretending to put his hand back in, "I'll make sure to come see you later at the bar."

Ashby gunned the engine once more and the man dramatically leapt back as if she were suddenly radioactive. His smiling colleague opened the gate and allowed them to enter.

As they drove into the courtyard, she activated her radio and announced, "Free parking."

Palmer smiled. "Come to think of it, maybe this phase should have been called *Community Chest*."

She flipped him the middle finger. "We'll deal with your alcohol and guns comment later," she said. And then, playing on his nickname, she added, *"Ass Kisser."*

He smiled as she brought the Land Rover to a stop outside the stone home's heavy wooden front doors.

"Just like we rehearsed it," she stated as she turned off the ignition and they both hopped out.

Removing trays of food, they walked up the front steps. Ashby went first, followed by Palmer. Before she even reached the doors, they were opened for her. Two more men stood there.

Ashby offered the trays to the taller of the two, but he shook his head. "Kitchen," he told her.

She started walking in the most likely direction and the other man put his hand out to stop her. He peeled back the lid on the top tray each of them was carrying, while the taller man gave them a quick pat-down.

When the taller man tried to give her a second pat-down, she side-stepped him and asked, "Where's the kitchen?"

The man grunted out directions and he and his colleague went back to their posts as she and Palmer walked down a wide hallway toward the rear of the house.

The rest of Durkin's pals, four more men in total, were gathered around a large TV, watching soccer and drinking beer. The man himself, though, was nowhere to be found.

"Excuse me, gentlemen," Palmer said. "Should we prepare eight plates? Or will there be others joining you?"

"Leave the food in the kitchen," one of the men said with a dismissive wave. "We'll get it ourselves."

A voice from Northern Virginia came over their earpieces. "We're picking up one additional heat signature in the northwest corner of the house."

"Understood," said Ashby. Quickly, she and Palmer unpacked the food, along with their weapons, which had been sealed in Ziploc bags and hidden inside.

With Palmer acting as a screen, she assembled a plate of appetizers and wrapped her suppressed weapon in a linen napkin underneath. She waited until the intensity of the soccer game began to pick up and then stepped into the television area.

"Who wants some?" she asked. "Compliments of Kau Tapen Lodge."

One of the men turned to tell her to shut up, but upon seeing her, his pockmarked face spread into a lascivious grin and he beckoned her over.

His attention flitted back and forth between the soccer match and the attractive young lady carrying a plate of hot food.

Something wasn't right, though. Was it the look in her eyes, or was it the fact that he could only see one of her hands and the other was hidden behind a napkin?

Ashby knew she was in trouble when the man gave up any pretense of watching the match. As his grin faded and his eyes narrowed, she saw his hand go for his gun. *It was on.*

"All teams go!" she said over her radio, and taking aim, she let the rounds from her weapon fly.

CHAPTER 71

As Harvath and Ryan came driving up the private road toward the gated ranch, thing one and thing two stepped out of the guardhouse. Matt Sanchez, hidden high above in the hills, watched it all unfold through the scope atop his rifle.

"You're all clear," he said over his microphone.

With Sanchez providing overwatch and Ryan in the passenger seat ready to engage any targets, Harvath leapt out of the 4x4 and opened the front gate.

Driving into the courtyard in front of the house, they received an update that not only had Ashby taken out the four men near the kitchen, Palmer had neutralized the two men just inside the front door. The only man left was the only man they were looking for.

Coasting to a stop, Harvath turned off their vehicle and removed the keys from the ignition. He and Ryan quietly climbed out and gently closed their doors.

They met Palmer in the entry hall and he signaled where he believed Durkin was holed up. Harvath nodded and gestured for him to circle around outside and make sure he didn't escape. Ashby would remain inside and make sure nobody sneaked up on them from behind.

With their weapons up and ready, they crept down the hallway toward Durkin and the northwest corner of the house.

A door at the end of the hall was open and a television could be heard from the inside. It was tuned to an American cable news channel. There was no other sound. Harvath didn't like it. How could Durkin have gone to all the trouble to set himself up at the end of the world with bodyguards and a gated retreat, but not have any intrusion detection measures? Did he feel that safe here? Or had he simply not gotten around to it because the ranch was never intended to be anything more than a fly-fishing getaway?

A few feet from the room, Harvath gave Ryan the signal to stop. He listened intently, his ears straining for any sound other than the TV coming from inside. He couldn't make anything out.

Removing a flash-bang from his coat pocket, he showed it to Ryan, counted to three, and pitched it into the room.

He and Ryan crouched down, closed their eyes, plugged their ears, and opened their mouths to equalize the pressure from the blast. As soon as the device had detonated, they swept into the room.

Durkin had been taken by surprise, but not by them. He lay on the floor of his study with a single gunshot wound to the back of his head, blood pooling around him.

Ryan looked at Harvath. "You've got to be kidding me."

Harvath reached down and touched his skin. "This is fresh. He's still warm. Come on."

Running toward the front of the house, he radioed Ashby and Palmer to meet him there.

"How do you know the guy's not hopping on a ferry?" shouted Palmer as he rushed to the Land Rover.

"I don't," Harvath replied as he jumped into the 4x4. "But we should assume he wants to get home as quickly as possible."

There were two airports on the island. Harvath hoped that he had selected the right one. Just in case, he sent Sanchez toward the other. Better to only have one person there than no one at all.

As he raced toward his airport, Harvath asked General Johnson's team to zoom their satellite out to try to help him find what he was looking for.

"There are vehicles coming and going in both directions," a voice from Northern Virginia said over their earpieces. "We need more to narrow down the search."

"We don't have more," Harvath replied. "The target could be in a car, a truck, or even on a motorcycle."

"Searching," said the voice. "Stand by."

Ryan looked at Harvath as he pulled the wheel hard to the left and then swung out onto the main road.

"If the house was under satellite surveillance, how the hell did anyone get in or out without being seen?" she asked.

"With the weather, they were relying heavily on thermal imagery. That kind of technology is no longer foolproof. In fact, if you have the right resources, anything can be beaten."

The analyst's voice from Northern Virginia came back over their earpieces. "We've now got a plane warming up at Ushuaia International."

"Get somebody to overlay a schematic for an Aerion SBJ," said Harvath. "I want to know if you get a match."

"The Fed helped Durkin escape, only to turn around and kill him?" Ryan asked.

"I think somebody doesn't want him to talk."

"Who?"

Harvath was about to reply, when the voice from Northern Virginia came back. "We've got a hit on that aircraft profile," it said. "You were right. Aerion SBJ. We also picked up a cell phone transmission between what we believe is the aircraft and a vehicle about fifteen miles ahead of you."

Harvath looked at Ryan as he stepped on the accelerator and said, "I think we're about to get all of our questions answered."

By the time they caught up with the blue Chevrolet Celta, they were less than ten miles outside Ushuaia. Harvath slowed his approach so as not to spook the driver.

"What do you want to do?" Ryan asked.

"We're going to box him in," he replied, as he radioed Ashby and Palmer to tell them what he wanted to do.

"Roger that," Ashby acknowledged. Punching the accelerator, she first passed Harvath's vehicle and then the Chevy Celta before settling into the lead position on the road to Ushuaia.

Palmer had wanted to see if he could get a look at the driver, but Harvath had warned him not to. He wanted to take him by surprise. It was bad enough that the Land Rover had the fishing lodge's logo emblazoned on the side of it. He didn't need a man who was no stranger to killing locking eyes potentially with another such man. He told Palmer to pretend he was asleep.

If the driver of the Celta suspected anything, he gave no indication as he maintained his present course and speed.

Getting back on his radio, Harvath told Northern Virginia there was one other thing he was going to need and that the Old Man better get back on the phone to his SAS contact quick.

Five minutes later, the Old Man came back to him with a safe house location. Immediately after, Ashby told Harvath she could see a stoplight ahead and that they should launch the ambush at the next red.

As Ryan plugged the location into her GPS device, Harvath saw the Land Rover up ahead and just beyond that, the stoplight.

"Put your head against the headrest," he told her.

Ryan did it and flashed him the thumbs-up.

Harvath calculated their speed. It wouldn't take much to surprise the driver of the Celta, but he didn't want to surprise him; he wanted to stun him if possible. He also wanted to make sure that he wasn't going so fast that his air bags deployed.

As the Land Rover slowed down for the next light, the Celta slowed as well, but Harvath maintained his speed.

When he struck the tiny car, he sent it skidding sideways across the wet pavement into a lamppost. Before he could even release his seat belt and glance at Ryan to make sure she was okay, Ashby and Palmer were already out of the Land Rover with their weapons drawn.

They immediately closed the distance with the Celta, threw open the door, and pulled its bloodied driver into the street.

As Harvath jumped out of his 4x4, he recognized the man immediately. He didn't know who he had been expecting, but William Jacobson, the Federal Reserve's security chief, definitely wasn't it.

CHAPTER 72

William Jacobson was a hard, stubborn son of a bitch. Trying to get information out of him had been like trying to get blood from a stone. The Old Man had pulled his jacket and there weren't any significant pressure points they could find. He had no wife, no children, no family. He was incredibly loyal to his employer. No matter how badly Harvath threatened him, he wouldn't part with even the smallest detail about what the Fed, and with it Monroe Lewis, had been up to.

If Harvath had to torture him, he would, but that was never the first card he played. He was starting to think, though, that it was quickly working its way up to the top of the deck.

Harvath had already played what he thought was one of his strongest cards. He had threatened to turn Jacobson over to the Argentines to face murder charges, and the man hadn't even flinched. No matter what downside Harvath outlined for the man, Jacobson simply shrugged it off or fixed Harvath with a cold, vindictive stare.

It was as if the man believed there was no force that the Fed couldn't overcome and rescue him from. This left Harvath with very few options.

"I have to tell you, Will," he said, "things are about to get even worse for you. You either start cooperating, or you'll only have yourself to blame for what happens. We're a very long way from home and nobody is coming to save you."

Jacobson laughed. "You have no idea what you're tangled up in, do you?"

"I have a pretty good idea. One of Durkin's guys, a man named Stark, had a lot to say before Sal Sabatini killed him."

"Durkin's guys are pros. They'd never talk."

"Everyone talks, Will," Harvath replied with a smile. "It's just a matter of when. For Stark, it was when one of Durkin's Swim Club psychos pulled up in front of his house and gave him a play-by-play over the phone of what his family was up to."

The smile faded from Jacobson's face.

Harvath pressed his advantage. "The killer is named Samuel. Ever heard of him?"

A barely perceptible tic registered on the security chief's face. Most would have missed it. Harvath didn't. "If you haven't met Samuel, you should. I think he'd like you. Or maybe not. I suppose it all depends with an unstable personality like that. But, I assume you know that. Salvatore Sabatini is another wack job. You'd love him, too."

"Sabatini is dead," Jacobson said. "You shot him."

"I shot him, but I didn't kill him. I merely clipped his wings. Everyone thinks he's dead, but that was so we could keep him safe. We have him in a very special cage in a very secret place."

"Both of them are nuts."

"I agree," said Harvath. "Completely nuts. What's amazing is that their stories are almost believable. You know who they sound a lot like?" he asked studying his face. "Besides Stark, of course."

Right then, there was another micro-expression that flashed across Jacobson's face. Harvath was definitely hitting close to home.

"The other person they sound like," Harvath continued, "is Tara Fleming."

"I have no idea who you're talking about."

The man had answered a little too quickly, a little too emphatically.

"Funny, because I have surveillance footage of you entering and leaving her apartment building two days ago. Didn't find much, did you?"

The vindictive stare was back again.

"You can give me the tough-guy stare all day long," said Harvath. "Or we can talk, man to man."

Jacobson guffawed. "I told you, you have no idea what you're dealing with."

"Why don't you break it down for me?"

The security chief was dead silent.

Harvath smiled. "Will, trust me when I tell you we're now quickly approaching my least favorite alternatives. Like I said, I don't want to hurt you, but it is on my list. Sooner or later, everyone talks."

The man chuckled again.

Harvath nodded to Palmer, who produced a pair of EMT shears and cut away Jacobson's clothing. Ashby came in with a metal pail filled with water and a stack of towels.

"Are you going to waterboard me?"

Harvath tilted his head. "Anything's possible. It all depends on you."

Palmer tore off two strips of duct tape from a roll and pressed one down onto Jacobson's gray chest hair and the other on his equally hairy left side beneath his armpit. He then grabbed a corner of each and ripped them off.

The security chief cried out as much in surprise as in pain. As Ashby placed adhesive pads on the now-hairless patch of skin, Harvath shared with him something he had learned from his file.

"You've been on both Crestor and Lipitor. Now you're on something I can't even pronounce. There are some other heart-related meds in your file, which tells me—"

"How the fuck did you get hold of my medical records?"

"It's a brave new world, my friend. You think Durkin's people are the only ones who can hack into electronic medical records?"

Jacobson glared at him.

"So," Harvath continued, "based just on your meds, I'm guessing you either have a bad ticker or there's a serious history of heart disease in your family. Either way, we're going to do a little stress test together."

No sooner had Harvath said the words than he noticed the tic race across the man's face again.

Wires led from the adhesive pads to a small, black Storm case whose lid was up and facing Jacobson. He couldn't see what was inside, but his instincts told him it was some sort of defibrillator on steroids meant to deliver increasingly unhealthy shocks to his heart. When the young female removed his shoes and socks and placed his feet into the pail of water, he knew beyond a shadow of a doubt that his instincts were right on the money.

"This part can get really uncomfortable," Harvath said. "You may find your mind going in a bunch of different directions, so let me help you out. Here's what I know.

"I know that Phil Durkin ran a host of black-ops programs out of the Central Intelligence Agency. One of those programs was a political destabilization team. Yes or no?"

"Fuck you," said Jacobson.

"Wrong answer," Harvath replied as he nodded to Palmer.

Palmer made ready behind the open lid of the Storm case as if he were about to throw some sort of switch. But as he did, Jacobson broke. "Wait."

"Yes or no?" Harvath commanded.

"Wait . . . I . . ."

Harvath looked at Palmer and said, "He's stalling. Shock him. *Hard.*"

"Yes," Jacobson said quickly. "Durkin handled the team and Tom Cushing ran it."

Now they were getting somewhere. It was time to see if what Stark had told Bill Wise in Boston was true. "Was Cushing's team involved with the Arab Spring?"

The security chief nodded. "Cushing's team *was* the Arab Spring. They organized all of it. Right down to that fruit vendor who kicked it all off in Tunisia."

"How about Jordan?" Ryan interjected. "Is Jordan on the list?"

It was the first time she had spoken during the interrogation, and both Jacobson and Harvath looked at her.

"Tell me," she ordered.

"I have no idea," Jacobson replied. "All those countries are the same as far as I'm concerned. I couldn't tell one from another on a map and I don't give a rat's ass."

"Was the prior Federal Reserve chairman, Sawyer, funding Durkin's black-ops programs before he died?" asked Harvath.

"Yes."

"Why?"

"Because he needed that destabilization team."

"Why?" Harvath repeated.

Jacobson fell silent once more.

Harvath looked at Palmer. "Turn it all the way up and juice him. I don't care if his heart does explode. I'm tired of being jerked around."

"No!" Jacobson shouted. "I'll tell you."

"You've got thirty seconds."

"The Saudis."

"What about them?" Harvath demanded.

"The Saudis were blackmailing Chairman Sawyer."

"Blackmailing him how?"

"The dollar has become worthless. The Fed has created too many of them and the U.S. government has run up hundreds of trillions of dollars in debt."

"Hold on," Harvath admonished. "The U.S. debt is nowhere near that number."

Jacobson shook his head and laughed. "You have no idea how bad things are. It's a house of cards and it is all ready to come down. The Saudis figured it out. Without our protection, they're going to be overrun. They wanted to create a buffer zone."

"Why would Sawyer care about what Saudi Arabia wants?"

"Because the only thing preventing our house of cards from falling is the fact that oil is bought and sold in dollars, *American* dollars. Take that away and everything goes bye-bye. The dollar collapses, the economy collapses, and civilization follows."

Harvath was stunned. "And that's what the Saudis threatened to do? Collapse the dollar?"

Jacobson nodded. "Normally, their intelligence services can't even rub two sticks together, but this time they came up with one hell of an idea. Think about it. When the United States collapses, Saudi Arabia is going to be at the mercy of its neighbors. Why not work to make sure *all* of your neighbors are sympathetic to your cause? Let me ask you, in all of the Arab Spring countries that have been overthrown so far, who has risen up to be the new government?"

"The Muslim Brotherhood," said Harvath.

"Which is loyal to which kinds of Muslims? The Shia Iranians, or the Sunni Saudis?"

"The Sunni Saudis, of course. Iran is Saudi Arabia's greatest enemy."

"The Saudis aren't stupid. In fact, they're quite cunning. They didn't bother taking their ultimatum to America's politicians, who are subject to reelection and the whims of the masses. They went over their heads and straight to the ultimate defender of the dollar, the Federal Reserve.

"What people don't grasp," Jacobson continued, "is that empires collapse. Ours will, too, if we don't do everything we can to keep it alive."

"And whose idea was it to go after the Fed candidates?" Harvath asked.

"Durkin's."

"Why?"

"Chairman Sawyer wasn't just funding Durkin's team for the Arab Spring; he was funding a ton of other projects as well. It was a quid pro quo. Durkin made the Arab Spring happen, and in return Sawyer secretly opened the money spigot for him. There was just one problem. He was growing increasingly uncomfortable with how Durkin was doing things.

"The chairman's tenure was coming to an end, and he was the one who had pushed the Board of Governors and convinced them that the next chairperson should come from outside the Fed. The five candidates were all people he thought could successfully firewall the dollar off from any further Saudi threats and, just as important, would resist Durkin."

"But Durkin found out about the candidates and had them killed," said Harvath.

Jacobson nodded.

"And then what? He keeps killing candidates until he gets one he likes?"

"You're not thinking like Durkin."

"Elucidate me," Harvath replied.

"He never set foot on the road to toppling any Muslim government without knowing exactly who he wanted to install at the top."

"We didn't get hired to prevent these murders, did we?" Harvath said.

"No. The Federal Reserve needed to be seen to be doing everything they could. Plus, we wanted to have an extra set of eyes and ears as close to the investigation as possible."

"Who's *we*? You *and* Monroe Lewis?"

There was a look on Jacobson's face that sent all of the tumblers in Harvath's mind locking into place. "That's who Durkin wanted as the new chairman, isn't it?"

Jacobson simply smiled.

"How were you going to do it?"

"The Federal Reserve has a lot of secrets. There's one in particular that would be particularly damaging if it was brought to light."

"You were going to blackmail the Board of Governors into recommending Lewis for the chairmanship?" Harvath asked.

"The governors are unaware of this particular skeleton in the Fed's closet. Lewis was going to not only bring it to their attention, but offer a rather clever solution to the problem."

"Which would result in his name being put forward for the chairmanship."

Jacobson smiled again.

"And you came down here to kill Durkin to tie up loose ends."

Jacobson's smile continued.

Harvath studied the man's face. "What's in this for you?" he asked. "Why did you go along with it all?"

"The world economy is crumbling. Something very bad, very dark is on the horizon. The chaos and anarchy the United States will face is like nothing history has ever seen. It's going to be beyond biblical," he said, pausing for a moment before adding, "The storm's coming and there's nothing anyone can do to stop it. I just want a seat on the Ark."

"And you didn't care what you had to do to get it."

Jacobson smiled once more and Harvath had heard enough. He had trekked far beyond his purview.

Stepping outside the safe house, he activated his satellite phone so that he and the Old Man could talk about it in private. This wasn't something he could make the call on. The President himself would have to decide what to do next.

CHAPTER 73

"You can call it whatever you like, George" said the President to his Director of National Intelligence, "but I call it treason. We're a nation of laws. That's what makes us a republic. We need to start enforcing those laws and making examples of those who think they're above them."

"And the financial system?" the secretary of the Treasury asked.

"We need to allow it to fail. That damn Federal Reserve has done nothing but allow banks to take bigger and bigger risks, and whenever they get in over their heads, it's the taxpayers and their hard-earned money that is used over and over again to bail them out. That needs to stop."

"So we remove all restrictions from the financial industry?"

"Hell no," the President said, rebuking him. "I want a top-to-bottom review in the next seventy-two hours. I want to streamline that entire industry. They'll succeed or they'll fail on their own, but they'll know where the lines are drawn and that they'll be enforced. No longer will we hold that any business is too big to fail, and I don't want to hear that any person is too big to jail.

"It is going to be painful, I'll give you that, but we need to take our medicine now, right now. If we don't, we'll never pull out of the nosedive we're in. Our creditors need to know that not only do we have our house in order, we are also going to begin paying off our debt. For every job that's been shipped overseas, we're going to see five more spring up here by this government creating the most pro-business climate in the history of the modern world."

"And what about the Federal Reserve?" the secretary of the Treasury asked.

"We're not renewing their charter."

"We're not?" the man replied, stunned.

"No. The power to print money was intended for the Congress, not to be outsourced to some banking monopoly masquerading as a government agency. You've got twenty-four hours to get back to me with a plan on how we disentangle ourselves from the Fed."

"But, Mr. President—" the man began.

"No buts. We've shut down central banks before in this country. It's past time we do it again."

"The shock to the economy could—"

"Be just what this country needs," replied the President.

They went over a couple of additional items before the President thanked the Treasury secretary for coming and excused him from the balance of the meeting.

Harvath, Ryan, Wise, McGee, and Reed Carlton were all then shown into the Oval Office. It was the first time any of them had met the President. He directed them to the couches in the center of the room and asked them to sit down.

"We saw the secretary of the Treasury on his way out," said Carlton. "He didn't look so well."

"Good," replied the President. "Have you seen the state of our economy? The man should go to bed every night worrying that tomorrow he'll be swinging from a lamppost if things don't get better. I know I do."

This President had been elected largely based on his common sense and a no-BS approach to problems. He was very charismatic and, unlike many of the slippery politicians in Washington, seemed to not only genuinely care about the condition that the country was in, but also to be truly confident that things could be turned around and that collapse wasn't inevitable.

"But you're not here to talk about what keeps me up at night," said the President. "First, I want to thank you for what you did. I understand there were a few others who helped you," he said as he peered down at his notes. "A Ms. Sloane Ashby and Messrs. Chase Palmer and Matthew Sanchez. Please also extend my thanks to them."

Carlton assured the President that it would be done.

"Excellent," he replied. "Now, on to business." Looking first at Ryan, then Wise and finally McGee, he said, "I don't know what the hell is going on at CIA, but it's going to stop now. It needs all of the deadwood cleared out and a brand-new culture instilled. It's filled with patriotic men and women who would go to the ends of the earth for this country if the bureaucrats gumming up the system would just get out of their way and let them do it.

"This whole Phil Durkin situation never should have happened. I have already asked the DCI for his resignation."

Ryan and McGee were shocked.

"Who's going to replace him?" McGee asked.

"You are," said the President. "Both of you."

"Codirectors?" replied Ryan.

"Unless you think one person can handle turning that agency around in the next twelve months."

The Old Man smiled.

"I take it you approve?" said the President.

"Yes, sir," replied Carlton. "In fact, if I may say so, it should have been done a long time ago."

"It's being done now." Turning to Wise, the President asked, "Do you have any desire to come out of retirement and serve your country again?"

"If my country needs me, I'm happy to come out of retirement."

"I think Ryan and McGee are going to have their hands full. They're going to need someone they can trust to help weigh who stays, who goes, what gets saved, what gets cut, et cetera. I can't promise you it will be glamorous, but I can promise that you'll have the appreciation of a grateful nation."

Wise nodded. "Thank you, sir. It would be my honor."

"Good. I have already spoken with His Majesty in Jordan. He, of course, feigned outrage that his intelligence service was blackmailing the CIA with an active terrorist plot in order to extract information about Durkin's political destabilization team. He assured me that the bombers would be apprehended immediately and that any and all information they have on the plot will be shared with us straightaway. Ryan, I'd like you to review it and brief General Johnson, who will in turn brief me."

"Yes, sir," Ryan replied.

"What else?" the President asked as he flipped through his notes. "I've asked the attorney general to give me recommendations as to how Sal Sabatini and this Samuel character ought to be handled. I have to tell you that I'm less worried at this point about the legal process than I am at the prospect that there could be others like them running around out there. Dr. Wise, I'd like you to make Swim Club, as well as all the other black programs Durkin had kept alive, your immediate focus at the Agency."

"Yes, sir," said Wise.

"Speaking of Durkin's black programs, I understand the last member of the destabilization team, a Tara Fleming, has been placed in FBI custody and is being debriefed. I expect to meet with the FBI director soon to discuss what, if anything, he believes should be done with her.

"Which brings me finally to Mr. Monroe Lewis of the Federal Reserve. The scandals be damned—he's going to stand trial for what he did. His security chief is going to be charged as an accessory as well. I think that does it," he said, glancing once more at his notes. "Am I missing anything?"

Carlton raised an eyebrow.

"I'll get to your request in a moment," the President replied. Focusing on the others, he said, "I want to thank you again for what you did. It took tremendous courage. It's that kind of bravery and sacrifice that is going to bring this nation back to prominence. Remember that when things get tough up on the seventh floor at Langley, because they will get tough."

"We will, sir," said McGee as he stood and shook the President's hand. "Thank you, sir."

Ryan and Wise joined him, and after they both shook the President's hand and said goodbye, they exited the Oval Office along with Bob

McGee. Harvath and the Old Man sat facing the Director of National Intelligence and the President.

The President looked at Carlton and said, "General Johnson debriefed me on what happened in Somalia and shared your request to pin the firefight and the casualties on Durkin. I'm going to grant the request. Run everything through the general's office, and as long as it all has his approval, I'm okay with it. Technically, though, this conversation never happened. Understood?"

"Understood," the Old Man replied, pleased that he'd be able to put the *Sienna Star* issue to bed and get their agency paid.

"I also understand that your firm lost its DoD contract and since that time has been struggling a bit."

"I wouldn't say we've been—"

"That's correct, sir," Harvath replied, cutting off his boss and answering the President's question.

"I also understand, Mr. Harvath, that you worked for a prior president and helped chalk up some big wins. How come the next administration didn't hold you over?"

"They had a different worldview, sir."

The President thought about that for a moment. "I am very bullish on America's future; I make no secret about that. But before we return to prosperity and abundance, I believe we are going to face profound darkness and be tested like never before in this nation's history. When that happens, the United States is going to need its very best and very brightest to push back the darkness and take the fight to any enemy that would see us destroyed, both foreign and domestic.

"I'd like to be able to count on your organization. I want you to be part of that fight. With some of the reorganization that General Johnson and I are planning for the intelligence community, we believe a place can be made for you. Would that be of interest?"

Simultaneously, Harvath and Carlton replied, "Yes, sir."

"I'm glad to hear that," said the President as he rose, signaling that the meeting was over.

As he walked them slowly to the door, he left them with one final thought. "A man who occupied this office years ago once said that freedom is never more than one generation away from extinction. We didn't pass it to our children in the bloodstream. It must be fought for, protected, and handed on for them to do the same, or one day we will spend our sunset years telling our children and our children's children what it was once like in the United States when men were free."

He then shook their hands and said, "I'm glad to know that you'll both be with me in this fight."

EPILOGUE

"I promise you," said Harvath. "I'm not going to let anything happen to him. Trust me."

"Says the guy who lied to me about not being able to swim."

Harvath smiled and pulled her close. Her skin felt warm and smooth against him, her body perfectly fitting with his. He kissed her neck, just below her ear, and then gave her a playful bite. She squealed and tried to get away, but couldn't. He was holding on just tight enough to make it impossible.

They had been at the beach for a week and Harvath couldn't remember ever being this happy. It had been a long time for Lara Cordero as well.

Harvath and Marco had been inseparable. They had walked the beach together, picking up buckets full of rocks and shells along with piles of sticks and huge pieces of driftwood. The little boy laughed when Harvath would pretend the pieces were too heavy and struggled to pick them up. They built sand castles with enormous moats, went for ice cream at least once a day, and rode bikes everywhere.

It was a perfect vacation, and Harvath and Lara had both needed it.

But the question bubbling to the surface was if they needed more than just a vacation.

As far as he was concerned, Lara was not only gorgeous, tough as hell, and accomplished in her own right, but she was also very smart. Though he'd been dead set against her plan for taking down Sal Sabatini, she'd been right and he had been wrong. A fact she found no end of joy in reminding him of.

Lara hadn't wanted a shootout in her apartment that could have killed her son or her parents. In fact, she had rightly put their safety above everything else. Neither of them had known for sure if Sabatini would still be in her apartment when they got there, but her instincts had told her he would be.

She had given Harvath the key for the apartment's back door and had made him promise that if he could get to Marco and get him out safely, he would do it. Harvath had honored that promise, waking up the first-floor tenants, giving them the boy, and telling them not to open the door for Sal as he returned upstairs to help Lara.

To her credit, she had instructed her parents to run as soon as Sal led her out of the living room and down the hall to Marco's room. He had come completely unglued by that point, and she was seriously worried that he might kill her. The only thing that gave her any comfort was knowing that Harvath had saved her son, and even if he couldn't get back in time to save her, at least her little boy would survive.

But Harvath had come back and he had in fact saved her. He had also honored the other half of the promise she had sworn him to, which was that he wouldn't kill Sal unless he had no other choice.

When asked why he hadn't simply taken the man by surprise and knocked him out with the butt of his weapon, Harvath replied, "You said I couldn't kill him. You didn't say I couldn't shoot him."

His sense of humor was just one of the many things about him that she had grown increasingly attracted to.

The second night on Cape Cod, after they had put Marco to bed, they opened a bottle of wine and talked. Or more to the point, she had asked questions and Harvath had talked. She wanted to know everything about him and he had told her, more than he had ever told any woman before.

Harvath wasn't a soft man, but he also wasn't so hard that he couldn't make room for someone like Lara Cordero and her son in his life. He was scared to admit it, but he'd fallen in love with that little guy the moment he saw him, and he was quickly realizing that the same might be true for Lara as well.

He didn't know where any of this was going. All he knew was that he wanted the two of them to be in his life going forward. As long as he could lug huge pieces of driftwood up and down the beach, he knew he could count on Marco being on board. Lara, though, was another question.

She had been slow to open up about her past and he hadn't pushed her. He didn't really care what was behind them. He cared only about what might be in front of them, and today was a watershed moment.

Harvath hadn't wanted to come to this stretch of beach. It had been Lara's idea. "I need to finally say goodbye," she had told him, and he had been okay with that. Closure was important, especially when someone so important in your life had died.

They had spent the afternoon doing all the things Marco liked doing on the beach, but they hadn't been in the water. Coming back to Cape Cod was a big enough deal as it was. Going into the water where she had lost her husband might be a bridge too far.

Harvath smiled at her again and, scooping up Marco in his arms, leapt to his feet. "I promise," he repeated. "It'll be okay."

Lara looked at him and slowly smiled back. In that moment, he thought or maybe hoped that he was seeing something fall away, much like the armor of her police persona, which dropped piece by piece on her way home at the end of the day.

Standing up from their blanket, she wrapped her arms around them both and kissed them. "I know it'll be okay," she said. "Why don't we all go in together."

ACKNOWLEDGMENTS

With each thriller I create, my goal is to stretch myself as an author and become better at my craft. I had a lot of fun writing *Hidden Order* and I hope you enjoyed reading it.

The acknowledgments section is where I get to thank all the people who helped me over the past year. Of those, I owe my greatest thanks to you, my terrific **readers.** I work for you, and it is the greatest job anyone could ever have.

Equally important are all of the wonderful **booksellers** around the world who continue to help sell and introduce new readers to my novels every day. Thank you.

Once again, my dear friends **Barrett Moore, James Ryan, Rodney Cox,** and **Sean F.** were incredibly helpful. Without them, this book would not have happened. Thank you, gentlemen.

A special thanks for their support and friendship over the last year goes to **Joel Brumlik, Dan Bitton, Mike Bitton, Ray Hamilton,** and **Shawn Landa.**

I owe an additional debt of gratitude to **Frank Gallagher, Steve Tuttle, Evan Jones,** and **John Levin.**

To those who contributed to the novel, but whose names I am not able to include for security reasons, thank you for both your help and for your service to our great nation.

In *Hidden Order,* the **Lydia Ryan** and **Bill Wise** characters are so named because of their real-life spouses, who generously gave to two very worthwhile causes. I thank both **Mrs. Wise** and **Mr. Ryan** for their generosity.

On the publishing front, you will find no better people in the business than the amazing team at **Simon & Schuster.** To that end, I extend my deepest thanks to everyone at **Emily Bestler Books** and **Pocket Books,** particularly my phenomenal editor, **Emily Bestler.** Not only are her contributions invaluable, but working with her has proven to be one of the greatest joys of my career. Thank you, Emily.

I have surrounded myself with the absolute best, and so much of my success is directly attributable to the unparalleled business acumen of my outstanding publishers: **Carolyn Reidy, Judith Curr,** and **Louise Burke.** Ladies, thank you for everything you have done and continue to do for me and for the Brad Thor novels.

When I speak to aspiring novelists, I explain that writing a novel is only 40 percent of the work. You can write the greatest book in the world, but if no one knows about it you won't realize much success. This is why you need an astounding publicist and why I am blessed to have the greatest one ever: **David Brown.** My thanks go to David and the rest of our outstanding **PR team,** including the world-renowned **Cindi Berger** and **Cara Masline,** as well as the second-to-none **Valerie Vennix** and **Ariele Fredman.**

I also want to thank all the stellar people on the **Emily Bestler Books/ Pocket Books sales staff,** including **Gary Urda, Colin Shields, John Hardy,** the awesome **art and production departments,** the marvelous **Sarah Lieberman, Desiree Vecchio, Armand Schultz,** and the **Simon & Schuster audio division,** as well as the fantastic **Michael Selleck, Kate Cetrulo, Caroline Porter, Irene Lipsky, Lisa Keim, Jeanne Lee, Al Madocs,** and **Tom Pitoniak.**

Heide Lange of **Sanford J. Greenburger Associates, Inc.** is hands down the best literary agent ever. Her sage counsel, deep friendship, and the example she sets as a consummate professional are but the tip of the iceberg when it comes to the qualities I cherish in Heide. Add to that, Heide's spectacular assistants **Rachael Dillon Fried** and **Stephanie Delman** and **everyone else at SJGA,** and you have my constellation of lucky stars that I am thankful for every day.

My dear friend and peerless entertainment attorney, **Scott Schwimer,** has my deepest gratitude for all he has done and continues to do for me in Hollywood. Thank you, Scottie.

This year, Thor Entertainment Group is honored to be joined by the extraordinary **Yvonne Ralsky,** who has helped take our game to an entirely new level. We have many, many exciting things planned, and Yvonne is key to making those happen. Thank you, Yvonne.

Finally, I would not be where I am without my beautiful wife, **Trish,** and our two wonderful **children.** They are my inspiration and I love them beyond words. They put up with my late nights and weekends at my desk, always greeting me with a smile, a hug, and a love that knows no bounds. I am truly blessed and could not ask for anything more. Now that the book is done, what adventure can we take off for?

For a look behind the scenes of *Hidden Order*, plus up-to-the-minute information on Brad, make sure to visit BradThor.com and sign up for Brad's fast, fun, easy-to-read newsletter.